The Empty Quarter

The Empty Quarter

DAVID MARION WILKINSON

BOAZ PUBLISHING COMPANY
ALBANY, CALIFORNIA

DISTRIBUTED BY
PUBLISHERS GROUP WEST

Address all inquiries to:
Boaz Publishing Company
PO Box 6582
Albany, CA 94706
(510) 525-9459

First Edition

Edited by Sarah Nawrocki and Elizabeth Lyon
Designed by Elizabeth Vahlsing

PUBLISHER'S NOTE
This is a work of fiction. Names, characters, places, and incidents either are the products of the author's imagination or are used fictitiously, and any resemblance to actual persons, living or dead, events, or locales is entirely coincidental.

Library of Congress Cataloging-in-Publication Data
Wilkinson, D. Marion
The Empty Quarter / David Marion Wilkinson
p.   cm.
I. Title.
PS3573.I44185E46   1998
813'.54--dc21   98-15700
CIP
ISBN 0-9651879-2-6

Printed in the United States of America

For my friends

Joseph Allen "Joe" McCue

Who lost his life to the oil fields,

And Thomas C. Southern and G. Michael Pugh

Who, in a way, saved mine.

Prologue

The earth—everything in and on it—was created from the debris of dying stars hurled into the expanding void of space astronomers call the Milky Way. Their burial shroud was the earth's nebula—the womb of all stars and planets. And thus, their end was the earth's beginning.

At first ethereal, formless, cloudlike, the nebula's cosmic clutter was drawn by gravity toward its center. The violence of random collisions sparked new nuclear reactions. The infant sun fused in its swirling center and the planets—originating from cooler, condensing elements swept aside by burgeoning solar winds—gradually accumulated around it until there were nine orbiting, continually accreting spheres. The proto-earth was the third from the sun.

Step by step the miracle unfolded. Whether one believes it took seven days or seven billion years, such a wondrous process bespeaks the hand of God. From its violent beginning, the cooling, homogenous earth was bombarded by smaller stellar particles. Blow after cosmic blow struck its waterless, dusty surface, and the planet began to heat anew. As temperatures rose, the earth's elements turned molten. Denser materials such as iron and nickel sank to its center, while the lighter metals and gases rose in volcanic eruptions to its surface. The earth's matter differentiated into a solid inner core, a liquid outer core, a mantle, and a cooling crust. Hydrogen and oxygen vented to form the first oceans. The lightest gases escaped to form the earth's atmosphere—one far different than it is today: it could not sustain life. But that would change, as everything on the earth has and will, over incomprehensible ages, with or without humankind. Only the earth, Solomon broods in Ecclesiastes, will abide forever.

The concept of solid ground is illusory. Everything, including the continents and the oceans, moves. The crust and outer mantle form a series of rigid, though shifting, tectonic plates that travel at *the whim of the heat-softened, slow-flowing rock layer that churns beneath it. The surface plates move not like icebergs drifting in a liquid ocean, but like glaciers creeping along a rock basin. The plates' center is relatively tranquil. It is at their edges—whether the plates are crashing together or being ripped apart—that geological violence occurs.*

Continents are transient components. Five hundred million years ago, there were two major land masses, poles apart. Oceans larger than any on the earth today lay between them. Over the next 250 million years, the two continents crept toward one another until they collided to form one—Pangea. For fifty million years, Pangea traveled the earth's surface alone. Then its many fused plates started to tear apart, eventually forming the seven continents that wander the earth today. In some distant age they will meet again.

Over the last twenty million years, the Arabian Peninsula rifted from Africa. The Red Sea formed in the parting wake and still grows. Someday it may rival the Atlantic. Arabia's eastern edge, which includes the Rub al Khali desert, creeps day by day toward the northeast at a pace a little faster than human toenails grow. The ocean plate in its path must yield.

The volume of water on the earth is more or less finite. What changes, as a result of drastic climatic deviations, polar shifts, and plate tectonics, is sea level. The oceans rose and fell over countless ages. Since the beginning of life, partially decayed microorganisms accumulated in the muck on the ocean floors. Layer after sedimentary layer settled above these remains, sealing them beneath a landmass that would one day emerge from the declining seas. Pressured from above, heated from below, the organic decay solidified into the waxlike substance known as kerogen. More pressure, more heat and time, and kerogen converted to hydrocarbons—oil and gas. The deepest of these deposits formed the lightest of the natural gases—propane, ethane, and methane.

Once the gases matured they were forced from the source rock and migrated through porous and permeable layers of sandstone and limestone. Almost all of these generated gases—99.9 percent— as a result of one geologic event or another, ultimately vented at the earth's surface. The remainder was trapped in folded and domed reservoir rock beneath some impervious layer or came to rest at a fault plane. These anomalous accumulations, cheated out of their usual fate, fuel the entire human race as our twentieth century wanes.

Seismic studies had identified a promising caprock dome—named Al Hisaab by geologists—about three miles beneath the Rub al Khali's dunes. Ungodly hot, superpressurized, contaminated by hydrogen sulfide, it waits for a shift in colliding tectonic plates, the roar of a volcano, the rumble of an earthquake, or the prick of a rotary drill bit. And then it will rush upward—powerful, ancient, and angry—following the path of least resistance to freedom, to complete the cycle it began sixty-five million years ago.

The question for those whose profession it is to probe such reservoirs once the technicians have found it is always the same. Could they control the beast once they set it free?

The Empty Quarter

Momentum # 127
—Legend—

1 Crown Block
2 Crown Runaround
3 Jack Knife Derrick
4 Gin Pole
5 Derrickman's Monkey Board
6 Traveling Block
7 Hook
8 Swivel Bail
9 Gooseneck
10 Swivel
11 Kelly Hose (High Pressure Mud)
12 Stand Pipe (High Pressure Mud)
13 Kelly (Hexagonal)
14 A-Frame / "Derrick Leg"
15 Doghouse
16 Drill Floor
17 Rotary Table
18 Drill Pipe Rack (Not Shown)
19 Draw Works
20 Electromagnic Brake (Auxiliary Brake)
21 Drilling Line (1 5/8" Steel Cable)
22 Driller's Console
23 Shale Shaker
24 Mud Tanks
25 V-Door / Ramp
26 Substructure
27 Cathead
28 Elevator (Not Shown)
29 Geronimo Line (Not Shown)
30 Emergency Slide

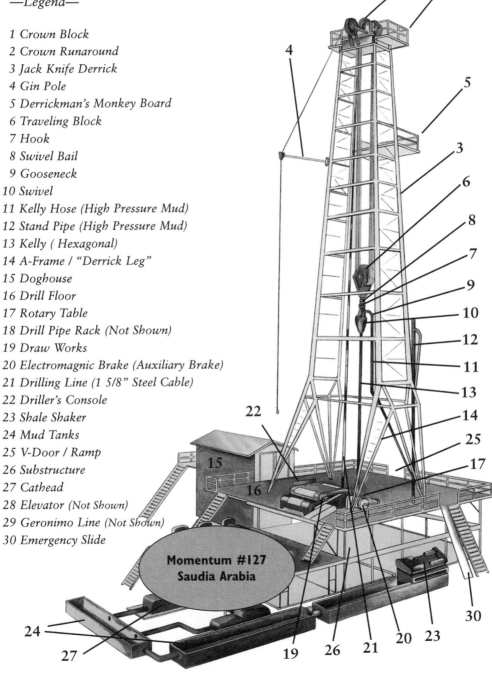

Momentum #127
Saudia Arabia

MOMENTUM DRILLING, INCORPORATED
Drilling with Excellence Worldwide

September 14, 1986

Mr. Logan "Doc" Wilson
901 Shelly Avenue
Austin, Texas   78703

Dear Mr. Wilson:

I have mailed two applications to you at this address and have received no reply. I also left several messages on your answering machine.

As you know, the Tulsa office's inquiry found no evidence of negligence on the part of either yourself or James M. Strong in the Saudi Arabia Division incident that preceded your termination in late August of 1985. At the time, we considered this action appropriate given the loss of life and amount of equipment destroyed. However, since you have been cleared of all responsibility for the mishap, coupled with the two letters of recommendation supplied to me by rig superintendent Elvin Barnes and Arabco drilling foreman Marshall Christianson, I am pleased to advise you that Momentum regrets its earlier decision and would like to offer you a new assignment.

Momentum has wellsite positions available in Indonesia, New Guinea, Gabon, and Nigeria. We are prepared to offer you a two-year employment contract at the standard driller's rate. Prospects for your advancement seem excellent.

Please let me know as soon as possible whether you are interested in any of these positions. I look forward to hearing from you.

Sincerely,

A. H. "Butch" Amistead, Director
Foreign Recruiting
Momentum Drilling, Inc.

ONE

AUGUST 1985

Logan stared from his bedroom window at the conical illumination beneath the corner streetlight. Moths, fluttering flecks of white, hovered about the alluring purplish glow, while larger insects shot through like meteors to vanish into the still and humid night.

He turned and stuffed the last of his things into the worn duffel. His connection to New York left at dawn the next morning. He'd packed clean white cotton socks, three pairs of tartan boxers, T-shirts and khaki shorts to wear around the camp, and carefully folded jeans and an oxford shirt for the return trip. Jumbled in there also was a large bottle of Pert shampoo, his shaving kit, and three good novels: Gabriel García Márquez's *One Hundred Years of Solitude*, Larry McMurtry's *Leaving Cheyenne*, and Caitlin's suggestion, Toni Morrison's *Sula*. Logan felt certain these would see him through. He stuffed a dozen packs of Levi Garrett chewing tobacco around the books. Next came the stethoscope in its thin rectangular box, two coiled western belts with absurdly long foreign names stamped in curling block letters—names he'd had to pronounce three times for the incredulous clerk, a wannabe redneck starched from head to toe, before deciding to spell them out on a counter notepad. Last, he crammed in the badminton set, complete with four rackets, three birdies, and a net, its four box corners poking through the canvas. Everything else he needed for the month ahead would be waiting for him in his locker.

He zipped up the duffel, snatched it from the foot of the unmade bed, and slipped quietly into the narrow main room of the garage apartment, where he knew Caitlin waited. The oak floor creaked beneath his bare feet, betraying his presence. He saw Caitlin sitting on the sofa with her legs curled beneath her, thumbing impatiently through the list. She looked up to meet his glance. The names and addresses of her friends and family she obviously knew well. It was his scant additions, the supposed labor of the last month, that he knew had irritated her. Logan avoided those cold brown eyes and passed through the room to place his bag on the kitchen table. He took another beer from the icebox.

"Is this it?" she called as soon as he'd plopped himself on the kitchen counter and twisted off the bottle top. White fumes danced in the longneck's narrow throat until he blew them out.

"That's it." He sighed, knowing by her tone that he couldn't put off the confrontation as he had hoped. He slid off the counter and walked back in, choosing to sit in the rigid corner chair, the most uncomfortable in the apartment. It suited his mood tonight. Caitlin swept the dark hair back from her face, her eyes glistening, and held up the paper. Her frigid glare could freeze a frog in mid hop.

"Six names, Logan?" she asked, cocking her head. "For a wedding?"

Logan swigged his beer. It was cold enough, but it lacked the punch he needed to confront her searing expression. "For a small wedding," he answered, his glance fixed on the floor. "We can send notices to anyone we want."

"And your father?"

Logan shook his head. "I don't want him around for that."

"He has a right to see his only son married, Logan. What harm could he do?"

"Plenty," Logan said. He'd spent seventeen years under that man's leaky roof. If he had his way, his father would not spend one day under his. "I don't think you understand the depths of my family's dysfunction. I'm used to it, of course. But it might take you a while. We're from Arkansas, you know. The family tree's short a few limbs if you know what I mean." He thought she would think it funny. She didn't. "If it's all the same to you, I'd rather not expose you to your new in-laws until after it's all legal-like. It just might queer the deal."

Stonefaced, lips pursed, Caitlin tossed the list aside. She fumbled for her Virginia Slims and plastic lighter, lit a cigarette, and flipped the pack back onto the coffee table. "What about the date?"

"You know my schedule, Caitlin," he said, settling back against the hard vinyl. "Pick any date you like."

"And what do you think," she said as her eyes narrowed, "would be my problem with that?"

It was the way she argued these days, making her point with questions, something she'd learned in her first year of law school, he guessed. It bugged him to no end, especially now when he was desperate for peace. Well enough, he thought. We can have us an argument now.

"I don't know," he said. "Why don't you tell me?"

She lurched forward and planted her bare feet on the floor, toes curled against hard wood. "You said you'd quit this damn job, Logan. You promised you'd get something here when we married."

The obvious response was that they weren't married yet. But it wasn't the correct answer if he wanted to get out of this without claw marks. Instead he said, "Like what?"

"You could get anything you want if you'd just try!"

"I don't see it that way." He fingered the mouth of his beer bottle, resenting the timing of this eleventh-hour pep talk. It looked to him like he had no choice but to go through his reasoning again. "I've got a liberal arts degree, Cait. Not much doing out there for those."

"You could start with the banks or the brokerage houses. You're interested in that. A sales job would be fine."

"I could do that," he said, "and we'd starve. Those jobs won't pay me near what I'm makin' now. You've got one more year of school. When you're out, I can look for somethin' else and start over, just like I promised. Until then," he said, and he hoped it was firm enough so she'd know the issue was decided, "I'll stay with my current career."

"Ah, Logan," she moaned, grinding a half-smoked cigarette into the tray. "That's not a career. It's just a job." She collapsed against the back of the sofa and ran her fingers through her hair. "And it's killing us. I hate it that you're gone better than half the time. And when you're here, you're in a terrible mood. The first week you come home exhausted. The next two you drink too much. The last you sit around here on edge, waiting to go back. I don't want to live like this anymore."

"Now, that I knew," Logan said, sliding forward in his chair. "And that's why I haven't set the date." He spoke more quietly now. "You're as edgy as I am with law school and all, Cait. There's a lot of pressure on us both. Things aren't settled. All bullshit aside, I think we should wait until they are before we set the date."

Caitlin threw her head back and closed her eyes. "And knowing that," she said, "you let me work on this list, make whatever plans your mother and I could make by ourselves, did nothing about trying to find another job—like you promised me, I might add—and now you tell me, after I forced the issue, when you're about to leave again, that we need to wait." She leveled her glance. "Is that it?"

Logan rubbed his temples, his beer bottle cradled between his thighs. "I guess that's it," he said. "I'm sorry."

"You won't quit?" It sounded like an ultimatum. Logan slowly shook his head.

"It's that bastard Jamie Strong, isn't it?" she said. "It's some kind of bullshit boy thing. Jamie's never going to grow up, and you won't either as long as you work with him."

"Leave Jamie out of it. I like what I do. I'm good at it."

"I know, Logan. You're good at anything you want to do. But I know you better than Jamie does. You won't let Jamie see you like I see you." She jostled another cigarette out of the pack and lit it. "Jamie doesn't know how you've cut yourself off from your friends and family, does he? He doesn't know about the nightmares. He doesn't know you're scared."

"It's a dangerous job, Caitlin." Logan rose from his chair. "We work under pressure. We're in a big field in a bad place. There's a world of things that can go wrong over there. It's no shame that I worry about it."

"And if you're worried, I'm worried." Caitlin leaned forward. "It's just time to quit. That's all I'm saying. You can find yourself something safer, a little more traditional. Come home and be my husband."

Logan noticed that familiar shift in her reasoning. It always worked its way from his fear, which he denied, to his need to change careers, which hurt him. "Are you ashamed of what I do, Cait?" He sank back into his seat.

"No," she said, her eyes widening, "but I think you are. Whether you'd admit it or not, it eats at you all the time. And it eats at us, too."

Logan's chin fell to his chest. She understood. Inside that gorgeous, often angry head was a perceptive mind. "I don't know what to do," he said. "Things haven't work out like I planned."

"That's the problem, Logan. You haven't planned much of anything. But that's all right. I'll help you. I *want* to help you. For now, I'd rather have you be lost here at home than halfway across the world." She managed a smile, the first he'd seen that evening. "Here I can keep an eye on you. With that son of a bitch Jamie Strong, there's no telling what might happen." She tapped the telephone with her index finger. "Call them tomorrow and tell them you have to quit. Tell them you've got cancer, that your whole family died, or anything, I don't care. But don't get on that plane. I've had a bad feeling all week."

She crossed the floor, curled up in his lap, and raked her fingers through his hair. One touch from her and everything felt better. "Let's get married," she said, kissing his ear. "Let's get on with our lives."

Logan exhaled. "I can't do that, Cait."

Her head shot back. "What if I try whining? I haven't tried whining yet. Bitching doesn't work. Sexual allure gets me nowhere."

"Why not give that sexual allure another shot?" Logan said.

"And if I did," she purred, unbuttoning her shirt, "would you make that call? Would you quit?"

Logan ran his fingers under her bra and cupped her breast. He caught the scent of her—not her perfume, her. She had a sweet, redolent musk about her that soothed him regardless of his mood. An ethereal essence that bound him to her, he would carry her scent with him during their month apart. "I just can't. It's not right to up and quit the company like that. I can't leave my crew shorthanded."

"Fine," Caitlin snapped, jumping out of his lap. "I can't put off my studies, either." She angrily stuffed loose papers, notebooks, and bulky, maroon law books into her backpack. "My group's meeting right now."

The group included Caitlin's ex-boyfriend, Adam Bellmeade, a tall, sandy-haired, blue-eyed jock Logan couldn't have liked even if he hadn't once been romantically involved with his fiancée. Should he refer to Caitlin as his fiancée? Things seemed a little tentative all of a sudden.

Logan had pumped Caitlin for the troubling details. Bellmeade was the kind of slick, positive, effusive bastard who knew he could get anything he wanted with his looks. And he wanted everything. On top of that, the son of a bitch was smart, too. And wealthy. His Dallas family was something out of a 1960s television show, with sit-down home-cooked meals and Baptist services on Sunday. He was the kind of dickhead who wore tennis outfits to class, the arms of his cashmere sweater tied around his tanned neck. There wasn't a scar on his athletic body, not a callus on his smooth hands. Twenty-five years on the same planet as Logan and no tragedy had ever touched him. He could've been a brain surgeon, a professional quarterback, an astronaut. What he'd decided to be was an attorney, and there could be no doubt that he'd rise to the top. Along his greased path, he'd formed a study group, like all law students did. But why, for God's sake, had he invited Caitlin to join it? And why had she agreed?

Logan thought he knew. Adam Bellmeade wanted her back, and he had a nose for opportunity. Perhaps Caitlin would be more susceptible now to his advances. Maybe it had been a mistake not to set the date.

"Ah, Cait," Logan moaned. "Not tonight. I've got to go in the morning."

"You do what you've got to do," she said, snatching her keys on her way to the door. "So will I." Logan heard the hinges squeak and then the rusting screen door slam. Angry feet on the warped wooden steps. He'd meant to nail them back down sometime during the last month. Like the rest of his planned productive activities, he hadn't quite got around to it.

He scrambled to the porch. "I guess it's a bad time to ask for some parting sex?" he called.

"Not a chance," she said. She wouldn't even look at him. "You stay, I'm a harlot. You go, I'm a law student."

"C'mon, Cait. I don't want to leave it like this."

"Oh, this is *exactly* how we should leave it. You need to think about what you're missing while you're over there." She piled her books into the backseat, bending from the waist. The lines of her long legs, curved hips, and flat stomach made his blood gush. She was so beautiful. "You leave me no choice. You think you can go on living like a teenage boy."

"A sweet boy," he said. "A kind, sweet boy with a lot of manly world experience, not to mention knowledge of various and interesting sexual techniques, some of which I've considered patenting."

No response.

"A boy who earns a pretty good wage, I might add." This caught her attention.

"This isn't about money," she said, cramming her key into the ignition. "It's about us. I only want what's best for you, Logan. And that's me. Sooner or later, you'll understand that."

She started the Toyota and backed out the driveway. Logan heard gravel crunching under the tires. "Damn," he muttered. He'd just about had her. There was a moment when she almost cracked a smile. She would study late at the library, until she cooled off. When she came back, he hoped like hell she'd wake him. The last hours he spent with Caitlin before his bi-monthly departures were usually the best. He went back inside the apartment, the smell of her still lingering in the cramped rooms.

He took a cold beer with him into the shower. When he finished, he toweled himself off and climbed into bed, wondering how he could merge his world with Caitlin's. He wasn't ready to abandon his just yet.

TWO

Logan hobbled alone through the gray haze, his clothes covered with stinging sweat and mud, his knee joint grinding with every step. At first he'd smelled the unmistakable stench of hydrogen sulfide, and now that he didn't he knew it had him. Soon he would feel exhilarated, then disoriented, and finally, if he failed to find fresh air, he'd sink to his knees and die where he fell.

Go on, Logan, he urged himself. *Strong's left you behind. Get yourself out.*

The others were dead or gone, he wasn't sure which. Twisted metal, pipe, and cable lay everywhere. The tower above, weakened by blow after shuddering blow, listed hard to the south, groaning in the desert wind. Soon, he was certain, its iron legs would shear from its stubby mounts and crash violently to the earth. If the gas didn't kill him, the structure's collapse would.

The roar of the well drowned out all other sound. A stream of hot gas as thick as an oak trunk rocketed from its center and dispersed into milky clouds. The wooden planks, slick with mud, grease, and human blood, trembled beneath his feet. He staggered on. If he wanted to live, he had to keep going.

A path opened to the stairway, a wavering tunnel shrouded in white mist. He turned to enter it. He felt the euphoria now, the deceitful gift of the poison gas, and though his mind told him he could easily make it, no need to hurry, what was left of his reason advised him that it was already too late.

He stepped through the haze and saw an Indian, his body crumpled on the metal grating like a discarded rag doll. He instantly recognized the face.

"Rahiman!" he screamed. The Indian lifted his head, his eyes bruised and puffy, his black hair matted with fresh blood.

"Where's Strong?" Logan yelled.

Rahiman shook his head. "Gone."

"Bastard," Logan said. "C'mon. We're goin', too."

But Rahiman didn't move. Instead, he pointed at the sky.

The main electrical line, the one that powered everything beneath the great mast, had drawn tight as a guitar string. The tower groaned, its steel buckling, its galvanized coating peeling like dead skin, and the cord stretched tighter. Soon, Logan knew, it would snap. One little spark and the whole location would explode.

Logan reached for Rahiman's arm. "Leave me," the Indian said, "or we'll both die."

"That ain't happenin'," Logan said. He lifted Rahiman, bending to drape him across his shoulder. His knee screamed from the burden. Logan wheeled, discovering that his path had clouded over. He panicked. When he looked up again, the cord snapped clean, its ends recoiling until they disappeared into the fog.

He saw the whiteness of that thin spark, the last communication between forever parting ends, and then the white expanded, with no beginning and no end, absorbing him. He felt the explosion, his body parting from Rahiman's and rocketing end over end through space. But he never left the whiteness.

Logan struck iron squarely, flipping again until he came to rest in a crouched position, his back against solid steel. He opened his eyes. The bones of both thighs shoved pink and jagged through the black fabric of his crumbling jeans. There was no blood when it should have been gushing. He watched as his flesh receded, bubbling away from the wound, and the shards of his broken bones began to burn like kitchen matches.

All his clothing, save his blazing lace-up boots, burned away. Skin peeled from his abdomen, his viscera dripping away like candle wax. Everything went black. He knew his eyes had been burned out of his fleshless face. He screamed in a blackness more terrible than the whiteness had been.

Then all went quiet. All was still. He felt no heat, no pain.

A cool breeze swept down from above, heaven's breath, and he looked up to face its source. He saw no bright light, as so many have predicted. Only a hazy, gray funnel in the middle of the black, swirling around him as if he were in the calm eye of a storm. It marked, he assumed, the beginning of his final journey.

"Help me," he called, hoping. *"Help me, please."*

He stared into the vortex, waiting for guidance before he took another step. He'd always said that if heaven meant having to spend eternity with his kin, he'd take his chances elsewhere. He regretted that now.

He heard a woman's voice growing louder. At first he thought it might be his mother. Then he imagined it was an angel sent by a merciful God. It was not a soothing voice, as he'd always expected, but an insistent one. And then it became angry. There was nothing angelic about it.

"Logan!"

He felt a cold hand on his calf and it startled him. He was being pulled the wrong way. He kicked his leg free and looked up again. Waiting, arms outstretched.

"Logan!"

Slowly the vortex cleared. He recognized the swirling blades of the Hunter ceiling fan above him. No mistaking that. He'd mounted it himself, unable to smooth out that frustrating wobble. He had meant to write the manufacturer about that. He heard the familiar whine of the window air-conditioning unit to his right. He brought his hand before his face. His fingers were of flesh and bone. He felt beads of sweat running down his muscular back; his abdomen, full and taut; his legs unbroken, big ugly feet on each end.

Far from standing naked before his Creator, he was standing in his boxers in the center of his futon. He exhaled and let his forehead collapse against his hand. Caitlin shouted his name again.

"Goddamn," he said. He shuddered and then sighed.

"What're you trying to do? Cut your head off? You scared me to death!"

He struggled for breath. "I'm sorry, Cait," he said.

"Was it that same dream?"

"Was it ever." He sank to the bed. She wrapped her arms around him. He felt her shake her head.

"Don't go, Logan."

"I can't leave them in the lurch," he said.

"Ah," she said, "I don't believe you." She drew back, her eyes meeting his, and wiped the sweat from his brow. "At least you're not scared, huh?"

"I'm scared now," he said, forcing himself to take deep, calming breaths, his hands shaking.

"And you're still going?"

Everything within him answered no. He'd worked overseas too long as it was. Something bad was going to happen. Like her, he could feel it. A sense of imminent disaster had hounded him all month long. But instead he said, "I have to."

"Logan." She hesitated. "I know this isn't the best time to say this. But I've been thinking. I've been thinking a lot. I don't know if we should get married right now." He felt a deep ache in his gut. "We'll have to think long and hard about it when you get back. I don't see things working out between us if you won't come home."

He put his finger to her lips. "Let's don't get into this now," he said. "It's all right to put things off for a while and see what happens. We'll work it out. For now, try to go back to sleep. You've got an early class."

He pressed her down gently and she pulled the covers over herself. She turned on her side, her back to him.

He lay there beside her for over an hour, watching the red numbers change on the digital clock. He thought about his future—their future, now, it seemed, at risk. A few hours ago he wasn't seriously worried about their relationship. The idea of marriage itself had a few kinks in it, but he wasn't concerned about their attachment to one another. She was the one constant in his life. He was able to do what he did because he had a home, and Caitlin was there waiting for him. He couldn't imagine himself apart from her. Now it was clear she had doubts.

But what he thought of most was his dream. How terrible, how vivid it was. Every sequence of the disaster as it would be. Every detail of the explosion correct. He could almost smell the stench of his scorched flesh as he burned alive.

He listened in the dark. Caitlin's breathing had grown deep. If he were careful, he could slip away without waking her. No sense in both of them going without sleep.

He showered again but did not shave. He wrapped a towel around his waist and faced himself in the mirror. Six-foot-three and slender, he was still proud of his physique. The ends of his light brown hair, streaked blonde from the summer afternoons he spent at Barton Springs, curled at his shoulders. Nose and cheekbones sharp. His green eyes accentuated by his sunburned face. Normally he'd look at himself and say, "You're a damn good-looking man."

But what he thought at this early hour was that he'd better wake up, boy. No mistaking the age lines etched into the corners of those anxious eyes. The tone of his pectoral muscles was a little softer than a year ago, the abdominals a little less defined, the paunch around his hips a little riper. His eyes seemed sunken and dim. If he weeded through those locks around his ears he'd find a gray hair or two. Twenty-six years old and going nowhere. Boy, you'd better wake up. You're about to lose her, and maybe everything else, too. *You'd best not get on that jet.*

He turned away from the mirror and spread the towel over the rack. Leaving the bathroom, he crossed the bedroom floor in silence. He dressed in the clothes he'd laid out on the sofa the night before. He tiptoed to the icebox and took two bottles of beer, propped up his feet on his sagging duffel, and twisted off the first cap. The only sound he heard was liquid washing down his parched, aching throat.

It was always bad when the time came to go back, but this was the worst. This time he couldn't shake his sense of foreboding and emptiness that accompanied the usual worries. This time he was truly afraid.

She was right to postpone the marriage. For two years he'd been drifting, his alienation from domestic life deepening until he felt his center was lost. The goddamn nightmares were a part of that, he was sure. And so, he thought, were the problems with Caitlin.

She had a good heart, uncommon in a woman of her looks and intelligence in Logan's experience. It had probably hurt her more than him to say what she'd said. He couldn't fault her for it. She'd been understanding of his indecision, more than patient with his moodiness. What, he wondered, did he offer her?

Whether she admitted it or not, Logan felt she had become accustomed to living without him. That's where the problem lay for him. He was either always gone or always there, and it seemed to him that Caitlin reacted coolly in both instances. Her life was blossoming just as his had begun to wilt. She had new friends and new prospects. She'd find her way without him, and he knew she had to wonder how his rough edges were going to fit in her tidy future.

He couldn't bear it. Everything he'd tenuously stitched together over the last three years was unraveling around him. Living in two worlds, he felt he belonged to neither.

As he opened the second bottle, he saw the lights of the taxi in front of their little pink apartment. He took his duffel down, tossed it in the backseat, and slid in beside it. The cab driver, a fat guy squatting beneath a black beret, cast a glassy eye at the longneck in Logan's hand.

"Early start or late finish?" he said as he set his meter. He smelled of coffee and cigarette smoke.

"I couldn't say." Instinctively, Logan checked the compartment where he kept his ticket. He opened the folder to check the itinerary. In it, he found Caitlin's note. It read: "Be careful, Logan. And for God's sake, don't get smashed on the way over! I love you."

"Hang on a minute," he told the driver.

Logan scribbled his reply: "We'll work it out, Caitlin. All my love, Logan." He got out of the cab, stuffed the note in the mailbox and slammed the car door shut.

"Let's go, man."

The cab driver popped his lever into drive just about the time a large insect plunged out of the darkness for the center of the streetlight, dallied briefly in its glow, and fell smoking, wings beating violently, to the pavement below.

"The airport," Logan said. "Hurry, if you don't mind. I've got a plane to catch."

THREE

Most of the passengers nested after the meal when the lights went down for the movie. But these flights were always loaded with businessmen, engineers, and technicians, and some of them gathered, ties loosened, pinpoint shirts unbuttoned at the neck, in the rear section of the aircraft to talk shop. They gripped clear plastic tumblers of bourbon or scotch. As it was for Logan and his crew, this cramped celebration would be their last hurrah before the mandated drought. Lines formed at the row of eight lavatories. Mothers saddled with cranky young children, and elderly passengers nursing arthritic joints, wandered the aisles of the jumbo jet. They smiled grimly each time they passed by Logan's seat.

Logan thought he might sleep, and after he scooted three empty little bottles of Johnny Walker Red along with his cup onto Jamie Strong's tray, he arranged his body as best he could to do just that. He'd no sooner closed his eyes than Strong elbowed him in the ribs.

"Where do you think you're goin'?" Strong's stentorian tenor, curiously tinged with Montana twang, was much too loud for Logan's docile mood. Strong matched Logan's height exactly, but he was twice Logan's breadth. His bulk, among other overcompensations, made him difficult to sit next to on such a long flight. "Party ain't over yet, Doc," he said, his sausage fingers putting the final touches on a fat joint.

"For God's sake, Jamie," Logan protested. He checked around to see if any of the other passengers had noticed Strong's art. They hadn't. Most were wired with stethoscope-like headphones to the arms of their seats, staring blankly at the movie.

Strong casually twisted each end of his doobie. He seemed pleased with his product. "What's happened to you, Doc?" he said, his eyes red and hazy. "That woman's turned you into some kind of wuss. It used to be about now you'd be up beatin' on the cockpit door wantin' to fly the damn plane. Wasn't it on that London connection when you and Charlie Gentry were rollin' around the aisles in your underwear? The pilots thought they'd lost an engine."

"I'm not proud of that," Logan said. He sank back in his seat, grateful at least that Caitlin knew none of that. Knowledge of such behavior could further tilt the scales against him. Logan struggled with reform. But it was clear that Strong, running the joint between his lips, had no such intention.

"I am," Strong said. "It was you at your best."

Logan massaged his pounding brow, worried about the scene Strong was about to make. And he'd made plenty in their four years together. Jamie Strong, to use his own phrase, didn't give a fuck for nothin'. Logan wasn't nearly drunk enough to share Strong's twisted view. He made one last attempt to reach what remained of Strong's reason. "Jamie, please. We can't smoke that here."

Strong pulled the joint from his mouth. "Relax, mama's boy. I've already made other plans. Jamie Strong's no fool. You've got nothin' to worry about."

Logan had plenty to worry about, but that didn't include worrying whether or not Strong was a fool. Strong was the poster boy of fools—loud, obnoxious, drunken fools. And Logan explicitly understood the criteria for judging him as such. He'd staggered around a time or two in that same club.

Strong elbowed Elvin Barnes, who gawked at the movie screen, quietly nursing his bottle of Jack Black. If Strong couldn't sway Logan, he assumed Barnes could. Barnes was stout and squat in his jeans, boots, and western shirt. He looked like a rancher, complete with bowlegged gait, which was odd considering he didn't ride horses and had never owned a cow. Elvin Barnes, like his daddy before him, was drilling oil wells before he was licensed to drive a car. Once Strong had their supervisor's blurred attention, he proudly displayed the joint. Barnes seemed impressed, which Logan deemed completely out of character for a leathery West Texas redneck ten years his senior. When Barnes tossed his headphones aside, unbuckled his seatbelt, and produced his lighter, Logan lost all hope. He dropped his head into his hands.

Strong turned back to him. "The question I've got for you, Doc, is always the same. Are you with us or not?"

"Ah, hell, Jamie," Barnes said. "Don't worry about ol' Doc. He got a late start. He'll come aroun' directly."

Strong twisted his head. "Are you sober?" he asked, incredulous.

"Not really. I'm just not insane."

"We'll fix that," Barnes insisted, refilling Logan's cup with a spare bottle of scotch. "This always happens when Doc don't fly in from Dallas with me and Werner," Barnes explained. "His pump don't get primed, so his valves clatter to beat hell in the early goin'." He raised the cup to Logan's lips. "Drink up, boy," he said. Now he was giving orders.

Logan took some cubes of ice from Strong's cup with his fingers, swirled them in his own glass and tipped it back. "Happy now?" he said in a growl.

"No," Strong said, again displaying the joint. "But that's what this is for. Let's go."

Strong and Barnes climbed out of their seats. When Logan hesitated, suggesting that he'd at least like to finish his Scotch, Strong pulled him to his feet. He prodded Logan ahead of him down the aisle, Logan sipping his whiskey as best he could. Barnes followed in their wake. Logan heard the clunk of his boots on the worn carpet.

They faced eight stalls in the rear section of the plane, and Strong picked one with great care. When the door flew open, he let the relieved passenger pass and shoved Logan in. Barnes made three. This, Logan observed over his shoulder, drew some queer looks from those already waiting. "We're frequent flyers," Strong explained to the blank faces. "We got rights." He slammed the door.

Strong faced Logan, as if they had any choice. "I judged you wrong," Strong said. "You're pretty damn hammered if you came in here. I never thought you'd do it." He brought the reefer to his lips and flicked the lighter.

"What about the smoke alarm?" Logan said.

Strong hesitated, then reached into his pockets, proudly producing two double-A batteries. "I was in here earlier," he explained with a wink. This time the flame reached the joint's tip. Strong stuck it first between Barnes's anxious lips. "Inhale, Elvin." He did. "Hold it, Elvin." He did. Out of caution, Strong brought Barnes to his feet, no easy task in the space available, and directed his head skyward. "Exhale, you fool, and then sit your ass back down on the toilet."

Billows of white-gray smoke engulfed the detector. To Logan's horror, it responded as designed by the manufacturer. Its raucous shriek sent electric shudders through Logan's body. All three recoiled like rats in a cramped cage. "Damn it," Strong hollered, staring at the batteries still in his hand. "Must've been the one next door."

"Great," Logan said. "Good job."

Barnes, obviously reeling from the effects of the first hit, his face blank and puerile, looked to Strong to manage the crisis. He seemed to Logan a poor choice. Strong fumbled with the squawking unit to no avail, ultimately pounding it with his fist. The alarm persisted, but the exhaust fan shorted out.

"Well, boys," Strong yelled, "we're fucked now. Might as well finish up." He stuck the joint in Logan's mouth, and there was little else to do but inhale deeply. By then someone outside was banging on the door. Strong showed no alarm. "Wait your turn!" he yelled. "It ain't my fault you ate all that airplane food." And they puffed away until visibility was cut to zero.

When the attendant pried the door loose with what appeared to Logan to be a fire ax, the smoke cleared enough to reveal Strong supercharging Barnes's ear with surprising vigor.

The purser's face pierced the dissipating cloud. Her facial expression changed from shock to smoldering anger. "What in God's name?"

Logan stepped aside to allow Strong, expert at explaining indefensible situations, to face her fury. Strong pushed the nozzle of her fire extinguisher aside and stepped calmly out of the lavatory.

"Okay to smoke in here?" he asked, childlike. Barnes, who had been oblivious the last fifteen minutes, started snickering like a cartoon dog. It didn't help. Logan fanned the smoke from his face, thinking that maybe the stewardess was about to use that ax a second time.

Before them stood three flight attendants, the beloved purser with whom Strong had tangled earlier over seat assignments, and a man wearing a skipper's hat and officer's stripes on his coat sleeve.

"I didn't have to look to know who it was," the purser told the pilot. "They've been trouble from the very start. They should never have been allowed to board."

"I'll handle it," the captain said, coughing into his fist. "Please step out of the lavatory, if you don't mind."

They did, Logan embarrassed, Barnes clueless, Strong appearing to stick by his tireless creed. Barnes somehow got a grip. "I'm not one to mind another man's business," he said with an impish grin, "but shouldn't you be drivin'?"

Strong laughed alone.

"They've been on my flights before," the purser continued. "It gets worse every time. My people can't do their job with this sort of thing going on. I want something done." She crossed her arms.

"I'll handle it, Liz," the captain said, massaging his temples. He was composed in the face of adversity, which Logan knew even Strong respected.

"Gentlemen," the captain began, and the sarcasm was not lost on Logan, "I can't have this."

"What?" Strong asked, immediately on the offensive with this, the next in a long line of adverse authority figures.

"No more games," the captain said. He seemed to recognize that Strong was the author and instigator of all this, and he squared off with him. "I'm perfectly prepared to set this bird down, say, in Cypress, and expel you all. There's a civil war going on there. I bet you'd like it. There, you may first explain to the local authorities what you were smoking in my lavatory—and I don't want to know what it was—and then you can tell whoever it is who hires people like you why you didn't show up for work." He straightened his coat and looked from one face to the next. "I'll do it in a heartbeat," he added, turning back to Strong. "You better believe I will."

Logan believed him, but he was pretty sure Strong did not. "Now don't get me wrong, men," the captain said with transparent officiousness. "I'm an old Air Force man myself, and I'm not opposed to having a little fun now and then..."

"You wouldn't know fun if it licked ya," Strong said. Logan elbowed him in the ribs.

The captain shrugged, "...but there's a time and a place, and you fellas are way out of line." He focused on Logan, who deflected his glance toward Strong. "Now, what's it gonna be, boys?"

Logan knew Strong was about to pop off. He warned Strong with his sharpest glare. When he sensed this had failed, he stepped between Strong and the captain. "I've got a suggestion," he said.

"Oh, I'd like to hear it," the captain said.

"It's a little out of the ordinary."

"Why am I not surprised?"

"I can guarantee you that there won't be any more of this," Logan said. He pointed to the busted lavatory door. The smoke was still clearing. "But you've got to do us a little favor in return."

"How can I help?"

"Give us more whiskey," Logan said.

The purser's jaw dropped. "Oh, sure," she guffawed.

The captain held up his hand. "Explain to me why I should do that."

"Because we'll pass out. That's it. Problem solved. You fly the plane. We'll drink the whiskey. Nobody gets hurt."

The captain shook his head. "Oh, I don't know."

"Look." Logan pointed to Barnes. "Look at this man. Believe it or not, he's our boss. On location we respect him like he's some kind of god. But right now he's just a drunken piece of shit. He's burnin' out like last night's charcoal. All he needs is just a little more fuel and then, that's all she wrote."

The captain deliberated, victory enough as far as Logan was concerned. But then Strong jumped in. "That's right, General. Give us more whiskey. All we can drink, and it'll be over. If not, radio ahead to Cypress and let us out. We'll take our chances there."

Logan rolled his eyes, wondering what the weather would be like in Cypress, what side of the war they should take, whether the local arms dealers would accept an American Express card for a good used AK-47 and a couple of hand grenades if their unexpected vacation got really rough.

The captain rested his elbow in his palm and stroked his chin. "All right, boys," he said. "I'll play ball. You all appear to me to be in pretty bad shape. I'll give you the whiskey on these conditions."

"Name 'em," Strong said.

"The drinks will be delivered only to your seats. No more

jumping around, no more hide and seek. We'll put you by yourselves, and by yourselves you must stay. You must not accost, forcibly remove, or hinder the movement of any passengers. There must be no more complaints. Not one. My crew must be treated courteously and with respect from this point forward. The lavatories are to be used solely for the elimination of wastes, and I suspect we'll see plenty of that. This one here," he said, slamming the door shut, "is closed for repairs. No more drugs. No more screaming. No skullduggery or gangland activity of any kind." He looked from face to face. "Do we have a deal, gentlemen?"

"Deal," Strong said, looking first at Logan, who nodded. Strong shoved Barnes front and center as an offer of good faith. "You see," Strong said, "it's already workin'. A little more and he's gone."

"Indeed," the pilot said, an expression of compromise tinged with disgust. "Now sit your butts down, boys. Your whiskey is coming."

Barnes spoke, though his swollen tongue, chalky from the marijuana, made it difficult. "I'd prefer beer," he said.

"No beer," the captain snapped. "The hard stuff only or it's no deal."

"Let's not push it," Logan suggested, and even Strong agreed that the time for conciliation had come.

"A little water, maybe," Strong begged him, "just at the start?"

"One cup only," the captain said. He clapped his hands together. "And then straight to the jet fuel. Is that clear?"

"You bet," Logan said. He turned to leave and Strong followed, herding Barnes along in front of him. They passed the purser, whose look of contempt defied denial.

"Captain, I..."

"Just do it, Liz," he said. "I'm sorry. But it's for the best. As quickly as you can, pour whiskey down these men's throats. Please."

Strong took it from there. "That would be Johnny Walker for Joe College, here. Jack Daniel's for this one. And for me," he grinned, "gin."

FOUR

THE NIGHT BEFORE

Even the captain looked a little worn to Logan as he greeted the departing passengers. "Thanks for flying with us," he repeated as they passed by in their crumpled clothes. When Logan's turn came, the captain gripped him by the shoulders and leaned close to his ear. His breath smelled of mint mouthwash. "Don't even think about choosing my airline again."

"I didn't choose it this time," Logan said. He ducked under the aircraft's door and stepped into the heavy night air. Barnes and Strong, eyes red and faces swollen, lumbered close behind. Logan led them past the soldiers, Pakistani mercenaries with automatic weapons slung across their pleated shoulders, who formed a corridor to the German-made buses. He and his crew squeezed in with the other exhausted passengers. The pneumatic doors closed with a hiss and then the large tires rolled over the three hundred meters of scarred tarmac to the terminal gate.

Logan's head pounded with each bump, his stomach nauseous, his fingers trembling. He wondered when he'd learn. As if twenty years of watching his father endure this very same condition, at least until the daily cycle began again around noon, had not been enough. No matter. He'd soon sweat out the alcohol.

He squinted from the ocher glare of the halogen lights that illuminated the entire airport and most of urban Dhahran. God, he felt miserable. But if there was any justice in the world, Barnes and

Strong should feel far worse. Strong, in particular, looked as if he carried a mortal wound.

The bus came to a brisk halt in front of the huge, sliding-glass terminal entrance. Logan surged with the rest as the bus rocked back on its frame and the doors hissed open. He shepherded Barnes to their spot in the immigration line, the only thing cold in Saudi Arabia in August. Logan wanted no part of Jamie Strong here, where guilt by association was good enough to convict. The fun and games were over. Serious business lay immediately ahead.

Into this country whose technological, petrodollar-fueled future warred with its religious past, entered the mercenaries—strayed Nasranis, or Christians, tolerated out of economic necessity by one faction, a walking abomination in the hard eyes of the other, and despised by both if Logan's scotch-dulled instincts served him. If the immigration line had an ostensible purpose for Anglo westerners—whose track record with the darker-skinned races spoke well enough of their arrogance toward their reluctant Middle Eastern hosts—it was to slap their faces while it stamped their passports. The message had always been clear enough to Logan: *Bend your knee, white man. You are not master here.* Now he would hear it again.

The Saudi passengers, of course, required no such orientation. Once inside the terminal, most fell to their knees on the prayer rugs provided. Whether they had reentered precisely at one of the five prayer times published in the newspaper each day or simply had some catching up to do after living in the land of infidels, Logan couldn't say. Yet he admired their devotion. He didn't find many Baptists or Catholics on their knees in JFK's chapel. After their prayers, they drifted through the immigration line like graceful ghosts, dressed in their rumpled white *thobes* and fine white summer *ghutras*. Logan watched them filter into the surging throng.

The immigration official, a young Saudi dressed in a drab olive-green military uniform, pounded his palm on the worn Formica counter. Logan, roused from his reverie, looked up to read the man's face. But the official only stared at the near-empty counter of his booth. The drumming of his dark fingers signaled for Logan's documents.

Logan slid his passport under the slot of the scratched plexiglass window and the Saudi took it, flipping through the pages like a child who has not yet learned proper respect for a book. Logan watched as the official came to the one-year government visa, checked the dates, found the renewal on the next page, and stamped the new exit and reentry visa required for all visitors. Then he flipped through the rest of the pages, checking all the stamps Logan had collected in his travels, in search, Logan suspected, of one from Israel or South Africa. A stamp from either nation would mean immediate deportation, or so Logan had been told. But his passport contained neither, and the official shoved it back through the slot and waved him through without looking up. He pounded his hand on the counter for the next in line, who happened to be Strong. Strong, true to form, banged his fist in response. Not a good idea, but so many of Jamie Strong's ideas weren't.

Next, two aging natives in traditional garb complete with horned daggers thumbed through the passports again to check current visas. They took the last section of the immigration cards the airline had supplied to its passengers, checking what had already been checked. No one really understood their function, but Strong had once speculated that they were relatives of some ranking official and in need of gainful employment, lest they take to raiding caravans again. Immigration was a natural second choice. But at least the old-timers were pleasant and gracious, smiling at Logan as they waved him through.

Now Logan faced the last phase of entry. Saudi Arabia was governed by Sunni Moslems, Wahabi fundamentalists who adhered to the most conservative interpretations of Islamic law. The Koran forbade the use of certain substances, many of which were in common use throughout the world. Travelers were warned not to have them in their possession when they arrived, and ignorance of local law was a flimsy excuse. It was forbidden to possess statues or figurines—dolls included—or anything else formed in man's image. No magazines, videos, films, or photographs that displayed men and women anything but fully clothed were permitted. International newspapers and magazines for sale on the airport racks had been censored by black felt-tipped pens long before they reached the stands. And certainly no firearms, or even camouflage clothing; no drugs other than those prescribed by a physician; and no alcohol or even distilling equipment, and the Saudis had learned exactly what to look for.

Fortunately for Logan, illegal alcohol possession usually meant in the bottle and not in the blood; he knew his liver could not possibly have metabolized his intake yet. He put on a brave face, as he would at a late-night traffic stop, confident that he had collected himself well enough to pass inspection.

In his experience, immigration officials worldwide were a humorless, efficient lot. Smugglers of drugs and illicit currency had plenty to worry about, regardless of who they were trying to fool. But in Saudi Arabia, every visitor had cause for concern. The process seemed especially arbitrary, its grim agents keen to find fault. If discovered, banned items were confiscated and destroyed, usually before the owner's very eyes. Should one be apprehended with whiskey, recreational drugs, or pornographic materials, one would be detained and probably arrested, a situation a gifted native company liaison might sort out over a week or two with supplicant diplomacy and ready cash. A repeat offender faced immediate deportation and possibly the lash if the *qadi*, the judge, didn't like the look in his eyes.

Public beatings of foreigners, though rare, did occur. The English-language newspapers reported the tally. Such accounts were threats, and as far as Logan was concerned, they were effective. A westerner could question the law from the safety of his own compound, and most did. But to defy it openly in the Dhahran airport was a grave mistake. It had become his habit to check his luggage carefully before he left home.

Logan placed his bags on the counter and waited. He knew what to expect. The soldiers rifled through his belongings, their hands protected by latex gloves. They asked him the purpose of this item or that, especially about the stethoscope and badminton set. They inquired why his nametag said Logan "Doc" Wilson when his passport said otherwise. They flipped through his novels to see if they might be too explicit or offensive, on the banned list, or if they contained references of any kind to Israel. He'd once lost a book about the Six Day War at this same juncture. They had offered no explanation. They had just pitched it to the floor. They chided him for bringing so much chewing tobacco, lit cigarettes dangling from their lips, and picked through his toiletries to examine prescription bottles. Finally, they checked the bag for secret compartments or a false bottom. When that was done, they shoved the entire pile aside, and it was Logan's responsibility to put everything back and be quick about it, too.

Once Logan had repacked, a soldier on the other end of the counter marked his bag with an Arabic figure in white chalk. The soldier beside him inspected the mark, another inspected the inspector, and a fat man was shouting into the phone just as he'd been doing two months before. Beyond that the corridor led to all of Saudi Arabia. At last Logan was allowed to walk it.

Even that last lane was not free of chaos. Throngs of taxi drivers, bus operators, and company lackeys waiting to pick through the new arrivals jockeyed for position. They thrust their handwritten signs or corporate placards with pernicious vigor at any white man who walked by. Most of them screamed as well to up the ante. It had become Logan's habit to wait for his crew and face the storm together. He paused at the exit just as Barnes and Strong's turn came at the inspection counter. Since they each had only one bag, they stepped up together.

The immigration official lurched back when he smelled the stench of alcohol on these demons from the West. He faced Barnes. Barnes glared back. Logan saw what was happening: Strong knew the rules, as he did, and Barnes's condition was borderline at best. Strong reacted, shoving Barnes aside to step in his place.

"Let's go, man. We're in a hurry," Strong said, smacking at the inspector, answering intimidation with intimidation, his forte. He stuffed a stick of Juicy Fruit in Barnes's mouth. "Here!" he said, opening both their bags. "Get after it. We're in a hurry."

The soldier reached for the bags, still staring at Barnes. He was watching, Logan knew, for the slightest waver, listening for the slightest slur. Strong rapped the counter with his knuckles. "C'mon, man," he said. "There's no problem here. He's fine."

The soldier hesitated at first, then began rummaging through the carry-ons. Strong elbowed Barnes to stand back. Finally, the soldier picked up the bags and dumped them on the counter, scattering their contents with his hand, picking at items that interested him. He nodded at Strong and shoved the whole mess down the chute.

"We were lucky," Logan told Strong as they strolled the corridor together.

"Since when?" Strong said.

FIVE

───────◈───────

It was after midnight when the Indian driver nudged the Suburban's nose through the compound's closed chainlink gates. He idled past the racks of pipe, spools of cable, worn-out pumps, and rows of dust-caked trailers and parked at the front door of the Saudi division office. Logan took his place in Momentum 127's crew truck along with Strong, Barnes, and the master mechanic, Werner Freitag. Abraham, an Indian Catholic, took the wheel.

Things settled down quickly inside the cab as they made the long, southward journey. They passed the famous Arabian oil fields of the central eastern province, drove by Hofuf, the ancient oasis and port, and then entered the windswept dunes of the Rub al Khali, the Empty Quarter.

There was little conversation now. There were no longer any streetlights to illuminate the strange landscape, no more cinderblock or mud-brick homes, nationalized gas stations, or even family *souqs* (a sort of Saudi Arabian 7-Eleven) to break up the monotony of the five-hour trek into uninhabited wilderness. Logan stared out his window, overwhelmed by the bleakness. Strong nudged him in the ribs with his elbow, his way of offering a freshly lit joint.

"You crazy bastard," Logan said, just before he took a deep drag. He saw no reason to quarrel this time. He thought it would soothe his nausea.

"Ssshhh," Strong hissed. "They're asleep. And if there's one thing I know about you, Doc, it's that you can keep a secret."

"I don't even want to know where you hid it," Logan said, grunting, holding his breath.

"No," Strong said. "You don't."

Abraham sniffed the air. His eyes widened in the rearview mirror. Strong, grinning like a raccoon with the joint between his lips, waved at Abraham. The driver panicked.

"Very danger!" he cried.

"No problem. No people here," Strong said. "Only company *gondos*"—an Indian word Logan loosely translated as "asshole." "You, me, and three more white asses only."

"Very danger," Abraham insisted. He had heard stories, obviously. "Police catch…" He slapped one wrist across the other, symbolizing handcuffs. "After, we going inside long time."

"Naw, Abraham. Nobody's goin' to jail. Police coming, Strong eating, dope goin' inside." He pointed to his stomach. "Police not find. Don't worry."

Abraham continued to protest, more quietly now, still emphasizing the handcuff gesture. Preoccupied as he was with Strong's activities, it was only a matter of time before he allowed the speeding truck, top-heavy with its metal crew canopy, to run off the pavement into the shoulder of soft sand. Logan saw it coming.

"Watch out!" he screamed.

Motor mounts struck frame at the first rut. Barnes's eyes snapped open.

"What the…" Barnes shouted, anchoring his arm behind the back of his seat. "Go left—left! Watch that big rock! You better hope we don't get stuck out here on crew change day. I'll have your ass!"

Logan could see that Abraham was in no mood for threats. Plowing through dunes at 110 kilometers an hour was worry enough. Between the sluggishness of the tires in the sand and the canopy leaning opposite whichever way he turned, Abraham had a tough time regaining control of the truck. He turned one way, and Barnes, who had also grabbed the wheel, turned the other. When they slowed enough, the big truck swerved back onto the pavement. Abraham let it coast to a stop and shoved the transmission into park. He collapsed against the back of his seat, gasping for air.

"You wanna tell me what that was all about?" Barnes said.

"Very nervous," the Indian answered in choppy breaths.

"I know you're very nervous, Abraham. I'm a little nervous my ownself. I was thinkin' we'd be stuck out here all day tomorrow in 130-degree heat with no food or water."

"They smoking *ganja*," Abraham said. He pointed behind him with his thumb.

Barnes looked perplexed. "*Ganja?* What the hell is *ganja?*"

The Indian put his fingers to his mouth and sucked at them. "Smokey, smokey."

Barnes sniffed the air. "Oh, I get it," he said. "They're smokin' dope."

Abraham nodded, obviously relieved to have the ranking supervisor in on the problem. Barnes turned around, stern faced, only to be greeted by a smoking, resin-coated joint smoldering in his face.

"Gimme that," Barnes said. He brought the roach to his lips and inhaled. Abraham slapped his hand over his eyes. "Strong, if I catch you with any of this shit on my location, you'll be stateside the next day. Am I clear?"

"That's the last of it, Elvin," Strong said. "I swear. Just enough for these hangovers. It takes the edge off."

"I mean it." Barnes exhaled. "This stuff's no good for our line of work. I won't stand for it. I've seen a lot of good people get hurt working on this shit."

"I know. I don't have any more."

"Is there enough for me?"

All of the white asses perked up at the sound of the last voice. Abraham simply shook his head in despair.

"Why sure, Werner," Barnes said, handing the joint to the old man. Logan watched in amazement at the copious inhalations of the master mechanic. Damn if he didn't French inhale.

"Whoa!" Logan said. "Go, Werner!"

"I worked in South America for many, many years," he said in a deep, nasal tone.

"Who'd have figured?" Barnes said.

"Very danger," the driver protested once more.

"You're the only danger I see. Now if you can't handle it, just let me drive. Otherwise, let's keep it between the lines. *Sabe?*"

"No problem." Abraham engaged the vehicle, and they drove on.

Soon Barnes was snoring. Strong and Werner had sprawled into comfortable positions. Abraham drove well enough between brief, rearview glances to ensure that no new evil had broken out. But Logan couldn't sleep. He found himself more anxious than usual—from the alcohol not yet metabolized and from the added effect of marijuana. He shouldn't have smoked it—yet another "shouldn't have" to add to his growing list. How easily he was swayed against his better judgment.

He stared out at the desert and thought of Caitlin. He wondered if she was thinking of him. The problem, as Logan now saw it, was that Caitlin understood the problem. She knew why he held on to this life. The truth was that he'd come up so hard with so little, he didn't know if he had it in him to make it back home. And he was pretty sure that Strong no longer believed he had it in him to make it *here*. Caitlin pulling, Strong pushing. Toward what, exactly, Logan had no idea. But it seemed both of the people closest to him demanded he change.

Goddamn Jamie Strong, Logan thought. Once Logan had loved him like a brother. They'd been inseparable that first year in the North Sea. They worked together as assistant drillers on a fourteen-day rotation. Days off they summered in Devon and the Costa del Sol, wintered in Innsbruck and Kitzbühel. Palma de Mallorca during the bullfight season was Logan's favorite. He'd spent many a Sunday in the *sol* seats, drinking iced beer out of a metal bucket. Strong was magnetically drawn to the seedier parts of Amsterdam, especially after he'd witnessed an onstage argument between two performers of a live sex show. With all of Europe at his disposal, it had been a highlight for him. But they'd gone where they pleased. It had been quite an experience for a twenty-three year old, and Logan cherished the memories. He just wished he'd had the good sense to leave Strong to his own manic devices and come back to Texas. Back then, Logan easily could have gone to work for any one of the domestic oil companies, which had been part of his one and only amorphous career plan. The door was open then. But with the world oil glut and the domestic layoffs that accompanied it, he'd waited too long.

Logan's problems with Strong had started with Strong's unfortunate marriage, a whirlwind romance by a whirlwind man. When this union soured, as everyone had predicted it would, his withdrawal began. Before Strong reached bottom, he had ruined both of their careers. Logan had never told a soul—not even Caitlin—what had really happened. He was too ashamed to share that burden. But every time he glanced into Strong's cloudy eyes, Logan was reminded of his most bitter personal failure.

He knew how easily it could happen again, but he was stupid enough to keep the secret to himself in the name of loyalty between fools who had once been friends. Now he'd thrown his lot in with a man he could never trust again. His apprehension, he was certain, contributed to the recurring nightmare.

Barnes, Werner, and Strong were all snoring, a sort of white-trash, nasal a cappella suite. Abraham stared at the road ahead like a zombie. Logan tried to shake off his uncertainties and gear up for the weeks ahead. The Empty Quarter would try to take everything he had left.

The crescent moon was up now, illuminating the alien formations around him. He could finally distinguish between rainless cloud bank and dune ridge. The truck plunged deeper into the gaunt landscape, whose vastness was sliced in half by the black asphalt ribbon that led nowhere but to its end.

SIX

The First Day

Logan left the catwalk to cross the flat of coarse sand between the substructure and the mud pits. He climbed the steps, slick from the steam that rose out of the dark, swirling fluid below. He found Gayland Buffarn in the cramped white metal office perched atop the active system. Buffarn sat next to the sink fumbling with the mud scale as if he were finally committed to learning how to use it. Logan feared it was a wasted effort.

Buffarn was a westerner, a thickset, square-jawed lump of overalled manliness from Utah. Logan had worked in the North Sea under his older brother, a competent, pious Mormon who never cussed or raised his voice regardless of the situation, a rarity in the oil fields. His little brother, it seemed, was more easily corrupted by his professional milieu. Buffarn acted like all the rest.

He was the kind of Mormon Logan wanted to ask, "Say, do you really believe that fella Smith found an extra book to the Bible in that cave?" And Buffarn would probably answer, "Naw, but we get extra wives out of the deal, so we don't bitch." He was the kind the Church's spin doctors don't let hang around Salt Lake City, and for whom they're all too happy to waive the one-year missionary requirement. Buffarn they kept hidden in the hills, resting a little easier in the knowledge that he had managed to find employment in the remote Rub al Khali. There was no doubt in Logan's mind that Buffarn's position had been arranged by his successful brother. Someone in Tulsa had done him and the entire Mormon faith a very big favor.

"Why hullo, thair, Doctor," Buffarn greeted him in his peculiar Utah twang. "Good time back in the States?"

"Just peachy, Buffarn. How're things with you?" They shook hands, then Buffarn began stuffing his calculator, pipe tally book, and smokes into the pockets of his tattered Carhartts.

"Oh, fine I guess," he said. "Say, you didn't fart a bunch in our room last night, did ya?"

Logan had to think a minute. "Can't say for sure, Buffarn. I was asleep. Probably did though."

"Well," Buffarn began, screwing up his face, "that Canadian son of a bitch relief of yours ate curry for two weeks straight and just about run me out of thair. It got to where I had to drive down after crew change and load up an expat plate and shove it down his nasty gullet. Course, a responsible pusher would've sent him to Dhahran to one of them A-rab doctors to get checked out. It's obvious his guts is rotted out."

Logan's mind went blank for a second. "Sounds bad," he said.

"Gawd, I hate livin' with that stinkin' Cannuck bastard. Might as well sleep with a cesspool vent crammed up my nose."

"Might as well." Logan dug into his fresh pouch of Levi Garrett and loaded the first chew of the month into his mouth. He shuddered. He enjoyed the sweet caramel taste, but not the way his head swooned from the first rush of nicotine. His stomach felt a bit dodgy for that. This would soon pass, until like any addict he craved tobacco above food. By the trip's end, he would chew a pack a day. "How's about fillin' me in on what's goin' on around here? I already know how bad our cabin stinks."

"Uh, yeah. Okay." Buffarn reached for a soiled notebook with rows of figures scribbled in pencil. "Here's the way it's been on my tour," he said. He pronounced it "tower" as they all did. "The mud weight's holdin' at ninety-seven pounds per cubic foot. And they are damn sure serious about wantin' to keep it there."

Buffarn explained that he had added the fine, powdery barite to hold the system's weight for maybe two hours, just trickling it into the active system. He supposed the mud engineer wanted to do a treatment in the afternoon. The system would require thinners and more bentonite gel.

"The mud's comin' back hotter 'n hell," Buffarn added, "'bout 140 degrees Fahrenheit, and so you gotta add water to keep it from dryin' out an' gettin' too damn thick. I got about ten barrels an hour tricklin' in the active pit."

He paused to look over his smudged notes. It took a while. "Looks like you got it, Doc," he said, starting down the steps. "I'm headin' for the house."

"See ya at midnight," Logan yelled to Buffarn, who waved but never looked back as he tromped across the location.

Logan had learned from experience to check the system for himself once on duty. As he crossed the metal gratings above the mud pits—four active tanks mounted on one skid, four reserve tanks of equal size on another directly adjacent—the steam obscured the lower half of his body. He broke out into an immediate sweat. The drilling fluid gurgled in the pits beneath him, its eddies driven by large propeller-shaped agitators. The mud looked like his mother's fudge as she whipped it in an old pan. He reset each of the rudimentary hand markers—nuts suspended on lengths of sash cord coiled around the handrails—so he could monitor the level of fluid while they drilled new hole.

This was crucial in any operation, but especially in exploration as was the case here. A sudden loss or gain meant serious trouble. Momentum had installed electronic volume sensors, but they were often fouled with caked mud and so were unreliable. The crude strings provided a trusted second opinion if the well decided to flow before it was supposed to. Electronic readings were sent to the floor to be read on one of Strong's gauges. But Logan, true to his teachings in the tricky gas fields of Galveston Bay, relied most on his little ropes.

Satisfied that he had a handle on the pits, Logan decided to inspect the mud pumps next. Only one of the triplex giants was currently in service; the smaller drill bit used at this depth did not require much pressure to achieve suitable hydraulics. In the shallow sections of the hole, both pumps ran to capacity to sustain velocities powerful enough to remove the tons of clay and shale that emerged from the bore, and were then filtered out over a series of vibrating mesh screens—the shale shakers—and dumped behind the pits until Brother, the Rhodesian crane operator, shoved them away with Momentum's huge bulldozer.

Logan examined the pump pistons thrusting in and out of their cylindrical liners for potential wear on the rubber pump parts, or expendables, that would allow leakage and loss of pressure. When a part wore out, mud that began as a trickle would soon spray violently for several feet. Once the rubber had eroded, the fluids could wash away the metal parts as easily as a blowtorch could melt steel. Logan had seen it happen many times, but it always struck him with a sense of wonder. He had developed a healthy respect for the power of fluid pressure. As much as the great pumps could deliver, it was a spit compared to the earth's potential. He'd seen that a few times, too.

A good assistant driller, an AD, watched for the tiniest drops of mud forming where they should not be and learned to listen for the telltale gasp of a leaking valve or the hiss of a wearing swab, much like a physician listened to a patient's diseased heart. Violent eruptions would soon follow these early warning signs.

Small leakages, especially those appearing just before a crew change, were often allowed to continue in the hopes that they might go undetected long enough to fall under the next man's watch. So Logan made it a point to check the pumps as soon as he went on tour. Buffarn had stuck it in his ass before.

The pumps seemed sound enough and Logan returned to the shed to recheck the mud's weight and viscosity. Inside, he found a muscular Indian wearing a University of Texas Longhorn football jersey Logan had given him. He leaned on the table, timing the fluid as it ran through the viscosity funnel. Logan stood next to him near the logbook, ready to record the results. The Indian smiled below his mirror sunglasses, also Logan's gift.

"Hullo, Doc-baby," the big Indian said. "How the fuck you doing?"

"Great, Abdullah-baby. How the fuck are you doin'?"

"Oh, number one," he said. "Only twenty-eight days more, I go to fucking India. Plenty jig-jig. No more *whanimidi!*" Abdullah gestured with his hands to signify masturbation. "Jig-jig" clearly meant the preferred alternative.

Logan kept his gaze fixed on the mud log. "Well, that's certainly something to look forward to," he said. "I guess." Logan would hate to be Abdullah's wife after he'd been gone for three months.

"Feeftee-too," Abdullah said. It had taken fifty-two seconds for the specified volume of mud to pass through the funnel opening. This was a measure of fluid viscosity, the ideal thickness specified by Huntley Cleftbar, the mud engineer and a known wanker. Logan recorded the numbers on the chart. Abdullah poured mud into the weight scales, tapping them carefully to remove all air bubbles. He placed the scales on the rack, working quickly with precise, nimble fingers.

"Nine-tee-seefen plus," he said. A cubic foot of mud weighed a little more than ninety-seven pounds.

"That sounds good, man," Logan said. Buffarn, God bless him, had done him right.

Abdullah rinsed the scales and the viscosity cup, dried his hands on a rag hanging over the sink, and offered his hand to his supervisor after a brief hesitation. Logan shook it firmly, smiling at the thought of how far they had come to accept such a gesture. None of the Indians, known as third country nationals or TCNs, relished the thought of having personal contact with a wicked race of men who wiped their butts with pieces of flimsy paper. The one point on which all Muslim, Hindu, and Christian Indians agreed was that the prophet Mohammed had a good thing going on the proper procedure for this private human function. Momentum had provided a TCN latrine, but the Indians would rather go blind than use it. Somewhere along the line, Barnes had abandoned it to the desert.

They much preferred the water line, a system of pipes joining a well some kilometers away staffed by a toothless Pakistani no one understood. Anglo expatriates referred to this region as "Turd Alley," and it was always avoided by the more seasoned staff.

The operation was completed, so Logan had been told, by using the contents of a bucket and the left hand. The right hand was left pure for eating and Logan felt at minimal risk to shake with any member of his crew. The Indians, however, discovered no such strict routine among the white asses, as they affectionately referred to the expatriate supervisors, and suspected they were ambidextrous. For months, they literally cringed at a white man's touch. Eventually they learned that some of the white devils washed their hands with reassuring regularity, but a pat on the back was by far their preference. Logan had worked for two years alongside Abdullah, the most Americanized of all the Indians, and he no longer seemed to mind a handshake so much.

Logan picked up the phone and paged the drill floor. Strong answered. "Strong here," he said. "Makin' hole is my goal."

"I got a lot goin' on down here. You ready to compare notes?"

"Shoot."

Logan explained that they were adding about ten barrels of water an hour, but evaporation in that heat would be heavy, so he didn't think Strong's indicators would show much gain. The mud cleaners were running to filter out the finer sediment, mostly sand, and they had the hopper running as well, in case they needed to add weight along with the fresh water. "So," Logan said, "unless somethin' changes on my end, your gauges ought to read steady."

"Okay, Doc," Strong said. "Your markers set?"

"Yep. What's your pressure like?" A constant reading was the sign of a healthy pump.

"Solid. Looks good."

"How's it goin' up there?"

"Not too good. Elvin's up here tellin' me about every hole he played on the golf course in Big Spring, Texas."

"Damn the bad luck." Logan laughed.

"You ain't seen my niggers, have ya?"

Logan hesitated. Strong's rare use of that word made it clear he intended to begin this hitch where he'd left off the last one. He was already unhappy with his roughnecks.

Why the change, Logan wondered. Strong had once cared deeply for the Indians. He had molded that sickly, emaciated group of strangers into a crew. He'd started by teaching them to tie the shoelaces of their Momentum brogans and worked his way up until they became roughnecks as good as any in the world. Strong worked with them, ate with them, lived with them. He became their friend and advocate. He was the one who argued with Tulsa for leniency in their merciless eighty-four-day working schedule. No expat could endure it. Why should they? He went to bat for Abdul Rahiman, suggesting that Momentum reward his abilities with an assistant driller's job. Tulsa turned a deaf ear, but Logan had marveled at Strong's patience, leadership, and compassion. Where was that man now?

"What niggers are those, Jamie?" Logan said.

"Don't start with me, Doc," Strong said. "I ain't in the mood. If you see my Indians, you send 'em up to the floor."

"You bet." Logan hung up.

After the exchange, no sound rose above the drone of the

Superior diesels. Logan felt hot wind on his face as he studied the derrick above. Momentum 127 was "big iron," designed to handle exceptionally heavy hook loads in deep holes. The kelly—the hexagonal shaft of high-tensile steel, so shaped to allow the rotary table to grip it and then turn—twirled at its steady, hypnotic rate, swaying from a mild bend along its forty-five-foot length. Penetration was slow but steady, with a new bit on the bottom that would last some time. Smooth sailing, Logan thought. Perfect conditions for the first day back.

He looked out at the mountainous range of golden, crested dunes. For such a desolate place, the Rub al Khali had its own beauty—a clean and powerful majesty that eclipsed the iron derrick. The wind strengthened with the afternoon heat, blowing dust across the location that obscured the distant horizon. The sky mirrored the hue of the desert below. The thermometer read 121 degrees and it was only one o'clock. By late afternoon, it would easily reach 130 degrees.

The sweat on Logan's arms had already evaporated, leaving distinct white high-water marks on his worn khaki sleeves. Logan craved water. He hoisted the plastic cooler and drank from the spout. Then he left Abdullah in charge to wander about the location. He'd already sweated out the alcohol. His body felt fatigued, but his mind had cleared, and a day begun was a day half done. Two hours into his first tour, Logan settled into the routine.

It felt good to be back in Momentum's shadow. He wondered why he had worried so much about coming back. Here he understood how everything worked and what was expected of him. If something broke, he'd probably know how to fix it. If something went wrong, he would probably know how to react. In the Rub al Khali, he had a trade and he was good at it. No such luck back home. In urban Texas, Logan felt lost. If Caitlin could see how he functioned here, she'd forget about asking him to leave. Her only image of him was sulking on her sofa, a bottle of beer in his hand. He could change that far easier than he could change careers. Caitlin's reaction was his fault.

No matter what happened, no matter how Strong behaved, Logan knew he was better off here. He had earned his place in the Rub al Khali, and it would require a serious upheaval to drive him from it.

SEVEN

———◈◈◈———

Logan wandered under the substructure of the derrick, a grid of square and angular girders that supported the weight of both mast and drill string. Centered beneath it was the pit, dug fifteen feet into the sand, its walls braced with inch-thick panels of reinforced steel. From its depths rose the mud-caked wellhead, treated to endure the rigors of hydrogen sulfide, which rendered common steel brittle and useless. Atop the wellhead stood the blowout preventer stack, twenty tons of iron rams actuated by hydraulic pistons, and the barrel-shaped hydril, designed like a basket to seal itself around the surface of moving pipe should the well decide to kick while they were drilling. In such cases, the well must seal and the pipe must move. The hydril's design met both conditions. Above the preventer stack sat the "possum belly," the bell-shaped reservoir that rose to just beneath the rotary table on the drill floor. Mud returning from the well flowed through it to a trough connected to the filtering shale shakers and then back to Logan's steamy pits, only to be pumped down again through the kelly to the drill pipe and blasted through the drill bit jets downhole. The cycle never ended as long as Momentum drilled on.

Logan surveyed it all, listening to the drone of the 750-horse-power electric rotary motor, broken only by the screech of the drawworks' brakes when Strong bored another inch or two of new hole. The weight on the bit would remain constant, as would everything else. Logan found comfort in the continuity. The oil field was the first place he'd ever encountered it.

Looking back, it had been a strange series of events that had led him to the Rub al Khali. Caitlin was correct; there'd been no plan. He'd left the university after his lackluster freshman year. He hadn't been much interested in his studies. In fact, he wasn't interested in much at all. But he needed a job to support himself and he knew he'd work as a galley slave before he returned to his parents' home.

That had been the year of their divorce. Too little, too late as far as he was concerned. The years preceding his nineteenth birthday had ruined that place for him. Not a day passed when he didn't find some evidence of his father's failed schemes or some token of his infidelities. The nights were worse. The continual arguments, the breaking of dishes in the kitchen, the slamming of bedroom doors. Collection agencies called every evening about some overdue bill. On the rare occasions when his father took an interest in his life, Logan couldn't help but smell the stench of alcohol on his breath or some floozie's perfume on his rumpled jacket. As time went on, things got worse. Logan's father couldn't possibly have been surprised the day the constable served him with the divorce papers. He'd had twenty years of chances and wasted them all. With his father out of the picture, Logan redirected his anger toward his mother because she'd allowed that man to contaminate the family for so long. And that's where he left it.

Caitlin knew none of this. Logan refused to talk about it. So she could never understand why once he got out of that house, nothing could make him go back.

He had heard of a job where a guy worked straight through for one week in exchange for one week off. The pay was good and he thought the schedule might suit his restlessness. He filled out an application and got a phone call three days later. That took him to the great drilling barges of Galveston Bay and a new world.

He rode the twin-screw supply boat, piloted by a one-legged ex-shrimper from South Louisiana, past the wellheads, reefs, and murky oyster beds to the island rig. He stood just over six feet at the time, weighed maybe 165 pounds soaking wet, his coat-hanger shoulders connected by gristle and bone to his pencil legs. He was a gangly boy with a lot of energy and a bad attitude. High school in Houston hadn't really rounded off his rough Arkansas edges.

He had no brothers. He played no team sports. He had maybe two close friends, both of whom were usually stoned. The only man in his life was, at best, a bad example.

Logan came of age with a sense that somebody owed him something, but by then he was pretty sure he would never collect. He crawled out from his father's shadow with little more than his hunger and determination. That crew boat was the first thing to come along for him where he sensed he'd use them both. When it anchored at the barnacled dock, he didn't hesitate.

He worked two days as a roustabout, a maintenance man. On the third, he was awakened by the motorman to temporarily replace an injured roughneck on the night shift. It was supposed to last only one hitch. As it happened, it lasted a year.

He rose to the job in body and spirit. His sinewy frame responded to the arduous work and heaping meals. Stranded on that iron island, he saw the chaotic world around him start to settle. He'd stumbled into his niche when he least expected it.

He earned his place on a drill crew. He became part of a team. He depended on other men, and they depended on him. He found no reason not to trust those in authority. The more responsibility he accepted, the more they gave him, and the promotions quickly followed. He roughnecked for six months, ascending to derrickman, the second in command on an eight-man crew. For the first time in his life, he saw himself as an achiever. He saw himself as a man. Looking back, nothing could have been more important.

After one year he left the drilling barge to try college again. On his last day his crew had stripped his clothes in a scuffle and "doped" him with gobs of pipe-thread lubricant, an oil field rite of initiation as old as the Hughes rotary bit. For him, it was the mark of pride. He stood naked and alone on the bottom deck as the sun rose across the still, bay waters, wiping the pipe dope from his buttocks and genitals with a rag soaked in a bucket of diesel fuel, laughing. He showered, dressed in street clothes, gave all his accoutrements to those who needed them—save his hard hat, which he kept forever—and left that old rusty barge with a whole new plan.

More assured, disciplined, and serious, he worked hard for his college grades. He spent his summers in the oil fields wherever he was needed, and sometimes Christmas vacations as well. He studied English literature primarily, but also geology, finance, and business, all interests sparked by his oil field tenure and the career that might follow it. After graduation, he accepted, of all things, an offer to work in the land office of one of the oil company giants. Few such offers were made that year, and Logan was proud to receive one.

Then a recruiter for Momentum, the largest drilling contractor in the world, called. How they'd gotten his name he had no idea, but they offered him an assistant driller's job in the North Sea. Fourteen days on, fourteen days off, stationed in Aberdeen, Scotland, a job that paid three times what the oil company had offered him as a jive-ass junior executive. The world had called, and Logan answered. He applied for his passport, advised Exxon that they wouldn't be seeing much of him around the watercooler, and boarded a jet for Heathrow.

At first the power of the North Sea daunted Logan, as did the great offshore installations that probed for her honey crude. Soon enough, they absorbed him. It was his first taste of big iron, and he liked it. He'd promised his college girlfriend he'd stay only a few months. But his days off with Strong led from one adventure to another, and two years flew by. Even then, he'd known that nothing—at least nothing that was coming his way—could equal the experience, and he clung to it with an energy he'd never known before. Somehow he'd cheated his middle-class fate. Logan saw himself as truly lucky, truly free.

Then came the debacle with Jamie Strong.

He'd had no choice but to return stateside, more exhausted and ashamed than homesick. He enrolled in graduate school just to catch his breath and lick his wounds. He had amorphous plans of collecting a master's degree to demonstrate what a smart boy he was. After that, he might knock again on the doors of the oil companies or maybe a law school or two. But graduate study in English literature couldn't match the European pace. He studied less than he needed to and drank more than he should have. He became restless and bored. He jumped at Momentum's next unexpected offer, an AD position in Saudi Arabia.

It was a second chance, and this time Logan knew exactly what he was giving up. The choice seemed simple. Better to spend his working days around this iron he knew so well than stumble around Austin lost, with a big hole in his resume. Three years as a bohemian was difficult to explain to a corporate recruiter. Momentum had rescued him from all that.

The money was still good, the Indian crews excellent, the Saudis not around. And the off days were his to spend as he pleased. Good enough, he thought. His generation had gone on without him, and he told himself he didn't care about it anymore. He'd be content to let the pieces fall where they may if Caitlin wouldn't push him to find something different.

Yes, sir. Logan was grateful that he had come to the oil fields. He remembered now that this place was his refuge and not his prison. With a little patience and perseverance, opportunity would come looking for him again. He was, after all, lucky that way.

He heard another screech of the brakes and turned from his reverie.

"Doc!" Abdullah yelled from the pits. "Pump all fucked up!"

Logan left the substructure, certain he could fix whatever was wrong with the machine.

Logan had eaten, showered, and cranked the window unit up to its highest setting. It had taken only a couple of minutes to wash the stale heat out of his room. He'd cleaned and conditioned his slip-on Redwing Wellingtons, the type he'd worn in the patch since his roughnecking days, and set them outside to dry. He was about to slip his body between cool cotton sheets when there was a loud knock at the door. A white man.

"Come in, goddamn it."

"Good to see you, too, Doc," Strong said, drops of water at the ends of his black curls. He handed Logan an envelope. Momentum never sealed them. "Telex came for you," he said. "Might be important."

"Thanks," Logan said. He opened the Momentum envelope. He wondered how Strong knew it held a telex and why, for God's sake, the bastard just stood there like a big nosy lug. He unfolded the crisp yellow paper. It was from Caitlin. It read:

I'M FINISHED THINKING, LOGAN. I LOVE YOU. I'M SETTING THE DATE. SEPTEMBER 15. IF YOU'RE NOT COMING, BETTER TELL ME SOON. OTHERWISE GET READY TO HONEYMOON.

LOVE, CAITLIN

P.S.: HAVE EXPANDED YOUR INVITATION LIST TO SEVENTY-FIVE. SORRY.

Logan reached for a pencil and scribbled his reply:

I'LL BE THERE. PATENTS PENDING. ALL MY LOVE.

LOGAN

In the morning he'd give it to Tate-Pixilate, the camp boss, to send. He couldn't imagine what seventy-five friends of his she'd found to invite to their wedding. He also couldn't imagine why Strong was hanging around.

"Good news, Doc?" Strong said.

"Yep," Logan said.

"I hope you'll be happy. I was," Strong said, as he started to leave. "For a little while." He let the door swing shut behind him.

EIGHT

DAY THREE

Logan stood beside Strong on the drill floor listening to the discussion that would decide their labors over the next few days. Behind them stood Marshall Christianson, the Arabco drilling foreman, and Mousa Onabi, the geologist, a Sudanese. Both men leaned over the geolograph, comparing its figures with ones Mousa had previously marked in his field book.

"What d'ya think?" Marshall said. His tone was brisk.

"We're into the dome," Mousa said, running a dark, skinny finger down a crumpled graph. "It coincides with the depth of the seismograph charts." He rose to his full height. "It's a thick shale strata, I think. Impervious and brittle. A perfect seal for a great reservoir."

"You wanna call it TD?" Marshall said. His only sign of pleasure at such promising news was the gleam in his nervous, searching eyes. His manner and tone never changed.

TD, total depth, did not mean to Logan that they'd reached the reservoir. The question was whether or not they'd drilled deep enough to run the next string of casing pipe, a protective liner of tubular steel that sealed off the uncertainties of the open bore. Momentum's final objective, the gas reservoir, lay far below the hard dome whose surface they had, perhaps, only scratched. The cuttings filtered out of the drilling fluid suggested they might have reached it, but the only way to make sure was through the use of technology Logan couldn't begin to understand. They had to log the well.

"Yeah," Mousa answered with a western inflection, assimilated from his many years working alongside Americans. "We should pull out and log it, Marshall. Then we'll know."

"All right, Mousa," Marshall said. He shoved his hands in the loose pockets of his worn khaki pants. "It'll cost us three days before it's all done. More if we find out we've got to drill deeper. I hope you're right." Logan marked the implied warning.

"I'm right," Mousa said, his impish grin cloaking his intelligence. Reserved, competent, and unflappable, Mousa Onabi had earned the drill crew's respect. The Sudanese was a diminutive sort, thin and spidery, crowned with a thick mat of bushy black hair that caused his hard hat to sit a full six inches above his scalp. Add to that his loose-fitting polyester shirt, high-water pants, and lace-up grandpa boots, and Mousa looked exotic enough for Marshall to call him the Witch Doctor, a name that seemed to amuse him.

"The Witch Doctor here's called it, Jamie," Marshall said. "I want you to pick up the kelly and ream back through the formation half a dozen times. Then circulate bottoms up." Logan knew he'd have to calculate the time it took for the mud blasting through the bit jets to rise up the well bore and reach the shale shaker screens on its long, steamy trip back to the active pits.

"Pull out ten stands to the last string of casing, run her back down again, and circulate bottoms up one more time," Marshall said. "When that's done, set all the pipe on the bank and rig up to run the nine and five-eighths casing. Got it?"

"Yep," Strong answered. "I got it."

"Keep that pipe movin' in the open hole, Strong," Marshall added, "same as you do on your time off."

He turned to Logan. "Good afternoon to you, cousin," he said. Marshall had been in Arabia for thirty-odd years, but he'd never lost the Arkansas inflection he shared with Logan. They were from the same county. Marshall knew of Logan's family. Logan, who'd been dragged out of state at fourteen, knew nothing of his. But their roots bound them, or so Marshall always claimed. Strong, who had none, leered.

"Marshall," Logan said, embarrassed by the preferential treatment. Then Marshall left the floor.

"Doc, will you share your calculations with me?" Mousa said. "I want to collect another sample before we pull out, just to make certain."

"Sure," Logan said, and he recorded Mousa's figures, noting the depth of the last string of casing run. He knew the diameter of the open hole (same size as the bit), as well as the diameter of the casing set above it. It was a matter of determining first the current well volume and then the number of pump strokes it would take to displace it. "It'll take just a minute. I'll send them down."

"Thank you," Mousa said, and he turned away for the elevator.

"We're gonna work tonight," Strong said, yanking the cable to the air horn to summon Nigel Ripley, Logan's co-AD. It would be Ripley's job to organize activities on the floor.

Logan found all four roughnecks sitting on the bench in the mud house, crowding Abdullah, who didn't seem to mind the company or the cramped conditions. The metal shack sheltered the roughnecks from the Saudi sun and hid them from Strong, who would be unhappy to see them idle. Roughnecks the world over had a gift for finding remote places to lounge, but the Indians, in Logan's opinion, were the most talented. They knew every Momentum nook and cranny, and they were just the right size to squeeze in.

"Hullo, Doc," they said in unison, this followed by a series of grinning white teeth. Their brawn seemed inconsistent with their slight skeletal frames. Hard bodies swelled beneath their shabby clothes—bodies Momentum had made.

"What's goin' on here?" Logan said, but there was no answer.

Abdullah threw up his hands. "These fucking peoples always here, Doc," he said with token exasperation. "Abdullah don't know what the fuck to do."

"I've got a notion," Logan said as he turned to the roughnecks. "Y'all find somewhere else to hide."

"No problem," said Putti, the pipe racker, but no one moved. They lingered, all eyes on Logan. They wanted something, and he'd already given them the stethoscope, western belts, and badminton set, promptly exchanged for Saudi riyals. What else, he wondered, could it be?

"We ain't goin' to Hofuf," he said. They always wanted to go. They'd spend their money and kick up their heels. For Logan, such trips were always a worrisome, sleepless disaster. Recapturing a wild Indian was damn hard work. He didn't have it in him to go again.

"We never ask," Putti said, his sly expression assuring Logan that they soon would.

"What then?" Logan demanded, and again the silence fell.

"Doc?" said Abdul Rahiman, the youngest. Despite his youth, he had emerged as the roughnecks' leader and spokesman. It didn't seem to matter that he was the smallest. The Indians deferred to him in any crisis or controversy. And Logan knew that Rahiman had learned how to deal with Anglo supervisors.

Rahiman was a handsome, dark, hard-eyed man of twenty-three. The sun had burned copper streaks in his raven hair. He was shrewd but temperamental, which Logan chalked up to his youth. Logan admired him, and he knew Strong did, too.

Strong had recommended Rahiman to take Ripley's place as AD when it became known that the Englishman had requested a transfer, and Logan had agreed to work at his side. Abdullah, the derrickman, was stronger; Putti, the Hindu, wiser; but Rahiman, a natural fighter, was the roughnecks' heart and spirit. Their trust in him was absolute. Logan had learned long ago that to deal effectively with his Indian crew, he had to deal with Rahiman first.

Now something was on Rahiman's mind, which meant that they had all been wondering about it, and he stepped forward.

"What is meaning 'neegeer'?" he asked.

Logan saw no anger in Rahiman's eyes. He exhaled, hesitating. "Don't you know by now?" He knew the issue had come up many times before. He'd always stepped around it in the interest of harmony. The Indians walked a hard road for Momentum. Would their journey be any easier if Logan added that ugly label to their burden?

Most of the Indians had come to Saudi Arabia from rural, poverty-stricken areas and had never even seen their neighboring villages, much less a drilling rig. Strong had worked with them from the beginning, and had gone to great pains to explain to Logan what the experience had been like. They had arrived sickly, frail, afraid, and deep in debt from the bribes they paid agents for the "opportunity" to work abroad. Many had to be treated for parasites and other disabling diseases that came to a head under the Saudi sun. Once healed, acclimated, and equipped, they went to work.

It hadn't been easy. The Indians were initially shocked by what Momentum expected of them. They thought they'd come to be houseboys and clerks, not roughnecks. Strong said he'd seen them quake at the breadth and height of the derrick, and at the massive tools they would learn to operate beneath it. Their elfin bodies were dwarfed by the iron all around them. They didn't possess the strength to latch a tong.

There were other problems. Since Saudi Arabia is the birthplace of Islam, preference once was given to foreigners of Arabic blood and Muslim faith. This changed after the *Intifadet-el-Haram*, the Uprising of the Holy Place, a coup attempt by religious extremists in 1979. Shaken by this bloody episode, the Saudi government was all too happy to consider foreign laborers of other faiths and non-Arab nations, at least those less likely to choose sides in the widening rift between mosque and state. This decision had opened the door for Indians, Sri Lankans, Pakistanis, Filipinos, and Koreans.

But on Logan's particular crew, Islam still predominated. Momentum employed Abdul Mohammed Rahiman, Abdullah Mohammed, Mohammed Abdullah, and the ringer Hindu, Vranesch Putti. Whenever Strong called for Mohammed, three men appeared, unless some of the roustabouts—Mohammeds all—happened to be within range also, in which case Strong would be mobbed. To alleviate the confusion, Strong nicknamed his Muslim floormen Moe, Curly, and Larry. In the interest of continuity, he called Putti, the odd Hindu out, Shemp.

At first the Indians had been suspicious, believing that the big American had named them something evil like the strange and unexplainable "motherfucker," a word they heard daily. But they came to trust Strong, especially after he brought along some Three Stooges videos to put their minds at ease. Logan enjoyed watching the saturnine airport censors view these. Much to Logan and Strong's delight, the Indians possessed a singular passion for slapstick, even learning to replicate the noises and gestures of their assigned characters.

In time Logan managed, as did Strong, to call his crew by their given names, at least in private conversations, which the Indians appreciated. Few of the Americans and British went to such lengths. The Indians were called by a variety of names and numbers (usually one through four) and didn't seem to care much until this word "nigger" began cropping up. Logan couldn't see how they possibly deserved it. There was no excuse, and Logan decided then and there he'd make none.

"Y'all really don't know?" he said.

"We guess," Rahiman answered, his eyes sparkling, "but we don't know. Same maybe like motherfucker, no?"

"No," Logan said, shaking his head. He knew that some of the Americans used the word only when they were angry or frustrated with their crews; some of the British, always. Brother, who at his core was kindhearted, used only this term or its African equivalent, *kaffa*. Now that the roughnecks had come to him to ask, believing that he would answer honestly, Logan couldn't disappoint them. "There is a difference," he finally said.

"What difference?" Rahiman asked.

"Well," he began, "in my place some white people calling black people 'nigger'."

"Black peoples?" Rahiman said. "Like us?"

"No. American black people."

"Ah. Same-same like geologist. He is nigger, no?"

"He might be called nigger, Rahiman. But he is no nigger. No one is."

"Is bad word, yes?"

Again Logan hesitated. "It's not good."

Rahiman cut his stare to the others. It said, "I told you so." They rattled back and forth in Hindi until Rahiman lifted his palm to demand silence. He would handle it. "Why do some white asses call us—Indian peoples—nigger? We no understand."

"Because they don't know any better," Logan said. "They're dumb asses, that's all. *Gondos*." They all laughed, slightly teetering their heads from side to side. It looked like they were saying no, but what they meant was, yes, we agree. This characteristic looked particularly odd to Logan when the Indians were wearing their plastic hard hats. "There's no place for that here, and nowhere else, either."

"And if they call us that, Doc," Rahiman said, "should Indian peoples be angry?"

Logan knew where this was going. Word got around that there'd been strikes on other rigs for similar reasons, all probably justified in Logan's view. The Indians knew they were being exploited and were expected to be quiet about it. All they asked for was a little respect, and Logan had just confirmed that they weren't getting it. They didn't know the strike organizers had been docked pay and unceremoniously sent home, a disaster with consequences far beyond life at the rig. Most of the roughnecks supported dozens of relatives and in-laws at home. Logan didn't want their families to suffer on his account.

"Look," he said, reaching for a paper cup and filling it with ice water from the Igloo. "You men do a damn good job over here, better than most. You should take pride in that and let this other thing go." He took a sip. The cold hurt his teeth. "It means nothing, do you hear? It's just a word."

"A bad word," Putti said.

"You don't have to listen to it. Just earn your money, keep your head, and go home to your family when you're ready."

"Say nothing, Doc?" Rahiman said, hands set on his hips, the definition of his biceps shadowed from the sun.

"Say what you want, but do nothing. What these people don't understand is that we're all niggers here. I'm a nigger, you're a nigger, and Strong's a nigger. Elvin Barnes nigger, also. Plenty niggers workin' for Momentum."

They all giggled at the thought, Putti especially. "Doc?" he said. "You a nigger?"

"You bet. Number one nigger, and proud of it."

They talked it over until Rahiman spoke. "Doc is proud to be nigger, Indian peoples also proud."

"There ya go," Logan said, "that's how you handle racism."

This stopped them cold. "What?" Rahiman said, his head cocked.

"That's how you handle this shit, okay? Nigger problem."

"Okay," Rahiman repeated, and they all seemed equally satisfied. "Being nigger no problem for Momentum."

"None at all. It actually helps." He clapped his hands. "Now. Strong wants his niggers on the floor, while Doc, a nigger, and big buck Abdullah nigger have work to do. Y'all find somewhere else to hide."

They got the message and walked off in search of a new place where Ripley would never find them. Ripley they could dodge all day. But if Strong called, they'd pop out of some crevice and shag their *khundies* to the floor. Logan watched them disappear in the shadow of the substructure, Rahiman and Putti holding hands like boyhood friends.

NINE

At sunset Strong's air horn blared, this time summoning the roughnecks. As Logan had predicted, Ripley hadn't seen them since he'd run them out of the mud house. The circulations were complete, and it was time to pull out of the hole. A merciful God had let the sun to go down before the trip began. The desert breeze was cool and clean, blowing away the day's dust and heat. Logan smelled the sweetness in the air. If there was anything wonderful about this country, he thought, it was the Arabian nights. Even Momentum's four plumes of black diesel exhaust couldn't corrupt them. Everything felt new at night.

Before the echo of the horn had died, the roughnecks emerged from the Bombay Teahouse, their bare, scaly ankles pumping in their unlaced Momentum-issue boots as they scrambled for the floor to take their positions. From his vantage over the pits, Logan could see Strong watching it all from above.

When the kelly rose high into the derrick, Logan heard Strong kick out the pumps. This was his cue, and he switched his valves accordingly. Strong, like any driller, was especially nervous with the entire drill string sitting at the bottom of the well. Without circulation, it was easy to stick the pipe. He wanted the slug—the heavy mud that would push down the lighter drilling fluid as the pipe rose from the bore—pumped as quickly as possible. Logan switched lines from the active pits to the slug tank and signaled Strong that it was done.

Even at sunset it was still probably 110 degrees. But near the pump skids, where there was no breeze, the temperature remained near 130. Logan heard the pumps engage, slowly at first, and building, until at last the swabs were thrusting, and the creamy lubricant for the chrome pistons blanched to steam.

Logan left the pump skids to stand over the rails of his slug pit and watch its volume drop, the only way to ensure he'd done it right. He had. Sixty barrels of warm, thick mud vanished in three minutes. As the level dropped below the last rung on the ladder, he signaled Strong that he'd pumped enough. He switched his valves back to the active system so Strong could chase the slug out of the intake lines, and left for the floor.

Logan found everything ready. Barnes, Marshall, Ibrahim Mustafa, the Saudi petroleum engineer, and the Witch Doctor were on hand to witness how the string would pull off bottom. With an exploratory well, this was their ritual.

Everything was clean and organized, as Strong willed. The crew broke off the kelly. The drill pipe standing bare in the rotary table slips gasped for air, a sure sign that Logan's slug was good and that the pipe would come dry from the well. They set the kelly back and sheathed it, the first stand of drill pipe latched in the elevators rising hot and black beneath the derrick's canary-yellow blocks. The roughnecks manned their tongs, brushed clean, jaws open and waiting with sharp, fresh dies. A set of metal slips sat ready on the rotary table, a bucket of pipe dope behind them. Putti stood with a piece of yellow chalk in his hand. Twelve thousand feet of pipe would come from the well in ninety-foot stands, and Putti would number them each in order. They could not speak above the roar of the diesels, the groan of the derrick as it assumed the string's weight, and the slap of inch-and-a-half cable spooling itself like tailor's thread on the great drawworks drum.

Strong, left hand on the master clutch, right hand on the brake lever, watched the weight indicator intently. All of the brass gawked over his shoulder at the same damn thing. The needle bobbed slightly, as Logan expected, but in general it read steady enough. The well bore was clean and the pipe pulled free.

"Don't pull up into nothin', Strong," Marshall said. "Slow and steady here at the first. This son of a bitch'll up and bite ya, I guarantee."

"It's fractured, Jamie," the Witch Doctor said. Logan tried to recall the chapters of his old geology textbook. He remembered the term. Fractured meant that the sedimentary layers deep in the earth were skewed and jagged, perhaps even perpendicular like a mountain range, the result of some powerful geologic event. The production zones in the North Sea had this same feature. Drillers often stuck drill bits there, and wells were abandoned because of it. Logan knew that Strong had lived through it and learned. Up rose the first stand, and the nervous weight indicator needle never blinked.

"How deep's the shoe?" Strong asked of no one in particular. He wanted to know where the last string of casing had been run, and therefore how much open hole he faced.

Barnes reached back to his hip pocket for his pipe tally book, flipping through the soiled pages until he found the figure. "Thirteen and three-eighths was set at 9,267."

"Figure the stands, Ripley," Strong ordered, and Ripley vanished into the doghouse to do just that.

The last joint of the first stand finally cleared the rotary. The roughnecks grabbed the three handles of the iron slips, the clamp that held the pipe in the rotary table, and Logan heard the hiss of the main clutch disengaging. The brake screeched under the weight of the string as the slips were dropped into the rotary around the pipe, assuming the drawwork's burden. In one motion, two sets of tongs slapped around the pipe joints and bit hard into the steel. Strong yanked the lead tong cable to the cathead, and the backup line, the dead man, the cable that held one tong set in place while the other turned, snatched tight. The connection broke, the tongs swung free, and the rotary spun out the first stand.

Logan watched Strong engage the block again to pull the loose stand free from the string. The roughnecks anchored their feet on the wet floor and pushed hard to place it where Putti ordered.

Logan looked up at the descending blocks. Abdullah—his body suspended ninety feet in the air and harnessed like an organ grinder's monkey—snatched open the elevators and pulled the pipe to its rack with a hemp rope. Even at that distance, Logan could see the big Indian's sweating biceps bulge with the strain. When Strong was sure Abdullah was clear, he threw up the brake handle and let the blocks freefall. The roughnecks guided the elevators around the next joint.

As the second stand rose into the derrick, Rahiman yelled in

Hindi to Abdullah. Logan assumed he was asking if everything was all right and if the elevators were turned as he liked, and if he had wanked the night before as was rumored in the Bombay Teahouse.

Abdullah's form, stretched to its full height, obscured the derrick's crown. He signed thumbs-up and coiled his sleeveless arms into two powerful arcs. Then he screamed.

Quicker than a cat, Strong kicked out the clutch. He chained the brake down and yelled back, "What's wrong!"

"More pipes, *gondos!*" the big Indian yelled. "Give Abdullah more fucking pipes!"

"Christ," Strong said, and he engaged it all again as quickly as he could.

"What's wrong with that coolie?" Marshall asked, his brow furrowing. He was clearly annoyed with the delay.

"He likes his job," Strong said.

"If he wants to keep it, he better shut his goddamn mouth," Marshall snapped. "More pipes, my ass. Tell 'em we got plenty."

"More pipes coming, asshole!" Strong hollered, and the roughnecks laughed. He turned to Marshall. "What a crew I've got, huh?" When no one replied, he said, "Watch this: Moe, Curly, Larry, Shemp—the cheese! The cheese!"

On cue, the crew performed in manners consistent with their nicknames. Strong, a Stooges aficionado, had coached them on slow nights. They slapped at one another until Rahiman poked at Abdullah Mohammed's eyes, blocked by Mohammed's hand turned sideways along the bridge of his nose. Mohammed Abdullah fell to the floor, running in circles on his side. Putti, always the loner, shuffled backwards on the pipe rack, whooping very much like Shemp, if Logan's memory served.

All of this fell on blank faces. "We got a forty-million-dollar operation," Marshall finally said, "and three-dollar-an-hour stooges just waitin' to fuck it all up."

"They're great, ain't they?" Strong said. "Eighty-four straight days in the heat and they still can't get enough. I don't see how they do it."

Marshall pointed at the weight indicator. "Watch your gauge, driller. I'll watch the goddamn show."

Rahiman back-kicked his way to the console. "We good niggers, no?"

"Number one niggers, Porcupine," Strong said.

Marshall just shook his head again. "What in God's name have you been teachin' these people, Strong?"

"What they need to know," he said, "and then a little extra just to pass the time." He held out his hand to shut down the bullshit. The Indians responded, returning to their positions to watch the black pipe slowly rise from the hole.

Satisfied that the trip had begun well, Logan left the floor to look after his own problems. First he changed out the water-soluble oil that lubricated the pump rods. Then he pulled the valve caps to check the seats. All were smooth, the valves sitting tightly. He reprimed them and reset the caps with a sixteen-pound sledgehammer. He flushed sediment from the desilter and desander cones and changed the leaky packing in the centrifugal pumps. By then it was dark. A yellow moon rose over the dunes in a haze. Logan raised the watercooler over his head and drenched himself. He wiped the sand, sweat, and grease from his arms and returned to the floor to check in with Strong.

Progress had been slow. They'd pulled only twenty stands from the well. The brass lingered, but they had at least backed away from Strong. They sat together in the doghouse, bullshitting about something. Bob "Bull" Jones, the elderly, hulking night pusher from Enid, Oklahoma, and Barnes's relief, stood next to Strong. His teeth were always grinding away on a stick of gum.

"How's it goin'?" Logan said.

"My clothes are gonna go out of style before we get this pipe on the bank," Strong said. Logan figured it was already too late for that.

"I'll tell ya what," Bull said, cramming another stick of Doublemint between his teeth. "I don't want to wait all night just to find out Christianson's run the goddamn cones off the bit."

Logan and Strong had talked earlier about this very possibility. A tungsten button bit was generally good for a hundred hours. Marshall had run this one 140 hours through rough formation. Bull was certain the bit, overused and torquing badly, had not withstood the extra duty. He figured it had come apart. "Let the big shots get gone," he said, "and then come on out like you want, Jamie. They think they're gonna run casin'. We'll spend the next three days fishin' for scrap metal, you wait and see."

"Just say when, Bull," Strong said, "and we'll have it out before your first nap is over."

"I already told you," Bull said, "when they're gone."

Logan watched Putti scribble the number thirty on a fresh stand. Marshall looked too, and then he stepped out to visit with Strong.

"That's it, ain't it?"

"Yep."

"Good," he said. "Is it takin' mud?" When the pipe came out of the well, mud had to go in to displace it. Down-hole pressures required a constant column of mud to keep them in check, a balance carefully calculated by petroleum engineers Logan would never meet. Otherwise any fluid under pressure in the open hole—be it water, oil, or gas—would begin to flow upward toward the least resistance, the preface to disaster.

Mud weight was everything in controlling a well. Too high and it would fracture a brittle formation; too low and it begged for a blowout. Over the years, Logan had learned to manage the desired weight of a ten thousand-barrel system almost casually. But he knew well that it was no casual thing.

"Ripley?" Strong called, for displacement was the floor AD's responsibility. Ripley would know to the decimal, as Logan did, how much mud was required to displace each foot of five-inch X-95 steel pipe, the sturdiest in the patch.

"Spot on," Ripley said.

"We're in the shoe," Marshall repeated for no one's benefit. "Let's shut down and watch her a while, boys."

For better than ten minutes, they peered through the rotary table with plastic flashlights. The steamy column held steady without the slightest flow or ripple.

"Pull her out, Strong," Marshall finally said. "I'm goin' to the house." He turned away from the well. "Any trouble, Strong, you send for me and Elvin. We're gone. Be careful."

"You bet." Strong shifted the transmission from low to an intermediate gear. It took two hands to do it, the sprockets grinding violently until Logan felt the familiar jar. Strong was just about to his next break when the brass scattered to their respective company trucks. Logan watched them drive off in a dissipating cloud of fine dust. On Logan's signal, Strong stopped where he was and shifted a third time, into high. He waved a single finger in the air, the universal sign for acceleration. The Indians smiled in response. Logan knew they were restless with the slow pace. The adjustment would make the time pass more quickly. As if they had somewhere else on earth to go.

Strong engaged the clutch and mashed the foot throttle to the floor. Metal clanked against metal. The next stand rocketed out of the well beneath the derrick and the plume of jet-black smoke that drifted through it. Logan heard the engines rev under the sudden strain. The Indians shouted, "*Haami-haami*, Strong!" the Arabic equivalent, Logan thought, of the Mexican *andale!*

"*Haami-haami*," Strong repeated, and out shot the pipe. He turned to the night pusher. "Stay and watch, Bull. I got me a crew up here now!"

"Is that what you call 'em?" Bull said. "They're mighty scrawny for my likin'."

"Maybe," Strong hollered above the engine's roar, "but pound for pound, they're the baddest sons of bitches on this earth, and tough, too. I'd take 'em over any crew anywhere, and that's a fact!"

"A pack of Okies'd work circles around 'em," Bull said, stroking his chin.

"No way in hell!" Strong yelled. He shook his head. "You gotta respect 'em, Bull. I damn sure do. They're the best I've ever seen."

Bull grunted. "Wait till the shit hits the fan," he said. "Then judge. Not a one of these midgets would stay with a kick. They'd scatter like spooked quail."

If Strong heard him, he gave no sign. Up came the next pipe connection, the slips went in, and they broke it. The rotary hummed as it spun out the free stand, and Putti racked it alone. The blocks fell almost in one blurring yellow line until Rahiman reached the elevator handles to guide them over the next waiting joint, the other roughnecks shoving the bales toward the pipe. They snapped shut in a dying clatter, and the blocks flew up again.

Bull looked apprehensive. "Take it easy, Strong," he said. "You ain't gettin' paid by the pipe."

Strong said nothing, standing maniacally at his console, hands almost too quick for Logan's eye.

"He's the fastest driller I've ever seen," Logan said to Bull.

Bull stood fast, watching. "Speed ain't the only requirement in a driller," he said, "not by a long shot. It's a matter of working as quickly as you can, as safely as you can, the whole shootin' match under control." He unwrapped another stick of gum, folded it, and crammed it into his mouth. "That last is what's gonna get Strong's goat."

"How's that?" Logan was more than willing to consider Bull's objection. What Strong did certainly affected him.

"Because he don't know the first thing about bein' in control. Some day it'll get him," he said, "and I hope to God I ain't around to see it."

"I've never seen him make the slightest mistake," Logan said, mostly out of loyalty and respect for Strong, who he considered gifted on the brake. For all that, it was still a lie.

"Out here, it only takes one," Bull said, "and we got us a whole crew of dead Indians. Makin' a little time just ain't worth it, no matter how sorry they are." He spat. "Strong's long overdue to find that out."

The old man waddled out to the console. "Slow it down, Strong. I don't want nobody tore up on my watch. You hear?"

"I hear," he said.

Bull turned to leave the floor. "He don't hear," he told Logan.

TEN

⬦⬦⬦

Logan and his crew raced on to midnight. The breeze had died an hour after sunset, leaving the floor enveloped by a stale heat. The Indians' skin glistened with sweat under the purple glare of the neon lights that lined the derrick legs. Yet they labored on, moving with mechanical precision, engrossed, as Strong seemed to be, by the rhythm of the swaying rig. There was no longer any laughter or horseplay. There was only the work, and it gripped them all.

Logan looked up at Abdullah, stripped to the waist, his body shrouded by gray diesel fumes. When the next stand was ready, he reached out and took it with his bare hand. His loose rope danced in the breeze. In one motion, pausing only for the belly of the stand to swing his way, he racked it as if the steel were made of straw. Few had such skill.

Logan turned to Strong to ask if he'd seen it. He had. "Yeah!" Strong cried. "You're a stud!"

"More pipes, *gondos!*" the Indian yelled. "More fucking pipes for Abdullah!"

"More pipes coming!" yelled Rahiman, and on they went.

"Goddamn," Strong said. "I can't get 'em up there no faster."

Ripley passed by the driller's console on his continual orbit. His cheap British boots never stood still for long. "The loggers are here, Jamie," he said.

Logan knew Strong couldn't care in the least, not while he was gripped in the fever of a trip. "Ripley, you and Doc here give my boys a smoke break. You hear?"

"Sure, Jamie," Ripley said, "but I'm off just now to wake Bull. He wanted to know when the loggers arrived."

"Wake him after," Strong snapped. "Ain't nothin' gonna happen till we're done here, and these boys need a break."

Ripley took Rahiman's place. Logan climbed the ladder to the derrick, its rungs still warm from the day's heat. He carried the cotton muslin sack over his shoulder, water for Abdullah—with no ice, as he knew the Indian preferred. Abdullah would refuse to come down until the bit sat on the oak planks of the floor. The big Indian was funny that way. At first Strong couldn't get him up there; now they couldn't get him down.

The black pipe turned silver, worn smooth and shiny from friction, the deeper they drilled. Next came the heavyweight drill pipe, ten times heavier than the X-95 that had preceded it. Abdullah's rope reappeared and Logan couldn't fault him. They racked back a dozen stands. The drill collars followed, fat and silver, grooved like big screws. The flanges of the stabilizers that joined them were matted with shale and thick clay, their bulk studded with fossilized seashells. Beneath the two and one-half miles of sand and rock deposits there had once been the floor of an ancient ocean.

The operation slowed when the collars, the bottom-hole assembly, appeared. Their weight made them much more difficult for the crew to manage; their taperless shape made them easier to drop back into the well. The Indians racked them opposite the drill pipe, eight stands in a row. When the bit finally came, it was worn but intact.

"I'll be goddamned," Strong said. "Marshall was right." He turned to Logan. "Now you can get Bull."

Logan found the old man napping at his desk. He slammed the door behind him, and Bull jerked awake. He fumbled for his hard hat and popped it on his withered head. "What's wrong?"

"We're out," Logan said. "The bit's on the bank. She's got all three cones."

The folds of pale skin around Bull's eyes rippled as he squinted at his wristwatch. "It's only eleven thirty," he said. "Y'all shouldn't have been out until around two."

"Strong," Logan said with no explanation. None needed.

"Crazy son of a bitch," Bull growled. He adjusted his hat and rose. "Them Frenchmen's here?"

"They're here," Logan said. "I gotta wake the Witch Doctor."

"I hate lookin' at that wild fucker at night," Bull said. "He's a nice feller and all, don't get me wrong. But he's got ugly he ain't even used yet."

If so, Logan thought, he must've loaned some to this tired old man. "He wants to see the bit," he said.

"Get 'em," Bull said, "but give me time for a couple of shots of coffee first."

Strong had broken the bit connection by the time Logan returned, but he left it screwed loosely to the foot of the last collar and racked it back next to the others. He chained down the brake and shut everything down. In the silence, Logan noticed the hum in his ears. It would stay with him until he'd been home a week.

"Tell them frogs it's time," Strong told him, and Logan went down to find the technicians already assembling their tools on the catwalk below. They worked within the narrow beams of flashlights. They always seemed ill at ease around the drill crews. Different labors. Different tribes.

Putti stood at the V-door, the ledge of the drill floor above the catwalk. He addressed a Pakistani in what sounded to Logan like Hindi. There was no response. He tried his English next. "Hey, *gondo!* Tugger needing?" He was referring to the air hoist, the winch that hoisted moderate-size materials to the floor. It took the crane for the heavy stuff. Putti held the hook of the air hoist chain in his gloved hand. One of the French responded with a terse "*Oui.*"

Satisfied things were progressing well enough on the catwalk, Logan climbed the stairs back to the floor. Strong stood at the V-door, his hands on his hips, as Putti and Rahiman lowered the hoist amid the clatter of three different languages. "It's the fuckin' tower of Babel around here, ain't it, Doc?" And indeed it was.

Strong stepped to the west wall and unzipped his fly. All activity stopped cold. There was only sand below, the wind was right, and Strong had been trapped on the floor since just after dinner. He had to urinate, and Logan saw right away that he didn't intend to wait.

Rahiman and the others saw it too. At first they sneered, save Putti, who snickered. Then they turned away from what to them was an abomination in progress. Strong should have known. In fact, Logan knew damn well he did.

"For God's sake, check below, Strong!" bellowed Bull. "They had a whole crew of rousties quit on 126 because some driller pissed on 'em."

Strong peered over the rail. "It's clear," he said with a grin.

Some of the Indians, apparently unconvinced that Strong would go through with it, peeked between their fingers. For a man like Strong to stand atop the tower and proudly let it rain down for all to see was unthinkable. It was shameful and unclean, and if they were amused, as Putti sometimes still was, it was because of its unabashed novelty. For Rahiman and the others, the novelty had come and gone long ago.

Strong turned, penis dangling in his hand, and wagged it. "Don't you boys wish you had a whopper like this?"

Putti turned to Rahiman, his head shaking in disbelief. They rattled to one another in their native tongue and Rahiman had the final word. His dark face reddened. The rest of the crew turned their backs on Strong.

"Put that thing away 'fore somebody gets hurt, Strong," Bull said.

"It's too late for that," Strong said. "It's left a trail of broken hearts."

Bull scowled. "Can't you see they don't think it's funny?"

"Aw, they're all right," Strong said as he closed the distance, zipping his fly as he walked. "They know me." He reached out to pat Rahiman on the back, but the Indian caught his arm at the wrist.

"Wash your hands," Rahiman sneered, his dark eyes flashing. The rest of the Indians immediately turned around.

Strong stood still. "It's all right," he said quietly. "Strong ain't gonna hurt nobody."

"Not all right," Rahiman snapped. "Do not touch me before you wash your hands."

Strong wrenched his wrist from the Indian's grasp. "What's the problem?" he said, his jaw set, stare hardened.

"I am Muslim," he declared, and he raised one finger as a warning. "It is forbidden for you to touch me in this way."

Logan understood the problem. Strong was oil patch and always had been. They worked for hours in the heat, the dust, and the mud. What difference could it make for one to touch the skin of his penis before he touched the sweaty back of a roughneck's faded Momentum coveralls? How could it make anyone more filthy than the job already had?

But Strong now mistook a cultural difference for a personal slight. He clearly didn't like the roughneck's abrasive tone. Logan knew he would view it as a questioning of his absolute authority. If there were humiliation in the making, Strong would be the last on the receiving end.

"I'll tell you what," Strong said, hands locked on his hips. "I'll wash when I get to the shower and not before. But if you boys are worried about clean, I'm happy to oblige you. I want every nigger here to grab a bucket and a brush and scrub this goddamn floor down to the metal. You got it?"

Strong stared from one face to the next. The crew hesitated, talking under their breath among themselves. They'd worked hard and this was how Strong rewarded them. They started to move, but Rahiman held them back. Another moment's hesitation was a moment too long.

"Somebody want to go back to India?" Strong was ruffled now. Even in the dull glow of the derrick lights, Logan could see the flush of his cheeks. "I mean right fuckin' now!"

They stood, defiant. Logan, who would rather latch a set of tongs around his head than reason with Strong when he was angry, stepped forward. "Look, Jamie..."

"Stay out of it Doc!" Strong snapped. "I don't have to ask whose side you're takin'. This is between me and them."

He took one step toward the Indians before Bull stepped in between them. "Calm down, goddamn it, Jamie!" Bull said. "Nobody's goin' anywhere. You brought this on yourself. All you gotta do is show these men the respect you said you do, and this kinda shit don't happen." Bull pointed south toward the Momentum office. "Now, you carry your big ass down to the office and cool your heels on them books. Me and Doc here'll finish up your watch."

"I'm done takin' shit off these people," Strong said.

"You're done tonight, period," Bull replied. "You just get."

Strong stood motionless. The rage drained from his face. It was replaced by embarrassment. He was probably thinking about apologizing, but Logan knew his pride would never let him. Instead, he stomped off for the stairs.

He paused at the soap bucket and looked back at the Indians. He stuck his hands deep into the water and brought them out into the desert air. Lather dripped to the floor as he wrung them together. "Happy now?" he said, and kicked the bucket over the railing. It landed with a clatter. An obviously startled French technician yelled in response.

"Tomorrow we'll start again," Strong said. "Clean."

Logan knew this was about as close to an apology as the Indians would ever get.

The roughnecks looked to Rahiman, who'd won them this little victory. Rahiman, chest still heaving against his open cotton shirt, fixed his angry gaze on Logan. Logan nodded that everything was all right.

"Dumb son of a bitch," Bull said. "Strong'll be the end of Strong."

ELEVEN

❖

DAY FIVE

Strong, in his thigh-length cutoffs and cheap rubber thongs, ceremoniously plowed a shallow circular trough about a yard in diameter in the sand with a rusted piece of angle iron. Then he laid strips of cotton rags in the ditch. Putti followed behind, dowsing the fabric with diesel fuel.

Strong pitched the metal aside. "Now," he said, wiping his hands on his shorts. "Does everybody know what's happenin' here?"

It was clear to Logan that Strong had smoothed things over with the Indians. They had been aloof after the incident, a little bitter maybe. Rahiman, always game, even chanced a provocative demeanor. But Strong didn't bite. He let their anger pass without a word, treating them kindly, giving them plenty of room, allowing them to rest for the balance of the day past and most of this one.

Luther Parnell, the driller opposite Strong, had ordered his crew to scrub the floor as the well logging went on, so Strong allowed his disgruntled roughnecks to piddle about as they pleased. Soon driller and crew were talking again. The jokes came next. A little horseplay after that, when the Indians actually allowed Strong to touch them without cringing. Strong and the stooges seemed as close as ever.

The day, however, had not passed without event. While the well was being logged, Marshall had gathered the expats for a doghouse conference. He wanted them to understand what would happen once the next string of casing was run. The time had come, he said, to tighten up.

The reservoir, Al Hisaab, was a gas reserve, much like the Al Khuff formations they'd drilled in the north. The Saudis, Marshall explained, were in need of gas production. Back when a barrel of oil brought forty dollars, they had refined enough natural gas from their oil reservoirs to fuel their power plants. Now that the price had fallen well below thirty dollars, they'd decided the oil was worth more in the ground than on the glutted world market. The decline of oil production had directly resulted in the shortage of gas. That had led to the Al Khuff development program, a field that had already proven extraordinary reserves. That bird in hand, Arabco had sent Momentum 127 to explore the Rub al Khali and Al Hisaab.

Marshall assured them Al Hisaab would be a challenge. More than likely, he said, the reservoir would contain some degree of hydrogen sulfide contamination, an eventuality for which he reminded them they were well prepared. Logan himself had seen the contract technicians checking the sensory equipment throughout the location. Air tanks were readily available to the crew. All expats had taken the H_2S certification classes on Momentum's dime. The crews had executed drills twice a month for as long as Logan had been in Saudi Arabia. Completion of the well, Marshall said, would be much like Al Khuff. The difference was that Al Hisaab, though an unknown quantity as were all wildcat wells, promised significant volume at extreme pressures.

"What do you mean extreme?" Barnes said. The exact question on Logan's lips.

"As much as four hundred million cubic feet per day," Marshall said without flinching, "give or take."

Logan flinched. He'd cut his teeth on gas wells in Galveston Bay. They'd come in about one million feet a day. Al Khuff had dwarfed them at an average of one hundred million apiece. Flowing those wells had been some trick. They'd had to run the flare lines three hundred yards into the dunes, buried under one yard of sand along their entire length, just to keep them from whiplashing under the pressure. Logan had felt the percussion of the explosion from his compound bunk ten miles away when they lit the flares. After that, there was a low rumble until they'd shut the well back in.

He had personally inspected the site when it was over. Two acres of desert were blown aside and scorched black. He found pieces of glass slag, superheated sand, lying in Frisbee-size chunks. The experience had stamped a grim impression on him, as his nightmares confirmed. His subconscious wasn't any happier about Al Khuff than he was.

Now, according to Marshall, they were sitting on top of pressures perhaps four times greater than the most powerful of Al Khuff, and Logan spent the last of his shift pacing the dunes, wondering if this would be a good time to become a stockbroker, theological student, fishing guide, or shoeshine boy. Hours later he was still wondering, watching Strong prepare his circle as if he didn't have a care in the world.

Strong didn't have any options either. He had tried his hand at a number of domestic occupations and failed. He didn't have the education for most; he lacked the patience for all. The oil field had left him little expertise with the population at large. More specifically, Logan believed, he didn't do well with hands-on management. A driller ruled the rig much like the captain of a ship. Strong consulted Barnes and Bull when he needed to, deferred to Marshall when he had no other choice, but the day-to-day operation of Momentum 127 was his responsibility alone. As a direct result, Strong hadn't acquired the art of diplomacy, the knack for office politics, the finesse of closing a competitive sale.

Logan had a clear picture of the corporate Strong. No doubt he told clients and customers how it was going to be and was as shocked as his employers when they—all of them—went elsewhere. Between oil field assignments, Strong had tried his callused hand at selling insurance and financial products—ideal occupations, he was told, for self-starters. He proved a quick finisher. Next he sold water filters and auto parts. It was construction contracting after that, and Strong had enough pride to see the job done right. But he couldn't keep carpenters and plumbers. He couldn't stomach the homeowners' constant bitching. And he couldn't bear to watch his oil field nest egg wither until he was broke.

That brought him back, time and again, to the oil fields, like a soldier in search of a war. Logan was pretty certain, Al Hisaab or no, that Strong knew he had run out of employment options at thirty years of age. If Momentum intended to drill into hell itself,

Strong would have no choice but to take his place at the brake and say, "Make 'em bite, boys. We're gonna make some hole."

Now the entire crew—roughnecks, roustabouts, welder, mechanic's helper, kitchen staff, and houseboys—gathered at this late hour, all showered and dressed in their loungee skirts for bed. Their ankles and chests were bare. Strong asked and they all nodded that they certainly understood what was happening. After all, it had been their idea.

"Well," Strong began, "for the benefit of those who are just too damn stupid to admit it—and you know who you are—we'll light the rag pieces here and get the fire goin' good. Then we'll put the scruppy here in the middle."

A "scruppy" was the Indians' misnomer for a scorpion. They'd caught one in the parts house just before quitting time. They were vicious-looking arachnids, black as midnight. You didn't pick up a chemical sack or turn over an old flange before looking carefully.

"Once this bastard sees that he can't get out," Strong said, "he's supposed to sting himself to death."

Logan knew the scorpion wouldn't do it. But the ceremony was entertainment for the TCNs, who went in for this sort of thing, and Strong was in an obliging mood. He stepped back, waiting for the fire to catch. The Indians, anxious, erupted into excited chatter. The flames grew to the height of Logan's knees, and Putti handed the coffee can to Strong. Strong reached out over the circle, fanned the heat and black smoke from his face with his free hand, and dumped the scorpion dead center.

The scorpion dashed one way and then the other. Each time it neared the flames, the heat drove it back to the middle. It crawled in a circle, its tail poised above its head, probing this point and that, all with the same result. After half a dozen aborted attempts, in the center it stayed.

Logan closed in with the others to see what the thing intended to do.

"Watch, all," Rahiman said. "It knows it is doomed. It will happen as I've said."

And damn if it didn't look to Logan like it would. The scorpion stood motionless, its tail slightly pricking the armor along the length of its ebony abdomen.

No one said a word when the scorpion started to move again.

It backed slowly against the flames until it paused. The Indians pressed closer, their eyes mirroring the flames, just as the arachnid dashed for the opposite side.

They howled, scattering when the scorpion broke free of the fire. Logan lost sight of it among the bare feet scrambling for the safety of the mesh walkway. Once away from the fire's light, he couldn't see his hand in front of his face until his eyes adjusted.

The Indians danced around, drawing their loungees tight against their ankles. Their excited voices bounced off the trailer walls, drowning out the compound generator.

"I told you, boys," Strong said, his gray stare scanning the sand. "It'll never work. They're tougher than you thought. You caught yourselves a scorpion with other plans."

"We try again," Putti vowed, "next time we find scruppy."

"Next time bigger fire," Rahiman said.

"Much bigger," Strong said. "He's gotta know he ain't goin' nowhere."

Logan watched his disappointed crew drift away from the dying fire, their long shadows absorbed by the night.

TWELVE

Luther Parnell, spotted with mud, grease, pipe dope, and teardrops of drilling-line tar, chained down the brake at the first sight of Logan, Strong, and their crew. The drawworks drum groaned as it ground to an abrupt halt. Parnell moved quickest at relief time, as Logan believed all lazy men did.

"It's all yours, Strong," Parnell said in his northern Mississippi accent, "and you can have it. Casin's a pain in the ass." He rotated his big head on his neckless torso, a poor range of motion for a man his age. "My neck's killin' me."

Strong, reticent on the ride to the rig, seemed petulant once he reached it. Logan understood the transition. Just the sight of Parnell's muddy, moronic face was enough to sour any occasion; to listen to his garrulous redneck crap only made it worse. The only thing Strong and Parnell had in common was a driller's title, and Momentum valued them both equally. This gnawed at Strong, who worked circles around Parnell, and he never missed an opportunity to let the Mississippian know it.

Logan knew he and Strong faced a slow, tedious shift on the floor, and then three more weeks of the same. There was little skill and much chaos in a repetitive casing operation; nothing challenging, nothing new. The well had been dormant for the days of logging and would remain so until they'd run the last string of casing. There would be nothing to interest either one of them, particularly Strong, who lived to probe the depths of the earth. And there would be nothing, Logan knew, to distract Strong's thoughts from his ex-wife and the blond-haired daughter she'd taken from him, or the expense and frustration caused by Strong's lawyer, who had accomplished little in the family courts to bring his child back into his life. One glimpse of Strong's grim expression in the galley and Logan knew he had spent his off-hours obsessing about his custody battle.

Parnell stepped out of the driller's console so Strong could take his place.

"You ain't run no more than this?" Strong said, as he scanned Parnell's tally. Logan had seen the stack of pipes waiting on the catwalk below. They told the story.

"We done all right, Strong," Parnell said. "Casin's a slow go. You know that."

"The only thing that goes slow around here is you."

Parnell snorted and flicked his wrist. Logan surveyed the operation they'd inherited piece by piece, as did Strong.

"Everythin' hooked up like it oughta be?" Strong asked, always his first question, and a proper one. But Logan knew it was really a threat. If Parnell had a brain, he'd know Strong didn't trust him.

"I run over three thousand feet of pipe in six hours, Strong," Luther said flatly. "Speaks for itself."

"And I'll run the rest in twelve," Strong said. He slapped Parnell's book between the T-shirted folds of his considerable paunch. "But that don't answer my question." He pointed to the casing scaffolds, the fill line, the pick-up cables, and the single-joint harness. "What I need to know is if all of this is set up like it oughta be."

"Damn straight," Luther said in a pout.

Strong raised his eyebrows and cocked his head in Luther's direction. "It better be," he said.

Parnell wheeled to leave the floor. "What's eatin' that son of a bitch?" he asked Logan.

"He don't like you, Luther," Logan said, wondering why it wasn't obvious.

"Well, it ain't nothin' to me. It's like I always say."

"What do you always say?" Logan asked, bracing for the worst. Parnell was as creative as a tong head. For colorful turns of phrase, he generally resorted to the hooks of country-and-western songs. All bad.

"Here stands the body of Luther Parnell," he said. "If'n you don't like him, enjoy the smell." He moved upwind so Logan could do just that.

Logan shook his head. Parnell was grinning, his square head bobbing on his listless shoulders. His face drained in disappointment when Logan didn't laugh. That all came to a stop the moment Strong's boot wedged in his ass.

"Get off my floor, fatboy," Strong barked. "We're gonna run some pipe."

Parnell turned back, glaring. "You best watch yourself, Strong."

"I'm watchin'," Strong said. "What's it gonna do?"

They squared off. Strong waited, steady and calm; Parnell's cheeks flared. "Me and you's gonna get somethin' settled someday," he spat.

"You say when and where." Strong reached out and bent Parnell's finger back. "It won't take long."

"It ain't gonna be here, son of a bitch." He stepped out of Strong's range to nurse his finger. "They run a man off for shit like that."

"Then what've you got to worry about?"

Parnell snarled. "You'll get yours, Strong. Everybody knows it's comin'."

"And when it comes, you dumb bastard," Strong warned him, "you best hope you ain't around. 'Cause when they run me off, I'm comin' lookin' for you. I got nothin' to lose after that, and I'm gonna beat the ugly right off your face." He looked at Logan and winked. "And it's gonna be some job."

Logan stepped between them. "Let it go, Jamie. We got pipe to run."

"I'm always lettin' it go," Strong said, slipping his gloves on his hands as he turned back to his console. "It just never goes nowhere."

Parnell huffed off. In the silence that followed Logan studied Strong, until Strong's gray eyes met his. "I'm all right, Doc," Strong said. "I just hate that son of a bitch."

"Really?" Logan said, his attention now turned to the operation. "No use in hammerin' Parnell. He ain't the cause of your problems."

Strong, who was already adjusting the throttle up a notch or two, stopped cold. "You just tell me who is and they'll get the same," he said, and unchained the brake. "Let's go to work," he yelled to the Indians.

At half past four, Logan returned to the floor to relieve Strong for a cigarette, as they'd agreed. The operation was a mess. The casing crew, all Germans, stood on their metal scaffolds in worn, sleeve-less coveralls, manning torque gauges and huge circular hydraulic tongs in grim silence. The Indians worked beneath their scaffolds as best they could. The entire floor was engulfed in white-gray diesel exhaust and desert haze. The sky, though cloudless, was an opaque brown. Logan rarely saw a clear summer afternoon in the desert. There was only the heat, so intense it choked him. Metal all around burned his skin at the slightest touch.

Casing crews all over the world are a rough-looking bunch, a prerequisite for their arduous lot. These sweating, grubby Europeans were no different, with the exception of one. Logan recognized him on the stabbing board suspended thirty feet above the rotary table. He was a tall, muscular, blond-haired man with hard, almost carved looks, maybe fifty years old, meticulous in his dress, graceful, and athletic. Logan had worked with him many times. His name was Buehler.

He'd been a circus performer, or so he once told Strong, who had nicknamed him the Lion Tamer. Logan thought it appropriate given the crew he ran; the only thing missing was the whip and pistol.

The casing crew spoke in thick German, the Indians in Hindi, and Strong in harsh English pocked with cusswords, as the casing, joint after greasy black joint, plunged into the depths of the silent well.

"Ready for a nail?" Logan asked Strong.

"Damn straight." Strong went over the operation in tedious detail.

"I got it," Logan said. "It ain't my first time, ya know."

"Let's just make sure it ain't your last," Strong said. He looked back in the direction of the office complex some two hundred yards away. "Bull's come early. I'll sit down there with him. I won't be gone long."

Thank God, Logan thought, as Strong headed for the stairway. The Indians gawked at him, as if they were terrified of a novice at the helm. Logan engaged the drawworks and pulled in the first joint of casing with apprehensive care. The operation went slowly since he didn't quite have the touch. He was a little jerky with the delicate coordination of clutch and brake. But he'd put in his time at the console; he knew what he was doing. The roughnecks congratulated his initial efforts with a gracious "Aie-whaa." The Germans looked tired and bored. Soon Logan had the feel and his pace quickened.

Forty-five minutes later Strong still had not returned. Logan's eyes watered from the diesel fumes clouding his view of the drill floor. How, he wondered, did Strong endure it? To compensate, he moved more carefully, slowly raising the free single joint from its place in the mouse hole until it hung an inch or two above the drill floor. Logan waited until the Indians had a sure grip, then started to pick it up, high enough to stab its threaded end into the joint waiting in the rotary. It was the Germans' responsibility to attach it to the string at the desired torque.

The Indians just about had the joint stabbed when Logan heard a wrenching noise somewhere above. He disengaged the clutch and crashed the brake lever down to stop the blocks, shielding his eyes from the sun's glare to see what was wrong. It took a second more for the blocks to stop moving, and even that was too long.

In an instant one of the pick-up sling cables ripped apart, loose ends fraying and wild. A pipe swung hard toward the rows of drill pipe like the pendulum of a broken grandfather clock. It slammed into the floor, the top end swaying back and forth.

"Look out!" Logan cried.

The roughnecks, who had developed a keen sense for disaster, reacted the instant they heard the cable snap. Each moved catlike for safe ground. Curly Mohammed moved the wrong direction.

The bottom of the wayward pipe caught the toes of his boot, and he shrieked in pain. Logan froze, waiting to see if the last cable would also snap.

He had seen accidents, terrible accidents, before. He'd always been calm enough. But this was the first where he held the primary responsibility. He was the driller, and the Indians looked to him with wild eyes. The floor took enough of the loose joint's weight that the lone cable held, its top swaying in the breeze. Mohammed screamed as Logan had heard no man scream before. He felt the sparks of inconsolable panic, a knee-jerk reaction he fought with what remained of his logic.

He knew he couldn't pick the pipe back up. It took every bit of the tensile strength of two cables to hold it. If he raised it the other cable would snap and the pipe would crash to the floor. Instead of injuring one man, he could kill them all. Although Logan hesitated for only a second, it seemed like hours. All he heard was Mohammed's tormented screams and the cries of frantic crewmen, Indian and German both. "Doc!" they shouted. "Pick it up!"

Logan stood there, paralyzed. If he chose badly, it would be much worse. He knew Strong, wherever he was, no matter what he was doing, was always watching the floor. One glance from the Momentum office and he'd know something was wrong. Soon he would come. Until then, Logan was alone with the dilemma, Mohammed's howls filling his ears. Tears of pain flowed down the Indian's dark cheeks.

"Get the bars!" Logan said, pointing to the tool board. "We'll pry it! All we need is an inch or two!"

Rahiman unchained the air hoist line.

"No!" Logan shouted. The hoist could not be tied high enough on the joint to pull it straight up. He knew it would move laterally and tear off what was left of Mohammed's foot. He looked up at the Germans. "Get down here and help us!"

Their boots hit the floor as Logan was positioning a block of wood as a fulcrum. He wedged the points of two five-foot iron bars beneath the casing's threads. Logan put his body on the other end. He saw Mousa. "Get over here!" he yelled. "It'll take us all!"

Logan had the weight of six men on the bars and still the casing would not budge. Mohammed's screams grew louder. Blood gushed and bubbled between the laces of his boot.

"Goddamn it!" Logan cried, his mind racing for alternatives. He saw a flash of white cloth streak past him. Strong was on the floor.

"What happened! Did ya hang it up?" There was the sound of terror in Strong's voice, and anger, and will.

"No," Logan said, "the cable busted. Just like that, with no warnin'." He felt like a child caught playing with matches. This wasn't his fault, but it also wasn't the time to say so. "Let's just get him out!"

"You hold on, Mohammed," Strong said. "I'm here."

Strong ordered Logan back to the console. "Pick it up with the one cable. Just enough to get him out."

"No!" Logan said. "It's not rated to handle that weight! It might fall and kill somebody, man!"

"All right," Strong said. "We'll get the crane in here to latch onto it. Hang on, Mohammed." Strong marched to the handrails to find the Rhodesian.

"Brother! Get that crane in here and pick up this loose joint! We got a man pinned!" Brother must have moved too slowly. "Now, goddamn it!" Strong bellowed. Logan was sure Brother had the idea then. He saw the mast of the crane swing toward the V-door. It stopped short.

"Strong!" Brother yelled. "I can't get to it from this angle! I'll have to move it about!"

"Never mind," Strong growled, already heading in another direction. "Rahiman, slack off on the air hoist! Help 'em, Putti."

Strong yelled up to the Lion Tamer, who was about to come down and help. "Buehler! Can you tie this chain just above the collar?"

The German nodded. He shed his harness and perched on the end of the board. Strong took the hoist cable from Putti and swung it across the derrick to the German's hand. Buehler hooked the chain into a loop and slipped in the toe of one boot. He gripped the chain, readied himself, and swung back across the full length of the derrick to the crippled joint of casing.

Hanging by one arm, Buehler deftly tied the hoist cable around the pipe. Then he climbed up the cable and signaled for Strong to proceed.

"Okay, Rahiman, pick it up. Easy." Strong held the injured crewman. "We'll have ya out, Curly."

Rahiman bumped the air hoist throttle until it took the weight of the pipe. When it hesitated, he bumped it again. The pipe swung free. It came to rest against the pipe rack. Rahiman put his full weight on the hoist's brake. Buehler shimmied down the casing, dropping to the floor.

"Damn good work," Strong said.

Mohammed collapsed in a fetal position on the muddy planks. Logan knelt beside him and began to ease off his boot. The crushed steel toe made it difficult. The Indian shrieked at the slightest movement. It shook Logan's tenuous resolve. The others huddled around to see. Logan worked in their shadow.

Finally the boot slid free. Blood gushed from the stumps of three toes, coagulating into puddles on top of larger pools of warm mud. They did not mix. Mohammed was crying, more from fear, Logan sensed, than from the pain. He'd seen the blood. He leaned his head forward to get a look at his foot, but Strong gently pressed him back down.

"It ain't as bad as you think," he said. "Not near as bad."

Logan tossed the Indian's boot aside on the drill floor. "I'm takin' him to camp," he said.

"No," Strong said. "Send the driver to camp for Pix. Maybe we ought not move him, Doc. At least until the bleedin' stops."

Logan slipped his arms under Mohammed's back and knees. "And what if it doesn't? I won't wait." He cradled the injured Indian in his arms. "I'm takin' him now." He rose unsteadily with Mohammed's weight.

This time Strong said nothing. Logan felt Mohammed's arm drape around his neck, his heart pulsing against Logan's sweating chest. Mohammed was sobbing so he could not catch his breath. Logan staggered to the elevator and saw Bull at the bottom, about to come up. Unwilling to wait, Logan headed for the stairs, feeling all eyes on his back as he passed.

THIRTEEN

⬥⬥⬥

The driver was propped up on the bench in the Bombay Teahouse enjoying a smoke when Logan burst through the doorway.

"Camp! Now!"

Abraham stared first at the bloodstains on Logan's calf, then at the mangled foot of his countryman. He stubbed out his cigarette. "We go, Doc," he said.

Logan laid Mohammed along the full length of the backseat. The blood should have clotted by now, aided by the heat of the afternoon sun. Instead it poured over everything. He sat beside Mohammed, applying pressure on his foot with both hands. The warm blood covered his fingers. Mohammed cried out, and the driver stopped to look back. "Drive!" Logan barked.

"Very bad," the driver said, running off into the soft shoulder.

"Watch the road," Logan said. Mohammed was reduced to whimpering now. Logan continued to squeeze, blood sticking to his fingers. "I'm sorry." It was all he could say.

The crew truck skidded to a stop in the soft sand next to camp. Mohammed slid out and tried to hop on his own. Logan stopped him and held out his arms. "I'll carry you," he said, "it's not far." He hoisted Mohammed against his chest. The grating nearly buckled from the weight of each footstep as Logan made his way to Tate-Pixilate's shack.

Logan knew what awaited. Tate-Pixilate, an Englishman, was generally out of sorts with the frustrating day-to-day camp operation. He often complained the Americans were ungrateful for his efforts; the Indians, on the other hand, drove him mad. Logan shoved Pix's door open without knocking, moving through the office to the clinic. He put Mohammed on the cot.

"Wait here," he said. "I'll find Pix."

He opened the door that led to the camp boss's living quarters. It was as dark and stale as a cave and just as cold. There was no sound except for the whine of the window unit on high. Luckily the light switches in every cabin were in the same place. After a little groping, Logan found it and flicked it on.

Pix was curled up on his bed like a sick dog. He was a pitiful sight, and if something less serious had brought him here, Logan would have let him know it.

"Get up! I got a man hurt out here!"

"How hurt is hurt, Doctor? I'm not in the best of shape meself." Pix's fat bottom lip curled as if he were asking his mum if he could stay home from school with a fever.

"He's lost half of his foot. And I can't stop the bleedin'."

"Oh, well, why didn't you say? I thought it was another Indian with a blister on his heel."

Pix rose with difficulty from his bed, the soles of his wide feet flapping against the floor. He dressed himself in front of the lavatory and washed his hands. Logan led him to Mohammed.

"Who have we here?" he said. "Ah, Mohammed Abdullah, isn't it? You've made a right mess of yourself, lad. Let's have a look."

Mohammed reached for Logan's hand. Logan could tell that Mohammed could not find it in himself to trust this Englishman. Pix had persecuted the Indians too many times. The Indians were powerless, at the bottom of the chain, and Pix understood that within the compound they were at his whim. There was always some extra privilege that could be canceled, some small benefit denied. The Indians hated him, believing he passed his time in the desert thinking of new ways to make their lives miserable. Everyone knew that as a retired RAF medical officer Pix had training and skill, but Logan sensed something important—something fundamental—was missing. Mohammed, who cringed at his touch, seemed to feel the same way.

"Doctor," Pix said, once he had washed most of the blood from Mohammed's wound, "you really must review your fractions. This is hardly half of this man's foot." He wrung the towel out in the sink. Crimson swirled against white.

"Give him somethin' for the pain," Logan said, "and then send him to Dhahran for a real doctor."

"Yes, Doc," Mohammed whimpered. "Dhahran."

"Well, the bleeding's stopped," Pix said. "I'll clean him up, dress the wounds, and send the little nigger on to the hospital for stitches. Near as I can make out, he's lost the better part of three toes." He looked down his long nose at Logan. "How'd it happen?"

Logan told him.

"Well, he's all right," Pix said. "He'll be able to walk once the wound's healed. Mind you, it'll be a bit tender for some time. I don't expect he'll be fit for rig duties. We'll find him something to do around the camp."

"See there, Mohammed," Logan said. "Light duty. No problem." He held tight to Mohammed's shoulder. The Indian reached for Logan's arm.

"You're okay," Logan said. "You go Dhahran, maybe some jig-jig with wild women, I don't know. After, easy money. Light duty. No more roughneckin'. I'll go to camp, fix with tool pusher."

Mohammed tried to smile. "Stay with Mohammed," he said.

"I can't," Logan said. "I gotta go. Pix'll look after you, won't you, Pix?"

"Indeed," he said.

Logan pulled his hand away from the Indian. "Give him somethin' for the pain. Or do you get your jollies from watching him hurt like this?"

"Please allow me to do me job," Pix said, clearly annoyed at Logan's tone. "You're not needed here. I'll see after our friend."

Mohammed winced again.

"Give it to him now," Logan said.

"In due time. Please."

Logan stomped over to the unlocked pharmacy cabinet. He saw American drugs with American names. He knew, as a result of his misspent youth, what to look for. He picked through the brown glass bottles until he came to Percodan.

He figured if his own foot were mangled, he'd probably take

three with another handy just in case. He weighed probably twice as much as Mohammed, so he adjusted his dosage accordingly. He placed the pills in Mohammed's trembling hand and went to Pix's sink to fill a paper cup with water.

"I'll fix you up, Mohammed," he said. "These worked wonders for me when I tore up my knee."

"Mr. Wilson," Pix said, his face screwed into a frown, "that's not your place."

"No, it's not," Logan said. "But I can keep a secret if you can." He knelt by Mohammed and tilted his head back. He dropped the pills into the Indian's mouth and put the cup to his lips. "Good man," he said. "I oughta loan you my Walkman. You're about to be in a better place, my friend."

Logan wadded up the cup and pitched it in Pix's trash bin. Smiling at Mohammed, he started for the door. The Indian reached up and caught him by the wrist.

"Doc," he muttered. "Stay. Please."

"You'll be all right. If Pix screws you around, just tell me. Me and Strong'll kick his British ass. Gimme five, brother." They smacked hands.

"I one tough nigger, no?"

Logan smiled again. "You the baddest nigger of 'em all, Mohammed-baby. I'll catch ya on the flip." He turned to Pix. "I'll tell the driver he's goin' in." He paused. "Soon."

"He's going," Pix said. "Soon."

Logan shoved open the door to the TCN lounge. The driver was sunk in the vinyl sofa watching an R-rated video, smuggled in by some unknown Momentum employee, in the hope that he would be there long enough to see someone's breasts, preferably female.

"Let's go, man," Logan said and ejected the cassette. "You're runnin' to Dhahran."

Logan borrowed an Arabco truck to return to location. He found Strong, Barnes, and Bull in the center of their unsettled TCN crew. The Indians were angry and agitated, and Logan was relieved to see that, although Barnes seemed indifferent and Bull was bored, Strong was sympathetic to their concerns.

"Look, I know you guys are upset," Strong said as he tightened a nut on the new set of pick-up elevators with a chrome crescent wrench. "I don't blame you. But Mohammed's all right. It could've been a hell of a lot worse."

As usual, Rahiman spoke for the others.

"One man injured! Why? Today, fuck it up, his foot. Tomorrow, maybe somebody die. We say fuck this job!"

"Look, the cable broke, men! I know you're all pissed off about Mohammed, but it was an accident. No one's fault."

"Today a cable, maybe later fucking rig blow up, we all die! We have families in India!"

Barnes stepped in, his lips tight, jaw set. Logan knew his agenda. Another hour of downtime and Momentum would go off their day rate—news Frank Blount, the Momentum division manager, would not want to hear.

"You guys wanna quit?" Barnes said. "Fine by me. We can march right down to my office, sign the papers, and I'll ship every one of you bastards back to Bombay. There's six hundred million screamin' sons of bitches over there right now that would kill for this job." He crossed his arms. "Now either we start runnin' this casin' or we go. No more arguin'. Which is it gonna be?"

"What's wrong with you, Elvin?" Logan said. "Can't you see they're scared?" He pointed to Mohammed's blood congealing on the floor. "You don't think they've got good reason to worry?"

Barnes turned to Strong. "A couple of toes ain't bad enough to shut the whole goddamn operation down. I got a deadline."

"And I'm ahead of it," Strong said. "What good does it do if you run my guys off because they're scared? Will it go faster then? These men work circles around anybody else."

"I ain't no babysitter," Barnes said.

"And these ain't no babies. I'll be runnin' again in ten minutes if you'll just get out of their faces and let me and Doc handle it."

Barnes snorted, shaking his head. "Just get it done, then." He trudged off to the doghouse to watch with his arms crossed.

"You heard him, boys," Strong said. "We gotta go on. Doc here will work in Mohammed's place." He turned to Logan. "Why don't you tell them how he is."

"He's okay," Logan said. "He lost three toes, no more. He's goin' to Dhahran, then back to light duty. No problem."

Strong's crew talked it over. Rahiman spoke angrily; Putti answered with calmer words. They went back and forth until at last Rahiman stepped forward.

"We will work," Rahiman declared, and they all nodded. But Logan sensed their resentment.

"Good," Strong said. He glanced briefly back at Barnes. "Today, Mohammed was the unlucky one. Now you all see how easy shit can happen out here." He snapped his fingers. "Just like that and it's all over. Momentum don't give a shit about you. And they don't give a shit about me. It's up to us to look out after each other. I'm gonna watch out for every man on this crew."

He rose and slipped his studded gloves back over his hands. It was Logan's first glimpse this trip of the Strong he'd once admired. "Now what d'ya say we run some pipes and make Momentum happy?" Strong said.

Logan looked at his watch. It had been almost two hours since the accident. The Indians, still sniping under their breath, slowly resumed their positions. "Here we go," Strong said as he retuned his rheostats. "Nice and easy."

Strong looked again at Barnes, who nodded his satisfaction. He pulled in another joint of casing and the operation began. Logan worked in Mohammed's place. He kicked the damaged set of elevators aside. That's when he saw it. He dragged the cable over to the console and showed it to Strong.

"You see the code marked on the bracket here?"

"Yeah, what about it?"

"It's red. The chart in the office says we're supposed to be using blue. This one should've been thrown out before we ever moved down here."

Strong's eyes narrowed. "Goddamn that sorry Parnell," he said, pounding his fist against his open palm. "Don't say nothin' to nobody about it. Not to the Indians. Not to Barnes. Nobody. Take it down to the dump and throw it away. I'll take care of it—my way."

"I gotta fill out an accident report, Jamie. I gotta mention it."

"Don't you dare. What good will the goddamn paperwork do? I said I'd take care of it, and I will." He turned to his crew. "You guys ready?"

They nodded.

"I'm proud of you guys," Strong said. "I know you're worried. I know you've all got families back home. I used to have one. I've got a little girl runnin' around, somewhere. There ain't gonna be no more accidents on this floor. I can promise you that."

Logan coiled the cable in his hand and walked off the floor. The Indians watched his every step and had to wonder.

FOURTEEN

───◆───

The casing operation lagged even though the night air had cooled. Mohammed's accident had sapped the fire from the crew, as Logan had expected it would. The monotony denied any momentum, and running the big pipes became a task to be endured, one grimy joint after another, with no sense of accomplishment or satisfaction.

Just before midnight, Parnell and his crew reached the drill floor for their turn. Parnell sauntered out to the console with his thumbs hooked under the suspenders of his overalls in a ridiculous parody of a farmer—which Logan knew for certain he was not. Farmers wouldn't have him. Where Momentum had found him, Logan had no idea. Foreign recruiting must have turned over every sleazy honky-tonk rock in northern Mississippi.

"Looks like you come up short, hotshot," Parnell told Strong. "I ain't the least surprised."

"We'll see," Strong said, just before he landed his fist under Parnell's chin. Parnell staggered backwards until his body hit the doghouse wall. He slid to the floor, dazed. The Indians of both crews froze. Every man was as stunned as Parnell.

"What's that for?" Parnell mumbled, moving his chin from side to side.

"One of my hands got busted up tonight because you were too goddamn lazy to change out the cables on the pick-up sling. He's lucky it didn't kill him, and you're lucky I don't kill you, you worthless piece of shit!"

"Damn it, Strong," Parnell moaned, his face flushed. "Don't get so emotional, ya hotheaded bastard. I looked at that cable like I do everythin' else, and it was fine. You must've hung it on somethin'. Don't blame me."

Rahiman heard and answered. "No. Cable no good."

Strong craned forward, nose-to-nose with Parnell. "Next time you rig up an operation that my crew has to work under, you better make damn sure everythin's safe, you sorry motherfucker." Strong shook in anger, his veins pulsing under the sunburned skin of his neck. "If one of my men ever gets hurt because of you, I'll come lookin' for ya down at camp. I won't wait till crew change. I'll strangle you in your bed!"

"It was an accident, Strong. I didn't know it was bad."

"That's the problem! You're too damn ignorant to know any better. And I won't stand for it no more!"

Strong backed Parnell into the driller's console. Parnell reached for the rheostats; Logan knew it was in his best interest to get busy. He was sure the man's head was still ringing. Strong had smacked him good.

Strong snatched up his things and went down to the office to fill out his portion of the day's drilling log. Parnell gathered his Indians. "The show's over," he said. "Let's run some pipe." He looked at Logan, who glared back but said nothing. As he walked to the stairs, the Indians followed in silence.

"Okay, Strong," Rahiman said when they caught up with their driller on the catwalk. "Now better."

"What's better?" Strong said, cupping his hands to light a Marlboro.

"We have justice, Islam justice. Parnell pays for mistake. Indian peoples satisfied. All is well."

"I guess." Strong exhaled.

"Parnell is dumb motherfucker, no?"

"The dumbest."

"We are sorry about Mohammed, Doc," Rahiman said.

"I'm sorry too," Logan said quietly.

"Accident not your fault, Doc," the Indian said, and Strong looked back and nodded. "Mohammed is very slow. We all hear cable breaking. Mohammed would not move. Better for him to get light duty. Same pay. Easy money. No problem."

Strong stopped dead in his tracks. "You hear that, Doc? It ain't your fault. Now get over it."

"Sure," Logan said, although he knew it would take some time. It was true that Mohammed was slower than the rest, less agile, certainly less wary. Logan knew how easy it was to be injured on a drill floor. If he'd had to predict which crewman was most likely to get hurt, it would have been Mohammed. It'd cost him three toes to earn light duty—a luxury, given that he'd no longer have to risk a much worse injury. Mohammed would come out of this mess all right.

But what about Logan? He had not responded as he'd always thought he would. The Indians didn't fault him; Parnell's aching jaw absorbed the blame. But the Indians didn't see the panic rippling beneath Logan's cool facade. They didn't know how shaken he'd been. They just knew he had failed them. For all his good intentions, he had yielded bad results.

Logan had always believed that Strong depended on him. He saw their professional relationship as one of balance. For years, two distinctly different and often clashing natures had meshed to form an effective, competent leadership for the crew. But now he realized that he depended more on Strong, whose commanding strengths compensated for Logan's weaknesses. It had taken Strong to make things right.

Mohammed's accident had tipped the scales in Strong's favor. And Logan was fairly certain, despite Strong's public refusal to blame him for what happened, that he privately faulted him for how poorly he'd reacted. Logan sensed that he'd just slipped an essential notch in Strong's hard measure of a man.

Logan's concern, he knew, should have been for his injured crewman. He was supposed to be the warm heart, the one white ass who thought of the Indians first. But Logan found himself questioning his own place in this newly skewed picture. How would Strong use the incident against him? And how would this offset what Logan knew about Strong? How would those Indians look at him next time he took Strong's place at the brake?

The desert wind swirled around him as he walked down the long catwalk. Dust stung his eyes. He had dreamed of becoming a driller the first time he'd set foot on a rig floor. Now that he'd failed at it, he was inconsolably disappointed. For his part, Strong had said nothing, which to Logan was even worse than telling him point blank he didn't have what it takes to command a crew.

FIFTEEN

DAY TEN

After a day of cementing, Logan sat in the galley. He shoved his plate away. For some reason the British simmered every bit of flavor out of a vegetable. The fare had been cooked that way in the North Sea. Tate-Pixilate, who organized the menu, instructed his Indian chefs to boil the bejesus out of everything in their pots. Only a week into his hitch and Logan was already tired of the food's incessant blandness. But he never ate well in Saudi Arabia's heat. He chalked up his lack of appetite to the sweltering weather and to the fact that he felt particularly lonely.

He passed through the expat lounge on his way back to his cabin. He intended to spend the last couple of hours of the day reading Márquez. Strong, Brother, and Ripley sat sunk in the vinyl sofa, watching a video. Strong pointed to the slotted bin next to the TV.

"Letter for ya, Doc," he said.

"What's this one say?"

Strong shrugged his shoulders. Logan took the unsealed Momentum envelope and left for his room.

He reclined on his bed and opened the envelope. It was another telex. He suspected it was from Caitlin, informing him that she'd increased the list once again. She'd probably rented Palmer Auditorium to accommodate the swelling number of guests. But it was from his mother.

Logan:

>Twenty-seven years ago on this day I gave birth to my only son. I was a housewife then, and my baby boy spent every waking moment at my side. I loved all my children. I never played favorites. But you and I always had a special relationship. In my heart I always knew you were the one who was most like me.
>
>This coming fall I'll see you married. Soon, God willing, you'll have children of your own. When that time comes, you'll understand why I made the choices I did. You'll realize that I put up with what I did to keep my family together. And then you'll forgive me.
>
>You and I will be close again. Be careful, son. And Happy Birthday!
>
>Love,
>Mother

Logan stared at the ceiling, the telex still gripped in his hand. He'd never thought he had much in common with his mother. For her to say so would have rankled him a year or two ago. But to hear it now struck him with a strange sense of pride. Arkansas tough, she possessed a quiet strength and dignity that had never wavered in trying times. He hoped like hell he'd inherited it. Maybe it was time to give her another chance. It was easier to focus on better times. The best memories of his childhood invariably included her. And yes, he thought, it would be nice if they were close again. His wedding would be the beginning of their reconciliation. He'd apologize for his behavior and let nature take its course. Saudi Arabia had taught him about loneliness. Best to repair those frayed family ties if possible.

There was a knock at the door.

"It's open."

In stepped Strong, Brother, Ripley, Putti, Rahiman, Abdullah, and all the roustabouts. The Indians had all raided their personal stash of Arabic Pepsi cans. Each man also carried one cupcake, except Strong. He carried two. He handed one to Logan.

"Happy birthday," they all shouted.

"Why do you insist on reading my mail?" Logan said to Strong.

"I've got no choice," Strong said. "I never get any. If I'd have known it was your birthday, I'd have doped your ass."

"Another reason to keep it quiet," Logan said.

They failed miserably at singing "Happy Birthday." Strong finally broke in and told them to shut up. Abdullah made himself right at home. He dove onto Buffarn's bunk, crushing Caitlin's card, which had come the day before. How it had gotten by Strong, Logan couldn't say. Not much did.

"Happy fucking birthday, Doc," Abdullah said, his mustache smudged with white icing. He tested Buffarn's springs. "Number one bed," he said.

SIXTEEN

Not an hour after crew change Barnes arrived on the floor. Logan watched him yell into Strong's ear. He heard every word from three feet away. "How's the cement feel?" Barnes barked, hands dug deep in his jeans pockets.

"It's a little spongy," Strong said. He let the bit take a little more weight so Barnes could see for himself. "But it ain't green if that's what you're wonderin'."

"Good. It looked a little soupy when them Canadians pumped it, but I guess it sat up all right. How long did it take y'all to drill out the first plug?" The plug partitioned off the cement from the mud above it, much like the plunger in a syringe. Their rubber construction always made them difficult to drill.

"About an hour and a half," Strong said. "It kept wantin' to bounce."

"Well, you'll get to the second one pretty quick," Barnes said. "Don't be afraid to set a little weight on it. Get yourself a good bite, and let's get on with it."

It had been days since the derrick was clear of the rows of racked drill pipe. The drill floor had been perpetually cluttered with the contractors' men, whose noisy operations and machinery had been given temporary priority over those of the Momentum crews. Logan heard at least a dozen different languages at any given time, and none, including English, directed at him. The last few days had been chaos, but now the kelly was turning again. The Rub al Khali location belonged to Momentum once more.

Logan and his crew had accomplished much over the last few days. The nine and five-eighths casing had been run into the well and cemented in place. Then the blowout preventers were disconnected and set aside, a process called "nippling down." Saudi welders, employees of the national oil concern, cut the casing at its desired point, then fit the new casing flange on top of the three set earlier, the massive Japanese wellhead squatting solidly beneath them all.

The Saudis were big, gregarious men who seemed to enjoy their work. They stayed hard at their tasks, dressed like rednecks in their khaki uniforms and silly welder's caps with the bills turned backwards, as all welders wore them. They only left their scaffolds to pray at the appointed times.

Logan watched them walk into the clean dunes of the Rub al Khali, away from Momentum's clutter, noise, effluvium, and filth, to kneel in the sand and face northwest toward Mecca. They returned to their labors as jovial as ever, one of them singing. The myth of the lazy Arab, given currency by most of the expats, certainly didn't apply to them. They were good-natured, hardworking, skilled tradesmen.

Once the new casing head was welded in place, the task of "nippling up"—the reassembling of the blowout preventer stack—fell to Logan's crew. They reattached the configuration of rams and hydril, possum belly, mud trough, tie-down stabilizers, and hydraulic control tubes until Momentum's iron totem was complete. They sealed the bore beneath the wellhead and pressure-tested the preventer stack. Each component held in its turn, save the blind rams, which leaked the white hydraulic fluid exerted against them. Logan was the first to see it pour like blood down the flank of the beast. This was not good, especially on a wildcat well like this one.

"Goddamn," Strong said. "Let's take it back off and send it to town." He ordered his crews to reattach the hoist slings. Barnes shut him down, calling Dhahran on his mobile radio to discuss the problem with Frank Blount. Marshall, always anxious, paced around the cellar.

"Tell Brother to bring the flatbed," Strong said to Logan. "They've got no choice but to rebuild the stack." Logan knew they were looking at two days of downtime. Marshall wrung his hands.

But Barnes, at Blount's bidding, ordered the blind rams retested.

"That's bullshit, Elvin," Strong said. "Send it in and get it overhauled. We can't take a chance like this."

"It was overhauled before it ever came out here," Barnes said. "The seals are new."

"But they ain't workin'," Strong said.

"Blount says they will. He thinks there's just some mud or grease around the grooves." It was clear to Logan that the matter was closed. Barnes opened the ram bonnets and cleaned the seals himself. Then the roughnecks rebolted the bonnets while Barnes raised the hydraulic pressure to the lines. The rams held firm to fifteen thousand psi for more than an hour. Marshall continually rapped the gauge with his knuckle just to make damn sure.

Barnes radioed Blount again with the results of the latest test and suggested they tear down the stack anyway just to be safe. But Blount was satisfied, and Marshall concurred, as long as they tested it again.

"Don't sweat it, boys," Marshall said after studying their drawn faces. "No reservoir could come at us with fifteen thousand pounds of pressure. Not with a full column of mud above it."

And so they went on, despite the fact that Logan had never heard of a reservoir of Al Hisaab's potential power. But who was he to argue with Momentum? He satisfied himself by remembering that the blind rams were used only if the well attempted to kick when all pipe was out of the hole, a rare occurrence.

Once the blowout preventers were set and tested, the crews returned to the floor. They broke down the bottom-hole assembly piece by piece, and removed the thirty ten-inch drill collars from the string and put them out on the pipe racks to rust in the sun. Brother and his crew would load the lot onto one of Momentum's flatbed trucks for return to the Dhahran yard.

Logan's crew assembled smaller-diameter drill collars, stabilizers, and jars. The drill pipe followed and back to bottom Momentum went. The entire operation took three days. The bit struck hard cement around 11,500 feet, and Strong set up to drill it out again. He made good time, and connections came fast and furiously. Now, at the end of the cemented bore, the process slowed. This was a good sign. A few feet more and they'd reach the final rubber cement plug.

Beyond it lay the sleeping Al Hisaab, and the unknown.

The automatic driller whined like a fisherman's reel when Strong attached its cable to the brake. "How far they gonna drill, anybody know yet?" Strong asked Barnes.

"Maybe two thousand feet deeper, but it'll be slow. There's supposed to be some hard rock down there."

"Why so far?" Strong said. "I thought we were just on top of the reservoir. No way in hell there's that much pay."

Barnes shook his head. "They think there's three zones. They want to flow the deepest one first, then back up to the other two and test each one by itself. Completion's gonna be the shits on this hole."

"Jesus." Strong lifted his plastic hat to scratch his sweat-matted hair. "These fuckin' Arabs, man. Are they sittin' on a pile of money or what?"

"Sittin's the right word," Barnes said. "Back home they're mortgagin' the ranch to drill wells just hopin' one might fart. Here ya can't dig a goddamn post hole without a hundred thousand cubic feet of gas a day. Don't seem right, does it?"

"Hell, no, it don't."

"It's like this, Strong," Barnes said, his expression as close to philosophical as Logan had ever seen it. "They got the oil and gas; we got the know-how. They get the know-how, and me and you'll be sellin' ladies' shoes in the mall." He stroked his chin. "And they're workin' on the goddamn know-how right now."

"I wouldn't sweat it," Strong said. "They don't like gettin' their hands dirty. It might not always be us workin' over here, but it'll never be them."

"I'm not so sure," Barnes said. "Marshall worked on national rigs for twenty years. He says they're damn good hands when it comes to those six-thousand-foot wells. As good as any, he says."

"Huh. That I'd like to see," Strong said. "That don't explain why they ain't out here on this one, does it?"

"Their rigs ain't set up to handle it, from what I understand."

"Their minds ain't set up to handle it either. The whole thing makes me sick. I got a notion to twist off."

"And go where?" Barnes said. "The glut's ruined everything. There's no work anywhere no more. They're layin' off hands back home. The Saudis got the only game in town."

"Looks like we're all stuck." Strong turned to Logan. "It's gonna be slow drillin' while we ream out this last chunk of cement. Have the boys clean up this floor and tell Ripley to save Marshall some rubber once it makes it to the shakers. He always wants to look at it for some reason."

"I'll handle it."

Strong had given the assignment. Logan, as he so often was, would be the bearer of bad news. The drill floor was the one place where Strong had complete control, and Logan knew he cherished it. To see it in such chaos unnerved him. For Logan to do nothing about it until he was told irritated Strong to no end.

But Logan knew what Strong wanted. His driller liked to see the huge pipe and crescent wrenches cleaned and hung by order of size on the toolboard. Their respective places were outlined there like the bodies of murder victims on a sidewalk. He liked to see the grain of the oak planks on the floor once the drilling fluid had been scrubbed out. He wanted to see the brightly painted machinery glistening in the sun from the trace of diesel fuel he had taught his men to add to their rigwash pails. He wanted the bits of tar the drilling line threw off to be scraped from the drawworks. He wanted the doghouse—soiled by the dirty boots and clothes of the service hands—sponged out. And most of all he wanted to see his crew start to work on it pretty goddamn soon.

"We'll be into new formation here directly," Barnes said, his tone deepening. "Keep a close eye on this one. It might come at us. Don't take no chances. And stop poundin' the hell out of Parnell! He looks like you hit him with a tonghead or somethin'. He cried in my office for half a day."

Strong packed his mouth with chewing tobacco. "We had somethin' to get straight, that's all," he muttered. "It's done."

"Thank God for it," Barnes said, and he left.

Strong reached over and flicked the cable of the automatic driller so it would slack off. That handy unit provided relief from the tedium of the brake when the penetration rate was slow. He plucked at the cable again and again. Finally, the drawworks screeched. The increased weight settled on the twisting bit—three toothed, circular heads biting at cement, designed much like the bit Howard Hughes's daddy had introduced seventy years ago. Logan heard the rotary motor groan under the torquing strain.

"Drill, you son of a bitch, drill!" Strong hollered. "We're gonna see what this bitch's got."

"Strong!" Logan recognized Marshall's booming voice over the intercom. "What's all that weight doin' on my new bit!"

Strong kicked the button on the automatic driller with his boot to disengage it and pressed hard on the brake lever. Then he answered. "Uh, it's just a malfunction with my auto pilot, Marshall. I'll adjust it." He wiped the mud from his boot off the unit.

"You fuck up my cement job and you'll catch a jet!"

"Yeah, I got it now, Marshall," he said. Marshall knew everything as soon as Strong did, providing he was watching the set of key indicators that read directly into his office.

"Just for once, try doin' what you're told!"

"No problem," Strong said into the little beige squawk box. He sat back down next to the brake after he gave the automatic driller another kick. "Dickhead," he said.

"I heard that, Strong! Don't think I didn't!"

Strong manually operated the brake lever until he had reestablished the correct weight. He restrung the automatic cable. Then he slapped the little intercom box as hard as he could, denting the metal housing. He turned to Logan, his expression blank. "Go on, Doc. You know what I want," he said. "Make it happen."

Logan searched three nooks frequented by the roughnecks with no success. He found them in the fourth. Once he had opened the sealed door, he saw the men through the haze of stinking cigarette smoke. They were lounging on pallets of rags, chemical sacks, and bulky burlap bags. The supply room sat directly below the mud house and the shale shakers. It was the place where gas was first separated from the drilling fluid. To smoke there was a stupid idea and they all knew it.

"What the hell do you think you're doin'?" Logan said.

"Not hell, Doc," Putti said, exhaling. "Rub al Khali."

"Problem, Doc?" Rahiman said. Always Rahiman.

"Big problem!" Logan said. "Put 'em out! Right now!"

The Indians continued to puff. "I mean now!" Logan shouted. Then he stomped around to each of them, snatching the cigarettes from their mouths. He ground them into the metal floor with the toe of his boot.

"You dumb bastards know better! This is a gas well, *gondos!*" He was so furious, his jaw ached. "You can smoke in the Bombay Teahouse, the mechanic's shack, and anywhere out in the desert. But not on rig! And not under mud house! Understand?"

Rahiman settled into his rags, his hands behind his head. "Now drilling cement, Doc," he said, scratching his chin.

"Now drilling cement. But soon drilling reservoir."

"But now drilling cement," Rahiman repeated. "No gas here."

The calmer the Indian was, the angrier Logan became.

"Look! You don't say when it's okay to smoke and when it's not. Maybe you know, maybe you don't. Maybe one time you smoke this place, some gas, big boom, three dead Indian mother-fuckers and one dead Englishman! Understand?"

"Okay, Doc," Rahiman said. "We go Bombay Teahouse for smoke."

"No, I don't think so. You go rig floor. All makey clean." Usually he would preface that with "*Strong say* all makey clean," so they would understand that it wasn't his idea. But this time he didn't feel such qualification was appropriate. He wanted it done as much as Strong.

"Fuck that!" Rahiman growled, his lips snarling. "Three days hard working! Today rest!"

Logan looked at the other men. Even Putti's face was stern. "Doc?" he asked quietly, always the diplomat. "Is necessary?"

"First is necessary to clean drill floor, after maybe some rest." Logan offered this as a concession. "Slow drilling. No problem."

The Indians talked among themselves in Hindi. Logan suspected Putti argued to do it for the sake of peace. But Rahiman, who was clearly tired, sore, and irritable, wanted to take further issue. Abdullah Larry could go either way. Logan waited, but no answer came.

He understood the problem. Once he'd been in their boots, and he remembered it well. He had been the young Rahiman of his crew, always in conflict with authority. Somewhere along the line he'd changed sides. Now it was his job to deal with a roughneck's resentment. To be heavy-handed and strict with the crew was alien to his nature, and the Indians knew it.

He was the weak link in the heavy chain of the West. He sensed the Indians perceived the uncertainty in his eyes, his tendency to explain rather than order, and they took full advantage. Had Strong found his men smoking under the shale shakers, justice would have come hard and swift. With Logan, they knew they could argue.

He didn't like it. He'd always sympathized with the Indians. And he had always been lenient with them, a decision that placed him perpetually at odds with Strong. His repayment, as Strong had always warned him, was disrespect. Now that he saw it clearly in Rahiman's face, it stung him.

He could see the wisdom in Strong's coolness now. Camaraderie requires trust, and that was the first of many human resources depleted by Momentum's TCN policy and the Rub al Khali's heat. Now, seeing how the roughnecks used him, hearing them argue over the most common task in words they would never use with Strong, Logan's sense of failure deepened. The Rub al Khali had never felt lonelier.

It should have meant nothing. They were, after all, drilling cement. The Indians had earned a brief rest. Logan could have walked away and let them finish their hand-rolled cigarettes. They would come in time, and he could make excuses to Strong as he always did.

But he wanted them to understand that they had pushed him as far as they could. "Look," he said. "If y'all don't give a damn, neither do I. I'm gonna leave it up to you. Either you work or we'll go to the office. I'll dock you. I'll hold your vacation time. If that doesn't do it, I'll run your asses off. No more bullshit."

These were the weapons Momentum had given him, and Logan wanted them to know that even he, the kindest American they knew, was certainly capable of using them. He crossed his arms and tapped the toe of his Redwing boot. "What's it gonna be, boys?"

The Indians completed their discussion, and Rahiman stepped forward to deliver the verdict.

"Okay, Doc," he said. "No gas here, but we don't smoke. Rules, you know."

"Oh, yeah." Logan sighed, relieved. "I know."

"We get soap, go rig floor and all makey clean. You happy now?"

"So happy."

"Goot. You white peoples too much fucking problem, man."

"Very, very problem," Putti added. Abdullah Larry bobbled his head in affirmation.

"Okay, *gondos*," Logan said. "We make deal. You all makey clean drill floor, I speak to Strong, maybe too much slack time tonight for roughnecks. Maybe sleepin', Bombay Teahouse, I don't know."

"Maybe," Putti answered. Such plans were always tentative as far as he was concerned.

"No promises," Logan said. "Maybe driller want more working."

"Ah," moaned Putti, his suspicions confirmed.

Rahiman started for the door. "What goot are promises from white asses?" he said. "Less go, boys." The others followed him out. Logan watched them wade single file through the deep sand.

"Christ," he said. He removed his hard hat and ran his fingers through his sweat-soaked hair. He was so tired of being squeezed between the Saudis and the West, Momentum and Arabco, Strong and his rebellious Indian crew. Every little task was a burden, every transaction a bitter negotiation. And every day the sun grew hotter.

He heard the squeal of the drawworks brakes above him. Strong was making progress. Soon he'd drill through the last of the cement and the plastic casing shoe. After that he'd enter the shale dome and new hole, and inch by inch they'd bore closer to the end.

And while that was happening, those roughnecks had best be scrubbing that filthy floor.

SEVENTEEN

Strong bored through the rubber plug into virgin formation quicker than they had anticipated. He kept fiddling with the controls, searching for the combination of bit weight and rotary speed that would allow the most efficient penetration. Logan stood nearby in silence. From time to time, Marshall called from his quarters to see how things were going. The roughnecks busied themselves with their brushes and pails.

The dust was up in the afternoon wind, hell on Logan's allergies. It wasn't good for Marshall's either, and it was Marshall who mattered. He ordered three tankloads of diesel fuel to be spread around location to keep the dust down, something he said he'd once done with Saudi crude. There had been a time, before the 1970s and whirlwind petroleum profits, when the roads were paved with oil, as they'd been in East Texas during the Spindletop boom. Saudi Arabian highways were made of smooth asphalt now; crude had become too precious to waste. Diesel fuel, however, was worth maybe four cents an Imperial gallon, a sum the Saudis could still part with, and Logan knew Marshall liked the very idea of it— a tribute to the old ways and a tangible measure of his current worth to his Saudi hosts.

Arabco sent the diesel out right away. The drivers sprayed the entire location, but the dust from the surrounding Rub al Khali still blew. Now it stuck to everything, coating every inch of metal with a greasy grit, the acrid stench overwhelming the clean sweetness of the desert.

Logan, nauseated by the fumes, sat on the bench in the dog-house with his head in his hands. With the penetration slow and the automatic driller engaged, Strong was free to join him.

"I hate it when he does this," Strong said. "The dust is better."

Strong sometimes liked to have Logan around for company. They'd just sit and talk. Other times, Strong probably suspected that Logan took advantage of their relationship by sitting on his ass. Logan sensed by Strong's cool demeanor that this was one of those moments.

"Find yourself somethin' to do, Doc," he said.

"You bet," Logan said, off like a shot to do just that. He knew what had to be done and what didn't, and he didn't fancy the idea of busywork. He figured it was Strong's way of reminding him who was boss. When they'd worked together in the North Sea, Strong hadn't kept busy to please their drillers. Here in Saudi Arabia, neither would Logan.

But he couldn't hang around the floor. Maybe he'd go down to Barnes's office to bullshit with him about deer hunting or the upcoming football season. Barnes generally had lots of entertaining ideas about both, and unlike Strong he didn't care if Logan stayed busy when there wasn't anything going on. Logan was not going to jump through Strong's endless supply of hoops just to keep him happy. Not anymore. And given their history together, he was fairly certain that although Strong might bitch about it to him, he wouldn't do much else.

He left Strong standing before his console, surveying all with his arms crossed over his chest, master of his thousand-square-foot metal island. The Indians toiled around him to suit his authoritarian whim. Rahiman looked up at Logan as he passed. He moved two fingers in front of his lips, as if he were smoking.

Son of a bitch, Logan thought. He'll get his.

Barnes, boots propped up on his desk, spread the fingers of both hands above his head to represent antlers, obviously exaggerated in size. "I mean, Doc, he was the biggest damn buck I'd ever seen, and he wouldn't step out from behind that goddamn mesquite tree. I kept the crosshairs on his outline and waited until..."

Kashian, the gentle rig clerk, burst through the door with uncharacteristic alarm. "Elvin! Doc! Come! Too many camels!"

"Camels?" Barnes said. "What kind of camels? Ain't no camels out here."

"Camel-camels! Hundreds! Come. See."

Barnes rose from his squeaky chair, the torn vinyl snagging his khakis. "Let's go, Doc. Let's see what the hell's goin' on around here."

No sooner had they turned the corner than they found themselves dodging one of the beasts. Behind it, in a line that disappeared into the dunes, were camels.

In the north, Logan knew, young Bedouin boys in Japanese trucks coasted along with the herds in search of better grass, but he didn't see any here. The animals meandered onto the location, sniffing trash cans and pawing at the grass growing around the water lines until they could snatch it up with their big yellow teeth. They jockeyed for position, edging one another away for the rights to the sparse vegetation, which also grew in the shade of the metal shacks. There were so many hungry animals and so little food that every blade of dried grass was contested. They took it all and moved on to the next dry patch.

Brother had to shut down the crane once the animals surrounded him, and Abraham's crew truck could not leave for camp. With the exception of the activity on the drill floor, the entire location ground to a halt. Only the beasts stayed busy.

Logan looked ahead to the lead camel as it traipsed through the middle of camp. Its legs were tethered at the knees, forcing it to take short, choppy steps. The rest of the bawling herd followed their leader's governed pace.

Barnes pointed to a figure three hundred yards away. Through the distortion of the heat waves, Logan made out the silhouette of a man, bobbing along on a humped back. "Looky here, Doc," Barnes said. "We got us a real live cowboy."

"I wonder what the hell's he doin' out here?"

"He's Bedouin, I bet. Gotta be. Nobody else knows how to live out here. Headin' north for summer grazin'. Of course, I don't know much about A-rab ranchin', but I know damn well there ain't no grass out here. Let's go."

"Let's go where?"

"Let's go see if he'll let us ride one, man. You know, for the folks back home. Wish I had my Kodak."

Barnes trotted out to the rider with Logan following, both slowing down the last few yards as if they were approaching an unfamiliar bull. Marshall once told them that the government had been trying to settle Bedouin tribes into villages for the last forty years. One glance at this one and Logan knew he was looking at a holdout. He rode right up to them and pulled back on his ornate reins. The camel lifted its nose to the air and bellowed.

The Bedouin had an old bolt-action rifle, military style, but only Werner would know for sure what make. It was slung across his back. Arabic scrolls were carved into the stock. The rifle was beaten and rough looking from frequent and hard use, but Logan could not see the first trace of rust.

Barnes held up his palm like an "Injun" in some old black-and-white western. When that got no response, he decided to bow.

"Christ, Elvin. What's that all about?"

"You got a better idea?"

"Yeah." Logan approached the Bedouin. "*As salaam alaykum,*" he said. He'd practiced with Mousa.

"*Wa alaykum as salaam,*" the man said.

"Hey, Doc, he's got his ears on now, baby. Ask him if we can saddle one up."

"Forget it, boss," Logan said. "I know how to say 'how ya doin',' and that's about it."

"What's goin' on out here?" Marshall had come up from behind. He spoke to the Arab in his native tongue. The language seemed guttural and coarse, but Marshall flowed effortlessly over every syllable. The Bedouin answered, and Logan marveled at the fact that Marshall seemed to understand him.

Barnes's jaw dropped. "Hey, Marshall. Ask him if I can ride one." He pranced around like a kid at a theme park. Marshall continued the conversation, pointing frequently toward Barnes. The Bedouin replied. Marshall smiled.

"What'd he say?" Barnes asked.

"He says you can go fuck yourself. He's too busy and life's not a game."

Barnes kicked at the sand. "He don't have to be ugly about it," Barnes said.

Marshall turned to Logan. "Doc, go to the north end of location and open the water lines for the stock to drink. He's come up from the coast. He says it's been a hard summer out here and his pasture's played out. He's come out of his way—thinks the camels smelled the water in the lines and followed them here. He hasn't had a drink in two days."

The Bedouin handed Marshall his canteen. "Fill it up for him, Elvin. Water. No ice."

"Let him get his own," Barnes said.

"We've got it," Marshall said. "He needs it. Go get it."

"All right, goddamn it." Barnes turned toward his office. "I don't recall my contract sayin' anythin' 'bout waitin' on no sand niggers."

Logan studied the Arab. He was cloaked in dusty robes. The only exposed part of him was his eyes, and they searched the location. "The stock's thirsty, Doc," Marshall said. "Let the water run till they've had their fill."

The rusted valve on the sixteen-inch line was frozen shut. They'd never used it before. Logan kicked it open with his boot until the water came. It gushed out of the pipe, poured down the slope, and settled into a depression in the sand. The camels came at a trot. They muscled for position, grunting and snorting, as they had for the grass, knocking Logan from his perch. The first thing Logan noticed was how bad they smelled. It was a sweet sort of stench, like rotten fruit.

"Easy now, you ugly bastards," Logan said. "There's plenty."

The lead camel, unable to run, was among the last to arrive. Logan saw the bare ring just above his front hooves where the rope had rubbed the flesh raw.

Logan backed away from the line to rejoin Marshall and their guest. He passed Barnes, who'd already delivered a cup of water and a full canteen. He'd lost all interest. Marshall, his hands behind his waist, was listening to the Arab. The Bedouin sounded angry. Arabic always did to Logan. But it was clear that the herdsman was upset about something. Marshall answered him in a soothing tone. When silence fell, Marshall extended his hand. The Bedouin took it, nodded, and let it fall. He polished off the last of Barnes's water, restrapped the canteen to his saddle, whipped his mount on its flank with a thin switch, and headed north.

"What's eatin' him?" Logan asked.

"He says he can thank us for the water, but he can't thank us for that." Marshall pointed at the derrick. "He doesn't like what he sees."

"How's that?"

"Well, for starters, he thinks the world's changing against God's will. He says that Nasrani infidels crave oil the way his camels crave water, and that the West has infected the House of Saud with its sickness. Now Saudi kings build cities of salt, to be washed away in a rain. He says the sages predicted that the oil would last one hundred years, now nearly gone and good riddance."

"Not your happy-go-lucky Bedouin, huh?"

"That ain't all," Marshall said. "He says only fools and devils worship an iron image made by their own hand, an abomination, and he wonders which we are. God will strike it down, as sure as a camel swats a fly on its ass with its tail. In the end all of that, the rig, means nothing—not to him and not to a vengeful God. Doom awaits any who travel apart from the Lord, as sure as night follows day. The reckoning, he says, is near."

"Oh," Logan said. "Great."

"Ain't it, though." Marshall, his head down, turned and walked back to his office.

EIGHTEEN

DAY FOURTEEN

Logan faced the short change. His crew would work a full twelve-hour shift, take off six hours, of which he might sleep three, and then return to finish Parnell's tour. The Mississippian would go on days off, but his Indian crew would rest for six hours and then return for another twelve with a fresh driller. It was Momentum's policy to put a new head on a worn body.

Logan always struggled to adapt. The short change left him disoriented and fatigued. His vision blurred. He felt hungry and dehydrated, but he couldn't eat with the burn in his gut and he drank little else but coffee to see him through. The benefit of the short change, other than marking the midpoint of the hitch, was that the heat was now behind him. Logan's crew would work from midnight until noon, when the Rub al Khali was most generous. On clear nights the temperature plummeted so drastically—fifty degrees or more from the 125-degree afternoons—that in the early morning Logan sometimes wore a flannel shirt. His head cleared with the cooler temperatures.

With the short change behind him, he would be on his way home. Everyone's mood improved once they'd made the adjustment, the expats anyway. Except for Strong, who didn't seem to enjoy the going any more than the coming.

As Marshall had predicted, the drilling was indeed slow. Arabco had run another tungsten button bit because of its durability. But it sacrificed penetration in exchange for decreased trip time. Every ten minutes or so, Logan heard the screech of the drawworks as the blocks slacked off a little more.

For Strong, who equated movement with action and penetration with progress, the snail's pace was agony. To sit idly at his console, plucking at the taut cable of the automatic driller, only mired him deeper in his own funk. He was anxious for his drilling break, a brisk acceleration of the bit's penetration rate and the sign that they were through the tough dome and into the softer porous reservoir. No such break occurred, though, and Strong seemed to take it personally.

Earlier that day, Strong had placed his customary call to his lawyer. It had left him in a foul mood. He complained that they'd quibbled over the payment of fees rather than discussing the progress of his case, which apparently was going nowhere. Logan knew Strong had long ago given up on joint custody of his only child. Now he was battling for visitation rights. Logan didn't understand the court's reluctance. But Strong dwelled on it hour after hour, his windy rendition sounding like the grinding of a rusty axe, and it didn't take Logan long to hear all he could stand. At sundown, when the wind quit and the brass went to camp, he wandered alone about the location, eager to leave Strong and his festering problems to himself.

Teatime came at nine o'clock. Logan watched the Indians pile into the Bombay Teahouse. The metal windows were wedged open to vent the steam from the electric kettle and the dense cigarette smoke. He heard their laughter.

He found a quiet spot on the pallets stacked between the mud pits and the motor house. A fastidious roustabout had already arranged the sacks in a comfortable fashion. Once he had checked for scorpions, coiled pit vipers, and the inevitable piles of excrement deposited by an Indian who had waited too long to make it to Turd Alley, Logan settled in nicely.

From this vantage he could view the entire location. He saw Strong pacing back and forth on the floor, arguing with his shadow. Over the last few days, Strong had pushed the crew to their limits, moved heaven, earth, and iron to get back to drilling. Now that they had, he was tormented. The pace proved too slow to placate his insatiable drive for fast and furious action. Logan pitied him; Strong's disappointments overtook him so easily.

In this way, Strong reminded him of his father. They were both volatile, moody, and so quick to anger. But he didn't think it fair to compare the two. His father was by far the weaker man.

Logan had been roughnecking in Galveston for six months when his mother had phoned to ask a favor. His first reaction had been to refuse and let her clean up her own mess. But as the details became clearer, he told her he would oblige. He had always believed the solution to his family problems was a geographic cure: he had to leave. He decided to test his hard-won immunity by one brief re-exposure to the disease.

He found the keys where his mother said she had left them. He stepped inside and almost shuddered. He hated the cramped, disjointed floorplan and stale atmosphere of his parents' home. The walls were tarnished with cigarette smoke and angry words, the carpets stained with spilt wine and children's tears. Now that he was here, he regretted coming. He feared he wasn't free of it yet.

Logan was sitting in his father's chair when he heard the knock.

"It's open," he said. In walked his father with some sorry friend. They'd brought beer along with their boxes. Logan saw the blinking lights of the U-Haul truck parked outside.

"Won't be long," his father said, offering his hand from the sleeve of his tawdry suit.

Logan held up the court-ordered list of his father's property instead. "Here's what you can take," he said. "And not a damn thing more." His father looked at him with familiar hollow eyes. Logan deflected his stare to the piles of clothes, books, lamps, and worn furniture. "I don't have all night," he said.

He watched them pack and load every item. It wasn't done neatly. When they were finished, his father scribbled something on a notepad with a leaky ballpoint pen. He looked at his friend and nodded toward the door.

"Here's where you can reach me," he said when they were alone, handing Logan the note.

Logan wadded it up and dropped it in the ashtray. "I'm done reachin' for you," he said. He saw the old anger flash in his father's eyes. How Logan and his sisters used to shrink from him. How many nights they huddled together in one bed waiting for the storm to pass. Logan had long been taller than his father. Now he was stronger as well. You just try and come at me, you son of a bitch, he thought. I'm not one of my sisters you used to bang around when it suited you, and I'm not a kid anymore. Raise your hand to me again and see what you get. He was sure his father read that exact meaning in his cool stare.

And he thought he knew how his father would react. The tension would build in his face and some stupid act would follow. A gouge in the sheetrock, splintered furniture, broken glass. Something pitiful. But his father stepped back, exhaled, and shook his head. "You know what hurts about this deal?" he said.

"I hope all of it," Logan said.

"Don't judge me, Logan. You don't know what I've been through."

"I got a pretty good idea. You drug me and my sisters through it with you for the last twenty years."

His father stared at his scuffed shoes. "What hurts is to see my only son give up on me. I can deal with this divorce. I knew it was coming. I got a good job now. I'll get by. But it breaks my heart to see how you've turned against me. I didn't plan on that. Where I'm from, you don't quit on the people close to you. You never quit on your own kind."

"That's just it, isn't it?" Logan said. "I'm not from where you're from. You saw to that."

His father held up his hand. "You think I failed you?"

"I know you did."

"The truth is, you failed me."

Logan snorted and pointed to the beer can. "You must've gotten an early start tonight, old man."

His father, face boiling, snatched the decree from Logan's hand. "You think this paper means it's over and done with?"

He was supposed to be an educated man. Logan admitted there was an eloquence about him, a veneer of refinement. But when he got riled, the Arkansas oozed out of him like puss from an infected wound. Logan marked the mean shift in tone and inflection, his choice of bitter words. The South had bred no gentility in this man.

"You think it's all square one?" he said. "That you're a free man? Well, you're dead wrong. There ain't no easy way out from this. You think treatin' me like some kind of dog's gonna make you feel better. It's gonna make you feel a hell of a lot worse." He slurped his beer. "Sooner or later, you'll learn that I am what you are."

The exchange surprised Logan. The old buzzard had some fight left in him yet. Logan slipped his thumb and finger over the papers and pulled them from his father's hand. "I need that," he said. "You got your stuff. If you hurry, you can still catch happy hour."

"I'm still your daddy, boy. You'll never get shed of me."

Logan glanced at the decree. "Does it say that in here somewhere?"

"I see how the land lies," his father said. He crumpled the beer can and let it fall to the floor in a clatter. "I may be divorced, but I've still got friends. But you, you're a quitter, son. Always have been. You match that with your cold heart and you'll find yourself a world of sorrow out there. Who would ever be loyal to you? You just ain't worth it." He turned from Logan and headed for the door. "You sit in my chair and gnaw on that bone for a while."

And Logan, despite better intentions, had gnawed on it for quite some time.

He heard the roar of Abdullah's laughter. He rose and dusted the seat of his pants so no one could prove he'd been lying on sacks of bentonite, an old habit he'd picked up from a Louisiana wino roustabout his first week in the Texas patch. It was amazing how many didn't know, and Logan caught them often in their little lies. A man's dusty ass often told his lazy story.

He left the shadows. A vile odor rose up and filled the air. One of the Indians hadn't made it to Turd Alley after all. "Son of a bitch," he said.

Logan's frame filled the doorway of the teahouse. Every dark gaze locked on him.

"Make room, ya blasted wogs," Brother commanded, as if he sat in a pub. "Make room for the doctor. We need a little more white in here anyway." Brother shoved aside Aboobaker, his number one roustabout. "Christ, Aboo," he said. "You're fat as a haggis, mate. I'll need the crane to move you about before long."

Logan squeezed in between them on the worn metal bench.

"Not fat," Aboobaker protested. "Water."

"Water, me arse," Brother said. He pinched Aboobaker's abdomen. "Water you piss away. You're just plain bloody fat, Aboo."

"Not piss," Aboobaker said. "Water."

Brother rolled his eyes. "I know you don't see much of this

where you come from," Brother said, still clinging to Aboobaker's roll, "but this is fat. Be proud of it, Aboo. It's a status symbol in your country."

"Not fat. Water."

"All right," Brother said, "you win. Water it is, you stupid nigger." He eyed the dented little tin that sat on the table. "Give us one of them biscuits, Rahiman," he said. "I could use a little water problem meself."

Brother tapped the biscuit on the table's surface. The blow didn't produce the first crumb. "Sooner or later, we've got to change pubs, Doctor," he said to Logan. "This one's gone to shite." He bit the cookie. "Fockin' hell! This biscuit was baked when bloody Lawrence was 'ere. How do you buggers eat them?"

Razaki, the wispy roustabout, a shadow really, rubbed his stomach. "Number one biscuit," he said.

Brother flipped his into the waste bin. "You lot could eat bloody rocks if we stewed them in curry. At least Razaki ain't got no water problem, eh, Aboo?"

"No problem," Razaki said, and Aboobaker nodded.

"Razaki never drink water," Aboobaker explained.

"Short change tomorrow," Rahiman said, a dark cigarette dangling from his chapped lips.

"Too much problem," Putti sighed.

"You roughnecks have it made," Brother told them, an old roustabout argument and one no one bothered to respond to. "Any chance Marshall'll pull out tomorrow, Doc?"

"Maybe," Logan said. "Depends on the bit, I guess."

Brother's face wrinkled up like a prune. "For God's sake, what's that awful stench?"

"Smell bad?" Logan asked.

"Bloody wretched."

"Like shit, maybe?"

"Exactly."

"Must be shit. I stepped in it on the way here." Logan looked at the Indians, who were rapidly yielding space. "You bastards take a good whiff. Maybe you'll start usin' Turd Alley like you're supposed to. I'm tired of findin' your piles all over the goddamn location."

"You been near chemicals?" Aboobaker asked.

"I'd like to know why you're asking," Logan said. Aboobaker

quickly lost interest, directing his attention to the biscuit between his lips, his eyes cast to the floor. "Don't shit on location, Aboobaker."

"Never," Aboobaker said.

The Indians giggled at Aboobaker's denial but refused to budge. They wouldn't give Logan the satisfaction. This time they'd pay dearly for their obstinacy. Logan sat quietly by the window, grinning like a chimpanzee.

Brother, with no such access, bolted for fresher air. "You've made your point, Doc," he said. "Twenty minutes more, boys, then finish load chemicals. All right?"

"Thirty," said Aboobaker.

"Talked me into it, you clever little nigger, you. Cheerio. Whew!" he said, disappearing into the night.

Logan sat, quietly sipping his tea. He watched Aboobaker's expression wither. The rest held their breath. "Ah!" Aboobaker sighed painfully, pulling the neck of his shirt over his nose.

"Doc!" Putti said. "Please!"

Now that they'd had to ask him, Logan was all too happy to step outside and hose off his boot. He'd nearly gagged twice. He stomped his feet in the sand on his way back. When he returned, they all sniffed the air. "Much better," they agreed, and the conversation resumed.

S. V. Chavan, a perpetually grinning, gregarious Bengalese, slid a curled photograph before Logan. Logan looked first at the Indian's beaming face and then at the picture. Because of the danger of gas, Chavan's welding shop—a euphemism for his shack of chemical pallets and sunbleached plywood—was on the edge of location. It was a favorite hiding place for all TCNs after they'd been discovered in the others. Chavan's was a lonely assignment, and he became very adept at entertaining himself, usually with his own goofiness. Just the same, Logan liked him. He studied Chavan's photo, a beautiful young woman—tall, thin, graceful—wrapped in a tight, floral sari that did justice to her curves.

"She's very pretty, welder," Logan said. "Who is she?"

"She will soon be my wife," Chavan said, posture erect, chest swelling.

Logan slapped him on the back. "That's great, Chavan. I didn't know you had a girlfriend. How long have you known her?"

"I never meet this girl," Chavan said. "My father fix for me."

"You're kiddin'," Logan said. The room fell silent as the indians focused on Logan's stunned expression. Rahiman, in particular, looked peeved.

"Not kidding, Doc." Chavan tapped the photograph with his index finger. "This girl soon my wife."

Logan was speechless. "What if you don't like her?" he finally said. It was the first thing that occurred to him.

"Oh, I like, Doc. I like very much." Chavan snatched back the photograph and passed it around to the others, no doubt for the dozenth time.

"Yeah, she's very pretty," Logan said. "But what if she's mean? Or stupid? Or likes to gossip too much or spend all your money? What'll you do then?"

Chavan's expression dimmed. "I don't know, Doc. My father fix. My mother is very good woman. My sisters also. My father know." He reached for the photo, studying it in silence. "She look good, no?"

Logan sensed concern in the Indian's voice. "Oh, yeah," he said, as encouragingly as he could. "She looks very nice."

He wished he'd kept his mouth shut. It was just that he'd never known a victim of an arranged marriage. The novelty of it caught him by surprise, and he reacted as he thought anyone would. But he could see his concerns were not appreciated. Not by Chavan, and not by the rest of the crew. "I'm sure she's a wonderful woman, Chavan. Really. There's nothing to worry about. Congratulations."

Rahiman reached for the photograph, staring coolly at Logan. He studied it briefly and returned it to Chavan, who wiped it with his one good sleeve. The other was burned to fragments from welding slag.

"She is a beautiful woman, Chavan," Rahiman declared in English, for Logan's benefit. "She will make a very good wife. Trust your father and never worry."

Chavan passed the photograph around again. Everyone looked, smiled, nodded approvingly, heads bobbing like baby birds in a nest. Her potential, they all remarked in one way or another, was beyond dispute. Chavan accepted all of this with a grateful reassurance until, at last, the photograph made its way back to him. He carefully placed it near the end of his Indian novel to mark his place. Momentum welders had a lot of time on their hands.

Silence fell. Logan studied the different expressions of the Indians one by one. It was all he could do to keep from laughing. Rahiman must have sensed it. Logan watched the anger creep into his severe face.

Putti was deep in thought. "You are married, Doc?" the Hindu finally said.

"Soon, I think."

"Your father went looking for you one wife?"

"God, no. He had nothing to do with it."

"Your mother, then?"

"Nope."

"Oh," Putti said, looking puzzled. "How you find this woman?"

"Well," Logan began, "it was like this." He told them he'd met this woman at a friend's party. They'd talked a while. There seemed to be a mutual attraction and Logan had quickly pursued it. The next step had been to ask her out. They'd gone to dinner, a movie, and later, drinks. Rahiman nodded his head when he heard this last, convinced, as all Muslims apparently were, that whiskey would play a part in it somewhere. The relationship was doomed, his expression said.

Things went well, Logan continued. Gradually they spent more time together, and everybody seemed happy. They felt like they had a future together, so after some time, they decided to get married. It had been a difficult decision, Logan admitted, one that he had taken very seriously.

Rahiman obviously was not convinced. "Her father never come to you and ask what you are doing? He never ask you why you shame his family like that?"

Logan laughed. "Never."

"He never ask why you, a single man, spend time alone with his daughter without his permission? He never come to your house also with one big knife?"

"Not yet," Logan answered, "although it's still early." He explained that it was entirely possible that his soon-to-be in-laws were disappointed by his and Caitlin's pending union. As a Momentum assistant driller, he was no prize. "They'll get over it," he assured them. "It's between me and Cait."

There were several questions for him, most out of genuine

curiosity, Rahiman's verging on contempt. To the Indians, an unarranged marriage was an ill-fated one. The elders knew best, and Logan's had not even been consulted.

A brief silence fell as they pondered Logan's story. Then water-ridden Aboobaker touched on another American failing.

"Jig-jig before marry?" He spoke so emphatically that he sprayed stale cookie crumbs across the table.

"Maybe," Logan answered, suddenly uncomfortable. He flicked away the crumbs that landed in front of him.

"Maybe?" Aboobaker said, glancing at Rahiman. "How you not know?"

"Okay, some jig-jig. No big deal."

"Ah," Aboobaker sighed, his worst fears now confirmed. The grainy Momentum videos they watched indicated this sort of thing was rampant in America, and now Logan, the only American they'd had the opportunity to interrogate, admitted without shame this soiling of flesh.

"Doc?" Rahiman said. "Before you marry, how many women you jig-jig?"

"I don't know. A gentleman never tells."

"You no gentleman, Doc," Putti said. "You nigger, and even you say so."

Rahiman leaned forward, elbows on the table. "How could you not know?"

"I didn't keep tabs."

"Tabs?" Abdullah asked. "What the fuck is tabs?"

"I don't know the number," Logan said.

"Aie-whaa!" Rahiman gasped, as did the others. "More than three?"

"Certainly more than three," Logan said.

"Maybe one dozen?"

"At least."

"All before marrying?" Rahiman asked, his sharp nose pointed at the bare lightbulb above.

"Yep."

"And now?"

"My wife only, as is right." It sounded strange for him to refer to Caitlin as his wife. He'd get used to it.

"Ah." Rahiman looked at the others before he turned back to

Logan. "Only after marry Doc worries about what is right."

"Yep. Before marrying," Logan said, "Doc jig-jig pretty much with anyone interested in jig-jigging him. I'm not proud of it, of course. Well, I'm proud of some. Some were pretty damn good-looking. Some not so good. Doc sometimes get drunk. Make big mistake." He grinned.

"Ah!" Aboobaker said, his nose wrinkling. "Filthy."

"In some cases, yes," Logan admitted. "But those were short-lived. I was very young."

"What the fuck cases?" Abdullah asked.

"Never mind."

"And your wife," Rahiman continued, "she also jig-jig with other mens before she jig-jig with you?"

Logan fidgeted on the bench. Not something he liked to think about, but he tried to retain some objectivity. If the Indians were curious about his culture, he felt it his duty, however uncomfortable, to be frank. Some duty this was turning out to be.

"Maybe," he said. "I don't know. What she did before Doc is her business. Some American women never jig-jig before marrying. Some do. Everybody different in my place."

Rahiman looked at the others. "Same like dogs," he quipped, and they all nodded.

"Not like dogs," Logan said. "Dogs take no responsibility. People with a lick of sense do. Jig-jig between a couple who care for each other is special."

"Not special enough to wait for marriage," Rahiman said.

"Marriage also special, Rahiman," Logan said. "Jig-jig no promise of good marriage."

"Too much jig-jig promise bad one," he said.

Logan shook his head in frustration. "My way and yours different. You'll never understand."

"Yes, we do," Aboobaker said. "We watch plenty video. Everybody jig-jig in America. Before marriage. After marriage. During marriage, maybe. All the time. Same like dogs."

"Same like dogs," Rahiman repeated. Aboobaker howled. The rest simply barked. "Very dirty," Rahiman said, and with that it grew quiet. "Now, Doc," he continued, keen to move on once he'd drawn blood, "what about dee-force?"

"Divorce. What about it?"

"How many divorce your place?"

"Maybe half."

"Aie-whaa!" he exclaimed. The rest looked stunned. "Why, Doc?"

"Many reasons," he said.

"I know number one reason," Rahiman said with characteristic confidence. "Too much goddamn jig-jig." The rest agreed.

"I don't think so," Logan said. "The problem with you guys is that you're culturally unprepared for the concept of responsible sex." This, of course, lost them, but Logan didn't mind. What they needed was a graphic example. He couldn't think of one, so he offered this. "We are worlds apart. I mean, y'all got cows walkin' around your houses and shit."

"What you mean?" Aboobaker demanded. He'd sniffed a slight. "No cows, my house. I am Muslim."

"It's just that we're different, that's all," Logan said. "One's no better than the other. Just different. Americans don't feel like they have to be married to jig-jig. It's not wrong. It's not right. It's just the way it is. That's all I'm sayin'."

Rahiman lit his cigarette. Logan smelled its crisp odor as he exhaled. "No, Doc." He fanned the smoke away from his face. "No matter where you live, no matter what religion, jig-jig before marry is wrong. Husband jig-jig with wife only, and no other. This is goot. In our country there is no divorce. We are here three months, home only for two weeks, and then back again. Our wives wait for us, and us only. Not like dogs in the street."

"Well," Logan said, "that's all fine. But first of all, I know your young ass ain't married, so you don't know what you're talkin' about. And second, most of our wives wait for us, too."

Rahiman's chin fell to his chest. "Not English crane operator, Chester and his wife," he said. "He is here. She jig-jig with young boy. He go home. She is gone." He looked up at Logan. "What is that?"

"I don't know, and neither do you. Maybe Chester is one big asshole." Aboobaker bobbled that this was certainly true. "Maybe his wife no good in the first place. Maybe Chester marry better wife this time. Maybe Chester never marry again. It's not my business, and it damn sure ain't yours."

"Who would want this business?" Rahiman said. "Chester

working Saudi Arabia, wife want jig-jig, she jig-jig with some-body—anybody—same like fucking dog." He waved his hand. "Never happen my place."

"And never happen in mine," Logan said, struggling. He'd often wondered about it. Caitlin was around a number of hand-some, ambitious young law students, including that known jig-jigger Bellmeade. They spent a lot of time together at mixers and late-night study groups. It could happen, he thought, very easily. She had offers. She'd warned him several times that she didn't like being alone. He shook it off.

"It happen to Strong, no?" Rahiman said.

Logan cut him off. "I don't know what happened to Strong. No one does."

"We know, Doc," Rahiman said. "He is longtime married, one yellow-haired woman-child—I see photo. Strong's wife say you get job our place. Strong say no, I working oil field. Too much money. He go to work, then he come back. She pick him up at airport with another man. They jig-jig too much. Strong angry. They fight. Strong nearly kill her. Police come. Big problem for Strong. She take child and leave with other man. He never see his woman-child. Three years pass, still fighting. He come to rig, he is angry. Always yelling at Indian peoples. And why? Because too much jig-jig in America. Everybody jig-jig."

"Same like dogs," Aboobaker said.

Logan was stunned. Strong had never told him the details. He knew of the divorce and the ensuing custody battle, but never of the third party. And he had never heard about the violence.

"Where did you bastards hear all this?"

"Strong say this one time," Putti explained. "Strong say that another. We listen. We understand."

"It's none of your business."

"It *is* our business," Rahiman said. "Strong is happy, we are happy. Strong is sad, too much problem for Indian peoples. Strong no longer care for Indian peoples. Same now like all white asses. And why? Because everybody jig-jig in America."

"Same like fucking dogs," Aboobaker repeated slowly.

"Would you shut up about the dogs, fatboy!" Logan said.

"Not fat," Aboobaker said. "Water."

"Whatever. If y'all know what's good for you, you'll keep your mouths shut about Strong. I don't think he would appreciate having his personal problems discussed..."

"What problem is that, men?" The voice loomed from outside the metal shack and quickly filled it.

NINETEEN

⬧◆⬧

T he Indians froze when Strong stepped through the doorway, scowling at each man until he looked away. He fixed last on Logan, who didn't feel he had the luxury of looking elsewhere. "I said, what problem is that, Doc?"

"Ah," Logan began after clearing his throat, "Chavan's dad found him a wife, and we started talking about marriage, that sort of thing. They were interested in how we did it, ya know, and things went on from there."

"I heard where things went," Strong snapped.

"Well, no you didn't, Jamie," Logan said. "You didn't hear it all."

"I heard enough to know I don't like it," Strong said, his teeth clenched.

"Well, they were just interested." Logan rolled his styrofoam teacup between his palms.

"Don't you think, Doc, that they oughta be a little more interested in their jobs about now? Don't you think maybe you oughta be a little more interested in yours?"

Logan didn't like where this was going. "It's been slow drilling. Everything's in good shape on the floor. I didn't think you'd mind if they took a little extra time down here."

"I do mind. I mind like hell. Do you know how long these men've been in here?"

"Not really. I came in from the pits," he said, a lie to which his clean butt would testify.

"It's been nearly an hour and a half. That's a little too long, ain't it?"

Logan didn't answer. A yes or a no would be wrong.

"Short change, Strong," Putti said, thinking it would explain everything. It didn't.

"I know it's the short change, Putti. What difference does that make? I go without sleep just like the rest of ya. But we ain't gonna sit out here and jerk off all night. If my AD can't find you some work, by God I can. You roughnecks get on back to the floor and get ready to make that connection. Abdullah, you carry your big ass back to the mud pits and let Ripley get a cup of coffee." Strong looked at Logan, who knew it should have been his job to relieve the Englishman. "He ain't had his yet. You rousties ought to be unloadin' them chemicals. That truck goes back to the yard at dawn."

Aboobaker peered at his watch. "Brother say work in ten minutes more."

"You go tell Brother that Strong say work right now. Get your fat ass up in the forklift and start movin' them chemicals around."

"Not fat. Water."

"I don't give a damn what you think it is. Just get it movin'. Now."

Logan watched the Indians scramble out the door. He heard them bitching as they crossed the sand. At least they were wise enough not to do it to Strong himself.

Logan thought maybe he should pick up his hard hat and scoot off to the floor. But he didn't want to tuck his tail between his legs because of Strong's bark. He sat with his fingers wrapped around his cup, waiting for Strong to say whatever he was going to. And he was going to say something, Logan was sure.

"Let's me and you have a little chat, Doc," Strong began, his expression as stern as steel.

"Shoot," Logan said, preparing to duck.

Strong poured himself a cup of coffee and threw his leg over the bench. He blew into the cup and Logan watched the steam rise from the black liquid. "I don't like what I'm seein'," he began without looking at him.

"What do you see?"

"Don't get smart, Doc," Strong said. "You know what I'm

talkin' about." He picked up a cookie, tapped it on the table, and tossed it in the bin with Brother's. He lit a Marlboro instead. "You lettin' them Indians walk all over you is the same thing as lettin' them walk all over me."

"Nobody's walkin' all over anybody. It's the short change. You always give 'em a break, and so do I. If you wanted it any different, you should've told me. When have I ever not done what you asked?"

"I'm tired of askin', Doc."

"Just tell me, then," Logan said, peeved. "I'm workin' for you."

"Well, that's what I'm always wonderin'. Who are you workin' for? I don't feel like it's me." He exhaled a plume of smoke. "Not anymore."

"What do you mean by that?"

"I mean I need help runnin' this crew. That's what Momentum pays you for. That's what I want. I don't want you buddyin' up to the goddamn Indians. All that buys me is trouble—more sass, more attitude. And it's all because of you."

"It ain't *all* because of me."

"I think it is," he said, exhaling. "And I don't like it."

"I'm sorry," Logan said, and he was. "But I'm not you. We see things different when it comes to the Indians. We didn't used to. But we do now."

"Don't make out like I'm some kind of bastard, Doc. I got a job to do."

"And you're damn good at it. I respect you for the way you run that rig. You've taught me a lot—everything, really. But I can't be one thing to you and another to the Indians. I am who I am. I'm sorry if that don't cut it with you."

Strong sipped his coffee. "I just wanna know—I need to know—that you're with me, Doc. That's the problem. There ain't no in-between like you think there is. Like it or not, it's us over the Indians, and all this buddy-buddy crap ain't gonna do nothin' but screw things up. I need to know that when push comes to shove, you're on my side."

Logan leaned back against the wall. Push had come to shove many times on Strong's crew and he was sick of it. "How long have we been together?" he said.

"Long time," Strong said. "Two years as ADs in the North Sea. Nearly two years here."

"We've been through the thick and the thin, haven't we?"

"I guess so."

"And all of a sudden, because I sit in here with the Indians, treat them like I'd like to be treated—just like I've always done—you think I've turned on you in some way."

"That's what it feels like to me."

"Well, you're wrong," Logan said.

"Look, Doc," Strong said. "I know you. I can tell by lookin' at you what you're thinkin'. I guess that's my problem. But you're next in line for my job, and it's my responsibility to make sure you're ready."

"What about Ripley? He's got seniority."

"Ripley will never drill. He just ain't got it. He could never keep an Indian crew. I know it and you know it. It's gonna be you."

Logan didn't think he wanted it. And it wasn't because he'd promised Caitlin that sooner or later he'd come home. He could run the rig as good as any, he knew, but that was only a small part of a driller's job. He couldn't stay focused long enough, for one thing. A moment of daydreaming could easily result in a lifetime of guilt. And he couldn't think as quickly as a driller should. The incident with Mohammed had convinced him of that.

It surprised Logan that Strong was touting him for a driller's job. Even if he wanted it, even if he could shove his doubts aside, he didn't think he had the experience. Not on this well. Besides, worm drillers were never candidates for exploration positions. And where did Strong think he was going? Something didn't add up.

What Strong was offering him had the feel of a bribe, and Logan hadn't known him to make many. The loneliness must have finally gotten to him. What better way to keep a friend than display a promise with one hand and threaten him with the other?

"That's why I want you to keep your distance," Strong said. "I've told you all this before. You're gonna be runnin' a crew soon—my crew—and this buddy-buddy shit's gonna be over. You'll end up havin' to send somebody home, you wait and see. I had to do it. I sent those men home to nothin', and I've never forgotten it. I fucked their world, and I wouldn't want you to have to do the same thing. I think about it every day."

"It'll be all right, Jamie," Logan said, because he knew it would. "I'm not goin' to have any problems."

"You don't think?"

"No."

"Why?"

"Because I don't think I want a driller's job. Not anymore."

Strong huffed and shook his head. "Then why are you here?"

"I been askin' myself that very same question," Logan said.

Strong flicked his ashes into the tray. "It's the woman, ain't it? I almost quit for one. It would've been the biggest mistake I ever made."

Logan knew for a fact that Strong had made much bigger. "It's not just her," he said.

Strong exhaled and tapped his finger against his cheek. "I don't understand you, Doc. You've got a degree. You could do anything. Instead you work over here with me. And now, when I tell you that I'm pushin' to get you a promotion, you tell me you don't want it. Man, I don't get it."

"I'm just sayin' it straight, Jamie."

"You don't know what straight is," Strong said. He massaged his temples with his fingertips. "I'd like to have what you've got. You come from decent people. When you're drunk you bitch about your dad, but at least you had one. Mine left when I was just a kid. You've got a good education. You've got a good woman waitin' for you back home, and you have no idea what I'd pay for that alone." He stubbed out his cigarette. "You could go places, and it seems to me like you're makin' a career out of rubbin' my nose in it. I just don't get it."

"I'm just makin' a livin'," Logan said. "The same as you."

"Let me tell you somethin'," Strong said, grinding his fist into his palm. "There ain't nothin' about me that's the same as you. I came up hard with no one to care about me. I quit school in the tenth grade to go to work in the patch. I ain't known nothin' but trouble. What I got I earned. I don't get no love letters, no birthday cards from my mama. This rig's my world. I want you to know that."

"I know it, Jamie."

"Do you, Doc? Do you really? Do you know what it's like to be stuck out here, knowing damn well that you can't go anywhere else? And I've tried to leave. You know damn well I have. The truth is, I ain't worth a shit anywhere but here." He lit another cigarette. "And I guess it breaks my heart a little, when I tell you—a man I still consider one of my best friends—that I want you to have what little I've got, to hear you say that it ain't good enough."

"That's not what I said. There's a bunch of reasons, and that ain't one of them." Logan crossed his legs. "Besides, there's nothing decided yet."

"Well, it don't really matter if it is or if it isn't. Now I know which way the wind blows." Strong stared out the window. "Me and you go way back, Doc. We had us a time in Europe, the best I've ever had. And I haven't forgotten that you once did me a big favor. In fact, I think I've repaid you many times. But I figure we're about caught up now."

"I've never said a word about it."

"You didn't have to," Strong said. "I feel it every time there's a little friction between me and you." He tapped his ear. "I hear you sayin' 'you owe me, Jamie Strong.' But that's over and done with now. I'm callin' it even from here out. Where you go with Momentum's up to you. You do your job and we'll get along all right. You don't, it's time for you to think about twistin' off and leavin' poor old dumbass Jamie behind." He stubbed out the cigarette. "That's all I've got to say."

"Fair enough," Logan said.

"Good." Strong rose. "My turn to fuck off. Get up there and make that connection for me. I'll make a driller out of you yet. Old Bull's too gone to screw the top back on a wine bottle. I'm gonna go down and fill out the books. You hold down the floor for the rest of the shift."

"I'll take care of it." Logan started for the door and fresh air.

"One last thing," Strong said. "I don't want them little bastards gossipin' about my personal life."

"I didn't let 'em."

Strong held up his index finger. "I heard what I heard, Doc. And I don't wanna hear no more. I'll dope the balls of the next man I catch talkin' about me and my ex." He took two steps and turned back. "I might just dope their balls anyway. I owe 'em that."

Logan didn't doubt that Strong ultimately would. Most people in the patch talked about doping somebody, usually in the crack of his butt. Strong, gifted at making anything worse, more specifically tuned his threat to the genitalia.

Logan walked across the sand to the elevator and rode it up. The Indians and Bull were waiting for him.

He took his place at the console just as the kelly was drilling down to the mark.

"What Strong say?" Rahiman asked.

"Shut up and man them tongs." Logan kicked out the automatic driller, shut the rotary down, set the power-train rheostats, and hoisted the block and kelly high into the derrick. He kicked out the pumps and ordered the roughnecks to set the slips.

He made the connection without a hitch, chains rattling, kelly spinner whining, deadman cables cinched tight. He gently set the bit back on bottom, the kelly again high and spinning, tuning the pump rheostats back to Strong's pen marks. Pump pressure steady. No torque as the bit gnawed into new formation. Everything looked good to him, and felt better. Maybe he could take a driller's job after all. Maybe it suited him more than he'd known. Why else, he wondered, had he stayed so long?

"That was real smooth, Doc," Bull told him. "Strong couldn't do no better."

"Thanks." Logan eyed his gauges and the Indians intently until he saw the crew truck headlights rise and fall with the desert dunes.

TWENTY

DAY SEVENTEEN

Logan's prayers for an eventless short change went unheard. Parnell had bequeathed them a bit that was torquing violently, its cones locked and bearings burnt. They pumped their slug at dawn and tripped through the remainder of the tour. They returned from camp at midnight to find three rows of drill pipe left in the derrick. Strong ran them all in less than an hour. Logan was relieved to see the kelly turning again. But it wasn't to last. At two o'clock on a warm, moonless morning, Strong lost all pump pressure, a sure sign of a wash, a leak somewhere in over two miles of pipe. They had no choice but to pull every last joint from the well without the benefit of a slug. Drilling mud blanketed everything on the floor, including the weary, disgruntled crew. They located the wash where they almost always found them—near the bit in the bottom-hole assembly. The mud pressure had burned a fissure the width of Logan's hand into a stabilizer. They broke out the damaged pipe and tripped back to bottom for the balance of the shift. And they drilled like demons for the two that followed. For Logan, the pace was exhausting.

The third week of his hitch returned Logan to the mud pits and pumps. It was his favorite assignment. He ran the show down there, out from under Strong's lurking shadow. He enjoyed his sense of control.

He was checking his pumps, his hard hat wedged between his ear and the iron monster, listening for the telltale hiss of a wearing valve, when he saw Marshall and his wife pass under the substructure lights on their way to the pits. He sprang to his feet and dashed for the mud house, hoping to mitigate the disaster he could not prevent. He knew it was already too late for that.

Unlike most drilling foremen, Marshall refused to delegate to lesser engineers or even rotate with one equally qualified. In Logan's view there were none. Marshall seemed to agree. He stayed with his wells from the first turn of the kelly to the last, leaving only after the Christmas tree was erected atop the stout wellhead and the Pakistani crews began laying the pipelines that connected with the central refinery at Abcaiq. Only then would Marshall go to his family in Ras Tanura. A week at best would pass before Marshall would arrive at the next wellsite, itching to start that kelly turning again. If his wife wanted to see more of him than that, she had to come to the sunbaked Rub al Khali.

She was a slight, delicate woman, dark featured with streaks of gray in her satin black hair. She wore a western-style dress long and plain enough to satisfy the *mutawwa*, the religious police. She carried in her hand a dull gray scarf, which she sometimes wore to cover her locks. Younger than Marshall, she walked with more grace behind him.

They were some pair: Marshall, the son of an Arkansas truck farmer, she the daughter of a Syrian merchant. They'd met, Marshall often bragged, while he vacationed in Damascus. It was an unlikely and exotic coupling but Logan sensed the endearing bond. They'd overcome the barriers of race, religion, and culture, and even an oil man's schedule which alone had mangled many an expat marriage. Marshall and his wife had beaten the odds, and Logan hoped he and Caitlin would be half as lucky.

The danger now lay in the form of the shirtless Abdullah, his sweaty muscles glistening under the rig lights, his surfer sunglasses (which he insisted on wearing day and night) hiding his joyous eyes but not his beaming smile. He waited to greet the couple at the top of the stairs. Logan was certain Mrs. Christianson knew her way around a drilling rig. It was meeting Abdullah that would come as a surprise.

Logan scrambled across the boggy sand, stumbling over the electrical skid. He'd reached the bottom of the stairs when he heard it begin.

"Hullo! Hullo!" Abdullah said. Marshall passed him without a word. His wife followed.

"Abdullah!" Logan called, bolting up the stairway, hoping to distract him. Abdullah turned, smiling, and then spun back around to greet his guest. He towered above her. She looked to her husband.

"Welcome to mud pits, *memsahib*!" Abdullah said warmly, if perhaps a little too loudly. His goodwill had the better of him. "How the fuck you doing?" He extended his hand. Her own, cautious at first, was immediately drawn behind her back.

Abdullah seemed puzzled. She was, Logan understood, quite stunned. At last, as a precautionary measure, she yielded two steps.

Abdullah, perplexed but undaunted, closed the distance, spreading his arms to the desert wind. "Beautiful fucking weather, no? Abdullah like it too much!"

Marshall shoved Abdullah to one side. "Back off!" he said. He reached for his wife's hand, and this time she gave it. "This coolie doesn't mean anything, honey. He doesn't know any better. Come on. He ain't gonna hurt you."

"Problem?" Abdullah looked at Marshall, whose glaring eyes answered for him, and then at Logan, who was now between them but unable to speak for lack of breath.

"Stick him back in his cage, Doc," Marshall said. Logan reached for Abdullah's belt and yanked him backwards.

"What problem?" Abdullah asked. "What the fuck Abdullah do?"

"Just shut up, will ya," Logan said. "Don't say another word." He turned to Mrs. Christianson. "I'm sorry, ma'am. He means well. The rig's all he knows. He's picked up some bad habits."

"You of all people should've taught him better, Doc," Marshall said. Logan took this as a compliment, of sorts. "Come on," he said to his wife. "There ain't nothin' here to see." They left for the rig floor, which Logan hoped they would find much cleaner. More sensible Indians, anyway. He noticed that one of the woman's heels wedged in the grating. She glanced back at Abdullah and climbed the rest of the way with one bare foot. Logan shook his head. She'd rather risk the pain than another encounter with Abdullah. A moment or two later Marshall returned, glaring at the big Indian, to collect the shoe.

When all was clear, Logan went to work on his derrickman. "Abdullah! How many times do I have to tell you that 'fuck' is not a good word?"

"I dunno," he said rapidly. "Everybody using."

"Everybody on rig using. Other people, nicer people, particularly drilling foreman's wife, never using. Understand?"

"No," Abdullah said, his expression pained. "Abdullah no understand. American peoples using, British peoples using, all Indian *gondos* using, no problem. Abdullah say one time, big fucking problem. Woman run away. Drilling foreman angry. Abdullah don't know what the fuck to do!"

"This is what you do, okay?" Logan said, wrapping his arm around the Indian's shoulder. "You don't talk to any peoples that you don't already know. No Americans, no Saudis, nobody, and especially you don't talk to no women. Never. Understand?"

"No problem. Abdullah no like English language. Some peoples using one word, other peoples no using. Abdullah say this word, everybody scared of Abdullah. Fucked up, English."

"For you, it's awfully risky, I admit. Just don't talk to anybody you don't know. Okay? You work. I'll talk."

"No problem," he said, and he dropped his bucket into the mud to catch his next sample. "Every time Abdullah speak to white peoples," he muttered, "some problem coming."

"It's okay, Abdullah," Logan said to comfort him. "Same thing happens to Strong all the time. It's best that we just keep to ourselves."

"No problem," Abdullah said again, taking the fresh sample to the mud shack for his tests. True to his word, he consoled himself in his own language for twenty minutes or more.

TWENTY-ONE

With Marshall's impromptu visit behind him, Logan settled in for the first quiet night he'd enjoyed in a week. The mud swirled below him like a swollen river, the slow drone of the diesels throbbed in his ears. All would go better now.

Then the shaker screens tore loose. Before he'd replaced them, the swab blew out in a violent gush of mud on the No. 2 pump. While he, Abdullah, and Ripley frantically repaired it, Logan heard the warning hiss of a valve leaking in No. 1. He notified Strong of the problem before Strong could have the satisfaction of notifying him. Logan switched pumps again and isolated the damaged unit. He bled off the trapped pressure before Abdullah beat the hammer caps loose with a sixteen-pound sledge. He reached into the cylinder, the mud burning his hand. He yanked out the valve and spring and tossed them aside. Abdullah displaced the hot mud with warm water. Logan was running his finger along the lip of the valve seat when he heard a commotion on the floor. The main kelly hose had sheared at its standpipe connection, spraying mud all over the derrick. "Big problem," Abdullah shouted, an understatement.

Strong was deep into the open hole, which left him no choice but to pull ten stands wet to reach the safety of the casing before he shut down for repairs. This drew Abdullah and Ripley away to the floor, so Logan, soaked in his own sweat and up to his elbows in mud and grease, labored on alone. Abdullah would have learned the appropriate use of a litany of American curses had he remained.

If that weren't bad enough, Huntley Cleftbar, the mud engineer, arrived with a full belly and a new additive list. Alarmed by the sudden loss of mud from the shaker screens and the ruptured hose, Cleftbar decided it was also time to whip up a new batch. Logan said he would get to it as soon as he could. Cleftbar insisted it be now. "Exploration, you know," he said.

"First the pumps," Logan said. "Then the mud."

Brother and his roustabouts had been assigned the task of repainting the Momentum substructure. The ruptured hose poured fresh, steaming mud all over the newly primed iron, where it dried in sticky scales. The disgruntled Indians bolted for the Bombay Teahouse, cursing their fate. Brother followed in their tracks, cursing them. "An hour off, lads," Brother shouted as they passed Logan's downed pump. "And then we'll start again from the beginning."

As daylight approached, a sash of violet breaking over the black dunes to the east, things only got worse.

When the kelly hose had been replaced, Logan lined up the active system on pump No. 1. Then he left for the pits to mix Cleftbar's mud. A moment later the squawk box summoned him with its customary obnoxiousness.

"You got a pump that can run ten minutes down there?" Strong asked.

Logan slapped the box. "What is it now?"

"Pressure gauge is jumpin'."

"It's a mystery to me. I just went through it."

"Line me up on the other one and get it sorted out. I've lost all the time I'm gonna. If you can't fix it, find somebody who can. I need that pump."

Son of a bitch, Logan thought, as he jerked open the butterfly valves that connected the active system with the intake of No. 2. He prayed to a God who used to love him it worked. He stood by to listen as Strong engaged it. It sounded all right.

He called Cleftbar and told him to stick his plans up his ass.

Then he tore down the fluid end of No. 1 in search of worn rubber, a fragment of a chemical sack, a piece of stone, or a body part of an Indian. He found nothing. He checked the supply lines, the valves, the pit levels. Nothing. He felt betrayed by his own experience as he pushed the intercom button again.

"I don't see what's wrong," he told Strong.

"Get Werner," Strong snapped. "I can't come myself." End of conversation. Logan, miffed, went in search of the mechanic.

Werner was moving slowly at that early hour, a styrofoam cup of coffee in his leathery hand. He wore boots and denims only, his metal hat listing slightly to the left. His puffy red eyes were set deep in his gritty face, the lines more pronounced from nearly three weeks in the moistureless Rub al Khali.

"I got problems," Logan said.

Werner lit his Tiparillo. "Don't we all," he said.

"I've got mechanical problems."

"Well, I guess that's different." He followed Logan out to the skids.

Logan went through his list of symptoms and all he had done to locate their source. Werner listened, not saying a word. When Logan finished, the old man focused on the intake manifold, although Logan advised that the problem was most likely somewhere else. Werner was not dissuaded.

"Here's your trouble," the mechanic finally said, stroking the flange with his thick fingers. A mechanic's hands were mangled bones sheathed in scars. Werner had fresh scabs all over his. "There's nothin' wrong with your pump, Doc. You've got yourself a hairline fracture in the intake flange, probably from the heat, and the pump's suckin' air. It can't prime itself."

Logan moaned. "Should I replace the whole thing?" It would take hours. The crane. Men Strong wouldn't spare.

"I wouldn't," Werner said, news Logan found encouraging. "There ain't no pressure back here. It only needs to seal. Just get Chavan to weld it."

Logan's disappointment returned. "Can't weld here. Might be gas. Marshall would kill us." Then he thought again about the labor involved in replacing the entire manifold.

Werner didn't seem in the least affected by Logan's gloom. But then, Logan hadn't known him to be affected by much at all. He simply pointed to two separate flanges. "Take it loose there. And there. Then haul it out with the forklift to Chavan's shack and let him have at it. That's the easiest way."

"I get the feelin'," Logan said, "you don't see yourself as part of this operation."

"Oh, I'd like to be," Werner said. Logan sensed his sarcasm. "But I've got other fish to fry. There ain't another hour's worth left in the day tank, and Strong's back on bottom, in open hole. It might be nice if his engines kept running," Werner said wryly. And then he listed a half-dozen things that had gone wrong overnight, all of which Barnes wanted repaired yesterday. The best he could do was loan him Samuel, his Catholic helper.

Logan thanked him for his diagnosis if for nothing else, and returned to his pits to see if Abdullah had kept everything running. Before he stepped twice, his foot sank into something he knew could not be sand. As he looked down, the fetid fumes punched him in the nose.

"Goddamn that Aboobaker," he cried.

The sun had risen above the bank of clouds, and already it was very hot. Strong was on the squawk box. Rather than being pleased that Logan now knew what was wrong with the pump, his only concern was how long it would take to fix it. "As long as it takes," Logan said and left it at that. He'd start right on it after he checked in with Caitlin. She would be worried if she didn't hear from him soon. He'd planned to call her for the last three mornings. Nothing was going to keep him from doing it now.

Logan found Marshall at his desk, sipping coffee, staring out the window at the derrick.

"Would you mind if I used your phone?" Logan said. Only Arabco equipped their drilling foremen with satellite connections. Logan could call Caitlin direct, without the hassle of going through the Saudi operators or the risk of Kashian broadcasting his conversation to all the TCNs.

"Keep it short," Marshall grumbled.

"Should I come back some other time?" It was unusual for Marshall to be terse with him. For all his quirks and unwavering sense of purpose, Logan knew Marshall was a generous man. They shared a natural curiosity about their unusual world. They spent a lot of time talking of the present operation, the oil fields, Arkansas.

Logan had learned much about all these things from Marshall. And although it was unpopular to say it outright, especially to Strong, Logan was fond of him. He'd never cared if Logan used his phone, and Logan had never abused the privilege. He called Caitlin once a trip, usually after the short change. He'd just caught Marshall at a bad time.

"Naw," Marshall said, failing at a smile. "It's yours. Talk as long as you want. Just don't tell them other bastards I let you use it."

"Deal," Logan said, and he picked up the phone as Marshall, hands deep in his pockets, left him to pace the catwalk.

Logan had a list of things he wanted to go over with Caitlin. He wanted to make sure she had enough money for extra wedding expenses. By now there would be plenty. He wanted to remind her that he'd left several blank checks on the top bookshelf. He wanted to help with any unmade decisions and, above all, assure her that the ceremony was very much on his mind. He wanted to tell her he missed her terribly, tell her not to make any plans for his first two or three days back. That time, he'd tell her, belonged to them. He would remember to apologize for not calling sooner. On this trip, he'd say, nothing had gone right.

There was an eight-hour difference in their zones. It would be close to eleven o'clock in Austin. Logan hoped it wasn't too late to call. Caitlin had early, grueling summer classes. Finals would begin soon. She needed whatever sleep she could get.

"Hello?"

Logan went cold. A man's voice. Comfortable. Confident. "Who's this?"

"Who's this?" the voice said, and now Logan recognized it. Adam Bellmeade. Law student. Ex-boyfriend. Home wrecker.

"Where's Caitlin?" Logan said.

"Oh, is this Larry?"

"Logan."

"Sorry. Cait's, uh, in the shower, Logan. We've been studying. I'm on my way out."

"That makes two of us," Logan said.

"Would you like me to get her for you?"

Logan hesitated. He imagined Bellmeade stepping into the shower in his clothes. Caitlin laughing while he held his finger to his lips. It's him, he would whisper, kissing her wet breast. His hand would stroke the curves of her hips, settling between her legs. Tell him, he'd say. Caitlin would begin tugging at his fly. There's no hurry, she would say.

"No, thanks," Logan said. "Just tell her I called."

He heard a door slam. "Damn it," Caitlin said. "I told you not to answer that. And what the hell are you..."

Logan hung up the phone and just sat there. He felt sick. He shoved himself from Marshall's desk and kicked open the door.

"Finished already?" Marshall asked.

"Looks like it," Logan said.

Logan stomped along behind the forklift, the cracked flange dangling from a chain. When Samuel engaged the air brake, the welder emerged from beneath a warped plywood box, a weathered tarp for its roof.

"Ah, my friends," Chavan said. "You have need of welder? Goot. Very lonely today."

Samuel tilted the forks until there was sufficient slack in the chain. The loose flange rested on sand. Logan, breathless, motioned for Chavan to come see.

"What problem you have for Chavan, assistant driller Doc?"

Logan was in no mood. "Shut up a minute and I'll tell ya." He showed him the fissure and what he wanted done about it.

"You want weld that?"

"I want to weld that. Quickly."

"Aaahhh," Chavan said. "A *haami-haami* job. Chavan's specialty. Number one welder. Very fast. You see."

"I've got every confidence in you," Logan said.

Chavan swung the visor of his welder's cap backward, donned his leather apron and the shoulder shroud above it, wiped the lenses in the fiberglass helmet clean, and shoved his hands into rust-colored leather gloves that ran up to his elbows. He was ready to conquer the Alaska Pipeline.

Once Chavan had strapped on and adjusted his accoutrements,

he presented himself, arms outstretched, to Logan. "Very goot, eh, Doc? Number one welding outfit."

"Impressive," Logan said, and he pointed to the waiting flange. "Do you mind?"

"Ah," Chavan said, "these Americans. Always *haami-haami*, these guys." The welder motioned to Samuel, still sitting at the controls of the forklift as a matter of expediency. Logan, who maintained no such illusions, sat in the sand, his arms across his knees.

"Samuel," the welder said. "My little Christian friend. Come help Chavan."

The consistently sulky Samuel, isolated by both his religious beliefs and his assignment as the mechanic's helper, seemed pleased by the request. "What to do?" he asked with enthusiasm.

"First, we start welding machine," Chavan said, and it made sense to Logan. Chavan ripped the tarp from the unit and flung it to the winds. He set the throttle with precision, yanked the choke knob, carefully checked his battery cables, scraping the corrosion away with his matted wire brush. Satisfied that all was in order, he disappeared to the other side of the machine. Soon Logan heard him furiously grind the crank. "One moment, please, Doc," Chavan said over the valve covers. "All will soon be well."

He nodded to Logan and pushed the start button. The unit whined, white smoke puffing from its rusted stack, but failed to turn over. "Not to worry," Chavan said. "Motor cold." He tried again. And again. Then he beat the crankcase into submission with his chipping hammer. "This fucking thing! It never work!"

Logan rose and waded through the sand to the machine. He found the switch, the one marked "On" in bold black letters, and flipped it. "You might have better luck now," he said.

"Aaahhh," Chavan said. "Assistant driller Doc also number one mechanic."

"It's a gift," Logan said. "I wish I could share it."

Chavan cranked the handle again and released the fly. The big diesel sputtered through its critical speed, white smoke turning black. Chavan made his final adjustments, tuning the rheostat on the welding unit to his precise standards. "Want to see picture again, Doc? My wife?" He reached under his apron for his shirt pocket.

"Want to see your ass weldin'," Logan said. He'd lost all interest in women. "I'm in a hurry."

"Chavan understand," he said. "Doc here on business. Show photo again teatime only." Chavan handed his wire brush and chipping hammer to Samuel. He demonstrated how the metal must be prepared, and how Samuel was to chip the fresh slag from the weld before it cooled. In the time it took to accomplish this, he could have welded ten flanges. Samuel nodded several times. Chavan slapped his visor down over his face. "We are now ready," he said under his helmet, and he leaned forward in confidence to strike the first arc.

He pecked again and again, but there was no spark. He opened his visor, only to find that he'd been pecking at the toe of Logan's Redwing boot. Normally Logan would have said something, but today he wasn't in the mood.

"Sorry, Doc," Chavan said. "Only joking." He turned to Samuel. "Please, my strange Catholic friend, very dark in helmet. Point Chavan's hand to crack in pipe."

In this assignment Samuel performed well. He directed Chavan's hand to the fissure, his head as close as Chavan's. Suddenly, Chavan struck the first bright white arc. Samuel fell backwards to the sand, his hands clasped over his burning eyes, the hair around his face singed like a mourner's veil.

"Close your eyes, Samuel," Chavan said. "Never look at welding."

"You stupid man!" Samuel groaned.

Chavan, now engrossed in his art, paid Samuel no mind. He started his bead and followed it, so close to his work that he must have felt the heat of the burning red steel.

Logan heard the crackling of burning rods. He smelled the acrid, sulfuric odor of the smoke. And then he smelled something else burning. He pointed at its source for Samuel's sake. Samuel peeked through a crack in his fingers. All he could do was blink his eyes.

"You want to tell him, or should I?" Logan said.

Soon enough, Chavan felt the discomfort. He swatted several times at his thighs but pressed on. At last the pain must have become unbearable. He jumped back and flung off his helmet. It was then he saw his shirttail on fire.

"Aie-whaa!" he shouted. "Fire is here!" He dove headlong into the half-barrel of stale water he kept to cool iron parts. "Why you no tell me these things, Samuel?" he said, water dripping from his soggy hat.

"I could not see," Samuel said.

Chavan climbed out of the barrel, wringing the water from his clothes. "Small delay," he said to Logan.

Logan staggered to Chavan's shack to lie down in the shade. Why hadn't she told him she wanted to see Bellmeade? Why all that shit about a wedding when that was her intent? He never once suspected she was the kind to operate like that. He picked up a two-by-four and hurled it at the flange. Chavan and Samuel, startled, spoke to one another in Hindi. No doubt they were comparing him to Strong. And maybe they should, Logan thought. Women had driven them both crazy.

"Hurry your ass up," he said.

At eleven o'clock, an hour from relief, Logan dragged himself up to the floor. With the manifold repaired and bolted back together and the pump running, he planned to coast to the end of his tour, collapse into his bunk, and never move until Daniel, the houseboy, came to wake him. He'd plot his double murder in the cool dark of his shack.

Strong sat alone at his console. Logan had only to look at him to know something was wrong.

"What now?" he asked.

"The bit's gone. Wore out." Strong crossed one leg over the other at the knee. "You didn't hear those pages?" he asked.

"I heard," Logan said.

"What's up? She's called three times."

"I got nothin' to say to her," Logan said. His stomach grumbled.

"Well," Strong said, "I feel better. I had six months or so of marital bliss. Your ass got hung up at the startin' gate." Strong pulled out his pocketknife and scraped the point of its blade under his fingernails. "Sounds like you need a change of plans."

Logan rolled his eyes. Marital advice from a wife beater.

"What do you say we reroute to Vienna, catch a train up to

Tyrol. We can ski that glacier this time of year. We'll bird-dog some sleazy German chicks." He winked. "It'll be like old times."

The last thing Logan wanted was to relive the old times. They'd nearly killed him. He couldn't count the mornings he'd woken up in some strange hotel with some strange woman and had to call the desk to ask where the hell he was. Sometimes they answered in French, sometimes Spanish, but that was always his first clue. Regardless of his location, he could generally depend upon Strong crashing next door in a similar state. No, sir. He'd received several American Express card statements full of itemized debacles like that. He'd lost his passport twice, his cash three times. Once, while he was drinking in the bar car, the rest of the train left him at the depot. He waved bon voyage to his friends, luggage, and ticket, vodka martini in hand. It had taken two days to iron out that little wrinkle. No, sir. Strong's manic excursions didn't interest him in the least. Not anymore.

He liked the new times better anyway. Quiet evenings in his own house. Clothes hanging in the closet. Friends you could call on the phone. Car waiting in the driveway. Mexican food. Microwave. And no Jamie Strong. No matter what happened with Caitlin, he had things to do in Austin. Like move out. "No thanks. Marshall gonna pull out?" Logan said, anxious to change the subject.

"He'd better." Strong pointed to the three men huddled behind him. "But who knows with them?" There stood Marshall, the Saudi drilling foreman Bin Saed, and the Witch Doctor, arguing about what should be done.

Logan heard the Indians shouting. The roughnecks, their clothes in filthy tatters from the night's disasters, were involved in a bitter dispute of their own.

"What's with them?"

"Big problem. They said they wanted to go to Hofuf. I told 'em it was fine by me, but I limited the spots to them and two others, their choice. It's gotten ugly, I think."

"Good luck with that."

"We'll need it."

Logan shook his head. "There ain't no *we*, Jamie." He remembered the horrors of the last time he'd gone. It would rain in the Rub al Khali before he'd make that mistake again. "No, sir," he said. "Doc ain't goin' to Austria. And Doc damn sure ain't goin' to Hofuf."

"Oh, yes you are," Strong said. "You damn sure are. You always talk about doin' something special for the Indians. You're their little buddy. This is what they want. And you're goin' with me."

It was tough to win an argument with Strong. But this time it would be worse to lose. Logan was about to dig in his heels when he saw Marshall's little forum disband. They drifted, jaws set, toward Strong.

"The bit's had it, ain't it, Strong?" Marshall said.

"Bank on it," Strong answered. Logan looked at the console to read the indicators himself. The torque gauge concurred. The stalling rotary motor seconded the motion. That made three.

"Goddamn!" Marshall snapped. "We should've been into the reservoir by now. Something's wrong. I can feel it." Logan had never seen him in such a lather. He looked irritated, but also gaunt, his expression drained of all enthusiasm, all hope. The look of imperial hunger.

"Nothing's wrong," Mousa said quietly. "The formation's harder than we thought, the reservoir deeper. Put the diamond bit on and let's drill ahead." He put his hand on Marshall's shoulder. "You should get some rest. You're tired."

"I'm not tired. I'm racked with doubt." Marshall massaged his forehead. "I don't feel right about this one," he said. "I don't think it's there."

"I've read the logs. I saw the seismic studies. It's there."

Marshall dismissed him with a flick of his wrist. "None of that technology crap means anythin' to me! I know it's there when I see that kelly drop a hundred feet in an hour, when that mud comes back to the shakers bubbling with gas. Them flares out yonder ought to light up the night. It ain't happening and it damn sure should've happened by now. We missed the dome, and Dhahran's gonna let me know about it."

"Put on the diamond bit," Mousa said, "and drill ahead. Don't worry."

Bin Saed shook his head. "We're barely making five feet an hour now. A diamond bit will cut that in half. It's twenty degrees hotter down hole than we thought it would be. We ought to switch to oil-based mud. More delays. More downtime. We're already over budget and overdue."

Marshall held up his hand to signal that he'd heard enough. He lifted his gaze to the derrick crown. "How long, Strong?" It was almost a whisper.

"How long for what?"

He lowered his gaze to glare at Strong. "What do you think? How long before you run for president? How long to trip the pipe?"

"Eight hours," Strong said. He snapped the blade of his pocketknife shut.

"That ain't so bad."

"Especially if you're tellin' and not doin'," Strong said.

"I suffer same as you," Marshall said. "In fact, I suffer more. It's a paycheck to you. But it's life to me."

"I bet there's a salary in there for you somewhere." Strong winked at Logan.

Marshall's face turned to stone. "By God, Strong, for such an able driller you strike me as an ignorant man. You know how to do it, but you don't have the first inkling of what you do. You don't know what's at stake here."

Strong was among an indiscriminate breed of men who viewed the word "ignorant" as synonymous with "fool." Marshall had just planted a bad seed in fertile soil. Logan watched the contempt grow in Strong's face. Bitter words hung on his tongue.

"I'm done with the chatter," Marshall said. "I'll get us a diamond bit out here. Slug it and pull out."

"Now?" Strong asked, his expression anguished.

"Right now. The bit's gone and we ain't deep enough. There ain't nothin' to argue about."

Strong didn't catch the hint. "My crew's wasted. We've had trouble all shift. In half an hour you'll have fresh meat up here."

"I won't wait," Marshall snapped. "We've got to know. If it ain't here, I want to move five miles south and try again. If we take too long—if we eat up too much money—Dhahran will send us back to Al Khuff." He pointed out to the dunes. "What you don't seem to understand is that there's been no major discoveries in the last fifteen years. There's nowhere else to look. This is the last place."

"Oh, I understand you all right," Strong said. "You don't give a damn about my men."

"I care. More than you know. But I care more about what this project means in a scheme no driller can grasp. My leash is short. Dhahran's skeptical. I've got to shave every lost hour off the schedule to keep the dream alive and I won't argue another minute about it with the likes of you. I want that bit on the bank! If you can't get it done I'll get Barnes to find me somebody who can!"

Strong slammed the brake lever down with his knee and chained it, his face crimson. "Let me tell you somethin', old man!" he roared. "All you ever gotta do is tell me what you want and when you want it, and then you ain't got nothin' else to say to me! And if I can't get it, there ain't no use in lookin' for somebody else."

"I won't listen to no sass, Strong!" Marshall said, his hands on his hips, his face ten inches from Strong's.

"And neither will I! It's Arabco's hole—Arabco's—but when I'm on the brake, it's *my* rig. I heard what you said. You don't want to wait. I got it. Now you stand clear and let a man work. You got a bitch about any of this, you take it to Barnes."

Strong turned his back on Marshall. "Rig up to pull out!" he bellowed to his crew. They stared back at him in disbelief. "Now!" he shouted. He turned to Logan. "I'll pump your slug in ten minutes," he said, and Logan knew he'd pay hell having it mixed by then. Marshall stomped off, his gaze glued to the floor.

The relief crew was racking the first stand into the derrick when Logan came down off the floor with Strong. Barnes waited alone outside the Momentum office. He should have been at camp having his lunch of stewed meats and vegetables.

"Y'all got a minute?" he said. "We need to talk."

"What's up?" Strong asked.

Barnes's cheeks puffed as he exhaled. "Marshall's been in here, Jamie. He ain't happy."

"He's never happy," Strong said.

"Well, he's just plain pissed now."

"Ah, he's just barkin', Elvin."

"Yeah, well, he's barkin' at Blount. Says you ain't workin' out on the brake. Says he wants a change."

Strong snorted. "We're almost into the formation. Who they gonna get to replace me now?"

Barnes poked the toe of his boot into the sand. Then he looked at Strong. "Says he wants Doc."

Strong said nothing.

"Now you both know where you stand." Barnes pointed to Logan. "Doc, you pay close attention to what's goin' on up there on that floor. I want you runnin' that rig every chance you get." He swung to Strong. "And you, dumbass, you let him. We'll see how it goes after that. *Sabe?*"

Strong glared at Logan, then nodded. "I guess it's a piss-poor time to ask if I can take the truck over to Hofuf, huh, Elvin?"

"No jokes, Strong. I'll try to smooth things over with Christianson. He'll cool off. But if you see fit to butt heads with him again, I'll send your ass to Dhahran. In a heartbeat." He paused, waiting for Strong to reply. He didn't. "You got it?"

"I got it."

"Don't let your mouth overload your ass," Barnes said. "Ain't nobody Momentum can't live without, includin' you. I'd keep that in mind over these next few days." Barnes was already walking away. "Y'all go on to camp."

Strong cupped his hands around his mouth and lit a cigarette. "Looks like you might make driller after all," he said.

Logan didn't answer. He started for the truck instead.

"Don't worry, Doc," Strong said. "I won't tell him about our discussion the other night. I guess it's my turn to keep a secret."

"Do what you like," Logan said, opening the door. "But if they offer me your job, I'll take it."

"How do you think I got mine?" Strong said. He pitched the cigarette.

Logan had just come out of the shower, still wrapped in his towel, toothbrush clamped between his teeth, when the Indians intercepted him. His skin was blotchy from the sun-heated water that came from the tank marked "Cold." Momentum had no need for water heaters in August.

"Come, Doc," Putti said, draped in his loungee.

"Where?"

"Scruppy. Come."

Strong was already there, lounging between the galley and the camp boss's skid, out of the sun. He said nothing to Logan, who silently joined the rest of his anxious crew.

This time Rahiman handled the ceremony. He dug the trench deeper, added more rags, poured more diesel. The circle itself, however, was more compact than the previous time, an obvious effort to pressure the scorpion. Rahiman had trouble lighting the fuel in the hot wind. But it was soon up and burning, a scant black veil dissipating in the brisk breeze. This time every Indian wore his boots. Without a word Putti dumped the scorpion in the center of the ring, and Indian and expat alike squeezed in for a better view.

The arachnid stood perplexed by its cage of fire. Then the wind blew the flames over its body and it obviously felt the heat. It darted from under the flames to those burning opposite. It scrambled along the entire circuit, looking for a way out, until it stood motionless again in the center, pincers tilted up and snapping, tail poised menacingly above its black head.

"Here we go," Strong said. The scorpion leapt through the flames, landing on the outside sand with its legs on fire. Tail coiled and ready, it darted toward the scattering Indians.

"Aie-whaa!" they screamed, scrambling for the metal walkways.

"What's all this?" Tate-Pixilate snarled, his big nose the first of him to emerge from behind his door. "Can I find no peace?"

The Indians, keen to avoid the scorpion, paid the camp boss no mind.

"Doctor?" he said, his pale stomach protruding above his boxer shorts. He stepped barefoot onto the sand. "What's going on here?"

"Pix," Logan said, "I wouldn't..."

Pix screamed. Logan saw the scorpion skitter across the arch of the Englishman's pale foot toward the sand and shadows.

"Might try a little cortisone on that," Strong said, cupping his hands to light another cigarette. The entire host of TCNs disappeared in snickers of delight.

"You really oughta wear shoes out here, Pix," Logan said, and turned to go.

"Hofuf?" Strong called down the narrow corridor.

"No way," Logan said. "No way in hell."

"You'll change your mind," Strong told him, opening his door. "You always do." He entered, then stuck out his head. "Pity about Pix," he said, before he slammed the door.

Logan heard his muffled laughter above the whine of the window units and the steady drip of condensation from the Freon coils.

What was she thinking? Logan asked himself as he slipped between the clean, cool sheets.

TWENTY-TWO

❖

DAY TWENTY-ONE

Logan, dressed in his boots and jeans, rounded the corner of the galley shack. Strong marched ahead of him. They came to a halt, shoulder to shoulder, at the edge of the parking lot.

"Would ya look at this, Doc?" Strong said. He belched.

"We're doomed," Logan said.

The entire crew, dressed in their polyester best, slick hair, and shiny shoes, mingled officiously near the crew truck. Abraham rested his head on the steering wheel. For the better part of the last three weeks, he'd cut a gritty groove commuting between the compound and the rig, and he, much like Logan, seemed loath to leave.

When Strong appeared, the Indians faced him with beaming smiles. Strong, frowning, waded in among them.

"I don't know what you guys are all grinnin' about," he said, holding up his hand, his fingers spread. "I said five Indians, no more."

The dismayed assembly mumbled among themselves. Very clearly, some of them had been told differently. Putti, as always, stepped forward to see what could be negotiated.

"Strong," he said, "they only want go shopping. Is necessary."

"Not to me, it ain't. I said five, I'll take five. I just can't handle any more than that. Five of ya load up in the back seat *haami-haami*. The rest of you get lost."

Strong and Logan slid in beside Abraham on the bench seat. Logan adjusted the air-conditioning vents. The Indians didn't move. Strong rolled down the window and leaned out. "Let's go, boys. We ain't got all day."

"Strong, there is room for all peoples," Putti said.

"Where?"

"In back. Truck is going Hofuf, Indian peoples should go in it. They need things. They get. Is necessary."

Strong exhaled. "Fine," he said. Logan cringed. "But there's only room for five small Indian peoples in cab. If the rest want to ride three hours in the back of the pickup in 125-degree heat, that's their business. Now get in and let's go if we're goin'."

Putti translated Strong's decision into Hindi, which brought new smiles. The roughnecks filed into the backseat of the crew cab, their place of honor as the expedition's instigators. Aboobaker, Razaki, Abdul Mohammy Godammy, and Shook Tendulkar climbed into the back without argument. Samuel, Chavan, Patel, the night cook, and two strangers who must have wandered in the night before filled the rear canopy to capacity. Logan suspected a few more stragglers stowed away as Abraham pulled out.

Logan awoke as the dunes of the Rub al Khali gave way to rocky flats, dotted with stands of palms and parched *wadis*, and tin shacks too rusted to reflect the glare of the sun. They passed by a group of Saudis—men dressed in white in one section, women in black in another—camped in the desert, just as Americans week-ended in the woods. Logan supposed the outing was a tribute to their pioneer past, better enjoyed with the convenience of Igloo coolers and air-conditioned mobile homes. The smell of the gulf, tainted by Strong's cigarette smoke, filled the air. For the first time in three weeks, Logan sensed moisture.

They crested a rise, and a city loomed in the distance. Abraham pointed through the chipped, nearly opaque windshield of the crew truck. "Hofuf," he announced.

Logan saw the mud walls of the old fort. There were several modern buildings, as there were in virtually every Arab city Logan had seen, but the old part of Hofuf had been preserved for posterity, like Williamsburg and Monticello.

The old warrior king Abdul Aziz ibn Sa'ud, of aristocratic blood and a Bedouin upbringing—thus master of both of Arabia's conflicting worlds—had captured the oasis city from the Ottomans early in his campaign to unify the Arabian Peninsula. He had first taken Riyadh, capital of Hejaz, central Arabia, and had then turned to Al Hasa, the eastern province, of which Hofuf, a port as well as an oasis, was the premier prize. From there he'd conquered all between the Red Sea and the Arabian Gulf, becoming the only man in the world to give his family name to an existing nation. The mud wall his raiders scaled at midnight still stood. So did the market and the buildings it had been constructed to protect—a monument, Logan figured, to Abdul Aziz ibn Sa'ud. His son Fahad ruled to this day.

Hofuf offered Logan the remarkable opportunity to see Arabia as it once had been. Logan's Saudi visa restricted his travel to to and from work only, not that he had the time to see more. But Hofuf was available, and now that Logan was here, it felt worth the slight risk of an illegal visit. The trip was also a diversion. He had been unable to think of anything but Caitlin since he'd hung up Marshall's phone.

In Hofuf he could walk in the footsteps of Abraham. According to Marshall, who knew Arabia's legends, some believed Al Hasa had been Abraham's birthplace. If so, he had certainly walked these mud-brick streets. Providing one could overlook the honking Japanese cars; the electric lines cobwebbing the streets; the stereos and televisions blaring from shop windows; the beehives of lamb, slick and greasy where they had not yet been sliced, revolving on stainless-steel rotisseries; the automatic weapons carried by uniformed Saudi soldiers, and all the other clutter of modern Arab life, one could still see what Abraham saw. The magic of Arabia was alive and humming in Hofuf.

Logan liked the bazaar best. Merchants spread their wares, as they had since before the time of the pharaohs, on worn carpets or along the dusty shelves of mud-walled nooks. Fruits, vegetables, clothing, rugs, urns, and even hand-forged swords were all displayed before him with no fixed price. Shopping was a sport in Hofuf. Novice Nasranis beware.

In the bazaar Logan saw faces from another age: an old man, his eyes shrouded in a white film, measuring grain against a balance of stone weights; a legless African who propelled himself on a wooden cart; two pudgy children with streaks of gray in their curly dark hair; tall, wispy women, draped like phantoms in flowing black *abayas*, their faces covered by golden masks save the warmth of their onyx eyes. Every time he came, he saw something different, something exotic, remarkable.

Logan decided to coerce Abdullah, who had learned Arabic as a student of Islam, to serve as his translator. He had long wanted a rug for Caitlin. Now maybe he wanted one for his new apartment. Strong could come along if he liked.

"Drive down by the square, Abraham," Strong said. "We'll park there." This was optimistic. Traffic choked Hofuf's bustling narrow streets.

"Okay," Abraham said, "no problem."

Strong turned around and tried one last time. All for naught, Logan knew. "One hour," he said. "I mean it. I need to be sure and tell those guys in the back, too."

"No problem," they all said.

"Here's a spot, Abraham." The bulky truck maneuvered into the narrow space with a dull groan, its cabin surging forward. Before it swayed back, Rahiman opened the door. Strong reached back and slammed it shut.

"Hold on, damn it," Strong said, staring down each one of them. "One hour."

Rahiman kicked his way through the doorway and the others flowed out behind him in a stream of shiny polyester shirts, like a fishing line being cast. Strong sprang around to the back of the truck to lecture the rest.

"Doc, damn it, they're already gone," he said. "I never saw a one of 'em."

"Probably never will again, either," Logan said, but it no longer mattered. Now that he was here, he was just as excited as they were. Momentum seemed a world away. And so did Caitlin. "Ready, Abdullah?"

"What the fuck you doing!" Abdullah shouted. "Less go!"

TWENTY-THREE

———❖———

Anyone who questioned the predominance of foreign labor in Saudi Arabia needed only to see the streets of Hofuf. They swarmed with Indians, Pakistanis, Filipinos, and Asians from God knows where. The only thing they had in common was the Saudi riyals stuffed in their pockets. The Saudis were the minority here. Logan and Strong followed Abdullah, who carved his way through the throng and into the dark adobe maze of the bazaar

First they came to the beggars, the blind and the horribly disfigured, squatting on soiled rugs, their arms outstretched for alms. Whenever they saw or sensed an American nearby, they called out "meester, meester," or sometimes "Arabco," and offered their tawdry wares. None of this troubled Abdullah, who seemed to know how to ignore them without offense. Logan followed his lead and walked by them all.

"You," Abdullah said, pointing at Logan and Strong, "too much fucking problem. Meester, meester," he mimicked, laughing. The supplicants had never once called to him.

"Just shut up and keep movin', would ya, Abdullah?" Logan said. "The rug place is in the back. Look at this poor bastard, Strong. Christ."

"That's why they call it a bizarre," Strong said.

They hurried through the static throng. Logan felt the stares and the hope as his group passed. When it was clear he had nothing to offer, the beggars' hands fell to swatting flies away from their gaunt faces. One didn't hear much about these, the poor of Arabia whom the oil profits never touched. Their plight meant nothing to Abdullah, who hurriedly pressed on through the dark inner corridors of the bazaar without the slightest glance. Logan sensed he had seen that kind of misery before—many times.

Finally they found the rug merchants. There were at least a dozen in the open market and twice as many in more established shops. The latter, Logan felt certain, would clip him clean. He set his sights on the hungry dealers who had no roof.

They came across a man with many rugs rolled and stacked against the mud walls. He was corpulent and shrewd eyed, but he seemed friendly enough—motivated, anyway. He rolled out his inventory without any prompting from Logan. Abdullah and Strong stood back as Logan examined the merchandise. The merchant sat down on one of his carpets and smoked a cigarette, waiting to see which rug would catch Logan's eye.

"Arabco?" he said. Logan knew that Arabco and white men meant dumb money. He shook his head, which confused the barefoot Arab. Not many tourists in Hofuf. Logan said "Momentum" instead and sensed that the distinction between producer and contractor was lost on the merchant, who cocked his head. "Oil," Logan said, and it registered. Technically he should have said gas, but why quibble? The Saudi had him pegged from the start.

"Ah," he said. "Today special price." He waved his hand over his ample selection.

"You speak English?" Logan said.

The dealer shook his head.

"Oh, just a couple of key phrases, eh? Well, how long is this one?"

The man did not understand. No matter. Logan grabbed Abdullah by the arm and dragged him over. "Ask him how long this one," Logan said, and Abdullah, seemingly aware of how the locals viewed imported laborers, did so with uncharacteristic restraint.

"He say twelve hundred Saudi riyals," he said.

"No, not how much! How long! We'll get to price later."

"Big?" Abdullah asked.

"Yes, how big, this one?"

Again, Abdullah discussed the matter with the Arab.

"He say he don't know how the fuck big this one."

"Great. Let's roll it out, then."

Logan spread the carpet on the coarse brick, nudging it with his boot. It was perfect. A rare scheme, navy blue woven into the more traditional scroll designs of deep maroon. It would go nicely in his and Caitlin's house, or wherever. Logan wanted it. The merchant smiled and asked Abdullah something in Arabic, something that clearly referred to Logan. The Indian nodded. The merchant smiled again.

"How much does he want?" Logan said, a little miffed that his Islamic translator was working both sides of the racial fence.

Abdullah questioned the Arab. "He say twelve hundred Saudi riyals."

"Tell him to go fuck himself, I don't think..."

Before Logan could stop him, Abdullah plunged ahead. He was a literal man. Logan noticed the change in the Arab's expression. He wondered how many lashes they gave for cussing an innocent man.

"Don't tell him everything I say, damn it, Abdullah," Logan said. He smiled weakly at the merchant. "Just tell him I'll give him three hundred riyals. Leave out the 'fucks.' See what he says."

The dealer answered in short grunts. Abdullah translated.

"He say you go fuck yourself. Not his first day at bazaar. He want one thousand riyals, no less."

"Tell him he'll take four hundred and like it. That's my final offer..."

But before Abdullah could consult with the merchant, the speakers in the prayer towers above the mosques blared *Allahu akbar*, "God is most great," summoning the faithful to prayer. In days past, Marshall said, the religious leaders climbed the minarets and sang to the people below. Now the songs were recorded and played at the five designated prayer times each day. The sound quality was reminiscent of an AM radio in an old truck. Nevertheless, it was effective. The townspeople dropped whatever they were doing and prepared for their prayers. Some of the Indians and Pakistanis did likewise. Those of other faiths simply disappeared from the streets, and Logan knew it would be wise if he and Strong did the same.

Before they could do anything, Abdullah sank to his knees and began his prayers. The rug dealer, facedown, occupied the space next to him.

"Looks like you lost him, Doc," Strong said. "What do you say we take a breather in that smokeshop across the street?"

Logan looked down the street at the approaching *mutawwa*. They wore khaki uniforms and carried long canes, which they banged on shop windows and doors to encourage the merchants to close down and pray. In Saudi Arabia, this meant everybody. No excuses. "*Salaat,*" they yelled. Prayer time. Now.

They entered the smokeshop just as the attendant was shutting the door. Logan perched on a big pillow beside Strong. Rows of water pipes lined the walls. "Two of your finest," Strong said.

Logan was snatched from his reverie by the sound of the mosque speakers signaling the end of the twenty-minute prayers. He popped up from the pillows, anxious to complete the purchase of his rug. He inserted the hose tip on a plug and called to the young Indian boy.

"Finish. How much?"

The boy held up all the fingers on his hand. Logan reached into his pocket for his wad of riyals.

"Here's a tenner for me and him," Logan said, and he and Strong dashed back out into the sun. Logan made out the form of Abdullah heading for the crowd.

"Hey, Abdullah!" he called.

The big Indian stopped stiffly.

"Abdullah!"

He stamped his foot and turned around.

Logan waved him back. "Where you goin', man?"

"Shopping," Abdullah said.

"First, talk to Arab *gondo*. Then shopping. Maybe five minutes more."

They crossed the street. Strong followed. The merchant was

back on his rug, calmly smoking a cigarette. Logan's choice remained unrolled, waiting.

"Bet you thought you'd never see us again," Strong said when he was within hearing range. The old Arab slowly walked over to them. He had time. He seemed to sense they did not. Abdullah tugging at Logan's arm like a puppy on a new leash, lent a sense of urgency to the entire affair.

"Now, where were we?" Logan said. "Oh, yeah. I was offering you three hundred riyals for the rug. Tell him, Abdullah." He looked at the merchant. "Now be fair, Mohammed. You've just spoken with God. Just let his love flow into this next transaction."

"This is all about love, man," Strong said, a Marlboro dangling from his lips.

Abdullah conveyed the message. "He say one thousand riyals," he said, clearly despairing at the distance between the two figures. He looked at his watch.

"By God," Logan said to Strong. "You gotta admire this guy. He's tough." He waved four hundred-riyal notes in front of the Saudi. "Tell him that's it. Take it or leave it! Plenty rugs for sale in Hofuf."

Logan noticed that the merchant's interest was in the amount returned to his pocket rather than in what was being displayed.

"This fucking man say now eight hundred riyals," Abdullah said. He sighed. "Fair price, Doc."

"How would you know?" Logan reached into his pocket again. It would've been nice to have a translator he could trust. "Tell him five hundred or we walk."

The dealer deliberated, answering only after he had studied Logan's face.

"He say eight hundred is good price. No less."

Logan wadded up the bills. "*As salaam alaykum,*" Logan said. "Peace be upon you." In this case, it meant *adios.* He walked away. Abdullah shot past him.

"Meester, meester," the old man called. Logan turned around, grabbing his translator. The Arab waved him back.

"He now say six hundred," Abdullah said with some reluctance. "Number one price."

Logan held the crumpled bills in front of his face.

"Five hundred."

The dealer paused a moment to think. Then he mumbled something to Abdullah.

"He say okay. No problem."

Logan smiled and handed the money to the Saudi, who straightened and counted the bills with his long fingers. Soon enough he smiled, too, which robbed Logan of his brief satisfaction.

"Tell him I like him, Abdullah, but he's a thief," Logan said as he rolled up the rug. When the merchant understood, he laughed loudly and then said something more to Abdullah.

"What's that all about?" Logan said.

"He say if the buyer is stupid, it is not for the seller to cry."

Logan crammed the rug under his arm. "How do ya like that, Jamie? The Momentum mentality everywhere you go."

TWENTY-FOUR

Logan, kneeling beside the parked crew truck, tightened the laces on the cheap tennis shoes he had bought to replace his boots. It had been a miracle they'd stocked his large size. He listened to Strong harangue the few Indians they had captured. At times he winced. Logan knew of no one who, when crossed, could get as personal and as ugly as Jamie Strong. The rig crew was unfazed, but Pix's kitchen staff looked stunned. Strong had shamed them close to tears.

Logan tested his new shoes. "I'm ready," he said.

Strong pointed to two of the eight Indians in custody. "You recognize these guys?"

Logan looked. "Never seen 'em before in my life."

"I'm takin' 'em anyway," Strong said. "Dhahran can sort it out later."

Logan checked his watch. It read 6:22. They'd been chasing Indians for two hours. His shirt was soaked with sweat. Now that he'd discarded his clunky boots, he felt certain he'd have better luck.

Strong grabbed Aboobaker by the collar and jerked him to the tailgate. "You sit your fat ass right here. Understand?"

"Not fat," he said. "Water."

"I don't give a damn what it is. You sit it right here. No one leaves. Anyone comes, they stay."

"No problem," Aboobaker said.

"Oh, there's a problem," Strong said. "And if you let one man step out of this truck while I'm gone, I'll kill you. I mean it. I'll squeeze the water right out of your big ass with a pair of pipe tongs. Got it?"

"No problem."

"Let's roll, Doc," Strong said. They jogged together along the stone alleys, searching the last of the tin-roofed malls and isolated shops for the rest of their mutinous crew. When that failed, they ran through the center of the bazaar. Logan, winded, leaned against a wall. He saw Rahiman crossing the street ahead.

"Rahiman!" he called.

Rahiman ignited down an alley. In his haste he dropped a package but didn't stop to pick it up. Strong was on him like a bluejay on a cicada. Logan let Strong have at him.

"You better not let me catch you!" he heard Strong holler, as if Rahiman didn't already know.

Logan's laziness was soon rewarded. Putti's head appeared around the corner, scanning one direction and then the other. He stepped out, tiptoeing toward Rahiman's things, which he repacked into their plastic sack. He checked all around and walked off in the opposite direction. When he drifted by, Logan snatched him clean and marched him back to the truck.

"Doc?" Putti said. "Too many things. Helping, please." He handed Logan three sacks.

"Sure," Logan said. Once the jig was up, the Indians seemed civil. Their passion was the chase.

He met Strong walking back to the truck with his hands behind his head, a beaten man. He looked more tired than angry, and he looked pretty damn angry.

"I don't know where he went," Strong said. He barely noticed that Abdullah, the derrickman and translator, and Abdullah Larry, the roughneck, had just passed them by. He stopped. They stopped. Putti warned them in Hindi.

"Hullo," Abdullah said, grinning. "What the fuck you doing? Shopping?"

"Dying," Strong gasped. "Let's go, boys."

"Abdullah need one more fucking thing," the derrickman said. "Gift for wife. Then go truck."

"No way in hell," Strong gasped. "You're goin' now." He

reached for Abdullah's shoulder to turn him around. Abdullah dropped the bags and raised his arm to knock Strong's hand away.

"You...no...touch...Abdullah!" He was so angry his jaw stammered as he spoke. "Understanding! You...never...touch." He drew his fingers into a fist and cocked his sinewy arm, a limb that rivaled even Strong's.

"Don't," Logan said, reaching for the Indian's arm.

Strong never blinked. He reacted as Logan had seen him do a hundred times before. All Logan could do was try to step between them. Before he could move, Strong grabbed Abdullah by the throat and tripped him. Abdullah swung and Strong blocked his arm. Strong rapped him hard on the back of the head as he fell.

Abdullah landed on the bricks before his packages did. He screamed in outrage. Teeth gritted, he planted both palms and tried to push himself up. Strong kicked his arms out from under him and pounced on his back. He snatched a handful of hair and used it to grind Abdullah's nose into the ground. Logan saw tears of rage well up in the Indian's eyes. With Strong's full weight on his back, he couldn't move.

"Now you listen to me!" Strong said between his teeth. "I didn't want it to be like this. I've never hit an Indian before, and I don't want to do it again. But if it's trouble you want, that's what you'll get."

Abdullah froze. Nothing moved but his heaving chest. His eyes filled with rage and Logan saw the first angry tear run down his cheek. He was too humiliated to speak. Strong wisely held him fast.

"Who's in the wrong here?" Strong said, his tone still firm. "Who put me in this position, huh? Maybe you don't like the way I treat you, and I understand that. I wouldn't like it either. But when I say it's time to go, it's time to go."

Abdullah would not answer. He turned his face away until his cheek rested on the pavement. He looked at Logan, as though to see if he had sided with Strong. Logan stood right next to Strong, sanctioning what he had done if only because he did not try to stop it. Abdullah closed his eyes. Logan closed his, knowing it was he who had delivered the final blow. Abdullah's struggle ended. He lay limp under Strong.

"All right," Strong said, and withdrew his hand. "Now I'm gonna let you up, and we're gonna go to the truck. We're gonna forget all about what happened and just go back and do our job."

"Only joking, Strong," Abdullah said, his voice gravelly and meek. Hearing it, Logan knew Abdullah's humiliation was complete.

"Naw, you weren't jokin'," Strong said. "You were pissed off. But I think you understand now. This ain't no game, man. I'm not your buddy, I'm your boss—on the rig and here in Hofuf. There's a limit to my patience."

Easily exceeded, Logan thought. But he said nothing. He could have handled Abdullah without any violence, yet he'd said nothing. There was a world of things he'd said nothing about. It occurred to him that he was more like his mother than he'd ever dreamed. He had been angry with her for appeasing his father. How, he wondered, should he deal with himself for appeasing Strong?

Strong lifted Abdullah to his feet and dusted him off, an attempt at conciliation. "I'm sorry if I hurt you," he said. "Let's just pick up your things and go."

Logan and Abdullah Larry gathered the crumbled packages and loose items. Abdullah gathered himself. Logan could see he was still angry, but he apologized for provoking Strong. Eighty-four days working, he said, what did it matter if they did not sleep one night? He was ready to go anyway, he said. He was coming to the truck when all of this happened.

"I'm sorry," Strong said again. "Are you okay?"

Abdullah nodded that he was, and Logan escorted them all back to the truck. He opened the door so they could load their packages, but still he did not say anything. He couldn't.

"That leaves Rahiman," Strong said. He checked his watch. "Let's call Blount and tell him we got engine trouble."

Logan shook his head. "We got a little time yet. Besides, he'll send a mechanic out to fix the truck. He'll find out we lied."

"The hell he will. I'll knock a hole in the oil pan. Then I'll drive this bitch around till it gets hot. By the time a mechanic gets here, we'll have engine trouble, by God."

"Let's do that when we have to," Logan said. "We'll never catch that quick little bastard on foot. Let's take the truck and cruise up and down every alley in this goddamn town."

"I'm with ya," Strong said. "But we need to leave somebody here in case he shows up."

"Who can we trust?" Logan asked. It was a difficult question.

Strong thought a minute before he spoke. "Abdullah?" he said. "Will you wait here?"

Without a word, the Indian opened the truck door and stepped out. The Indians gawked in disbelief. The prisoner was now a trustee. Logan was likewise stunned, but for a different reason. He thought Abdullah would tell Strong to stick it up his ass. "Not my fucking job," he'd say. What he saw was complete submission from a man who couldn't look another—white or brown—in the eyes.

Logan had been on hand to watch Strong, the agent of Momentum, break another one. This time it had been the strongest of them all. Abdullah was the one Indian Logan felt he could call a friend. To see Abdullah like this crushed him. He wished he'd never come. Not to Hofuf. Not to Saudi Arabia. Not to the oil field. Sooner or later, in work or in fun, Momentum took everything from a man. It was only a matter of time before it would get him.

Abdullah sat down against an adobe wall and locked his arms around his knees, his gaze distant. Somehow he seemed smaller. Every Indian in the cab stared down at him. Logan slid into the truck next to Strong. All they had to do was find Rahiman and it would be over. But Logan didn't know how well Abdullah would heal. He'd never once seen him injured before. Without his pride, what would Abdullah be?

"Let's go, Abraham," Strong said. "Start her up."

TWENTY-FIVE

⬦⬥⬦

The truck idled menacingly along the narrow streets. Strong peered through the windshield. The Indians were busy looking through their bags and admiring purchases. The crowd had thinned, and Strong seemed thankful for that at least. Abraham was nervous about the whole operation and drove like an old lady. In a country where the leading cause of death was rumored to be traffic accidents, Logan knew he had good reason to be cautious. To make things worse, Strong pestered him to no end.

"Turn here—left—left," Strong ordered him. "We ain't been down here yet."

Logan was so tired his vision blurred. He rubbed his burning eyes. When he was able to focus again, he spotted Rahiman trotting across the street. He hadn't seen the truck. "There he goes!" Logan said.

"Where?"

Logan pointed. "Down the alley."

"Let's go, Abraham." Strong slid his foot over the drive train until he reached the accelerator. He pushed it to the floor. This left Abraham with only one hand to steer. The other tugged at Strong's ankle.

"Look out, damn it," Strong said.

"No, please..." Abraham protested. He was watching Strong more than the road.

"Let me drive, Abraham," Strong said. "You're too slow."

"You no have Saudi license."

"By God, I'd like to know how the hell you got one. You're the worst goddamn driver I've ever seen. Get out of the way!"

"There he goes!" Logan yelled.

"Go, Abraham! Catch him. Left or right, Doc?"

"We'll see when we get up there."

The truck was headed for a main thoroughfare. There were a number of cars on the street and still a few pedestrians. Logan heard Strong's foot pump the accelerator again. Abraham was pale.

"Hang a left," Logan said. "He went that way."

Rattled, Abraham swerved right. Strong grabbed the wheel to turn it himself. Abraham pulled against him, fending him off. The truck plowed straight for the middle of the congested intersection. There was nothing to do but hit the brakes. Whose foot managed to do it, Logan couldn't say.

The canopy's weight threw the truck into an uncontrollable skid. Every man in the cab braced himself as best he could. The men who were jostled in back just screamed. The only obstacle between the truck and a mud wall was the sizable khakied posterior of a Saudi traffic cop. The headlights focused on the strike zone like a laser, everyone wide eyed and yelling, horn blaring, four hands wrestling with the steering wheel, the truck obeying no one.

The grill struck the policeman squarely, launching him twenty feet. Logan heard the distinct thud of metal against flesh and bone above the screech of the tires. The cop landed spread-eagle, face-down. The truck rocked on its frame. The Indians, fingers dug into vinyl, froze.

Strong was the first to find his voice. "I really can't believe what just happened!"

"You think he's hurt?" Logan said, afraid of the answer. The man never moved.

"He's dead!" Strong gasped. "We're all goin' to prison, man! I wonder what they cut off for negligent homicide!" He released the wheel. "Maybe we oughta get the hell out of here."

"That's a bad idea," Logan said. "There's not another truck like this in the whole country. They'll nail us for sure."

"You're right," Strong said, slapping his hand to his solar plexus. "I was just panicking there. Maybe we should see if he's all right." He hesitated. *Maybe,* Logan thought. "Yeah, let's do that."

They threw open the door, stepped out of the cab, and

approached the body. Some of the Indians came from the back of the truck to see what had gone wrong.

"Get back in there!" Strong yelled. "All of ya. If I go to jail, you bastards are goin' with me!"

Logan knelt down to check the victim and noticed that his mouth was moving. He was mumbling something, maybe a prayer. The officer's eyes opened and he slowly pushed himself off the ground. Logan reached down to assist him, but the Saudi swatted him away. He wasn't praying. He was mad as hell.

Strong reached out for his elbow. "You okay?" he said.

The Arab removed his hand. "I think so," he said. His eyes were glazed over, shining in the neon lights.

"You speak English," Logan said, relieved. They could at least explain. Or try to, anyway.

"Of course," he mumbled. "Why is it that you ran over me?"

"It was an accident."

"Naturally," he said. "Can you explain how it happened?"

"Uh, we're havin' a really bad day, Officer," Logan said.

"That makes three of us."

"Our driver lost control. He hit the brakes and we went into a skid. We're sorry. We couldn't stop." Logan felt the urge to touch him competing with the one that told him to run away, and fast. "You aren't hurt, are you?"

"No, but I'm not happy either. I don't think you belong here. By rights, I should take you in and fine your company." The officer massaged his backside where the truck had struck. It seemed to swell before Logan's eyes. "The law in this country is very clear on that matter."

"Well," Strong said, "if it's all the same to you, we'll just pay you right here. How's that? We're in a hurry." He dug into his pockets and pulled out a wad of cash. Logan glared at him in disbelief. Strong persisted, handing the entire amount to the officer. "How does eight hundred riyals sound?"

The officer folded the bills and slid them back into Strong's shirt pocket. "Let's not add insult to injury, eh?" he said, an angry glint in his eyes.

"We're sorry," Logan said. "We don't know the laws here."

The policeman shook his head. "That explains why you keep breaking them."

"What do you want us to do?" Logan asked. "You just say."

"I want you to go back to wherever you came from. I don't ever want to see you in Hofuf again."

"Not a problem," Strong said. "We're already gone."

"Not fast enough," the officer said. "But please drive carefully."

"It won't happen again," Strong assured him.

"Frankly, I don't see how it could."

Logan thanked him and headed for the truck. Strong tapped his knuckles against Abraham's window. The Indian rolled it down.

"What he say?" Abraham said. He looked terrified.

"He say rear passenger tire is flat. Can you help me fix it?"

More bad news. Abraham skulked out of the truck and walked around to see for himself. Strong followed. When they reached the tailgate, Strong pitched him into the back with the others. Logan was too late to help.

"I'm drivin'," Strong said, as if there were any question. He jumped in and engaged the transmission. "Ain't gonna be no more of that."

Traffic clogged the only way out. The officer was working to smooth things over, but Strong could not move the truck. He stuck his head out the window. "Say, Officer! Could you, uh...?"

"Yes, yes," he said, flapping his arms. "The sooner, the better."

Finally Strong had room to maneuver his way off the median. The truck hit the pavement with a clunk and they were on the hunt again.

It took twenty minutes more to locate Rahiman. They found him by the bazaar, licking an ice-cream cone. Strong skidded to a halt, grabbed him, tossed him in the back with the rest, and barreled down the dark streets. On the way out of town, they stopped to pick up Abdullah, who was offered his place in the cab. He meekly declined and climbed in the back. Where exactly, Logan had no idea. It was wall-to-wall Indians in the canopy. The wheels spun as Strong fishtailed back onto the main highway out of Hofuf. No one spoke. Night fell on them like a cloak.

The last part of the disastrous journey was on unpaved roads. Normally, because of the dust, drivers took it slow on this leg of the trip, but Strong powered out of every sinkhole and dune. The Indians under the listing canopy banged on the walls and screamed every English obscenity they knew. Strong, lips snarled, eyes staring, gunned ahead.

The truck came to a dusty stop in the compound parking lot. The Indians, their faces powdered, looked like ghosts under the glare of the halogen lights. They clung to what was left of their pur-chases while they slapped the ash-colored dust from their best clothes. Although they had yelled and screamed for the last hundred kilometers, they didn't have much to say now.

"It's eleven twenty," Strong said, cornering his crew. The kitchen staff filtered into the shadows as quickly as they could. "We leave for the rig in twenty-five minutes. You guys ain't here ready to go, you're run-off motherfuckers. I'll work kitchen boys on the floor before I'll put up with one word of back talk from any of you." He stomped off.

Logan watched the Indians collect their things. They still managed their polite smiles. With the exception of Abdullah, they'd had a wonderful time, and he knew they were tough enough to work their shift without skipping a beat. That was good. Strong would certainly give them the chance to prove it.

Logan went to Abdullah and put his hand on his shoulder. "I'm sorry," he said.

But the Indian wouldn't look at him. He jerked away. "You are not sorry for fucking Abdullah," he said. "Strong shames me and Doc does nothing."

"Ah, Abdullah," Logan said, "you gotta understand."

"Abdullah understand," he said, his eyes like black ice. "Abdullah think maybe Doc special. All fucking Indian peoples think Doc special. Now Abdullah know. Strong. You. Same-same." He turned away.

Logan watched him walk into the shadows that dissected the Indian shacks. Abdullah stopped in the last of the light and peeled the Texas Longhorn shirt from his back. He wadded it up and pitched it into the sand. Logan stood where he was until he couldn't see him anymore.

TWENTY-SIX

DAY TWENTY-ONE

Logan met Johnny Townsend and Graham Hampton on the catwalk. He knew both assistant drillers well. They'd worked together in the North Sea. With them, Logan never worried about what had been left to him when he arrived on duty. These husky Brits were especially good hands—industrious, experienced, spirited, and smart—in Logan's opinion as good as any in the oil field and better than most. Disciplined products of the Brent and Ninian fields, splendid examples of British manners and British cool, they left the location in perfect order. He often wondered what American roughnecks would think of them. ("I say, chaps. Would you mind terribly making those tongs bite?") They would complement a crew anywhere a kelly was turning, but Logan was damn glad they worked opposite him.

They commented on Logan's haggard appearance—"knack-ered" was their word for it. He explained it to them as best he could, and in so doing hoped he could explain it to himself. He'd asked for it, they said, and Logan agreed. They said there was no way they'd put themselves in such a position, and Logan replied there was no way he'd ever do it again. He knew he'd seen Hofuf for the last time. What he wanted from now on, he'd find in the *souqs* of Al Khobar or Dammam, both near the Dhahran airport, on his way home. Wherever that was.

"It seems," Townsend said in his thick Newcastle accent, "Strong's always sucking you into his messes, Doc."

Logan knew Townsend was not referring just to the Hofuf fiasco. He was speaking of the incident that had driven Logan and Strong from the North Sea. They knew, as did every Momentum hand on the Ninian Central, from the division manager in Aberdeen to the wormiest Welsh roustabout. They hadn't forgotten. They had been cool to Logan when they met again in Saudi Arabia. But he had worked hard to regain their trust and then their friendship.

"It seems that way to me, too," Logan admitted.

"Why not ask for a transfer?" Hampton said. He was from Devon, his English accent far softer than Townsend's. "You don't need to put up with that kind of crap. Leave Strong to sort out his own problems."

"I heard Marshall's about to sort them out for him," Townsend said.

"We'll see," Logan said.

They spoke of the well. The drilling went on, the penetration rate steady but slow, as if they were boring through granite. Logan was lucky, they said, as the bit probably would be on bottom for the six days he had left. They mentioned amorphous plans of visiting Texas, which Logan encouraged. Caitlin would like them, Logan thought. Very much. But then again, it seemed unlikely they'd meet now. He scribbled his mother's address and phone number in Townsend's pipe tally book. "This woman will know where I am. Y'all are welcome to stay with me anytime," he said. "I'll set you up with friends if I'm overseas."

"Friends with tits, perhaps," Hampton quipped.

"Those you'll have to find yourself," Logan told him, certain they would. Scottish women hung all over them both in Aberdeen.

He left for the floor. The two crews of Indians mingled at the base of the elevators, exchanging cigarettes and tales of recent Hofuf adventures. Logan took the stairs to avoid them. The crews split when they saw him, and Rahiman, Putti, and Abdullah Larry rode the metal basket to the floor. Logan arrived when they did. They'd no sooner rounded the derrick leg than Strong, slouching in his chair, motioned for them to come to him. His face was sullen and drawn.

Putti didn't hesitate. "Yes, Strong?"

"Take this thermos, all makey clean. Then fill it up with white-ass coffee. *Haami-haami.*"

Putti took the thermos and rode the elevator down.

"The rest of you," Strong ordered, "rig floor, all makey clean. Understanding? Get yourselves some rigwash and get your asses back. No smokey-smokey. No bullshit."

The Indians stood straight, silent, their gazes fixed to the floor.

"You finish one job," Strong said, "Doc finding another. We're gonna work, all night long."

Rahiman spoke. "You still angry, Strong?"

"Goddamn right! What did you think would happen? I'm gonna teach you bastards to treat me like that." Strong crammed the first wad of Redman behind his gnashing teeth. "When I say work, you work. Any problem, any back talk, and I'll run every one of you bastards off." He stuffed the tobacco pouch into his shirt pocket. "Now get after it. I wanna see assholes, elbows, and *gondos*."

The men disappeared to fetch the required materials. Logan stood behind Strong and said nothing. He'd anticipated the sentence. Just the same, his silence must have rankled Strong.

"You with me on this, Doc?" Strong said, fooling with his rheostats. "'Cause if you ain't, you're on the wrong crew. Things're gonna change. They'll do it the first time they're told or I'm gonna change their faces." Logan smiled at this oil field euphemism, used all too often, for replacing one man with another. Strong leaned forward to spit through the grating and turned back to study Logan's face.

"Hell, no," Logan said, "you're right, Jamie. I feel the same way." And he did. His quarrel was with Strong's management of the crisis in Hofuf. But it was all right to make the Indians pay for their disobedience. Abdullah was the only real casualty, and Strong's sanctions didn't affect him. "I was out chasin' them little bastards, too. All I got in Hofuf was an overpriced rug and a headache. They gotta learn."

"Damn right, they do." Strong nodded. "Here's what I've got in mind. Let's work 'em steady through breakfast. Then we'll keep 'em on the floor the rest of the day and let 'em bake in the sun. The heat'll do the rest. Don't tell 'em, though. Let 'em think they're in for it all tour. I'd like it if it happened like that."

Putti arrived with the coffee. He took it to its usual place inside the doghouse.

"Bring it here," Strong said. "And a cup, *gondo*."

Putti stood waiting while Strong poured himself a full mug of coffee. In the absence of a breeze, the vapors rose up around his face. He handed the thermos back to Putti.

"Well, what're you waitin' for?"

"What?" Putti asked with false innocence.

"Get yourself a bucket, *gondo*. All makey clean. *Haami-haami*."

"Strong. Is necessary?"

"You're goddamn right it's necessary." Strong's eyes brightened. "You know what else is necessary? Ball dopin'."

"No," Putti gasped, spooked by the threat. Logan knew it was baseless. The tradition had faded for obvious reasons, litigation among them. Logan assumed he'd been one of the last to be so anointed. In a weird sort of way, he was proud that the graybeards had found him worthy.

Overseas, American crewmen threatened it often, although Logan had never seen it done. The very mention of it made the British nervous; they formally banned the practice. But if there had ever been a reason to resurrect the infamous rite in Saudi Arabia, it was now. And no one knew better than the Indians that Strong was entirely capable of carrying it out.

"No necessary," Putti said, rapidly putting distance between himself and Strong.

"Oh, yeah," Strong said, his gaze narrow and lean. "I'm gonna dope your balls, Putti. Not now, but soon. Count on it. For now, you get your black ass to work!"

Strong placed a boot in Putti's behind just to hurry him along. "Doc, I got a plan for you," he said. "It's clear to me we can't stay awake for thirty-six hours. I ain't what I once was. I think we should take turns catnapping in the doghouse, say, for one-hour intervals, at least until the mornin', when Elvin and Marshall wake up. We'll have to wing it after that. What d'ya say?"

"Sounds good. Who's first?"

"I got me a fresh cup of crude here," he said, tapping the cup with his finger. "Why don't you take the first kip?"

"I was gonna suggest that," Logan said, all too happy to oblige.

"Better hurry. If Bull comes up here with another story, the whole crew'll be laid out."

"I'm gone."

Logan took the jackets and spare coveralls hanging on hooks in the doghouse and arranged them into a makeshift bed. They smelled of diesel and stale musk. Then he walked to the elevator to check the office. Bull was passed out facedown on his metal desk. Probably had the alarm set for thirty minutes before Barnes was due to arrive. Logan was already settling into the clothes on the bench when he saw dark forms drifting by the windows.

The Indians had returned with their five-gallon buckets foaming. They had new brushes. Logan smiled. In a pinch, they must have broken into the roustabouts' tool locker again, a cause for great strife in the past. Brother would be up in the morning to protest this latest raid on behalf of the aggrieved rousties, who generally had the foresight to stash the best. Logan would order all supplies returned, a little worse for wear. Peace would be restored.

The roughnecks set upon the drill floor with the industry of ants, scrubbing the lower places first, squatting as only they could squat, working together. Their energy was limitless.

"No, no, no," Logan heard Strong yell. "Split up. One man working one place. That's how it's gonna be from now on."

Without a word of defiance, the crew took separate positions and continued their work. They saw Logan lying in the doghouse, his hands behind his head, peering through the open door. Logan grinned. He wanted them to know this time he wouldn't help them.

Logan looked up at the yellow blocks swaying like a pendulum beneath the silver steel tower. Above the derrick he saw only cool and solid black. At regular intervals he heard the automatic driller cable drawing back the brake handle and he knew the spinning kelly would sink an inch at most. Hofuf was behind them. The Indians' transgressions had allied Logan with Strong. At least for now. Tonight they were again of one mind and one purpose, just as they'd been years ago.

Logan would go down and patch things up with Abdullah before long. The Indian didn't have enough malice in him to stay mad at anyone for long. And it was useless to obsess about Caitlin. What would come would come, and Logan couldn't do a damn thing about it while he was over here. Body exhausted, hard formation, diamond bit, slow drilling. All week long. Logan would coast back to Texas rested and five thousand dollars richer. Other than the fact that he was womanless, homeless, and directionless; that his entire crew hated him; that he'd once again thrown in his

lot with a known sociopath; that he saw himself as God's labora-
tory rat scrambling through life's maze for a cookie crumb, things
couldn't be more perfect. He could sleep with all that.

He thought of one thing more. He felt certain he'd defied the
haunting dream. He knew Momentum's timetable very well. If they
didn't drill into the reservoir soon—very soon—the other crews
would catch the completion of Al Hisaab. When he came back to
Saudi Arabia the entire Momentum 127 operation would be trans-
ported somewhere else to begin another well in another place. The
déjà vu that had plagued him throughout the hitch had run its
course. The scene before him no longer matched his dream. The
kelly high, the bench warm, the clothes stinking but soft enough,
Logan drifted off.

TWENTY-SEVEN

Logan felt a hand jostle his shoulder. He slowly let go of his dreamless sleep. He smelled coffee and diesel exhaust and then the unique sweetness of the desert breeze. He remembered where he was.

"Doc?" Strong said.

Logan sat up, rubbing his burning eyes, as the rig came into focus. "Yeah?" he grumbled, his throat parched. His body screamed for water.

"It's your watch, man. Get out of my bed."

"Yeah, okay," Logan said, wiping the cold sweat from his forehead. "What's happenin'?"

"It's two o'clock and we're pokin' a hole in the meanest gas well in the world. Ain't nothin' to it."

"No problem," Logan said. "I got it."

He staggered out to take his place at the console, then staggered back to get the thermos. He drank out of the bottle, pouring the coffee, lukewarm and bitter, down his throat. He gargled with the last little bit and spit it out. It was a wretched brew.

Logan massaged his temples with his fingertips. His head throbbed, his stomach gurgled, his eyes still burned. A slight breeze blew from the black night, and the lights of the derrick drowned out the stars overhead. Four more hours before he'd see the sun. Ten before he'd find a real bed.

The Indians paused in their labors as he took his place in the driller's chair. He thought maybe they would bullshit with him, but much to his surprise they worked on. They weren't the type to carry a grudge. They generally forgave and forgot in short order, especially when it came to him. But Logan knew from their behavior that such was not the case tonight. Fine with him.

He checked his gauges. Pump pressure steady at thirty-four hundred pounds, rotary turning at sixty RPMs with minimal torque, fifteen thousand pounds resting on the diamond bit, the flow gauge—the rate of mud returning from the bore—steady at thirty-seven percent. Then he checked everything again hoping to God nothing had changed.

Putti was the first to approach him. "Doc? Three o'clock. Time for tea."

"Fifteen minutes," he said curtly, his gaze never leaving the instrument board.

"No problem." Putti waved to his crewmen to follow. Logan watched them go. They'd worked up a good sweat in what little breeze there was. Their copper frames looked bedraggled. Hofuf had been hard on them all.

Logan felt sleepy. The coffee was gone, and he was glad of it. He decided to walk around a bit. Maybe it would clear his head. Ripley stood over the pits, well rested, nibbling a biscuit. Ripley was always eating something. Logan halfheartedly waved to him and backed away. A full moon lit up the location. Nothing moved. Now he understood Strong's problem. It was about as lonely as it got on the floor in the still of mid-morning. It would be a long night. He tipped back his head and yawned.

It happened just like in the training manuals and the simulators at well-control school. He had just resumed his seat when the automatic driller slacked off in a steady whine, like the drag on a reel when a big bass takes the bait and runs with it for deeper water.

He checked the weight indicator first and saw that the weight on the bit was not increasing. A tingle ran the length of his spine and the hair on the back of his neck bristled. His fingers fumbled with the switch that disengaged the automatic unit, which could no longer keep up with the bit's drastic descent. The formation had given way.

He wasn't sure how to handle it. Not on this well. Should he drill through it or stop immediately and check for well flow? Both approaches had risks. The kelly plummeted, ten feet in the span of a minute, as if the bit were boring through balsa wood. His gaze shot to the indicators. No fluctuation in well flow. Pit volume constant. Okay so far. He'd drill to the connection and pick it up there. That should be all right. Then he remembered he had no hands on the floor. He reached for the air horn and pulled it three times. Its blare faded into the blank of the desert.

Before he could think of anything else, Strong's body swept in before him. Logan stepped aside. Strong had come alive like a sleeping dog when it hears a strange noise, his face alert, his expression grave. Logan didn't see the first hint of concern or doubt. What he saw was undaunted confidence turned on like a switch.

"Whatcha got, Doc?" Strong studied the gauges for himself.

"Drillin' break. A big one."

Strong eyed the kelly. "Christ, it's just fallin' through. Where's the roughnecks?"

"Havin' their tea."

"We better take a peek at her when I pick it up," Strong said. "How many feet has it been?"

"Maybe twenty or so. Just started all of a sudden."

"Whew!" Strong said. "Never seen a diamond bit make hole like this. Might need to wake Marshall and Bull." Strong blew the horn again. Soon the sulky crew dragged themselves back to the floor. When they saw the kelly sinking, Logan knew they understood why they'd been summoned early from their tea.

The kelly cock dropped to the rotary bushing as they instinctively took their places beside their open-jawed tongs. Rahiman smiled at Strong.

"We want to check for flow!" Strong yelled above the roar of the diesels. They nodded.

The blocks were nearly to the crown when Strong chained down the brake and stepped out to the rotary with Logan. He grabbed a flashlight from the console and pointed its hazy beam down the flow line. Logan could not see for the steam rising off the fluid column. Strong dropped to his knees. Logan and the Indians crouched beside him.

"What's it look like?" Strong asked.

"No flow," Rahiman said.

"Dead as a hammer," Logan said.

"All right. Let's make the connection and put her back on bottom. Tell Ripley to reset his pit markers and watch 'em close.

We'll see soon enough if this is just a pocket or what we really came for. Let's go."

Logan no longer felt fatigue. He expected no one else did either. The time for quarreling was over. This odd group of men, so often bitterly divided, became a crew. He got on the phone to Ripley while Strong made the connection. To sever the kelly from the drill string was a great risk. The Indians knew, and together they muscled the muddy kelly atop the waiting pipe joint and stabbed its threads on the first try. Strong feathered the kelly spinner while he pumped the brake. Pipe dope oozed at the joint. The instant the tongs tightened the connection, Strong engaged the clutch and stomped the foot throttle, and up she rose from the mouse hole, a new joint added to the long, steamy string. The Indians hosed fresh mud from the floor they'd just scrubbed. The wind kicked up. Clouds of dust drifted through the derrick.

Strong reamed back to bottom. Even when Logan knew he'd reached new formation, the weight indicator read otherwise. The kelly dropped as if nothing were there.

"Go get 'em, Doc," Strong ordered, and Logan left without another word. He propelled himself forward on the slide from the handrails, airborne until he was a third of the way down. The shriek of the drawworks still echoed in his ears. His boots hit the sand with a dull thud and he sprinted across the shadowless flat to the Arabco shacks, knocking first on Marshall's door. There was no answer. Logan swung the door open against Marshall's bunk.

"Who's there?" Marshall growled.

"It's Doc. We got trouble on the floor."

"What kind of trouble?" Marshall fumbled with his lamp. "Strong get his ass stuck?"

"No. We've hit sixty feet of drillin' break and it ain't stopped yet. It's just fallin'."

"That's not trouble, son. That's money!" When the light struck Marshall, Logan felt as if he looked upon the face of a pharaoh's mummy. "Strong ain't lettin' it come in on us, is he?"

"No. We checked it, Marshall. It's not flowin'."

"Not yet, you mean." Marshall swung his legs across the cot and stuck his pale, knotty feet into his Redwing boots. He climbed from the bed and followed Logan out of the office in his boxer shorts, grabbing the aluminum hard hat that hung by the door.

"Better get the Witch Doctor," he said. "I'll go on up. Maybe we'll make us a well after all."

Logan found Mousa's bunk and told him about the new development. He left him dressing and went for Bull.

The old man was still asleep at his desk.

"Hey, wake up, old-timer. We need ya up on the floor."

He looked rumpled and gaunt. The years had a firm grip on the old roughneck. He claimed he was sixty-three, but everybody knew better. He might have rolled back the odometer a notch or two on his Momentum application, but his chassis and frame showed his true mileage well enough. Logan thought he ought to be sitting on a Lazy Boy in front of a television somewhere, not working graveyard in the Rub al Khali. But like many he'd known at home and abroad, Bull was too old to work and too poor to quit. And so there he sat, massaging his arthritic knees and kneading the curve in the small of his back.

Logan poured him a cup of hot coffee and added the four sugars he knew Bull liked. It took him a while to come around. Only at Momentum would he have to jump-start the toolpusher to witness the most magnificent drilling break he'd ever seen.

"This better be good, Doc," Bull said. "I dreamed I was gettin' laid." He shoved his hands in his pockets and moved things around. "Them kind of dreams is few and far between these days."

Logan set the coffee in front of Bull, wondering what kind of medical school cadaver would be caught dead in a dream like that. The old man combed his sausage fingers through his wispy gray hair. "Now. What's all the fuss?" he said.

"We drilled into the reservoir, Bull. Marshall's up on the floor. Thought you might want to come up, too."

"Oh, hell, I want to—I just don't know if I can. I'm stove-up. I feel like an old pipe wrench, I'm so stiff."

"Well, come up when ya can," Logan said, springing for the door. "I gotta go."

"I'll be up directly," he said, "once I get my engines idlin'." Logan heard him slurp the first of his coffee.

Logan beat Marshall to the floor. The Indians laughed when the drilling foreman arrived in his underwear and hard hat. Marshall confirmed what they always believed: westerners had no shame.

Marshall paid them no mind, marching straight to the console.

"Makin' a little hole, are you?" he said, just as cool and casual as the best of the old company hands back home. And just like them, while he said it he studied every gauge on the board.

"This kelly down makes about eighty feet of break," Strong said.

"You reamin' through these connections good?"

"Yeah, but there ain't no drag. It's like nothin's there, man. It's unreal."

"Nothin' means somethin'," Marshall said, watching the kelly dive. "Now I'm sure."

Strong made the next connection. Logan watched it fall like the three before it.

"Goddamn, man!" Strong yelled. "I ain't never seen nothin' like this."

Marshall motioned for Logan. "What's bottoms up, cousin?" he said. He needed to know when the mud at the bit would return to the surface.

"About two hours," Logan said, estimating his calculations.

"Tell Brother to check the flare lines," Marshall said. The orders came staccato, like the beat of a snare drum. They sounded strange coming from a skinny old man in a hard hat and boxer shorts. "He needs to fill both barrels with diesel and make sure they'll burn the next twelve hours or so, and then keep his boys clear. And tell him to get us some more drill pipe laid up in the V-door. I want to chase it to the end if there's no drag on the pipe and she don't come in on us." He nodded toward the mud tanks. "That Limey on the pits?"

"Yep," Logan said.

"Make sure he's got his head out of his ass, Doc. Tell him to go ahead and route the return mud through the gas buster so we can get an accurate reading on our mud volume in case this well wants to flow. But tell him to wait till he sees Brother's flares burnin' before he does any of that. We'll see gas-cut mud for sure here directly."

Logan shuddered when the alarm went off in his head. Gas-cut mud was a problem. Down hole, under pressure, it wasn't so bad. But on the surface the gas expanded exponentially, threatening the balance of the well's hydrostatic head. Gas-cut mud weighed far less than uncontaminated drilling fluid, inviting the reservoir to vent into the well bore. There was no place for it to go but up. It was the prelude to a kick and the first step toward disaster.

"Oh, and wake up that mud engineer," Marshall added, counting the penetration marks on the geolograph. "He may want to mix some aluminum stearate or somethin'. He'll figure it out." He farted. "Sorry," he said.

Logan got on the phone and relayed the foreman's orders. Strong stuck his nose in the neck of his shirt. If it had been anyone else, Logan knew he would have said something. When Logan hung up the phone, Strong grabbed him by the arm. "I hope the hydrogen sulfide sensors don't go off," he said into his ear. "It'd be damned embarrassing."

"I need a cup of coffee," Marshall said, "or maybe a kick in the ass." Logan knew which one Strong would prefer.

"I don't need either," Strong said. "This well's got me jumpin'." Logan saw it was impossible to keep any weight on the bit. The kelly plunged into the well, and Strong let her fall.

"I love it," Marshall said, beaming. "It's everything I hoped for."

"I'll love it more when there's a Christmas tree sittin' on top of this bitch instead of me," Strong said. "I've never seen one go on like this."

"Just ride with it, son. The mud's plenty heavy enough to hold her back if we deal with the gas. I don't anticipate any problems."

"I like the way you talk." Strong's gaze fell to the drilling foreman's waist. "Nice underwear, too."

"Ah, the wife buys it somewheres." His eye twitched. "Mind your business, Strong. We can talk fashion later."

"I better send for Elvin," Strong said. "He'd want to be here for this."

"Naw, let him sleep. We can handle this. Go ahead and make the connection. If you set the kelly too damn low, we can't get anythin' on it if you get stuck. And by God, in this formation you just might. Watch it close."

The Witch Doctor arrived, shivering like a wet dog in a cold wind. Marshall pounced on him. "See what he got, Mousa," he said.

The Witch Doctor counted the penetration marks, a wedge of solid blue ink, on the geolograph chart. "Over two hundred feet in depth now, and falling," the Sudanese said. "Remarkable."

"Well, we'll see," Marshall said. "Bottoms up here in a bit." He turned his wristwatch to the glare of the lights. "We might have some contamination from all these connections. If she wants to flow, it oughta happen while the fluid column is stagnant. Otherwise, nothin' ought to enter the well bore. If it does, I'll have that mud engineer's ass. He was warned."

Marshall looked out across the desert toward the flares. "Why ain't them goddamn things burnin'?" he asked. "Go down and get it sorted out, Doc."

"Right, you savages," Brother was saying. "Get me some diesel, Aboobaker. Two drums should do. Shook, find some rag pieces for the flare. Right, has anyone got a lighter?"

The four roustabouts produced plastic Taiwanese lighters and sparked their flints, only too happy to please.

"Have you lost your fockin' minds?" Brother said. "We're not fifty feet from the great Kahuna, and you're over 'ere flickin' your bloody Bics. If you lot keep on, we'll be lookin' for pieces of you to send to Bombay in a shoe box. Now piss off and get me the fuel!"

Brother turned to Logan. "I know it don't look it, mate. But Brother's got it all under control. Tell Marshall he'll have his flares in time."

Logan reached the floor, gasping for breath, just as the kelly fell to its bushing. He'd lost count of how many had gone before it.

"Pump pressure's fallen off, Marshall," Strong announced, a sign to Logan that Al Hisaab was sure enough coming.

"Pick her up," Marshall said, "and shut everythin' down. I want to see it for myself."

Strong raised the blocks high into the derricks, not ten feet from the crown, until the tool joint stood just above the rotary, the classic position for engaging the blowout preventers. He chained down the brake and kicked out the pumps in one smooth motion. Then he joined Marshall, the Witch Doctor, a disoriented Bull, and Logan around the rotary to observe the well. There was no space for the Indians in that crowd.

The mud continued to flow, which was normal this soon after

the pumps had stopped. But the longer they waited, the more unset-tled Logan became. The men looked at each other, then back into the well. The mud flowed on in thick, gushing, steamy ripples, like an angry river.

"Sure ya got the pumps off, Strong?" Marshall said.

"Yep." Strong seemed equally calm. "She's doin' that on her own." Then the pit warning buzzers sounded, like the wrong answer on a game show. More mud was coming out than had gone in.

Logan looked over at Marshall. All he did was stare into the well. Could he not see it? Didn't he hear what Strong had said? Didn't the pit volume alarms make it clear enough? It was a kick, sure as hell! Why did the man hesitate?

"I'll be damned," Marshall said. He spit into the rotary. "She's sure enough kickin'!" He looked up into the derrick to estimate how far they were off bottom. Logan knew it would have to do. "I've seen enough," Marshall said. "Shut her in right where she's at."

TWENTY-EIGHT

———◆◇◆———

Strong trotted over to the blowout preventer masterboard, a series of levers against a schematic overlay of each valve in the stack, choke, or kill lines. It was obviously designed with human panic in mind. Strong yanked the hydril handle to the "Close" position. The hydraulic lines gasped as their pressure began to squeeze the hydril, the segmented iron and rubber ring at the top of the blowout preventer stack that sealed itself around the drill pipe. The accumulator, the tank of hydraulic fluid that supplied the preventers, responding to the sudden drop in pressure, engaged with its syncopated beat. Logan's heart pounded to the machine's broken rhythm. Mud slammed against steel. The entire derrick shuddered with the blow.

Instantly the flow ceased. Marshall stood by the rotary a minute to make sure. He seemed satisfied, and if he was happy, Logan was happier. Marshall motioned for Strong to join him over by the choke control panel, but before he left he cut the engines. Everything stopped dead. Arabco had a "hard" shut-in policy. Closing the hydril, or any set of rams, trapped the pressure between the preventers at one end and the bottom of the well three miles below at the other. It was so quiet that Logan heard the wind whistling through the girders overhead.

He knew they wanted to see how much, in pounds per square inch, the fluid would resist its sudden confinement. This would tell them exactly how much the kill mud should weigh to stabilize the well. It was that simple. Find out what it takes, and pump it down there. The gauge told them everything.

"I like these kicks when you're on bottom," Marshall said. Logan wondered how many he had sampled to develop a preference. "It's when all your pipe's sittin' on the rack that you're really screwed. We nipped this one in the bud."

Strong lightly hammered the gauge with his fist. Logan watched as the needle bobbed a little and then began to climb. "Here we go," he said.

Marshall peered through the lower lens of his bifocals. He didn't seem as impressed as Logan was. "Hell, that ain't near as bad as I thought," he said. "It was really gushing out of that hole. Another ten minutes of that and it'd been blowin' through the rotary. I've seen it happen just that quick."

Logan knew it was true, how quickly things went from bad to worse. Strong's head bobbed like some kind of ass-kissing fool, a rare event. Marshall looked out into the desert and frowned.

"Brother needs to get them flares lit," Marshall said, turning back to his gauge. "You sure you didn't swab this in on us, driller?" Sometimes kicks were simulated by a bit acting like the plunger in a syringe. Marshall impressed Logan by considering all angles while he was under the gun. It's what made him good.

"Nope," Strong said with confidence. "There was no indication." It was true. Logan had seen none.

"Well," Marshall said, "either the mud weight's a little low or else that formation's under a lot more pressure than we figured. We'll find out which here directly."

The mud engineer appeared, clothes disheveled, face puffy, eyes filled with sleep and confusion.

"Cleftbar," Marshall snapped, "how quick can you have me some kill mud fixed?"

"Don't know, exactly," Cleftbar said, squinting from the derrick's glare. "How heavy do you want to go?"

Marshall pointed to the choke gauge. "There's your pressure. Figure me an equivalent mud weight. Get your true vertical depth figure off the geolograph."

The Englishman scratched the figure into his notebook, checked the geolograph depth, and returned punching numbers into his calculator. Then he did it again just to make sure.

"The weight we need will place us very near the fracture gradient for that last formation leak-off test," Cleftbar warned. Earlier, just after they had run the last string of casing, they had pressured up on the formation to establish how much it could withstand before breaking down. It was a precaution for the event they faced now.

"Very near it," Marshall said, "but not over. Right?"

"Yes, but it's never a good idea to get close to breaking down the walls of the formation. The one we've just come out of was hard but also brittle. If the bottom bursts out, we lose our fluid column. She'll blow through the crown."

"You best mind your figures, then," Marshall said. "You know what she can take."

He assured the others that there was nothing to worry about. It was just a kick, and they would circulate it around to see what happened. All they needed, he said, was to stabilize the pressures with heavier mud. Marshall alternated between well-control theories and practical matters with equal confidence. He never demonstrated the least bit of anxiety. "Now," he said, "does everybody understand what's goin' on up here?" Strong nodded. So did Logan. Cleftbar looked ill.

"Get with Ripley and mix the kill mud," Marshall said to Cleftbar. "I'm gonna start circulating around with the active system. We'll just keep her moving to stay safe." He looked at Strong. "You got a slow pump rate handy, driller?"

"Yep." Strong reached for his tally book where he had recorded the figures earlier. He and Logan checked them every day at the beginning of their tour. They told him precisely what the pressure should be at any given rate under normal circumstances.

Marshall himself would adjust the choke valve as the sequence began. The more kill mud pumped down hole, the less the pressure ought to be. When the pressure's zeroed out, he said, she's dead. Until then, they'd keep a constant balance—Strong at the pump gauge, Marshall holding back pressure on the choke—and around they'd go until the choke manifold gauges registered nothing. Marshall would flag Strong as they went along to increase or decrease the pump rate. Logan saw Brother's flares ignite in the distance, their glow mirrored in Marshall's eyes. Marshall, his hand on the choke, directed them all to their stations. "All right," he said. "Let's dance."

He opened the choke, its hydraulic pump sounding exactly like the beat of a human heart. On Marshall's signal, Strong engaged the pump and focused on his console gauge. Too much pressure could blow a line—or worse, fracture the formation. Once circulation began, Logan heard the mud hissing through the choke manifold. The entire system trembled from the pressure. Next the drilling fluid was piped straight to the towering gas buster where it rained down across the baffle plates that separated the gas from the mud. Ripley and Cleftbar would weight it up once it returned to the pits, and then they would pump it down hole again.

"Easy now, Strong," Marshall said. "Nice and steady. Doc! Come over here. I want to teach you somethin'. You can't be a damn hippie all your life."

Logan joined him at the choke controls.

"You know how to run this thing?"

"Yeah," Logan said, wondering why Marshall would ask. He'd never seen anyone below a rig superintendent operate the choke valve. Drilling foremen usually insisted that they do it personally. "I went to blowout school twice in the North Sea, once in Tulsa," Logan said. "I know how it works."

"Good. I never got past the eighth grade myself. I gotta go take my mornin' constitutional. You got yourself a kicking well here, son. Don't screw nothin' up while I'm gone. I'll be back directly."

Marshall, hunched up, trotted across the floor for the elevator.

"Now where's he goin'?" Strong said, incredulous.

"Shit needing," Rahiman said, always observant.

"Yes, is necessary," Putti added. The Indians snickered. Rahiman held up his personal bucket for Marshall to use, quite a concession, but Marshall was already scampering across the desert in his boxers. His hard hat blew off, but he didn't stop to get it.

"Jesus," said Strong. "I guess the crazy son of a bitch's just gonna let us fuck with it. Go figure."

Logan focused on the twitching needles, opening or closing the hydraulic choke as the pressure dictated. The valve needed continual adjustment to read steady. He checked his watch. Gas-cut mud should have been coming out of the well for the last twenty minutes or so. He looked at the flare. Nothing. At least Brother and his crew were on their way back now, out of harm's way. It was risky to circulate the well with them anywhere close to the flares. For a conservative man, Marshall sure liked to take chances. Brother and his men were walking back to the catwalk, punching at each other.

Logan was just beginning to get the hang of his job when the explosion knocked him from his perch.

TWENTY-NINE

$\diamond\!\diamond\!\diamond$

Logan's hard hat blew clear to the mud manifold. First he saw the glow. Then he felt the searing heat. He climbed to his feet and checked his crew. Strong was scraping himself up from the grating. Rahiman lay prone on the pipe rack and Putti was balled up in front of the doghouse. Abdullah Larry peeked out from behind the air hoist. He looked up, as though to see if the sky was as angry with them as the punctured earth.

Logan gripped the handrail and searched west toward the flares. There was no mistaking the pulsing blue flame. Hydrogen sulfide. Poison gas. The separators must have finally channeled enough gas to the flare lines for ignition. When it reached the burning barrels of diesel, it blew.

Logan thought of Brother and his roustabouts. He couldn't find them in the flares' illumination. He'd go down and hunt them up as soon as he had a tank strapped to his back. But first he had to think of the roughnecks, of Strong and himself.

"It's come up H$_2$S!" he yelled.

Strong stood at his console, checking his pump pressure one last time before he did anything. He motioned for Logan to do the same with the choke. Then he ran to the phone and switched on the intercom.

"This is Jamie Strong!" he said, his voice echoing from the Momentum office to the dunes. "We have hydrogen sulfide on location! All nonessential personnel evacuate immediately." He waved to Ripley. Ripley waved back. "You and that mud man stop what you're doing now and don breathing tanks! Then clear your area of all TCNs!" Ripley signed thumbs-up.

Strong dragged Rahiman to the phone. "Tell all Indians desert going!" Strong ordered. "Into the wind! *Haami-haami!*"

Rahiman looked puzzled, a little shy maybe about using the intercom, which no Indian had ever done. But he gave it his best. "All Indians desert going! *Haami-haami!*"

Strong rolled his eyes. "In Hindi, idiot!"

"Oh," the Indian said. "No problem. You never say." Once Rahiman broadcasted Strong's instructions, Indians ran from every dark and quiet place, pausing only to check the wind sock over the Momentum office as they had rehearsed many times. After that, they were running again toward the safety of the eastern dunes.

Strong reached above him and pounded the red alarm button with his fist. It began its obnoxious pulsing blare, the first time Logan had heard it in Arabia. Those who had dallied after the evacuation notice now scrambled like scalded cats.

The roughnecks, knowing they would be needed, stood fast. "What're you guys waitin' for?" Strong bellowed. "Go on! Get. Very danger here! Desert going!"

One after another, the roughnecks hit the slide. Logan heard their Three Stooges noises, performed for Strong's benefit. Abdullah joined them out by the pipe rack. Ripley had sent him away as well. They took a position upwind two hundred yards away. Rahiman was walking backwards, staring at the floor. Logan motioned for them to go further and be quick about it. Finally they reached the dunes where some of the roustabouts, helpers, and rig clerks were already waiting. When Logan saw they had gone far enough, he went looking for Strong.

"Get a tank," Strong ordered.

"You don't have to tell me twice," Logan said. Strong took his place.

Logan jerked one of the plastic, suitcase-like containers out from under the bench in the doghouse. He hoisted the tank over his head, slid it down his back, and buckled the straps across his chest. He reached behind to open the main valve and checked to see that his mask was operating properly. Then he strapped it around his head and cinched the straps tight. He knew he had thirty minutes of air. The alarm would sound at twenty-five, allowing him five more to find another tank or a better place.

He returned to the choke while Strong strapped on a tank. Logan was torn between staying with the well or searching for Brother and his men. "All right," Strong said, his voice muffled beneath his mask. "We're ready for this bitch now."

Logan eyed the needle on the choke. Steady enough—at least steadier than he was. "I gotta go look for Brother," he told Strong. Strong waved and pointed. Logan saw Brother and his rousties crossing the flat upwind of the flares on their way to the dunes. By Logan's count, that was everybody safe. Brother's bunch cleared the pipe rack and stepped into the gold-blue shaft of light, hands over their ears, smoke rising from their tattered clothes. Next time they'd move quicker.

The kill procedure was running smoothly when Marshall returned, still composed, still in his underwear, to the floor. He rapped on Logan's air tank.

"What the hell's this all about?" he said.

Logan pointed to the flares. "H_2S."

"Oh," Marshall said. "Damn if it ain't." He looked at the choke manifold gauges. "The pressure's already droppin'. I think it's just a big bubble."

"There's another tank in the doghouse, Marshall," Logan said. "You best put it on."

"That's all right. The flares are burnin' off what's come up, I think. I didn't hear the sensors trip. And I wouldn't be up here if I had." He looked down at the pits. "I see them boys on the mud tanks have sets on. They're the ones that really need 'em. You and Strong were right to order 'em out, though. You did good."

Barnes bolted through the elevator gate. "Looks damn serious up here," he said, looking at Marshall. "Came as soon as I heard the blast. At least I had time to put my pants on." He turned to Strong and planted his feet. "Why wasn't I told?"

"Marshall said to let you sleep."

He shook his head in disappointment. "I don't give a damn what Marshall says." His jaw worked like a bear trap. "If it's important enough to wake him, it's important enough to wake me. I'm on call twenty-four hours a day. Whenever somethin' out of the ordinary happens—say, like when my well wants to blow out—I wanna be on this drill floor. You got it?"

For a short man, Barnes could be terribly intimidating. He was an amiable enough drunk. Generally pleasant around the rig. But it was a mistake to cross him. He buzzed around Strong like a wet hornet. Logan yielded space between him and his driller. He didn't want to catch a stray sting.

"Don't get pissed, Elvin," Strong said. His face looked especially sheepish inside that mask. "It didn't kick until an hour or so ago."

"Then I should've been up here an hour or so ago. If you send for Marshall, you send for me. Am I clear?"

"Yeah," Strong said. "I got it."

"Christ, I can barely understand ya in that spaceman suit. How's it goin' up here?"

"Shut-in pressure's droppin'. Marshall thinks it's just a bubble."

"Good. Did it swab in after a connection?"

"Why does everybody think I did it?" Strong said. "Hell, we drilled through two hundred feet of reservoir. Why shouldn't we get a mean-ass kick?"

"Two hundred feet? Jesus!" Barnes surveyed the floor. "Where's your crew?"

"Evacuated. Brother's with 'em."

"Who's on the pits?"

"Ripley and Cleftbar."

"They still alive?"

"Don't know, it's hard to tell. Ripley's looked dead to me for over two years."

"They're still movin' around, ain't they?"

"Yep. They're mixing kill mud. They've both got sets on."

"All right," Barnes said. He shut off the alarm. "That's enough of that racket. Let's get a look at the choke."

Barnes marched over to the well-control unit. He looked worried. The first thing that caught his attention was the flare pulsing in the distance. Logan figured he must have heard the roar ever since he stepped out of his cabin door at camp.

"What've we got, Marshall?"

"Oh, just a fart, I think," Marshall said. "We've about circulated it out. Pressure's droppin', and the flare's taperin' off a little."

"Any sign of H_2S?"

"Enough to worry about. We drilled through plenty of reservoir and we ain't finished yet. Had to shut down when it started to flow." Marshall rubbed the stubble on his chin. "Your crews handled it real good."

"I wouldn't know," Barnes said. "Sons of bitches didn't include me." He glared at Logan.

"That's my fault."

"No," Barnes said, "it ain't. Strong knows better."

"He does now anyway," Marshall chuckled.

"Looks like you've got yourself a whopper," Barnes said.

"Yep. I believe so." Marshall signaled for Logan to take his place. "All yours, Doc. Me and Elvin's gonna go down and talk to that mud man. We'll get the system stabilized and put that bit back to bottom by noon." He thumped the gauge. "We ain't got nothin' here no more."

Three hours passed before Barnes and Marshall returned to the floor. Logan was glad they had finally decided to come. They'd called on the goddamn phone every ten minutes. It'd gotten old. They went straight to the choke.

"That's it, Elvin," Marshall said. "We're clear. It was just a bubble like I thought."

"Must've come in durin' a connection."

"Well, let's continue to circulate through the chokes for a while. When we get the same weight all around, we'll drill ahead."

"Suits me," Barnes said. "Let's go get us some groceries, and you some pants."

"Yeah, okay. Hey, Strong, circulate bottoms up twice more, and we'll see what we got. Be sure and work your pipe. I don't wanna get stuck this early in the mornin'."

"You got it."

"We're gonna eat," Barnes said. "Be back in two shakes."

They left. Every pressure gauge, save the pump's, pegged at zero. The flares had died away, their shooting flames replaced by the smudgy black smoke of the burning diesel. Strong went to the far corner of the floor and yelled for his men to return from exile. Then he took his seat by the console. He started to take a chew, but put it away. Breakfast would be here soon. Logan went down to see if he could help Ripley weight up the mud.

It was just after six when the sun, warm and blood red, rose above the dunes. For the first time since he'd been in Saudi Arabia, Logan was glad to see it. The whole world was bathed in its clean light. Everything was still in the Rub al Khali. The well was dead. And Logan had six more days to go.

THIRTY

DAY TWENTY-TWO

Shortly after the all clear sounded, the Indians showed up on the floor. They emptied the sand from their Momentum brogans, wiped the dust from their bare ankles, and took turns gulping handfuls of ice water from the Igloo. They splashed the last of it on their faces. Then they swarmed Strong.

"More gas coming?" Putti asked, slipping his scaly feet back into his boots. He didn't bother to relace them. It wouldn't have made much difference if he had.

"Not today," Strong said. "No problem."

"No problem?" Putti said, incredulous. "Very danger! You very goot, Strong. Never worry. Always knowing." Strong held up his palm and Putti slapped it just as Logan had taught them to do. It'd taken them a while to get it. Grown men who held hands couldn't believe that banging them together meant the same thing.

"You number one driller," Rahiman added, likewise clapping his hand against Strong's. It pleased Logan to see how they admired Strong—not only because he'd managed the kick so well, but also because his first thought after sealing the well had been of their welfare. Logan knew the Indians would never understand the complexities of Jamie Strong, and neither would he. But they trusted and admired him, the highest compliment a crew could pay their driller. Strong's shortcomings paled when compared to his cool expertise. Al Hisaab had roared, and Strong had roared back.

"I'm proud of you guys, too," Strong said. "You stayed with me until I sent you away. You don't know what that means to me."

"It means we assholes," Putti said.

Logan laughed. The man had a point.

"You're probably right," Strong said. "But you're my assholes."

It seemed to Logan that things were even again in this still, desert dawn. Strong had earned yet another fresh start with his crew. Logan liked the very idea of it, the sense of pride and camaraderie that bonded this unlikely group. How quickly, he thought, everything changed between men in the immutable Rub al Khali.

Strong turned his face to bask in the sunlight. Like the Indians, he didn't show the first trace of fatigue. Logan himself felt alive, clear headed, and connected. They'd both see the end of the sleepless tour in good spirits while Marshall decided what would come next. Until then they would continue to pump mud around until the system stabilized beyond all doubt, working the pipe up and down every so often to keep it from sticking against the formation's brittle walls. Now that they were into the reservoir, completion wasn't far off. They would be busy from the next day to the end of the hitch. But for now all was peaceful on Momentum 127.

The Indians continued to laud Strong for his cool, asking him to explain the kick blow by blow—what had happened and what it meant. Strong did so in a patient, playful manner. Soon, however, they pointed to their watches. Logan understood that with the danger behind them they were anxious to return to the routine. The morning sun was up and glaring. Logan felt the first hot breath of wind on his neck. It was time for breakfast.

Strong nodded and waved them away. They scampered for the Bombay Teahouse to slurp their porridge and powdered milk. Abraham, obviously still harboring resentment over the hijacking of his truck, delivered the white-ass breakfast to the floor without a word.

Logan peeled away the aluminum foil to find steak, beans, and eggs. Very British. Very cooked. He carried his plate back out to the console to eat with his driller. Strong drove a Phillips screwdriver through the lid of a liter can of apple juice with the heel of his hand.

Ripley, a stranger to the floor during his pit tenure, hit the doghouse in a flurry to inhale his two boxes of cereal. It took maybe five minutes. He trotted off to the pits again, signaling thumbs-up to his driller. Strong returned the gesture, a piece of meat hanging from his teeth.

"Strange bird," he said when Ripley had gone.

"Good bird," Logan said. Strong could take him or leave him. His hygiene and eating habits disgusted Strong—no easy feat. It was true Ripley wasn't a tidy man. His clothes were always disheveled and grimy, his fingernails dirty, a sheen of human grease covering his pocked face. The Indians knew for a fact that he didn't wash his hands after he used the toilet. That was the end of it for them. But Ripley was steady and predictable, and innocuous enough to compensate for Strong's volatile moods. For Logan, Ripley made the arrangement work.

Logan was busy gnawing on a bone when Werner Freitag and Sidney Greene, the English electrician, poked their heads around the derrick leg. The drill floor operation was priority for the tradesmen, and Logan knew they came there first each day.

"How's it goin' up here, Jamie?" Werner said. The old man looked tired, but sincere. Greene, his absurd hard hat dented beyond its original oval shape, its metal visor bent upward, had only a cursory interest, or so it appeared to Logan. Greene was as slack as Werner was thorough. He couldn't wait to get off the floor.

Strong went over his list, none of which Greene gave a fig about. He wasn't about to tamper with the explosion-proof seals of the driller's console, he explained, not on the very day the well had kicked. He said he'd deal with all of these things during the rig move, which meant to Logan that he'd leave it to his relief. That said, mechanic and electrician left the floor.

Strong picked at his breakfast. Logan yawned.

"Bored?" Strong asked.

"Yep. Last night is a hard act to follow."

"Who would want to?" Strong said. "I guess there's nothin' to do but tool the Indians."

Logan grinned. "They ain't paid for Hofuf yet."

"Nope." Strong winked. "Not by a long shot. We got all morning. We'll start slow and work our way up."

"Or down."

"You got the idea," Strong said.

THIRTY-ONE

~⬦~

Strong was pitching his plate into the tub when the Indians returned from their breakfast. He belched and hung from the doghouse rafters to stretch. He waved the Indians in with his free hand.

"Come in, boys," he said. "Somethin's come up."

Abdullah Larry, by far the most gullible, instinctively obeyed. The others, frequent victims when Strong had too much time on his hands, were more cautious. Putti, obviously alerted by Strong's supplicant tone, grabbed Abdullah Larry by the arm. Rahiman peered safely through the window.

"Come, boys. Big political problem in your country."

The Indians huddled together to talk it over. In the end, Logan figured they'd decided it was a bad idea to let their driller corner them anywhere, let alone in the confines of the doghouse. They spread out, content to take their chances in the open air, all eyes fixed on Strong.

"Don't you trust me, men?" Strong said. "This is serious. We have to talk."

"Ball doping?" Putti said, still motionless and wary.

"Naw," Strong said, closing his eyes, a tight-lipped smile on his face. "I wouldn't think of it. Driller only want to talk to his Indian friends."

They looked at each other. Then three bodies moved as one into the doghouse.

"What you want?" Rahiman said, still suspicious.

"Well, I'll tell ya." Strong reached for Logan's *Time* magazine, the dog-eared international edition. "Doc was reading here that there are too many problems in India."

"Yes," Putti agreed. "Many."

"Well, you guys aren't gonna believe this, but it says here that prime minister of India talked to Queen of England, and he want British to come back."

The Indians looked at each other blankly.

"No," Rahiman gasped.

"That's what it says in the magazine, here," Strong said. "Five boatloads of British soldiers coming to take over country. Stop all problems."

"No," Rahiman repeated. "British assholes never coming back!"

"Yeah," Strong said, holding up the rolled magazine. He flipped through several pages. "It says right here. Too many problems. British people fix for you. You should be happy."

"No needing British," Putti said. "No necessary."

"Well, Doc," Strong laughed, "at least we found somethin' that Putti doesn't think is necessary."

"Who'd have ever thought it'd happen?" Logan said. It never had before.

"Let me see paper," Rahiman said. He read English better than the other TCNs.

"No," Strong said, "this is white-ass paper. Black-ass paper in Bombay Teahouse." Rahiman reached for the magazine. Strong held it back. "It's a good deal," he said. "You guys can't get ironed out over there. Why not let some white people take a stab at it?"

"Ah," Rahiman said, "bullsheet." He looked at his feet and snatched the magazine from Strong. He flipped through it quickly, scanning the pages. "Bullsheet, man." He looked at his crewmen. "Nothing. Strong bullsheet. No British coming."

"They come. Big problem," warned Abdullah Larry, unconsoled. "Indian peoples fight."

"Now that's for sure," Strong told them.

"Strong," Putti said, "our country is beautiful. Not too hot, not too cold. Many peoples, yes. Many problems, but beauty all around. Not like fucking Momentum. Not like this fucking desert. No problem with these fucking flies," he said, swatting at the one crawling up his cheek. Even in August, the flies in Arabia were like a biblical plague. "The flies in India come, but not so many like here. Always biting these flies. Too much problem."

Strong looked at Logan and smiled. "Are these guys some patriotic sons of bitches or what? Even the flies are a cut above."

"Number one flies," Putti said, grinning.

"Y'all are one up on us there," Logan said. "American flies ain't worth a damn."

"He's right," Strong said. He put his hand on Rahiman's shoulder. "See how honest we are? We'll look you right in the eye and tell you that our flies suck. You guys can trust us, can't you? The British are coming. Be happy."

"They never come to India," Rahiman said, pulling away. "You big liar."

Logan looked out the window. Tate-Pixilate and Owen Oxley, camp maintenance man, were waddling up the stairs. "Well, they're coming here," he said.

"What seems to be the problem here, then?" said Tate-Pixilate as he entered the doghouse. Logan had to smile at the way his bright red plastic hard hat, melted on one side from being set too close to the stove, bobbled to one side of his black, wavy, oiled coiffure. People who never wore hard hats looked like fools when they did. But the rig crews didn't look right to Logan without them.

Oxley looked odd regardless of his attire. Strong had nicknamed him "That Sort of Thing" for his peculiarly British speech impediment. It was cruel, Logan thought, but appropriate. Two minutes of conversation with Oxley could drive him into the dunes.

At first sight of the Englishmen, the Indians retreated to the opposite corner. Their smiles disappeared and they grew solemn. Strong's merits occasionally allowed him to rise above their discontent. Pix, who had none, never could. As he stepped forward, the Indians crowded together a little closer, not wanting to mix their air with his, his endomorphic frame casting a shadow on their dulling faces.

"How're all my children, then?" he said, leering at them with his bloodshot, popeyed nervous stare. They gazed coolly at the floor and said nothing. "Shy, eh? Even you, Rahiman? Cat got your tongue?"

"Give 'em a little air, will ya, Pix?" Logan said. He opened the magazine. "Which reminds me. We called for you because we had to use the air tanks last night. They're empty. There's two more to fill on the mud pits."

"We'll have to take them back to camp. That's where the compressor is. Was there an emergency of some sort?"

It was no surprise to Logan that Pix hadn't heard about the kick. "Of some sort," Logan said.

"Any other difficulties to report?"

"The warning buzzer on the tank to the left failed."

"Strange," Pix said. "Have a look at it, Owen."

Oxley knelt down to examine the tank. He selected a screwdriver from his leather pouch and removed the cover.

"Good morning to you," Pix said to Strong.

"Ah," Strong said, tossing the magazine aside, "Dicks and his twin half brother Sludge."

"Ah, Mr. Wrong," Pix said. "Living proof that a little education will get you absolutely nowhere, especially when that's where you belong."

Strong belched in his face. "And you can take that to the bank, you wanker." When he hiked his leg as if he were about to pass wind, Pix backed off.

Oxley finished tinkering with the valve. "There. That ought to do it. Someone," he said, meaning someone else, "neglected to set it and that sort of thing. I simply adjusted the calibrator sort of thing and it should work properly, you know, as it should, sort of thing."

Strong looked at Logan as if to ask, "Can you believe how this man speaks?" Logan felt a little sorry for Oxley. At least he meant well. Pix, he was certain, did not.

"Rest easy, my pleasant American friends," Pix said. "We'll take the empty tanks to camp and test them. Will that make you happy?"

"Nothing you can do makes me happy," Strong said. "But you and Stammerin' Stanley need to check every goddamn tank on this location. We're gonna need 'em. And I wouldn't want to be you if one of them tanks fails."

The Indians burst into laughter. Pix glared at them and their laughter ceased. Even Strong could not protect them in Pix's apartheid domain. Putti alone continued to snicker in defiance. But he did it without looking at Pix.

The Indians didn't move until the Englishmen began to repack the tanks, and then they huddled around Rahiman. Rahiman motioned to Logan and Strong.

"Want to fuck camp boss," Rahiman said.

"Yes, very very," Abdullah Larry said.

"All right by me," Strong said.

That was all it took to animate the Indians. Pix and Oxley surfaced from the doghouse giving Strong the old thumbs-up. He returned the gesture.

"Asshole," Strong said.

"Jerk," Pix said.

The two Englishmen boarded the elevator, grasping the sides for the perilous ride down. The empty tanks lay at their feet.

"Now!" Strong shouted.

Putti tripped the elevator breaker. The carriage stopped cold. Stranded midway, the riders searched for a way off. As fat as they were, there was no possibility of climbing down.

"Doc, please," Pix said. "No games today. We're occupied."

Logan shrugged his shoulders while the Indians dragged high-pressure hoses from both corners of the drill floor. When they were ready, the roughnecks signaled for Strong to open the valves. The blast from Rahiman's hose blew Pix's deformed hard hat from his head and it fell beneath the substructure where Pix would never venture. The streams indented both men's flaccid stomachs. At Strong's signal, the Indians dropped their hoses and shut them off. Putti flipped the breaker and the elevator engaged.

"Have a nice day, boys!" Strong said. He waved good-bye to the English as they tramped down the skids in soggy boots, their shirts flapping because the buttons had been blown away. They headed for the Momentum office, no doubt to complain. It would be, Logan knew, a wasted effort. Barnes couldn't give a rat's ass what his crews did in their slack time providing no one got hurt. Pix would probably vent his anger on his kitchen staff, who had weathered many such petty storms before.

"Number one," Rahiman said, his white teeth flashing.

"It's good for you boys to get a chance to tool a prick like that," Strong said. "Makes you feel better."

"Oh, yes," Rahiman said. He mumbled to his crewmen in his native tongue. And then, one by one, the Indians reached for their hoses and turned to glare at Strong.

THIRTY-TWO

⬖⬗⬖

Logan dove for the water valve about the time the dual streams struck his chest. Their joint force blasted him from his feet, washing him along in the torrent until his body slammed against the railing. "Jamie!" he hollered. But all hope for assistance vanished when Strong's body washed up beside his.

"Damn." Logan shielded his face with his hand. What had begun as a national conflict had suddenly turned racial. "I can't believe they've lumped us in with Pix."

"They'll regret it," Strong said, spitting the water out of his mouth. He began crawling against the force of the water toward the Indians, who were shouting instructions to each other in Hindi. Strong veered for one group, Logan for the other. Logan wormed his way up the fire hose until he reached its middle. He bent it in half, cutting off the flow. Strong wrestled his nozzle away from Putti and Rahiman and blew them against the drawworks. Things seemed to settle until Abdullah Larry dumped a bucket of rigwash over Strong's head. Then it all started again.

Soon the hostilities spread to other parts of the location. Rahiman, sneaking down the substructure like an assassin, hosed Ripley and Cleftbar, who were resting peacefully on the handrails by the little house. Ripley, caught off guard, collided head on with the open door of the shack. He looked dazed, but he recovered enough to man the water cannon above the mud pumps, all the while rubbing his aching head.

Once on line with his weapon, his retaliation was relentless. He rained justice down on the outgunned roughnecks until Strong intervened with the threat of a good ass-kicking should the avenging Limey wet the drawworks brakes.

Ripley swung the cannon on fresh targets elsewhere, focusing his blast on Abdullah, who was trying to get a mud sample from his pits. Ripley blew Abdullah's bucket over the handrails; his body soon followed.

"What the fuck you doing, you crazy English!" Abdullah shouted.

Logan leaned over the rails to check on Abdullah, who was brushing the sand from his clothes. "You all right?"

"No problem," he said.

"Here's one little problem." And then Logan hosed him good. The derrickman ran out of his range, laughing, until Ripley hit him again with the cannon.

"Everybody crazy, this job," Abdullah said, disappearing behind the darkened dunes.

Samuel, fresh as always at the beginning of his shift, was busy checking oil levels in the agitator motors when the great stream of water pasted his dark frame against the orange handrail and blew off his cotton shirt. He threw down his tools in disgust and trotted for the safety of the Bombay Teahouse. Logan had never seen the morose Indian move so quickly.

Cleftbar, who had sought refuge in the metal mud house, peered through the shutter to find Ripley's cannon trained on him, waiting. A short, authoritative blast slammed the shutter door on his fingers. He fell to his knees.

"For Christ's sake, Ripley! Act your age!" he yelled from his new position under the rusted sink. He rubbed his throbbing fingers.

"Sorry, ol' chap," Ripley shouted in his best Victorian accent, ridiculing the exclusive education Cleftbar liked to remind everybody about. Ripley had been sent to the trade schools at age thirteen, and Logan knew he'd never gotten over it. "For Queen and country and all that rot, you miserable wanker!" He washed Cleftbar out of the mud house along with the scales, cooler, and viscosity funnel.

"Bloody idiots," Cleftbar said, just before Logan drilled him in the back of the head. Logan saw the white of his scalp. Cleftbar ran for the dunes.

No one had to encourage the roustabouts to join in the fray. They smelled blood and were drawn to it. Aboobaker attacked the nearest white man, who happened to be Brother. Shook and the skeletal Razaki stalked Ripley, who was busy burying Chavan in a fresh pit. When they closed in, they signaled Aboobaker, who turned on the valve to their fire hoses. Ripley, caught by surprise, flipped over the handrails to the desert below. The roustabouts drove him into Chavan's pit, where the struggle turned hand to hand. Aboobaker climbed up to the cannon in Ripley's place and hosed them all.

Things went well enough for Aboobaker until Brother arrived with the forklift, its bucket raised high in the air. Aboobaker brought his cannon to bear on the machine's cab. Brother turned on the windshield wipers, which, Logan thought, were seeing their first day of use in the Rub al Khali, and edged forward. When he was close enough, Brother tilted the bucket and a wall of water washed Aboobaker from his perch. Logan took his place.

"Technology's the thing!" Brother shouted, and Logan gave him thumbs-up. Brother opened the window to return the gesture when Logan let him have it with a sustained blast.

"Treachery's better," Logan said.

Brother floored the forklift and headed for the well.

Logan watched the shafts of crystalline water arc across the hazy blue desert sky. He could hear the roaring laughter of the combatants, many now reduced to throwing wet sand. Logan saw Barnes start down the long catwalk, only to be blown back by an indiscriminate Indian. Barnes, Logan was sure, threatened the man with his job, only to be answered with a brisk blast in the face. Barnes gave up, snatching the receiver of the nearest phone.

"Strong!" the intercom echoed. "Get your crew under control!"

Strong answered with a powerful stream of water. Barnes threw the phone down and walked away.

The sand around the location looked only a little darker. The desert drank the water, and the dunes absorbed the laughter of lighthearted men. How glad Logan was to be here, in this place, with these drenched people. At twenty-seven years of age, he could still have fun—good, clean fun—in the oil fields. He faced the sun, raising his arms toward its warmth, allowing the hot breeze to bathe him. He would have stood like that for hours if Aboobaker and Razaki hadn't smacked him in the back with blobs of stinking, rotten, coagulated drilling mud they'd found by the pumps.

"Fuck you, white ass!" Aboobaker yelled, his hands grubbing for another round.

Logan reached for his cannon, cocked the valve, and blew them both back to the Bombay Teahouse. He was wheeling his bore toward the derrick in search of another victim when he saw Marshall storming up the catwalk, shouting angrily with each step. Every hose on location petered out.

"I want every one of you bastards up on the rig floor!" Marshall yelled. "Right now!"

Logan arrived, the last of the stragglers, and took his place next to Strong. Not an advantageous position, he thought too late. Strangely, they'd lined up expats and Indians, each to their race. Marshall looked from face to snickering face.

"Don't you people understand this well kicked this mornin'?" he said. "What are you thinkin', Strong! We can't have this kind of shit goin' on at a critical moment like this!"

"Uh," Strong muttered, actually looking a little ashamed, "we were just funnin', Marshall."

"I noticed." Marshall nodded his humorless head. "I'll teach you about funnin'. Y'all just stand where you are until we get this crew back under control." Logan knew what to expect. Threats of termination. Blue incident reports headed for their personnel files in Tulsa. Marshall turned. "Go ahead, Elvin."

Barnes jumped around the corner, a hose in his hand, grinning large. "Yeah, you sons of bitches!" he hollered. "It's our turn now!" He trained his stream on the Indians. Marshall, who selected the main fire hose, worked on Strong first, then Logan.

"This here's what you call executive privilege," Marshall said. It worked, for a while at least, until Rahiman broke ranks and dumped a bucket down the back of Marshall's pants. After that it was every *gondo* for himself, just as it had been before. The only difference between Indian and expat, as far as Logan could tell, was that Marshall, Strong, and Barnes would study the console gauges whenever they were close enough. The Indians didn't give a damn.

THIRTY-THREE

⬥⬥⬥

Logan, exhausted, sat next to Strong in the doghouse, their forearms resting across their knees. He looked at the Indians chatting quietly near the V-door. Every now and then one of them would look back at Logan and grin. They'd enjoyed this day as much as Logan had. He was looking forward to twelve hours off. He was so tired that all he had to do was close his eyes and he'd fall into a trance. Things looked kind of fuzzy in the last of the morning sun.

Strong should have been weary, too. Every twenty minutes or so he dragged himself out to his console, engaged the drawworks, and worked the drill string, just as he'd done during the water fights all morning. Logan had taken a turn or two at it when Strong was otherwise occupied hosing Indians across the floor. It had been some tour, and Logan was glad it was ending.

Strong rose, glanced at his watch, and drummed his knuckles on the toolbox. Where he got his restless energy Logan couldn't imagine. But it made him a pain in the ass to be around. Logan wanted to coast quietly to the end and here was Strong, itching for action. Logan could see it in the nervous pulse of his eyes.

"Another half hour to go," Strong said, slamming the shield on the geolograph chart. There had been no good reason to open it.

"Yep," Logan said. He wished Strong would sit down and shut up.

"The Indians had themselves a time this mornin', didn't they?"

"Yep."

"They look happy," he said, hanging once again from the I-beam rafters to stretch. "Too damn happy. I don't like it when roughnecks look happy. It's the sign of a shitty driller. Makes me feel like I ain't doin' my job."

"What do you want to do about it?"

"I guess we oughta scare the shit out of 'em."

"How?" Logan said, when he knew he should have asked "Why?"

"Let's make 'em think we're gonna dope 'em."

"No, Jamie," Logan moaned. "No...no...no..."

Strong pulled Logan from the bench. "C'mon. They're gettin' cocky. One more gag and we'll call it a day. It'll take us both."

"Jamie," Logan said, "don't do this. They're whipped. I'm whipped. I don't know why you aren't."

"Ah, c'mon, Doc. It's just a game to pass the time." Strong smiled. "It'll be a kick. Are you with me?"

Logan deliberated as long as he could. Strong raised his eyebrows. Logan was about to refuse when Strong spun him around and pushed him toward the door. They eased out of the doghouse together.

The Indians scattered at first sight of Strong, whose malicious grin forecasted his intentions. Putti was the only one who didn't run. Strong snatched him by the arm.

"What you doing?" Putti said.

"Remember Hofuf?" Strong wrestled Putti to the floor. "Ball-dopin' time."

The game began, although Logan didn't quite understand what part he was to play in it. The other roughnecks grabbed their fire hoses. Rahiman concentrated on Strong. Abdullah Larry blasted Logan in the face. While Logan shielded his eyes, Rahiman came up behind him and kicked him in the butt. After that, Logan no longer needed Strong's coercion. He wrestled Abdullah Larry's hose away from him and forced each loose roughneck back with a fierce blast. Strong lay spread-eagle on top of Putti, pressing him flat to the floor.

"Get the bucket, Doc," Strong said.

Logan grabbed the dented five-gallon tin of Jimmie Gray thread compound. All he had to do was dip the applicator and twirl the dope—sticky as molasses from the Saudi heat—in front of Putti's face. Just the sight of it would produce the desired effect. Putti's imagination would do the rest, and that would be the end of it. Before he could step toward Strong and Putti, however, Rahiman snatched the bucket away. Logan chased him, but he proved too quick. Logan bent over and put his hands on his knees to catch his breath.

Rahiman paused at the pipe rack. He swung his slight hips from side to side, pointed his rear end at Logan, and shook it. "You," he taunted, "too much whiskey. No goot."

Logan lunged at Rahiman. But he lost his footing and skidded across the rotary table on his stomach. Rahiman ran across his back and the chase resumed around the drill floor.

Strong fared no better. While he wrestled with Putti, Abdullah Larry calmly walked up behind him, latched his sizable arm around his neck, and raised him to his feet. Strong gasped for Logan, but there was little Logan could do. Rahiman had scaled the derrick ladder with the dope bucket. He yelled in Hindi to the roustabouts below as he climbed, stopping at the first girder to tie off the bucket with a piece of sash cord he had around his neck. Then he slid down a tong line cable next to the fire hose and promptly blasted the three bodies—one Anglo, two Indian—now staggering together around the drill floor.

"Let him go, number one asshole!" Rahiman said, stepping in closer with his hose. The force of the water indented Strong's forehead. He closed his eyes, looked away, and held on to what he had. "Doc!"

Logan could have sorted them all out if the roustabouts hadn't attacked. Two were dashing up the steps; two more were arriving on the elevator. Logan grabbed a free fire hose and forced the stair climbers back with a thick bead of water. They rolled end over end for the last ten rungs or so. Aboobaker and Razaki bolted out of the elevator and climbed yelling onto Strong's back. They had trouble finding a place.

After that, the fighting was hand to hand. Logan successfully eliminated the support fire of Rahiman, hosing him across the greasy metal floor and down the slide, where he landed sideways in the wet sand. Logan strafed the area around him until Rahiman was blinded, his body mired in a sloppy mess.

Confident that Rahiman could not return to the hostilities soon,

Logan dropped the hose and began yanking loosely clinging Indians from Strong's back. Once they were free, Logan dragged them to the slide and flung them down its length. They landed in a heap. Tired, sore, and entangled, they were slow to regroup. Rahiman shot angry glances toward the rig floor, turning away to rub the sand from his eyes. Strong held fast to Putti's bony frame. No sooner did he grab hold of one loose limb than another one broke free. Putti, knowing he was now alone, struggled with everything he had.

Strong pressed on. "Christ, Doc! I can't hold him! He's strong as hell!"

"Take him to the floor, Jamie! We'll get him there."

Strong fell on his knees and pulled the Indian down to his level. He weighed twice as much as Putti, which he used to his advantage by rolling on top. The terrified Indian began to scream.

"Hurry, Doc!" Strong hollered.

Logan started up the derrick ladder until he remembered there was a new dope can in the supply bin. He pulled up his hose and watered down any attempt by the routed to return. He pried open the can with his free hand. The Indians below divided their forces. Logan knew he couldn't possibly guard them all.

There wasn't much time. Once the can was open, Logan grabbed it and the matted brush that was always near the rotary. He dropped the hose and hurried back to Strong.

"C'mon, Doc. I can't hold him much longer."

Strong pinned the Indian with his legs while he began stripping Putti's trousers from his waist. Logan thought this was taking things a little too far. All they really had to do was show the Indians that they could do it if they wanted to. It seemed to Logan that Strong had forgotten his own intentions. Strong looked too determined.

Logan set the bucket down on the floor in front of Putti. The Indian's eyes widened. He found strength from somewhere, struggling more wildly than before, forcing Strong to use his free hand to restrain him. Soon enough, Putti kicked Strong square in the jaw with the heel of his boot.

"You're fixin' to get doped, you son of a bitch," Strong said between clenched teeth, fending off whichever of Putti's appendages came at him next. With some effort, Strong flipped him facedown, his nose smashed flat against the planks of the pipe rack.

"Fuck these job!" Putti screamed. "Fuck these job!" He swung, screamed, clawed, and gnashed as Strong yanked at the colored bathing suit he wore as an undergarment. The Indians even showered in them, Logan knew. Finally, Putti's dark buttocks lay bare in the sun. Strong slapped them as one does a calf before branding. He held Putti's head to the floor and threw his leg across the small of the Indian's back.

"There," Strong said, huffing. "Dope him good." He sat back and waited.

Logan wanted to get this thing over and done with. He daubed the brush into the mixture, twirled in its tin like margarine in a fresh plastic tub. All he intended to do was dangle it in front of Putti and then slap his bare ass. The debacle of Hofuf would be avenged.

"C'mon, Doc!" Strong cried. "I can't hold him all day."

Logan stood over the Indian, rotating the dope brush so that none would drip onto the floor. Putti's screaming had stopped. He just moaned, "Fuck these job," as he had all along. But now Logan saw tears streaming down his anguished face. They'd shamed him.

Logan thought about these people, these Indians, with whom he lived and worked. He thought about their shyness and quirks. They would travel three hundred yards across the heat of the desert to urinate in private, kneeling in the sand. Logan looked at Putti lying there on the floor, Strong on top of him, squirming to maintain control.

"Do it, Doc!"

Logan shook his head. How, he wondered, had he gotten himself in such a position? What kind of game caused such suffering?

The other Indians rounded the derrick leg ready to fight. They halted, aghast at the sight before them, and stayed there, watching as a herd of deer will do when one of their number falls to the wolf. Even Rahiman, seeing Putti's body stripped bare and the brush poised, ready to strike, stood trembling in angry acceptance. Logan looked at them all.

"What's the goddamn problem, Doc?" Strong snapped.

Logan exhaled a moment before he answered. He looked at the floor, Putti's skinny bare ass, the dope brush. A glob of pipe dope welled up on the end of the brush and dropped onto Strong's pants.

"That's enough," he said as quietly as the rig would allow. "Let him go."

"No way in hell. You dope him!"

"That's not what you said." Logan let the brush fall back into the bucket.

"I don't care what I said. He like to break my fuckin' nose. I'm gonna dope his ass for it."

"We can't," Logan said. "We just can't."

Strong reached for the brush. "I goddamn sure can!"

Logan nudged the tin with his toe just out of Strong's reach. "Just let him go, Jamie. It's ain't funny to him. He's cryin', man."

Putti began struggling again in the lull. Strong dragged him by the ankles toward the bucket.

"You're gonna get doped, boy," Strong said. "One way or another."

Logan knew Strong as a man who did what he said, regardless of the cost. Maybe he'd come up short today. The Indians watched, their faces grim. There was nothing to do but let events run their course. Strong reached the brush and held it over Putti's bare ass.

I don't think so, Logan thought. As Strong lowered the brush, Logan grabbed his wrist. He twisted the handle from Strong's grasp and tossed the brush over the side to the dunes below. "You don't want to do that, Jamie," Logan said. "Just let him go and forget about it."

Strong, exhausted and cursing, lay back on the floor. Putti rolled away, catching his breath, hiccuping from his tears. He rose to his feet and pulled up his bathing suit and khaki trousers. Then he ran across the floor, whimpering. He couldn't look at anyone. Logan was devastated to see Putti—the oldest, wisest, and most reserved of them all, the one closest to Logan save Abdullah—shamed in such a disgraceful way. And he had taken a part in it, in the very same way as when Abdullah had fallen the day before. He'd stopped it, true, but he'd stopped it too late. The damage was done. He closed his eyes and shook his head, disgusted with himself.

The other Indians watched Putti pass, then turned to Logan, nodding in silence. They leered at Strong. Strong ran his fingers through his black curls and wiped the sweat from his forehead. "What the hell was that all about? I don't know what's goin' on out here anymore!"

"You, Strong," Rahiman growled, "crazy."

Strong's face flushed. He glared at Logan, eyes narrowed to angry slits.

Logan tried to think of something to say. Nothing would make any difference. "I'm sorry, Jamie. We," he said, letting Strong know that he intended to share the blame, "were in the wrong. They don't think of it like we do. We should've known better."

Strong's face boiled. Logan stood by him and said nothing more. But he hoped he could get Strong off the floor and back into normal operation. He had his books to fill out yet. That was something he could do alone. The Indians stood as if they might pounce. Logan held out his open palm, a gesture of peace. "It's all right, boys," he said. "Everybody's okay."

In a day or so all would be forgotten and forgiven. It usually was. Everyone was exhausted and grouchy, the easiest time to get crossways with each other. The thing to do was separate the crew, give the Indians and Strong a little room, allow the tension time to subside. He needed to help Strong save face, remind him that they'd both made the decision to tease Putti with the dope, and then get Strong to see how wrong it was. Strong would listen to reason once he got past his rage. First Logan would help Strong. Then he'd go and see about Putti. He knew he could heal the crew. He'd defused dozens of volatile family situations as a kid. He knew he had the knack. He could handle this one if he acted quickly.

He leaned over to help Strong up. He offered his hand, but Strong wouldn't take it. "C'mon, Jamie," Logan said. "Why don't you tend to the drilling report?"

Strong sat still, his face twisted in anger. Logan leaned in closer. "C'mon," he said. Strong pushed him away. When Logan put out his hand once more, Strong reared back and swept his leg across the floor. His boot struck hard against the side of Logan's bad knee.

Logan shrieked in pain. His leg buckled. He collapsed, drawing his leg to his chest. The Indians stood their ground and watched him fall. He closed his eyes and gritted his teeth. The pain was so fierce it made him nauseous. When he opened his eyes again, he saw Strong. Strong's face had gone pale, just as it had in the North Sea years ago.

Logan had been hurt plenty of times before. But this time the pain was different, deeper. It rocked him. Its only equivalent was the time he'd come to blows with his father. He had caught him with his little sister up against the kitchen wall. He was too late for that one, too. Logan could tell he'd already slapped her. She had her hands around her face to protect herself. But Logan decided then and there that it wouldn't happen again. He snapped a broom handle across his father's back. When his father came at him in a rage, he told his sister to run. With one swipe of his arm, Logan's father sent him tumbling into the dinette set. His father kicked him in the stomach as he lay on the floor. Then he stood with his full weight on Logan's knee until Logan's sobs returned him to his senses. The pain he felt now was like that. The kind that comes out of nowhere from someone close. *All right,* Logan thought. *All right.*

"Doc, I'm sorry, man!" Strong said, scrambling to his knees. His eyes were wild. "Are you okay?"

He crawled across the greasy floor to Logan's side. Logan, writhing in pain, waited for him to come. When he was close enough, Logan grabbed Strong's collar and cocked his arm for a decisive punch.

"You stupid son of a bitch," Logan said. Strong looked dumbstruck. Logan could see that his words had crushed Strong more than any gesture. Had it not been for his blank expression, Logan would have broken his nose. He had fought many times over things more senseless than this, but he could not bring himself to hit his friend. Never a friend. He released his grip as the pain overwhelmed him again.

Strong reached under his arms to pull him to his feet, but Logan pushed him away, lightly boxing his ears.

"Let me be, you dumb bastard," he said, his whole leg numb and throbbing. The knee itself burned. "I'll go myself."

Strong stepped back, looking confused. It was the first time Logan had ever seen panic on his face. Strong turned to the Indians, who continued to stare at him coldly.

"Aboobaker! Go to camp and get Pix!"

Aboobaker did not answer.

"Now, goddamn it! Can't you see what's happened?"

The Indian did not respond. Strong, infuriated, reared back his arm to slap him. The Indians moved in tighter, seeking force in numbers. This time they seemed prepared to go as far as Strong pushed them. He would make his move, then they, together, would make the next. Strong hesitated.

Logan managed to stand on his one good leg. He hopped over to stop Strong before it was too late.

"Don't make it any worse," he said, tugging at his arm.

Strong looked at Logan. The light drained from his eyes. His arm fell to his side.

"It's all right, ain't it, Doc?" He seemed relieved to see Logan standing.

Aboobaker pushed past Strong, ducking his head under Logan's shoulder. Together they moved slowly toward the elevator. Logan looked back at Strong, who was still waiting for his answer. Still waiting for his vindication, for relief.

"No," Logan said. "It's not. Not this time." He hobbled past the Indians onto the elevator. His knee couldn't bear any weight at all. The motor engaged and the car began to descend. He heard Strong's heavy boots cross the floor.

"I'm sorry, Doc!" he shouted. "I didn't mean it. We're still a team!"

"I'm twistin' off," Logan answered. "I've had enough."

"Ah, c'mon!" Strong groaned, and Logan heard the despair in his voice. "It ain't that bad! You know how I am. Sometimes I don't think! I can't help it!"

"It's not you," Logan said. "And it's not the leg. I've just had enough."

The elevator stopped. Logan limped across the thick sand and hopped up on the skids. His knee throbbed with a pulsing pain. He thought he might vomit.

"Doc!" Strong pleaded. "Just give me another chance! I'll make it right."

Logan closed his eyes, sighing, before he turned back to Strong. "You can't, Jamie. I gotta go."

Logan, with Aboobaker's assistance, resumed his course.

"Paining knee, no, Doc?" the Indian said.

"Paining, yes. Like a son of a bitch."

"Very problem, Strong."

"Not anymore." Logan heard the sound of footsteps in the sand behind them. Razaki and Abdullah Larry trotted up, each wrapping an arm around Logan's shoulders. The four of them hobbled toward the pusher's shack. Barnes, who must have seen them coming, stepped out of his office.

"What happened to you?"

"Worm bite," Logan said, oil field parlance for an accident

caused by a crewman who did not know any better. Enough said, he thought. "I need the driver."

Barnes ordered Kashian, the rig clerk, to go find Abraham. Kashian buckled the chin strap under his silly plastic helmet and went out to look for his man. Barnes motioned for the Indians to bring Logan inside. Logan took out his Old Timer pocketknife, the one he'd carried since his first days as a roughneck, and slit his pants leg up the sides. He wanted to get a look at his knee. Red on the sides, purple behind, it was already swollen to twice its size.

"Christ!" Barnes said. "You busted yourself up pretty good, Doc! What the hell happened?"

"I already told you." Logan bummed a smoke from Barnes and lit it. He hated cigarettes, but he needed something to do while he waited for Abraham. He didn't want to talk to anybody. He settled into the swivel chair and tried to relax. The knee wouldn't have it. It screamed with every beat of his heart.

Barnes studied his face. "You gonna be all right?"

"Not really," he said, and exhaled.

The phone rang. Barnes wheeled his office chair around and answered it.

"Momentum 127," he said. "Who? You're kiddin'. Okay, ma'am. It just so happens he's sittin' right here."

He handed the receiver to Logan. "It's your mom," he said with a grin. "Probably wants to know if you're eatin' right."

Logan rolled his eyes. In four years overseas she'd never called. She telexed on his birthdays and Christmas. They'd spoken a time or two on days off and they never said much then. Whatever was on her mind, Logan knew it couldn't be good news. "Hello?" he said.

"Logan, honey? This is your mother. I'm sorry to bother you. I hope it's not a bad time."

"No, Mom. Everything's fine. How did you get this number?"

"I phoned Tulsa, and they got me in touch with that nice man in Dhahran."

Logan wondered what nice man that could be. "What's up?"

"Well, I got a call from Caitlin, son. She was in tears. Says you got the wrong idea when you called the other night. It's all a big misunderstanding between you two, I think. You know she's in a study group with that Bellmeade boy. It was her turn to host."

Host, he thought. That was a funny way to put it. "I don't care about the study group. It's the subject I've got a problem with."

"Law?"

"Anatomy."

Barnes smiled. Anybody else would have got up and left. But Barnes couldn't stand missing it.

"Logan!" It was the first time in years he'd heard anger in her voice. She seldom risked it in her brief conversations with him. "This isn't the time for jokes. You know that girl loves you. She's been beside herself for a week. If you'd talked to her, you'd know she didn't ask that man to stay. They'd all gone. She went into the shower, and he invited himself back in. He caused this trouble. Not Caitlin."

Logan had never considered that Caitlin might be innocent. He knew Bellmeade was not. He'd do anything to derail this marriage. Logan tried to open his mind to the possibilities, but he couldn't override his nagging sense of doubt and his instinct for betrayal. The pieces fit. If it smells like a rat, it's probably a rat.

"There's not much time to smooth things over," his mother said. "She's already sent out the invitations and, by the way, they look lovely. You need to call Caitlin today and work this out."

"Look, Mom," Logan said, drawing on the cigarette. "I can't worry about this right now."

"When, then? The wedding's in three weeks!"

Why hadn't Caitlin canceled? He couldn't understand it. Did she really think he would go through with it now? "Did she tell you that?"

"She knows y'all will get it worked out, Logan. Nothing's wrong. Y'all just need to talk. I'm trying to get you to understand that. You shouldn't screw this up. She's a nice girl. She's good for you."

Like an IRS audit or hemorrhoids, he thought. "Look, Mom," he said. "There's not gonna be any wedding. Caitlin knows that. You're probably disappointed to hear this, but I plan to move out when I get home. I'm not sure what happened and I don't care. She shouldn't have even been around that son of a bitch in the first place. I saw this coming. Now it's her word against his, and I guess I'm not a very trusting person. I can't help that. And I'm not about to marry someone I can't trust. I've seen a lifetime of that, if you know what I mean."

"Oh," his mother said. She was silent.

"This is a bad time to talk about this stuff. I'm extremely busy right now. Believe it or not, I've got other problems to deal with before I get to this one."

"None of which are more important than your future, Logan."

"I know. And I appreciate you callin'—more or less. Please tell Caitlin what I've said. She'll understand."

"That's not my place. You'll have to take care of that yourself."

Logan's stomach twisted at the thought of hearing Caitlin's voice. "I can't do it from here, Mom," he said. "Will you just tell her to postpone the wedding for me? That's all I'm askin'. I'll sort out the rest when I get home."

"No, Logan," she said. "You do it and you do it today."

"Fine," he said. "I'll telex her from camp."

She hesitated. "You're an idiot, Logan. A damn fool. I wish you'd think this through before you hurt her. I hope you will. But whatever happens, I love you. And I'm here if you need me."

"Thanks, Mom. I guess," he said, looking at Barnes. Barnes puckered his lips. "I've gotta go."

"Good-bye, Logan."

Logan handed the phone back to Barnes.

"Rough trip, huh?" Barnes said.

"Yep," Logan said. He stared angrily at Barnes. "Is there anything about my personal life you want to know? Anything at all? I feel a deep need to be open with you."

"I think I about got the gist of it." Barnes handed him Momentum's accident forms, then pointed out the window. "Your ride's waitin'."

THIRTY-FOUR

DAY TWENTY-THREE

Logan lay alone in his shack, his knee propped up on his Arabian rug. Tate-Pixilate had examined his leg, for what little that was worth, and strongly suggested he seek treatment at King's Hospital in Dhahran. But he had been there before with a broken rib, a lengthy, bizarre, and ultimately frustrating experience, and he didn't see much use in going again. He'd felt whatever ligaments and cartilage he still had attached after the original knee injury tear loose from the joint. He needed surgery, and he opted to have it done at home. They couldn't book him on an early flight without routing him through London, and he was concerned about managing the rail connection between Gatwick and Heathrow. That left him with no choice but to load himself up with Vicodin and wait out the five days he had left. Thank you, Jamie Strong. If he could coax a little Percodan from Pix for the direct flight to Houston, he'd get home to his own orthopedist soon enough.

Now he lay there, his body relaxed but his head buzzing from the codeine, the room dark save the funnel of harsh light from his reading lamp. He felt nothing of his swollen knee other than its obvious bulk. He'd gone through all three of his books; Strong had provided him with plenty of free time. Desperate to read, he'd borrowed one of Pix's British spy novels. He had no interest in the genre and his own history kept creeping into his thoughts. He persevered anyway.

When he couldn't remember who was betraying whom let alone why, he tossed the book aside. He thought of his own betrayals, where he was, how he'd gotten there. The mistakes he'd made and what had come of them. It all led directly to Jamie Strong.

Logan had arrived on the Ninian Central in January of 1981. It was the largest and most forbidding structure in the British sector of the North Sea: twin Momentum standard derricks, two massive cranes, four flare booms puffing fire like dragons—all balanced on one perforated cement leg sixty miles northeast of Unst, the northernmost of the Shetland Isles.

Logan had just turned twenty-three when he first set foot on the Ninian, and Strong was four years older. Strong, the senior AD, had worked land rigs in the overthrust plays of Wyoming, Montana, and Colorado. He'd drawn a driller's pay before, so he was usually the likely choice to relieve their driller on the brake.

Logan was still an apprentice then, a green hand fumbling under those heavy gray skies, and daunted by the mass of that operation. Each derrick was scheduled to drill twenty-four wells, three hundred men buzzing about like bees in a cold metal hive. Logan was more than willing to defer to Strong, who had nine years total in the patch. Strong was the same back then—confident, capable, ambitious. And aggressive. Shouldn't leave that out, Logan thought. But there was a balance to the man in those days, or so he had believed.

Their relationship began as student and teacher. Logan hadn't been on the platform twenty minutes before he realized he couldn't do what Momentum expected of him. Everything on the Ninian seemed alien to him. It was impossible to trace pipelines between the rig floor, mud pumps, and two separate sealed pits. An AD just had to know which valve connected what—and there were dozens. And the mud pumps of German manufacture were totally beyond Logan's scope. He couldn't understand the thick Aberdeen and Glasgow accents of his Scottish crewmen, and the English he just plain didn't trust: on his very first day they'd sent him to places that didn't exist. He often got lost just looking for parts he didn't know how to replace anyway. His youth was also a liability. Logan was two years younger than the youngest roustabout, and the drill crews treated him like some snot-nosed kid wearing knickers and a beanie. It was easy to fail in the North Sea. Of the three new expats Momentum shipped in with Logan, two washed out within a week.

Strong seemed to sense his uncertainty right away and took him under his wing. Whenever Logan made the wormiest mistake—like filling the reserve system until its fluids ran out the vents, pumping barite over the side rather than into the bulk tank, or dropping a one-ton nipple flange onto the spider decks—Strong was there to help him clean up the mess. He never bitched about the added burden. He coached. Through Strong's efforts, Logan learned. Without Strong, Logan knew he never would have made it on the Ninian Central. This kindness and patience was the beginning of their friendship. Logan's trust in him was absolute.

They traveled together, ingeniously dodging Momentum's mandatory seminars on their off time, steering instead for Austria or Spain. They were inseparable for the better part of ten restless months, which solidified their bond. Then Strong married and Logan traveled alone or with vagabond South Africans and Australians who, like Logan, sought the sun.

Strong changed after his marriage, becoming more abrasive and taciturn. Logan overlooked it and easily mediated the inevitable disputes between Strong and his crew. But as the months wore on, Strong got worse.

He became downright militant on one particular evening in 1982. It was December. Daylight lasted for maybe six hours. Logan was pulling his weight and more by then. He'd drilled ten directional holes from start to finish. He understood and anticipated every coming phase of the operation. He'd learned to balance the pressures from Momentum and his surly crew. He'd even garnished his face with a beard to look older. He knew every custom, dictum, and nuance of the Ninian. And although he still feared the North Sea, he had learned to love it. Strong saw no reason to make similar adjustments. Entering his third winter of perpetual night, searing winds, and sudden storms, Strong remained steadfastly Strong.

That evening he was at first withdrawn, speaking to no one. He and Logan had dressed for work side by side in the locker room, usually a time for idle chatter, but Strong seemed particularly glum. Logan left him alone, but before he'd laced up his boots, he saw Strong wipe a single tear from his chin. They'd had mail call that day. Logan's slot was empty, but he'd noticed a letter, an attorney's office as the return address, waiting for Strong. Whatever it was, Logan thought, it must have gouged his coarse hide deeply.

They were tripping pipe out of an eighteen-thousand-foot

directional well. It had started slow and gotten slower. With Devine, the driller, off to a warm galley for his tea, Strong and Logan faced a disgruntled crew. Sleet followed snow, and bits of ice dangled like crystal daggers on the derrick girths and angled braces. The wind howled above the whitecapped sea. The Ninian rocked with the ocean's swells. The roughnecks, bundled in their Norwegian thermal underwear and Momentum parkas, had to kick through drifts of snow on the floor to find a pipe wrench or a set of drill collar slips. But the blocks ran on tracks to defeat the winter wind, and Momentum shut down for gales only. Bitterly cold, the crewmen were miserable in their work. Logan relieved them around the rotary so they could take turns warming their hands. Strong, switching clutches and brake in a heated Plexiglas doghouse, never skipped a beat.

At his best Strong had never mixed well with the British crews. To his way of thinking, they were better at bitching than tripping pipe. In foul weather Logan figured they had just cause. Strong didn't see it that way. The more they dawdled, the quicker he snatched their tong lines and the slower he picked up the string to lessen their burden with the slips. Gibes went back and forth between the driller's console and the rotary table.

Finally one of the Scots, the lead tongsman, an ex-fisherman named Murray McHendricks, had had enough. He shut down and confronted Strong about his attitude. And this sort of treatment, the Aberdonian concluded, from an AD! Strong told the Scot in no uncertain terms that he was to resume his place at the rotary and like it, and the trip went on, the next stand broken slower than the one before. Strong marked the widening lines on the geolograph with angry dissatisfaction. He was bucking for a driller's job.

"Why don't you let me run a few?" Logan said. "Get yourself a smoke and a cup of coffee."

"I got it," Strong snapped, his narrow stare focused on the crew. Logan stepped aside. He could see by the way he'd set his jaw that Strong had come to some sort of decision.

Strong didn't set out to hurt anybody. Logan was sure of that. Often drillers used their clutches and levers to make their point. Roughnecks generally got the idea. Logan certainly had, back in his rebellious days. Under a derrick, a crew was at the mercy of the driller's whim—especially so in a country suffering a twenty percent unemployment rate. However warranted, it was stupid to provoke him.

But this British crew seemed oblivious to reason. The fact was, Strong was a particularly disliked American in a place where Americans weren't liked. Strong's ambition, brawn, booming voice, and go-get-'em attitude undermined his best intentions. The Brits saw in Strong everything they detested in their uncouth, redneck American employers. In America, to be considered a cowboy might, depending on the circumstances, instill a sense of individualistic pride. To the British, it meant charlatan, chancer, or fool. They nicknamed Strong the Cowboy, and Strong knew it had nothing to do with his Montana roots. To make matters worse, Strong was working another man's crew, and the roughnecks never missed an opportunity to let him know they didn't have to put up with his crap. Logan watched the muscles in Strong's jaw quiver with each insult, each small act of disrespect.

They'd just broken a connection. The roughnecks stepped in to release each other's tongs. Logan saw Strong's hand move to the rotary rheostat a little earlier than normal. Before the tongs were released, Strong jerked his wrist far beyond what was needed to spin out the threads. The motor engaged.

The tong arms, five feet of solid iron, torqued violently with the rotary. The roughnecks never had a chance. Logan had learned to stiff-arm his tongs, so if they came at him he moved with them. The Brits did no such thing. The tongs' arc leveled them, cold iron against muscle and bone, knocking their bodies to the icy floor, where they collapsed in pain.

"What did you do that for?" Logan growled. But Strong didn't say anything and Logan assumed he didn't really have an answer. A mean stunt in itself, Logan saw that it was actually much worse. Not one of the four crewmen rose to his feet. The Scot shrieked loud enough to raise the hair on Logan's neck. Blood leaked through McHendricks's Momentum coveralls, and the tip of his thighbone, shattered like a green twig, poked through the fabric. Warm blood speckled drifts of snow.

Logan ripped the canister of nitrous oxide from the doghouse and strapped the mask to the Scot's screaming face. When the gas had soothed McHendricks, Logan tore his woolen scarf from his neck and cinched a tourniquet just above the wound. Strong stood

frozen at the brake, never moving save the trembling of his fingertips.

"Call the medics, Jamie!" Logan yelled. Still Strong did
nothing. Logan snatched the intercom and called them himself.
With the medics came the Momentum brass and the OIM, the offshore installation manager.

Logan helped carry the wounded to the chopper pad. Momentum
shipped all four to Lerwick for treatment, but not before they had
told the OIM their version of the incident. The OIM informed
Momentum that he intended to pursue a full inquiry. Strong, the
alleged perpetrator, and Logan, the only real witness, would be con-
fined to quarters until the kangaroo court the following day. Logan
knew his friend Strong would never keep his job.

Sequestered, Logan had lain in his bunk for the rest of that aborted
shift, reading, listening to the radio piped into his carpeted suite,
swaying with the concrete platform in the winter wind.

He was about to doze off when he heard a commotion overhead. He was aghast when the ceiling tile above him disappeared
and the hole filled with Strong's head.

"Good," Strong said. "I finally got the right place."

"What are you doing?" Logan said, unable to mask his irritation.

"We need to talk."

Logan shook his head. "No we don't. How'd you get up there
anyway?"

"I was here when we put this place together. I know my way
around. I guess I miscounted the rooms. Didn't you use to bunk
two doors down?"

"I switched after Williams went home." Strong's head receded,
replaced by his boots as he descended from the ceiling. "Don't do
it," Logan said. "Go back the way you came."

Strong bounced off the springs, brushing his boot prints from
Logan's blanket. He crammed his flashlight into his hip pocket.
"Sorry," he said. He plunked himself down in Logan's lone armchair with the obvious intent of staying for the long haul. Logan
pinched the bridge of his nose and sighed.

"Just wanted you to hear my side," Strong said. He studied Logan's face. He couldn't have found it encouraging. "Them tongs didn't release like they should've. I figure the cold had somethin' to do with it. Worn dies, maybe. I've seen it happen just like that before. Bad luck's all we're lookin' at here."

Logan leaned back on his pillow, his fingers meshed behind his head. He never figured Strong for a weasel. "If that's all you've got to say, you best be leavin'. Me and you got nothing to talk about. Shimmy on back through your hole and be quiet about it. I don't want my ass in another crack because you can't obey orders."

Strong lowered his head. "All right," he said, his voice solemn. "I'll tell it to you straight. I owe you that."

"I don't want to hear it," Logan said. "We'll tell what we know to the OIM tomorrow."

If Strong heard Logan, if he understood his intent, he gave no sign. "Last time off my wife left me for some other guy," he said. "I guess I should've seen it comin'. Things weren't goin' too good anyway."

He braced his forearms across his knees. Logan watched his Adam's apple bobble. "She didn't take all my money or anythin' like that. She just took enough to get by. But what hurts is that she took my little baby girl and moved out of state. I'm torn up about it, Doc."

"That's rough," Logan said. Strong never talked much about his personal life. Logan never guessed he had one. But it came as no surprise that the marriage was troubled. The shocker was the look of anguish in Strong's face. In the wide range of emotions inspired in him by Jamie Strong, Logan never thought he would arrive at pity.

"I'd do anything to get them back," Strong said. "She won't call me. I don't even know where she is. I went up to see her mother myself, try to get things back on track. She took her side. I didn't know where else to go. I ran out of time. I had to leave things as they were and come on back to work."

He lit a cigarette and leaned back in Logan's chair. "Then I got this letter from her lawyer. She's filed for divorce. She wants full custody over my daughter." His speech grew thicker as he started to choke. "Hell, Doc, it just about broke my heart. And then them roughnecks started in with their flack. It just got to me."

"I understand," Logan said. "I know you meant to brush 'em back a little, but it didn't turn out like that. They're hurt bad. You saw yourself."

Strong shook his head. Logan wagered he still heard the screams. That sort of thing stuck with you. It had with him.

"You should've talked to me about your problems," Logan said. "I could've picked up your slack. I owed you that. And you damn sure should've let me run the rig. As it is, you're in a hell of a mess."

"Well, I gotta get out," Strong said. "I can't afford to lose this job. I need the money for lawyers and to settle with my wife. Looks like I've got child support to pay."

Logan sat up in his bunk. "Look, why not tell 'em what you've told me? They'll go easier on you."

"They run drillers off for bumping the blocks against the crown around here," Strong said. "What chance have I got?"

"None here. But you'll get out clean. You've done a good job. Take a leave of absence and then ask for a transfer."

"I tried that already," Strong said. "I was hopin' to get a twenty-eight-day rotation in some other division. Thought it might smooth out the trouble at home. Momentum's got nothin' overseas. Saudi Arabia's gonna open up in a few months. I've got a shot there. Until then, I've got to stick it out here."

"I don't think you can," Logan said. He'd seen the OIM's face when he interviewed the injured. The inquiry was a formality.

Strong's tone shifted. "What's done is done. It's my fault. I admit it. But those men'll be cared for, paid in full. I can guarantee you that them sorry bastards would rather lay up in a warm hospital bed than freeze their butts off out here. How does it make things any better if I get run off? I've got to live with what I did. I've never hurt anybody before. I never will again. I want the chance to prove it. Momentum won't lift a finger to help me." He fixed his stare on Logan. "Only you can do that."

Logan stroked his beard. "We don't know what's gonna happen."

"I know. And so do you. Me and you's always been close, Doc. I helped you and I was glad to do it. Now I'm askin' you, as a friend, to help me. I'll make it right. I swear it."

"What do you want me to do?" Logan said. "You want me to go in there and lie for you?"

"I didn't put it quite like that."

"You didn't have to." Logan ground his fingertips into the corner of his eye. His windburned cheeks felt hot. "You're puttin' me in a bad way here," he said. "A favor's one thing, but this is somethin' else. McHendricks is hurt bad, and there's a lot of people that're pissed off about it."

"But they don't know what happened," Strong said. "You're the only witness."

"I know what I saw," Logan said.

Strong worked his tongue across his teeth, then his gaze met Logan's. "Am I good at my job?"

"Yeah. You are."

"Then help me keep it. I'm beggin' you, Doc. Are things gonna be any better if they send some worm to take my place? You've seen these bozos they're sendin' out here. Me at my worst is still better than any of them. I'll make up for my mistake. All I'm askin' for is another chance."

"You're askin' the wrong person."

"I don't see it that way," Strong said. "Just do what you can, Doc. That's all I'm sayin' here. And no matter what happens, we're still friends."

Logan moved aside so Strong could exit through the ceiling. Instead he headed for the door. "No, Strong," Logan hissed. "The way you came."

"It's late," he said. "There ain't nobody movin' at this hour. Besides, my legs are crampin'."

He walked straight out the door. Mickey Flinn, the Irish roustabout pusher, happened to be passing by. He stopped dead in his tracks. Looked at Strong. Looked at Logan.

"Beat it," Strong said. Flinn walked on, but Logan knew he couldn't have had worse luck. Flinn was a terrible gossip. Not five minutes would pass before the Irishman was whispering in someone's ear. No telling how far it would go. Logan spent those long hours weighing his dilemma and listening to the storm outside. It never broke.

By dawn he knew what he had to do.

Around ten the next morning, the company liaison knocked at Logan's door. He escorted Logan to the main office where he was announced to the Ninian OIM, the Momentum drilling manager, and a uniformed representative of the labor board or some arm of law enforcement, Logan didn't really know for sure. But he knew now that Strong had much more at stake than his job. One glance at the handcuffs attached to the guy's belt and Logan changed his mind.

He faced the three men across a desk. It was as cold in that cramped room as on the drill floor. He'd visited before with the OIM, an ex-naval officer. He was a good and personable man. Logan had never spoken to the Momentum manager on his short visits to the platform, and the cop had no air of humor about him. He sat grim and still, his pencil poised above his pad.

The OIM handled the interview. Damn if he didn't begin by swearing Logan in. He asked Logan to state his full name, home address, Social Security number, birthdate. They asked about his education, seemed astonished that he held a college degree. They were interested in his oil field experience, his current position with Momentum and how long he'd held it. The cop never stopped writing.

"At this point," the OIM said, "we'd like to commend you for your actions and first aid. By all accounts you conducted yourself admirably throughout this incident. Well done."

"Thank you," Logan said. "Momentum trains us to do so." He hoped that answer would please the division manager. He looked like he needed something to be happy about.

"Very well," the OIM said. "And now let's get to the specifics of the accident."

"It happened quickly." The words just gushed out of Logan on his cue, and they weren't the ones he'd rehearsed. "We were tripping pipe, pulling out of the hole. Everything had iced over. The driller was away, and Jamie Strong relieved him."

"Is Mr. Strong, in your view, competent to command the rig?" the OIM said.

"Without a doubt," Logan said.

"Please go on."

Logan crossed his knee over his leg, trying to look comfortable when he was anything but. "At any rate, the rotary table spins to unscrew the pipe. When it did, the tongs failed to release their grip.

We call it backbiting. They swept the floor and injured the crewmen."

"Had they backbit before?"

"It happens a lot back home," Logan said.

"More specifically, has it happened here?"

"No," Logan said. "Not that I've seen."

"What caused it?"

"I don't know."

The OIM looked at the officer. The officer glanced back at him, then turned back to Logan. They weren't buying it. Logan focused on deep breaths. "Was Mr. Strong arguing with his crew?" the OIM asked.

"I wouldn't say arguing. The roughnecks were grumbling, as roughnecks often do. It's hard work. The weather was bad. They weren't happy."

"Were they referring to Mr. Strong in a derogatory manner?"

"I'm sorry. I don't understand."

"Were they calling Mr. Strong," he checked his notes, "cowboy, Jethro Bodine, wanker, that sort of thing."

Logan cleared his throat. "I believe they were doing that, yes sir."

"And what was his response?"

"None that I noticed."

The OIM rubbed his palms together, slightly cocking his head. The Momentum manager stared straight ahead at Logan as if he had blinders on. "Mr. Strong doesn't take offense at unusually derogatory names?"

"There's nothing unusual about that. In our line of work, everyone refers to everyone else in unflattering terms. Mr. Strong's quite used to it, I'm sure." Logan knew they'd believe it. Momentum workers were at the bottom of a long chain of technicians, production staff, riggers, mechanics, electricians, computer nerds, engineers, and pilots. The clean seldom mixed with the dirty. Only Momentum hands entered the galley in their filthy clothes. Logan sensed the contempt in the cool stares of the skilled tradesmen. It would come as no surprise that the wretched often turned on each other.

"Is it your testimony here today then that all of this was an accident?"

"I'm afraid so," he said. Afraid was the correct word.

The OIM swung his head back toward the officer, who made no response, and sorted through his documents before he looked up at Logan. "Do you understand, Mr. Wilson," he said, "that the man with the compound fracture will require a number of surgical procedures? That he faces at least six months of rehabilitation before he returns to work? If he returns at all, that is." He held up three or four papers stapled together. "The doctor says it's quite possible he faces some degree of permanent disability." The report fell from his fingers. "Is that all quite clear to you, Mr. Wilson?" The room fell silent.

"Yes, sir," Logan said, looking the OIM in the eye. There was no use in trying the Momentum manager. He'd come up the ranks from the field. He would know better. Only overly worn tongs backbit, and Momentum's were brand new. Logan took his chances with the OIM.

"So what we're asking you, Mr. Wilson," the OIM said, looking down his long nose, "is whether or not it was an accidental or intentional act. That's the issue here."

"It was definitely an accident," Logan said, his arms crossed. "Certainly avoidable, but an accident nonetheless. There's no way that driller intended to hurt those men. No way in hell."

The last was the only true statement in Logan's testimony. He could look his manager in the eye with this one. A good place to end, Logan thought. No such luck.

"How was it avoidable?"

"By stiff-arming the tongs. When they move, you move. I've told those men time and time again. It would have helped if the driller had moved slower with his controls. But he's under pressure to perform."

"I see." The OIM coughed into his fist. "Would it surprise you to know that we have conflicting testimony?"

"In what regard?" Logan said.

"About most of what you're saying, I'm afraid."

Logan noticed he was gripping his shirt. He let go. "You'll have to be more specific."

"To begin with, no one else believes it was accidental in the least. No one else believes the tongs failed. The consensus is that they weren't given time to release them. Furthermore, they say there was a bitter argument going back and forth among the crew, and this was the way Mr. Strong chose to end it." He leaned back in his chair, flipping the tip of his nose with his index finger. "How do you respond?"

"Mr. Strong's not popular with his crew," Logan said. "I'm sure the others believe he meant to shatter Mr. McHendricks's leg. I don't." For the first time, Logan leaned forward in his chair. "That's what you're asking me, isn't it?"

"Yes, it is. And I likewise understand that you fare far better than Mr. Strong. You are considered a favorite among the expatriates. You've earned your crew's trust. They thought you would see things as they did. That's why I'm puzzled that your recollection is, well, inconsistent with theirs."

Logan swallowed hard. "Listen. I care about those men. I consider them friends. I'm not happy about what happened to them. I understand their anger and Strong makes an easy target. But I've got a duty to be objective here. I'm the only man on that drill floor who observed Mr. Strong's actions. I saw every move he made. There's no way what he did was intentional. That's all I can tell you."

The OIM studied him. The cop stopped writing for once and stared, too. The division manager never blinked. Neither did Logan. He heard the seconds ticking on one of their wristwatches, the subtle squeal as they shifted in their chairs.

"Very well," the OIM finally said, shoving his file aside. "Noted. We'll prepare your statement for your signature. For now, you're dismissed."

Logan walked out of the room and let the door swing shut behind him. Case closed.

Momentum shut down operations while they reorganized the crews. Logan stayed alone for the balance of that day. He dealt with his guilt. He felt he'd opted for the greater good, but the process dimmed him. Why should a fifth man suffer because four had? Strong belonged in therapy, not a prison cell. Logan had made his decision and he intended to stick by it. What choice did he have now?

The division manager left that same afternoon, but not before he received the crew's petition demanding the termination of Jamie Strong. Someone had slid a copy under Logan's door. It said that they refused to work with Strong aboard the Ninian. Why Logan's name wasn't on it, he had no idea. But Strong was on a chopper for Unst before the sun set. They never spoke.

Logan reported to the drill floor at six the next morning. His crew was cool to him, as he had expected. Even the expatriates had little to say to him. But it wasn't until teatime that he felt the weight of his decision.

Both rig crews shared the tearoom. It was Logan's favorite place on the rig. It had the atmosphere of a lively pub. Something was always going on. There was a bulletin board for company memos, safety slogans, and the like. These rarely lasted. What Logan saw instead were cartoons and silly photos ridiculing crewmen. His favorites were the poems. They'd ream some poor bastard for slack, thrift, drunkenness, or impotence. Regardless of how they started and how low they went, they usually ended the same way: "His chatter is a pack of lies./ He'll steal the pennies from dead men's eyes."

Logan heard them going on in there. There wasn't the usual laughter. It had the feel of a conspiracy. When he opened the door, it all stopped. Twenty pairs of eyes fixed on him. Logan could hear the wind blow against the platform's outer walls. Drops of condensation fell from the ceiling to the metal floor.

"Morning, boys," he said. He moved toward the kettle and grabbed a bag of Earl Grey. When it was clear he intended to sit with them, they spread out, leaving no place. Logan turned an empty bucket upside down and sat on it.

"You've got your bloody nerve comin' in 'ere," Coleman said. He was cutting a piece of twist, jet-black tobacco used by British coal miners. Coleman had once been one. Logan wished like hell the son of a bitch was in some deep hole today. The only men bigger and uglier than Coleman were the two roughnecks sitting beside him. The Ninian Central housed a rough lot. Coleman, leering at Logan, stuffed the bit in his snarling mouth.

Logan looked from face to glaring face. "I know y'all aren't happy," he said, dipping his tea bag. "I did what I thought was right. I'm not afraid to come in here and tell you that."

"What was right, did you say?" Coleman asked. "Who are you to say what's right! He's mangled Murray!"

"The question put to me," Logan said, "was did he mean to do it."

"But he did mean to do it! They'd have dragged the bastard away in fockin' chains if it hadn't been for you!"

"You've got no idea what happened! None of you do. You heard from the others."

"I heard from Flinn, mate," Coleman said. "You bloody well know what he saw. When push comes to shove, you Yanks stand up for each other. No matter what the cost. Four men down! It's nothin' to you lot! Nothin' at all."

"You're not welcome in here," someone said.

Logan closed his eyes and shook his head. The room began to empty. He heard the thud of heavy boots, the swishing of parkas brushing one against the other, the crumpling of paper tea cups. He sat still, rolling his cup between his palms. He sought warmth where he could find it. When he opened his eyes, only Coleman remained.

"We can't make you go, Doc," he said. "But we can make you wish you had. I'd keep my eyes peeled if I were you. Accidents happen, eh?" He leaned over and spit a viscous black stream in Logan's cup. He started for the door.

"Why didn't you just put my name on the petition and be done with it?" Logan asked.

"It's better this way," Coleman said. "Momentum'll see to Strong. He'll get what's coming to him." He pointed a finger and winked his eye. "But you're our little mate, Doc. We'll see to you ourselves." He closed the door.

Logan sat alone, thinking. He'd saved one friend and lost fifty. He rose to return to the rig floor. He'd hang with the Americans if the Americans would have him. In one month more he'd complete his contract. He knew what he had to do. The Ninian was dangerous enough without two crews gunning for him. As he tossed his tea cup into the bin, he saw a Polaroid of himself stabbed onto the bulletin board with a paring knife. Across it, in black letters, was written: "Liar!"

January 1983 was the loneliest month of his life. He decided to twist off from the oil field. He had money in the bank; maybe he'd give graduate school a shot. Regardless of what he did, he knew he could no longer stay in the North Sea. Momentum agreed and let him go, contract bonus in his hand. Blood money to be rid of him.

He did his best to put the whole affair behind him. It hadn't been easy. He had to look those men in the face every day. He lived with the shame, the guilt, the ridicule, and the acrimony of Strong's bitter legacy. He also dodged an occasional pipe wrench dropped out of the derrick. Strong himself never had the pleasure. Momentum sent him on to Saudi Arabia. Logan had always assumed he could let the oil field go when the time was right and never look back. He just never figured it would be on such dubious terms. He licked his wounds and went on.

How was he to know his path would again cross Strong's? He'd run out of money before he earned his master's, the result, he felt sure, of oil field spending habits in a grad school milieu. He was searching for a job when Momentum called. It seemed his record of North Sea accomplishments had not been overshadowed by its final blight. The division manager, in one act of mercy, had stamped his file "Recommended to be rehired." Tulsa was on the line again. Momentum had an opening for an AD in Saudi Arabia. Would he take it? Yes, oh yes, Logan said, buried under a stack of overdue bills. He put his amorphous career plans on hold once again, kissed a stunned Caitlin farewell, and boarded a flight for Dhahran. It was one last chance for adventure, one final respite before he joined the middle-class masses. "It's not for long," he promised Caitlin.

He reported to the drill floor on that first day, his first time on a land rig. And what a gargantuan creature it was, engulfed by even more forbidding land. He'd known Barnes and many of the others in the North Sea. Americans and British alike never mentioned the Ninian Central incident. Logan knew they'd given him a second chance. It had all come together rather well. He thought of himself as lucky again on his way to the floor to meet his new driller.

But there was one little hitch.

"Well, hello, Doc," Jamie Strong said, perched atop his console stool. "Welcome to Saudi Arabia. I told you I'd make it right."

And now Logan, massaging his swollen knee, was pretty sure he had.

THIRTY-FIVE

◈◈◈

There was a knock at Logan's door. An Indian, he knew from the delicate rap. "Go away, Daniel," he said. "I'm resting." The door swung open with a drawn-out squeak. Putti's head emerged from the light and the heat.

"Leg okay, Doc?" His voice sounded so quiet away from the rig. The man himself seemed at peace.

"Leg okay," Logan said. "Much dope taking."

"You can walk?"

"I can walk." Logan pointed to the crutch Owen Oxley had fashioned for him. "That Sort of Thing" had been kind to him, but Logan didn't know why. He certainly hadn't earned it.

"Come, Doc," Putti said. "Scruppy."

Logan studied him. "You aren't angry with me?"

"Never," he said, and Logan felt new shame. How forgiving these gentle people were. "Come."

Logan hobbled out to the site, where he found the Indians in solemn preparation. There were no smiles, no laughter. They were doing it this time for the meanness of it, to assuage, Logan thought, their own anger. It seemed to him that any member of that Momentum crew was every bit as helpless as the scorpion. Maybe the Indians wanted to learn how to endure by its example. They wanted to see it run through the fire one more time.

Rahiman clawed a circle in the sand with his hands. Abdullah carefully arranged the rags, soaking them all with a bucket of fresh foamy diesel. Abdullah Larry lit the rags, which glistened from the fuel. The hot wind carried the flames around until the circle roared. To Logan, the ritual lost some of its mystic charm under the glare of the noon sun. What remained, in broad daylight, was its cruelty.

Putti took the coffee can, its plastic lid punctured with a series of holes, and showed it to every man. Then he removed the lid, positioned it over the center of the circle, and let the scorpion fall to its fate.

Logan gasped. It was the largest scorpion he'd ever seen. It looked more like a crawfish than an arachnid, its shiny armor as black as a moonless desert night. Like the others before, it stood still, as if to survey its dire situation. Then it, too, began to search for a way out of the fiery ring.

Logan sensed another figure silently watching the rite. Strong had come, but he said nothing, standing apart from his crew.

The scorpion probed the walls of flame, first one side and then the other. It backed its tail against the burning trench and the gathered crew gave it room to run. It dashed into the fire, lost for a moment. The Indians scrambled for the gratings. But Logan saw it crawl again to the center of the ring, pincers and front legs burning, and collapse on the sand, tail poised above its black head. The Indians pressed in.

Then the scorpion did it—pricked itself in the segment between its thorax and head. It never moved again. The flames engulfed it, and its black body was reduced to black ash.

Logan watched it burn. He was stunned. He never thought he'd see it happen. The Indians said nothing until at last Rahiman spoke.

"You see," he said. "It's as I told you. Big ditch. Big fire. And the biggest are the first to fall."

And then, one by one, the Indians drifted from the dying circle to their shacks. Logan turned to go too, and Strong kicked sand on the flames with the toe of his boot.

Strong never spoke. Not one word. And Logan had nothing to say to him. From now on he'd let Strong put out his own fires.

THIRTY-SIX

THE LAST DAY

Logan waited until nearly two in the morning before he limped into the mess hall and eased into a dinette seat. He'd have the place to himself. His crew was on location; the other shift had already showered, eaten, and trudged off to their shacks. Logan had heard their weary footsteps on the grating outside his door. He had tried to keep to his normal schedule, sleeping from noon to whenever so that he wouldn't be out of kilter with his crew. The Vicodin helped with that. Pix had put him on the injury list as one of the walking wounded so he could piddle around the rig if he wanted to, although Pix advised against it. He warned it would make a bad situation worse.

"Hullo, Doc," the server said, adjusting his paper hat. He seemed grateful for Logan's company at that late hour. "Still paining, your leg?"

"Good evening, Jacob," Logan said. "No more paining. What's for dinner?"

The Indian pointed at the board behind him, every other word misspelled. It listed, as Logan expected, stewed potatoes, stewed peas, stewed corn, stewed every goddamn thing. He thought of home and a fresh plate of cheese enchiladas. "We have everything but shepherd pie," Jacob explained. "British eat it all."

"The question," Logan said, "is why?" He studied the menu. The past two days of lethargy had left him feeling bloated. He no longer worked off the heavy British foods or sweated out his fluids.

Already his jeans felt a little snug. He was concerned about irreparable harm to his slim physique now that he planned to work at more sedentary professions. His father had bordered on obesity by the time he was thirty. Logan would have to learn to eat lightly once his days in the oil patch were over. Caitlin would have been pleased to learn that he hoped to find a position that would allow him to expend far fewer calories. Maybe he'd wear a suit for once. A suit would be nice. Just to be safe, he'd buy one a little big.

Caitlin, he thought. I should've called her. He wasn't angry with her anymore. When he thought of her, he just felt sick. Their relationship hung over his head like everything else in his life. Big changes coming. He supposed it was time. Everybody said so. And Strong, in a predictable moment of ignorance, had sealed the deal. Logan had already filled out Momentum's forms. He would be on leave of absence status, citing his knee as the cause. The problem was that Logan had no idea what to expect next. Now that he was alone, his future haunted him. He couldn't picture himself without a hard hat on his head. He couldn't imagine what life would be like without Caitlin. He knew he'd just have to suck it up and squeeze in wherever he could. But he didn't know where to start.

Jacob stood by patiently until Logan made his selection. "I'll have one small meat-piece, please. No gravy. Maybe six steamed carrots. One small bowl of salad with only two spoons of Thousand Island dressing. And some peas."

"How many peas?" Jacob said.

"Don't get smart."

Jacob returned with a plate and set it in front of Logan, then vanished into the kitchen. Logan picked at the food. He'd been worried about eating too much and now he wasn't even hungry. The codeine made him nauseous. He'd ordered the food just to give himself something to do. Impulsive bastard, he thought as he labored to chew the food for Jacob's sake. He didn't want to disappoint anyone else on his way out.

Halfway through the meal he dropped his aluminum fork and shoved the plate away. He rose from the table and limped out to the maintenance shop behind the kitchen. There he found Oxley working on his cane, a less bulky alternative to the crutch for the long flight home. Pix stayed up with Oxley for company.

Odd hours these camp people kept, Logan thought, always up

and down and looking ragged, their foreheads slick and oily. They were multiphasic, like white-tailed deer. Their days were filled with whatever they could scrounge up to fill them. Logan did not envy them at all. The regimen of the rig had always suited his restless nature. He would miss it.

"'Bout got her, Doctor, and that sort of thing," Oxley quipped, his hands busy. "It's a bit long for me, mind you, but it ought to be spot on for you, sort of thing."

"I'm sure it's fine," Logan said. He looked around the shop. Oxley was sanding down the oak plank he'd scavenged on location. Although he was skilled at plumbing, air-conditioning, and electronics, he loved working with wood best, and he had most of the tools he needed at his disposal.

Logan, at Strong's bidding, had once peeked into Oxley's shack. He had trimmed the entire interior in oak and pine from the chemical pallets. It was quite ridiculous, the hours the man must have put into such a project, and for what? Momentum could be ordered out of the country in a week's time if they ran afoul of company officials over operational or contractual disputes. Someday Momentum wouldn't be needed. If Blount happened to get a glimpse of Oxley's cabin, he would cut his wages by half. It belonged up in some mountain hideaway, not here in the Rub al Khali. The eastern province was littered with the forsaken shacks of former compounds.

No wonder it had taken two days for Oxley to craft this ornate cane. His concept of time had been distorted by twenty-eight days of looking for something to do, waiting until someone told him it was time to go home. The boredom had obviously taken its toll. Logan thought Oxley was a little too detached, his affectations often inappropriate and poorly timed. The only other human being with whom he regularly interacted was Pix, and he was a poor, equally lonely sampling.

And then there was that pesky speech impediment. How did Pix stand it day in and day out? They were like some old married couple, immune to each other's flaws, passing the time through another eventless day. What an injustice Strong had done him, caging him with these queer birds in this suck palace. Like them, he now had too much time on his hands.

He felt himself decomposing. Wherever he went, they were there, waddling along, asking silly questions, wanting him to sample a new recipe of stewed beans or stewed okra ("We've added pimento, Doctor, for a little flair"), or inquiring about the dining and sleeping habits of his men which hadn't changed the slightest in two years. He'd heard at some length all about their Costa del Sol holidays with "the missus," the inequities of the British tax structure, and the prudence of those ugly Swiss shoes both men preferred. If it weren't for the drugs, Logan would have hidden a thirty-six-inch pipe wrench and bashed them over their heads when they craned their necks into his room. It had come to that.

If they would just give him that damn cane he would travel far enough away that they could not find him. They must have suspected as much. That was why it was taking so goddamn long. Not often they had a fly in their dusty web.

"There, that ought to do it, sort of thing, Doctor," Oxley said, and blew the fine sawdust from the cane. "I'll just rub some linseed oil, sort of thing, on it to protect it. If you can wait until tomorrow sort of thing I'll put a proper coat of lacquer on it."

"Oh, that would look nice, Owen," Pix said, his prodigious buttocks enveloping the stool on which he sat. It creaked in complaint.

"Thank you, no," Logan said. "It's perfect just the way it is. The simpler, the better." He felt sure they would believe it, coming from an American.

He took the cane from Oxley, who was still rubbing it with a cloth. He poked the floor with it a few times to please him. "It's great. A fine job. Thanks."

"No trouble a'tall, Doctor. It's me job, sort of thing."

"And no one does it quite like you." Logan pecked his way around to Pix. "Say, I didn't see the new videos out. Did they make it in?"

"'Fraid not, Doctor. Maybe tomorrow. It's grocery day. I'll lend you another book."

Logan had slogged through two of Pix's spy novels over the slow hours of the last three days. They bored him beyond words. He wasn't interested in what problems writers could manufacture for his entertainment. He had enough of his own to sort out. And he was damn tired of piddling around Momentum's camp with these piddlers, waiting to return home and discover where he was and what he must do to move forward. He felt as if he were stranded at some marathon family reunion, swarmed by old-lady relatives he didn't really know but obliged to be civil. All Pix and Oxley needed was blue beehive hairdos, a thick smear of rouge on their leathery cheeks, and the acrid scent of mothballs, and the sensory experience would be complete. Thank you, Jamie Strong, you son of a bitch.

"I don't think so, Pix," Logan said, heading for the door. He could go no further down this dead end.

"Where are you off to?" Pix said.

"To the rig."

"Why?" He raised his eyebrows, which accentuated his blood-shot eyes. "You can't possibly work."

"No, but I can't possibly not work anymore either." Logan took a step or two with the cane. It was too damn short, a clear sign that he'd slipped from the surface of the earth into hell sort of thing.

"Fancy a game of backgammon then, Owen?" Pix was already arranging the pieces on Oxley's newly crafted board, triangles of dark, lacquered wood inlaid against light. Logan had to admit it was a fine piece of work. It must have taken days. "Give our love to Strong," Pix said as he rolled the dice.

THIRTY-SEVEN

ogan went straight to the drill floor and stuck his head into the first conversation he found. Marshall flipped through the folds of computer paper the French well-logging company had sent him, his brow furrowed in ridges as coarse as old rope, the age spots on his face glowing purple under the derrick lights. The Witch Doctor, bug-eyed from exhaustion, stood calmly at his side.

"Why hello, cousin!" Marshall said, brightening. Logan saw Strong's head jerk in his direction. "Heard about your worm bite." He cast a malicious glance Strong's way. "You gettin' along all right?"

"Yeah, I'm okay," Logan said.

"Strong don't know what to do with himself without his better half. You can barely get a word out of him, and when you do, you don't like it." Marshall returned to his graphs. "I know you've got to take medical leave. But me, you, and Blount's gonna have a little chat when you make it back. We're gonna make some changes around here." He glanced up at Logan. "Might involve you."

"I don't want to make any changes, Marshall," Logan said.

"Well, we'll see." He showed the graph to the geologist. Mousa nodded, eyes widening after a slow blink. He looked like he was about to fall over. No telling how long he'd been up.

"Amazing, Mousa," Marshall said, his eyes shimmering with delight. "Three hundred and twenty-seven feet of production sands. That's gotta be a record."

"It looks very promising," Mousa said. "How do they want to perforate?"

"Dhahran wants to flow the bottom section first when we test. If it's strong we'll probably run two strings of production tubing off one packer. The shorter string will flow the rest of the reservoir. They do it back in the States all the time."

"There is no well like this in the States," Mousa said, an understatement as far as Logan was concerned. There was nothing even close.

"That's why I came over here. That's why I've stayed. This is what I'd hoped for." Marshall closed off tighter with Mousa and tapped the graphs with his finger. "I knew it'd be down there waiting for me. This game is far from over. We're fixin' to open up a whole new field. It's gonna buy us some time. You wait and see."

Logan, feeling squeezed out of that conversation, turned toward the driller's console for the only other game in progress. Bull was in the middle of another story. Strong's languid expression warned Logan that it was less than gripping.

"...and I told him, hell! How was I supposed to know she was the mayor's daughter? Man, we lit outa there like...why, hello thair, Doc!"

"Evenin', Bull." He nodded toward Strong. "Jamie."

"Ah, shit," Bull said. "I done forgot to call Dhahran and make sure that production tubin's on its way out here. I best tend to my bizness. Barnes'll have my ass in a vise come daylight."

"We ain't got no vise out here that big, old man," Logan said. Bull punched him in the shoulder on his way to the elevator.

Strong checked his gauges, then the skies. "I owe you one, Doc," he finally said. "You saved me. That was an Okie prom night story, if you can believe that. I don't know who's had it worse, me or Bull."

"You," Logan said.

Strong snorted, his lips cracking into a tight smile. "Yeah," he said. "I imagine so."

A strained silence followed. They had not spoken since Logan's injury. He'd feigned sleep the three times Strong came around to smooth things over. He didn't want to hear anything Strong had to say. Strong's apologies didn't matter anymore.

"How's the knee?" Strong had gone without mentioning it for

as long as he could. Logan sensed the regret in his gray eyes. He wagered Strong sensed the smoldering anger in his.

"Ah, there's a few loose parts rattlin' around, but it's not so bad." That was a lie. Strong had fixed him good.

Strong turned his attention back to his gauges although Logan knew there was nothing there to see. "I'm sorry, man. I don't know what to say."

"It's okay." He lied again. He still wanted to wring the neck that supported that ignorant head. Every cell in his body ordered him to choke the life out of this arrogant, violent fool. But if nothing else, over the last few days Logan had learned to think through his impulses a little. Strong could never master it, and Logan tallied the cost of his deficiency. Logan's knee was the latest in a long string of damaged bodies Strong had left behind. His wife had been foolish to marry him. To leave him had been a damn good idea. Come what may, Logan couldn't wait for his turn.

"Well, we'll be home soon," Strong chattered, eager for conversation, "and you can heal up for the next round. You'll miss one trip. Maybe two. They'll pay you."

Yes, Strong, Logan was supposed to answer. It's just a paid vacation. I'll get over it and I'll be back. Nothing will change. Instead, he offered a couple of pecks on the metal grating with the tip of his cane. He looked out over the floor. The Indians, huddled by the air hoist, were watching him now.

"Yep," he finally said. Strong nodded. A little hopeful, Logan thought, that he was not going to quit on him.

"How're the stooges?" Logan said, anxious to change the subject.

"Oh, they're kinda quiet," Strong said. "They won't talk to me and they never talk to Ripley. I apologized about the dopin' and all. They ain't over it yet. They just kinda keep to themselves. They been workin' like wild men, though. I got no complaints, I guess."

"I guess I don't either," Logan said, the third lie in as many minutes and the one he could tell Strong embraced the most. "Guess I'll see what's up with 'em."

Strong nodded, adjusting the visor of his hard hat until it shaded his eyes. Logan, having said more to Strong than he'd intended, drifted off to the darker regions of the floor.

"What doin', *gondos*?" he greeted the Indians.

"Hullo, Doc," Putti said. "How your leg?"

"Oh, number one. How your ass?"

Putti's head bobbled in affirmation. "No doping that place. Strong promise."

"Happy now?"

"Happy, no. But maybe keep job one more year."

"Good, Putti," Logan said. "You buy more farmland?"

"Is necessary." Putti grinned and Logan smiled back. Putti's entire extended family worked his rice farm while he slaved in the desert. Putti spoke of ambitious plans for doubling its modest size. It pleased Logan to know that somebody was accomplishing something over here. Over the last few days, he'd decided Saudi Arabia had been a waste of two years for him.

Rahiman looked as though yet another prying question hung on his lips. Logan waited for it.

"Problem with you and Strong?" he asked, and Logan knew nothing would please him more.

"No," he said, keeping his voice casual. "Accident."

"Accident, fuck! He kick you, man!"

"For him that's an accident." How similar his testimony was to the one he'd given in the North Sea. He was the victim this go-around, but the judges' reaction was the same.

"He is number one asshole!" Rahiman said. All Indian heads oscillated in agreement.

"I'd get over that attitude in a hurry if I were you. Things are bad enough as they are."

"We never talk to him," Rahiman said, lifting his sharp nose to the breeze.

"That'll teach him." From the corner of his eye Logan saw Strong watching. He could tell Strong didn't like the way the Indians were responding to him. Logan's rapport with the crew represented yet another gift Strong had been born without. Logan wrapped his arm around Putti just to goad Strong a little more.

"You won't have time to bitch here in a little while," Logan said. "The work's fixin' to start."

"For us," Abdullah Larry said, "work is no problem. That is why they bring Indians to this place."

"You don't have the foggiest idea why they brought you to this place, you idiot. You just came. Same like Doc."

"Yes, we know. Needing number one roughnecks."

"If they were needin' number one roughnecks, they'd have sent some Americans over here." It was so easy to chide them.

"Shit," Rahiman said. "Maybe soon Indians coming to America for rig jobs."

"Well, I got news for you. They're already comin'. Maybe not for rig jobs—there aren't any—but for everything else."

Putti cocked his head. "Indian peoples coming?" It was news to him.

"Yep, it's a goddamn rampage." He thought this would lose them, but they seemed to get the idea.

"Goot. Maybe Putti coming also. Make big money."

"That'd be great, really. We could join the same country club."

"What's country club?" he asked.

"Don't worry about it."

Rahiman surveyed him, pointing last at his knee. "What you do now, Doc?" he asked. Logan knew the young Indian wanted to return to the subject of conflict between the whites he knew best. That's where his interest always lay. "Leg all fucked up. No working rig job."

"Twist off." Logan stacked one fist on the other, turning them in opposite directions. It didn't matter if the Indians understood the gesture. Strong would. Logan had just answered his driller's earlier question.

"Because of Strong?" Rahiman said.

Logan shook his head. "Because of Doc." Their expressions turned grave. "It's time to go home."

"Maybe time for Indians to go home also," Putti said, looking from face to face as each considered it.

"Don't you dare. Putti needs two more hectares of farmland. Abdullah Larry needs to buy Bombay taxi. And Rahiman here," he said, punching Rahiman's stomach, "needs money to finance Islamic revolution." They all smiled save Rahiman, who wasn't sure whether or not he'd been slighted. "Get what you came for first, boys. Doc already has it. The mistake I made was staying too long."

"Aie-whaa," Putti said. "Soon also our time comes."

Mousa joined Marshall by the console. Strong was leaning back in his chair, listening. Logan stuck his head in behind them, resting his weight on the cane. A decision had been made.

"Mousa here thinks we've got an inordinate amount of drill cuttings settled into the bottom of the well. If that's true, loose fill like that might screw us up when we go to set the packer." Marshall slid his glasses up the bridge of his nose. "What we think we'll do is pull out of the hole, remove the jets from the bit, and run it back in there wide open. Then you and your wild bunch'll trip back to bottom and run the shit out of them pumps for a couple of circulations. We'll see what comes across the shakers. When they're clean, we'll pull out layin' down drill pipe and run our tubin'. With a little luck, we oughta have this well flowin' in seventy-two hours." He slapped Strong on the back. "You and Doc'll be lit up in some foreign country by then."

"I'm lit up in one now," Logan said, rattling the bottle of Vicodin in his shirt pocket.

Marshall returned to business. "Pump yourself a mild slug for the trip. I don't want any heavy spots in the fluid column. When you get out, don't close the blind rams on the preventers. We want to see if it'll try to flow on us again. I don't want to find out when we open the rams to run in the hole. I want a man watchin' that well at all times, you got that?" He thought about it a second. "Somebody that speaks English, damn it. Not one of them coolies." He turned to Logan. "Let Doc here do it. He ain't much good for nothin' else."

"We'll take care of it, Marshall." Strong had traded his cocky bark for officiousness. It didn't sound right coming out of his mouth. He'd finally decided to hook his suction hose to Marshall's mud pit. It would do him little good now. Logan noted the word "we" in particular. Strong was making an effort at team play.

"See that you do," Marshall snapped, his eyes nervous in anticipation. "Pull out just as soon as your slug is pumped. And Strong, as soon as you get the bottom-hole assembly into the casin', I want you to run this damn thing flat out. Time spent trippin' is time wasted, as far as I'm concerned. I think you know what I want. Now, I'm gonna lie down. Come and get me if anythin' out of the ordinary happens. Al Hisaab," he said, pointing to the rotary, but referring to the well beneath, "is big and mean. Don't let it get a bite out of our ass." He left the floor, the torpid Mousa in tow.

"You wanna work, Doc?" Strong said.

"You bet."

"Call Ripley and tell him to mix us up a slug. I'll send one of the 'necks down to help him."

"Roger," Logan said. He picked up the phone and paged to the pits. Strong motioned for his roughnecks to gather around him.

"We're gonna pull out. Putti, you go down and help Ripley mix slug. The rest of you guys get ready to trip. We're gonna blow and go." He raised a single finger in the air. *"Haami-haami!"*

Logan watched them set out on their appointed missions: pump a couple shots of grease into their tongs, change a dull die, dope the slips, connect the kelly pull-back sling to the air hoist. Then he looked after his own affairs amid the hustle and the hum of a busy rig. It felt good to be back in the thick of it, if only for this brief moment, one last time.

Ripley, huffing, at last answered his page. No telling where he'd been or what he'd been doing. "Nigel, this is Doc. Yeah, good to hear from you, too. Look, we're pullin' out. Mix us sixty barrels of slug twenty points heavier than your active system. We're ready to pump it when you say."

THIRTY-EIGHT

⬦⬥⬦

Logan's crew worked alone. The well had been dead for the days of logging. They'd drilled no deeper. Marshall's rare absence from the floor assured Logan that even the drilling superintendent wasn't concerned about how the string would pull off bottom tonight. Logan expected a trouble-free trip. Strong spun out the kelly without the tiniest squeal from the bright silver threads. Logan, at the air hoist, jerked it back above its sheath, and Strong slid it in like a big black dagger. The blocks jolted free of the kelly hook. The elevators lowered and Rahiman turned to the position Abdullah preferred. Putti latched onto the first stand of pipe and the long trip out began.

Logan locked down the air hoist brake and went into the doghouse to calculate Strong's figure. He stepped out to the console and yelled into Strong's ear, "Fifteen stands to the shoe!" The end of the open hole. He ceded one stand extra to the good. Strong nodded as the pipe crept upward to the crown. The Indians stood silently at their positions. It was too loud for gossip. There was only the occasional cough as the diesel exhaust choked them, tears from Abdullah Larry's irritated eyes streaking his dark cheeks.

A dozen stands soon rested on the pipe rack timbers. Putti was numbering them with a yellow paint stick that melted in his hand from the heat. It dyed the palm of his glove. "In English, damn it!" Logan shouted, and Putti numbered them again after he had rubbed off the Hindi characters. When they read fifteen, Logan heard the transmission gears grind as Strong downshifted. He engaged the clutch and stomped the foot throttle against the metal floor. The next stand rocketed out of the hole three times faster than the one before.

"Moe! Larry! Shemp! The cheese!" Strong called, but the Indians merely gawked back at him.

"I guess they ain't in the mood!" he yelled to Logan. Good guess, Logan thought. Strong shrugged his shoulders and focused on his machines, which were always receptive whatever the mood.

Logan had never seen Strong run the rig so smoothly and so rapidly. He maniacally shifted levers and twisted knobs, engaging drum, cathead, or cable, any of which could mangle a man in an instant. His style appeared almost wanton, though his expression was curiously grave. He looked like some street punk popping credits on a pinball machine, knowing just how far he can shove it without a tilt. He damn sure had the knack.

Pipe after pipe, row after row, the long silver joints rocked together with the rhythm of the rig. They came from the earth looking as new and fresh as the day they left the Japanese foundry, soon dulling in the dry air. Their walls a little thinner from the well's heat and the rotary's friction, Arabco would use them for two or three more holes, then they'd be pitched aside to rust in the desert alongside the rubbish heaps of abandoned workmen's camps that pockmarked Saudi Arabia's eastern province.

The tongs, freed by fresh grease and constant operation, clicked effortlessly for the master roughnecks around the scarred tool joints. Each crewman helped the other without a word. There was only room on the huge floor for three. Everything around them moved menacingly. Strong's catheads engaged, sleeping cables jerked alive and pulled taut. They were released just as quickly and were laid coiled on the floor. The tongs swung free again, easily dodged by the agile Indians. Ninety-foot lengths of drill pipe—each weighing fifteen hundred pounds—bit the oak planks of the pipe rack, chewing off strips of soggy, rotting wood that floated on congealing mud until one of the Indians paused from his regimen to wash the sludge away with a hose. A slip now and they'd work at camp beside the toeless Mohammed. Logan heard Strong gun the five diesel engines that powered the drawworks, their roar dying as the blocks freefell to the floor. Strong slammed the brake lever down as the Indians latched the elevators around the next joint to rise. Brown smoke, residue from the scalded asbestos-padded brake bands, danced above the drawworks drum.

The Indians moved comfortably amid the violence. For three hard years this was all they had known. They had grown accustomed to it, as Logan had in his youth. For him, this was the strangest aspect of this odd profession, that a human being could actually adapt to something like this and think nothing of it. A stranger watching the fury of a bit trip would shudder. But the Indians never flinched at the chaos that engulfed them. It was as natural to them as anything else. And it should have been that way for Logan, too. But, like that unaccustomed stranger, Logan caught himself startled by the crack of a tight connection or the shock of the slips as they absorbed the drill string's weight. Had those few days at camp made that much difference? Was he already out of place?

Sweat soon soaked the Indians' torn work shirts. Logan watched their arm muscles twitch as they gripped their waiting tongs. He limped over to the doghouse and flipped on the fans that faced the floor. The roughnecks, shirttails flapping in the artificial breeze, smiled in gratitude.

Logan wanted to work. He wanted to grip that iron and assure himself that it was still his. That he could work those tongs as well as he had when it was his job. That he was leaving a world he had belonged to, a world he had once loved. He pulled down his pants, tightened the elastic brace around his knee, pulled them up again and cinched his belt. Then he found a coffee can and filled it with cool water. He hobbled out to the rotary and handed it to Rahiman, gently shoving him backward so that he could take his place while the young roughneck drank. Because of his knee, he worked slowly. But he felt little pain, and he couldn't bear being idle any longer.

Rahiman gulped down the water and refilled it for the next crewman, assuming his position so he could drink. Once all three had rested, Logan filled the can a fourth time and set it carefully on the elevators for the ride up into the derrick. He didn't consult Strong, although it would require his cooperation. Strong seemed chagrined at having to alter his pace. Logan enjoyed making him slow down.

Logan watched through a hundred feet of dark haze strafed with white diesel smoke as Abdullah reached out from the monkey board and took the can. He poured the water down his throat and leaned outward across the tower, trusting his life to his harness and those skinny ropes that held it. The roughnecks shielded their faces from the drops of water that dripped from Abdullah's dry mouth, but they were blown far away into the dunes. Abdullah threw the can out into the desert and stood waiting for the next stand. Normally he would have used this opportunity to scream for more pipes. But, like the roughnecks, he wasn't in the mood.

Logan resumed his place on the chair. He'd done all right. He'd passed some time. Worked up a sweat. He felt a little fresher from the work. More connected anyway. What hadn't changed was that gnawing anger he felt whenever he watched Strong—sound, focused, and full of purpose—working a crew that by all rights belonged to them both. Strong had pried—or better yet, kicked—Logan away from them and everything else he'd known. He was leaving this life as a victim. Not the terms he'd imagined. Maybe, he thought, he should return to Saudi Arabia, if only to keep that appointment with Marshall. Logan could rob Strong of his job if he wanted. Marshall had made that clear enough. Then it would be Strong who faced an uncertain future. Logan had the power to turn Strong's world upside down, and by God, he just might do it out of spite. Wouldn't that even the score? He caught himself. He was obsessing. Strong's disease. Let it go, Logan, he told himself. You're gone forever in two days. Stay busy. Let the work absorb your frustration. Just let it go.

"I don't want you workin' out on the floor, Doc," Strong said flatly, irritated. "You might hurt your knee."

"It's hot." Logan's tone matched Strong's. "They were thirsty." He wondered how Strong could think he might hurt his knee.

"They can get their own water," Strong said. "I don't want you out there. It's bad enough as it is."

Strong expected an answer, Logan knew. An acknowledgment that he would obey. He wouldn't give Strong the satisfaction. Oh, but he wanted to tell him a thing or two. It took energy and discipline to sit there and say nothing. Every time Strong spoke, it was like another turn of a tightening screw. Let it go, Logan.

Logan directed his attention to the floor, attempting to ease his

mind with the magic of his Indian roughnecks at work. He wanted
to take this image—the best moments of a precise, disciplined crew,
tuned as finely as a Rolex watch to perform this odd, century-old
ritual—with him when he left. One didn't often see such things in
the American oil fields, and Logan didn't think he'd ever see it
again. He warmed knowing he had a hand in their performance.
He'd taught them all he knew and he felt joy in seeing his efforts
come to this. The Indians were very good.

Strong shifted gears, accelerating what was already a blistering
pace. Logan knew the geolograph would look like a blue tornado,
bereft of white spaces, when the trip was over. No one ran a rig like
Strong, and no one prided himself more on that solid triangle of
cobalt—the indisputable proof of his unmatched talent. This was
something for Logan to remember also, that he'd once worked with
the very best. Never mind that at the very moment Logan came to
this conclusion he also knew he hated Strong. It made no difference
to him that Strong was cursed with so many flaws, and that one of
those flaws had recently claimed Logan's career. As a driller, the
man had none.

The substructure trembled beneath his feet. The derrick rocked
above him. Pipe after pipe shot up from the depths of the well.
Muscled arms the color of old pennies gripped hot, burnished steel,
and on they worked as if they'd never see another dawn.

Logan's watch read half past five. For some reason Pix had sent
breakfast out early. The crew had sat on their asses and drilled for
days and the breakfast had arrived routinely just after six. Today,
when they were tripping, shorthanded, Pix decided to send it out
ahead of schedule. Logan knew Strong wouldn't like it.

Abraham brought the white-ass meals to the floor. They cooled
slowly under aluminum foil. Twice Strong motioned for Logan to
eat, but he would not go. He knew the roughnecks were preoccupied with images of the roustabouts, who always followed the
chow wagon onto location like cattle following a truck filled with
bales of fresh hay, consuming the greater portion of porridge and

scrambled eggs while it was still warm and quivering. The roughnecks were hungry, but they were also a man short. It would be a
while before they got a chance to eat. Meanwhile, the next joint to
break waited in the rotary. Strong motioned for them to get their
tongs latched around it and make it quick.

"Doc, go down and find Ripley," Strong said. "Tell him to get
his ass up here and relieve these hands for breakfast."

Logan nodded and rose from his chair, pleased that even Strong
wouldn't make the roughnecks wait much longer. Strong grabbed
his arm as he passed. "On second thought, don't tell him nothin'.
Just get him up here."

Ripley returned to the floor, bouncing ahead of Logan with
gangly, pigeon-toed steps. He consulted with Strong and received
the ill tidings and then steered an unwavering course to his waiting
meal. Logan heard his smacking when the diesels lulled. He imagined Strong did as well. Normally they would have commented on
it to each other.

Logan watched as Ripley hung his hard hat on a metal peg in
the doghouse, wiped his mouth with his soiled shirtsleeve, and
scaled the derrick, his bloated belly spilling out of tight, dope-
stained European jeans. They never looked right. Ripley paused
twice to belch and climbed on, hand over hand.

Logan knew Ripley preferred laboring alone in the derrick to
working alongside the roughnecks on the floor. He'd never come to
trust the Indians, as Logan had. His loss. Abdullah switched out his
canvas harness with the Englishman and flew down the derrick
ladder in his counterweighted cabled belt, his boots touching the
steel rungs only twice, just as Strong had told him not to do a thousand times. He bounced off the floor and onto the slide for the last
sandy stretch before the Bombay Teahouse. For all that had happened, Abdullah was still Abdullah—spry and strong—and it
pleased Logan to see his favorite appear content. He worried about
who would protect Abdullah and all the rest of the TCNs once he
was gone. But then again, Logan had done a sorry job of that.
What service had he provided them? The Indians would be better
off without his inconsistent meddling. They'd close ranks and face
Momentum together as Rahiman always preached. Who was
Logan to say that this wasn't the better idea? What could he teach
them about how to endure?

The others continued working and waited. Strong waited, too. Barnes would be along in forty-five minutes to relieve him for his meal. Of course, Logan could run the rig for him, but he knew Strong would never ask. He would cite his knee, but Logan knew better. The real problem was that Logan was too slow. Strong wanted that blue geolograph tornado, the measure of his skill, to be consistent from its thick beginning to its fine tip. Marshall had mandated speed, and Logan didn't have it. Any white spaces on the graph would be Logan's doing, and he knew Strong would wait until his empty stomach wrapped around his spinal cord before he'd relinquish control of his clutches and brake. He hungered more to regain Marshall's favor than for his scrambled eggs, beef sausage, and burnt toast.

Not ten minutes passed before Abdullah returned to the floor. Logan smiled at him warmly. He could have stayed a half hour before Strong would have bitched, but Abdullah wasn't the kind to lounge in the teahouse while the others went hungry. Any other time, Logan knew, he would have dawdled in there a good hour. Logan had seen the seasons change while he waited on Abdullah. The Indian nodded to Logan and went up the derrick. Ripley came down. He retrieved his hard hat and stepped out to the floor like a lost child on the corner of a busy street.

"Who's next?"

The Indians all pointed to each other, and Ripley quickly grew impatient.

"Will it take a bloody election?" he barked, screwing up his face. He stepped into Abdullah Larry's place. "You go," he said, and Rahiman and Putti nodded acceptance of the white man's wish. Abdullah Larry stepped over the cables and chains coiled like serpents and left the floor.

Meanwhile, the drill collars emerged from the well, marking the near end of the trip. Things were going well, Logan thought. Never smoother, and shorthanded, too. Strong should have been pleased with his crew's performance, but Logan saw no such indication in his stern expression as he feathered his cathead clutches, his way of letting the roughnecks know they weren't moving fast enough to suit him. Asshole.

Logan felt a hot wind on his neck. Sheets of dust whisked through the derrick girders, dulling the illumination of the fluorescent lights. The outward structures lost their definition in the chalky gusts. Logan couldn't make out the dunes at all. The wind felt to him like the beginning of a *toz*, a sandstorm. They sometimes blew for two days or better, rearranging the dunes and burying the location under drifts of fine sand. There was no escaping the dust. It even penetrated the door and window seals at the camp. The stewed meats and stewed vegetables would be seasoned with sandy grit.

Putti tied a clean rag around his mouth and nose. He switched off the fan. "No necessary," he said.

THIRTY-NINE

In a few minutes, Abdullah Larry returned to take Putti's place. Rahiman, leaning over his set of tongs, watched them coordinate the exchange. Logan pulled the clean pair of work gloves he had gotten from the office out of his hip pocket and slipped them over his hands.

"What d'ya think you're doin'?" Strong said, squinting from the dust.

"I'm gonna relieve that hand so he can eat." Logan raised himself up from his chair.

"Keep your seat, Doc. He'll eat soon enough."

Logan took the first uneasy step. "He's hungry," he said, glancing back. "He can eat now."

Strong, jaw set, lips pursed, deliberated for only an instant. "Stay off the floor," he snapped. Logan knew it was a warning, one he would have instinctively heeded in the past. Now that he was leaving, he didn't give it a moment's consideration. What he focused on instead was Strong's surly tone. He'd heard enough of that.

"Look," Logan snapped. "This man's hungry. I'm gonna let him eat."

Strong shook his head and bumped his clutch, another warning. "I said I don't want you out there, Doc."

"I don't care what you want. I told you, I'm quittin'. You just work them levers there. I'll worry about me."

Logan, glaring at Strong, moved toward the rotary. Strong

stood at his console and said nothing, but Logan knew exactly what was going through his head. The Indians were watching. A precedent of defiance was being set, and Logan knew Strong could never abide it. Not on his floor. Logan heard the click of the geolograph marking the first space of white in three hours.

Logan couldn't have cared less. If Strong chose to make an issue out of some chickenshit deal like this, he'd picked the right time. For once Logan intended to do exactly as he pleased. The man was hungry and his breakfast was getting cold. Logan would relieve him and Strong couldn't do a damn thing about it. The geolograph clicked for a second time.

He had tossed his cane against the mouse hole and taken a step or two toward the rotary when he heard Strong chain down the brake. "Hey, Doc!" Strong spat. "Maybe you didn't hear me."

"I heard you. I just don't give a shit." Logan turned his back again. He felt the full weight of Strong's hand clamp down on his shoulder. Strong jerked him backward toward the console. Logan's upper torso gave with the opposite force, but his legs remained planted. When his hips rotated his knee gave way. He shrieked.

All he felt was a nauseous wave burning from his knee into his thigh and reverberating in his gut. He bit hard, growling. It hurt far worse than the original injury. Strong darted around his equipment, chains, and cables to steady Logan's body. Logan saw the look of horror on his face, instant regret replacing instant anger.

Furious with pain, Logan cocked his arm. His fist caught Strong squarely on the jaw. Strong's teeth clicked.

The big man wavered, stunned, and staggered backward into the wall of the doghouse. He shook his head. Logan came at him on all fours, dragging his bad leg behind him. He no longer felt pain—he intended to inflict it. He lunged, striking Strong repeatedly on both sides of his face. Strong retaliated halfheartedly until he pulled up his arms to protect his battered head. Blood ran from his nose and mouth and lacquered the lower half of his face. Logan pounded him again and again, grunting with each blow, until he was too tired to swing anymore.

Strong raised his right leg, cocked like a scorpion's tail. He kicked Logan hard in the stomach. Logan doubled over, his wind gushing from him. He crashed into the derrick leg and coiled into the fetal position. Strong looked at him with a strange expression of fire and ice, blood dripping from his chin. He spat and waited to see if Logan would come at him again. And Logan intended to, just as soon as he caught his breath.

"Do you see what it's come to, you son of a bitch!" Logan yelled. "Do you see what you've made me do!" He pointed to the obscured dunes. "That's the Empty Quarter out there, man! The end of the fuckin' earth. You can't push me any farther. And you best think twice before you try."

Strong wiped the blood from his face with the tail of his T-shirt. "What's wrong with you?"

"What's wrong? Everything in my life is wrong. And you better believe I'm ready to fight about it. I learned that from you."

"Listen to me now, Doc," Strong pleaded. "Let's not do this. I can forget all about it. I know you're pissed about your knee and I don't blame you..."

"I don't have a knee!" Logan ripped his pants leg apart at the seams and yanked down the wrapping so Strong could take a good look. "It's gone. Like everything else, it's just wasted. I don't have a father. I don't have a wife. I don't have a job. And I don't even have a fucking home anymore." Logan tasted the bile clogging his throat. He hawked it up and spit it out and glared at Jamie Strong. "All I've got is you and this," he said, racheting his thumb toward the dunes. "And I'm sick to *death* of you. You said you wanted to make things right. Come a little closer, you dumb son of a bitch, and I'll make it right."

Logan could see that his words had finished what his fists had started. He knew the chinks in Strong's armor. Strong's face shriveled as if he smelled something vile. He looked for a moment like he'd crumple to the floor and bawl. He ran the heel of his hand across both cheeks. His chin collapsed against his chest as he slowly shook his head. He looked back up. He took in the rig—his rig— as if he didn't know where he was. Then he gathered himself. His cheeks flushed crimson as he chewed his lip. He blew the mucus from his nose one nostril at a time. He spat out the blood and gripped Logan with a darkening stare. "I hear you, Doc," he sneered. "Let's get it settled."

Logan knew what was coming. Knee or no knee, Strong owed him for this. If such a ceremony was how Logan chose to leave the Rub al Khali, Strong would certainly oblige. Strong waited until he was ready, until the blood had cleared from his eyes and he found his balance in that sanguine haze. Then he stepped forward to even the score.

Rahiman knelt at Logan's side. "Okay, Doc?" the Indian said. Logan couldn't answer. He tried to get to his feet and ready himself to meet Strong, but his knee wouldn't let him. The crippling pain overwhelmed his anger. Strong loomed closer, his eyes wild with rage. When Rahiman saw him approaching, he rose and jumped in front of the big man's path.

"Strong! No! What you doing, man!"

"Stay outta this!" Strong reached down and snatched Logan by his collar, dragging him to his feet. Logan hurt too badly to fight him off. He stood limp and helpless, hanging on to Strong's shoulder, awaiting the force of the inevitable blows. Strong drew back his fist to strike when Rahiman jumped on his back.

"Run, Doc!" Rahiman shouted. Strong revolved like a bull out of the gates and tried to throw him. The Indian held tight. Strong landed an elbow to his ribs, and Rahiman slowly slipped down, clutching his stomach and gasping for breath.

But Logan could not run, and furthermore he didn't want to. The Empty Quarter was truly the last place. He lay there next to its barren, hollow core while its wind stung his eyes. His knee pounded. And his anger burned. "Goddamn it, Strong!" he cried, seeing the Indian doubled over on the floor. "Don't hurt anybody else! This is between me and you!"

Blood ran down Strong's face in steady streams.

"That's just it, motherfucker! He got between me and you."

Logan looked at Rahiman, whose face was contorted in pain. It was bad enough that they'd fallen against each other. Strong was stupid enough to drag the Indians into it, too. He turned again to Logan to finish what he had started.

Logan rolled onto his stomach, pushed himself up, and with everything he had left, rammed his head into Strong's abdomen. He knocked him clear to the mud manifold. Logan was on him before Strong could wipe the fresh blood from his eyes. He snatched Strong by the hair and drew back his fist to break his nose when he felt someone grab his bent elbow. It was Putti.

"No necessary, Doc!" he shouted, and dragged him away from Strong. Logan couldn't break free of his sinewy grasp. Abdullah

Larry clamped his arm around Strong's throat. Rahiman jumped up from the floor to dive on him. Ripley ran from group to group trying to figure out exactly what was going on.

"Bloody hell!" he screamed. "You're mad! You've both gone mad!"

Three Indians jumped on Strong's back to weigh him down while others swarmed him like bees. One of them alone could not possibly hold him. He was twice their size. But working together they did a pretty good job. Whenever Strong was able to shed one, another took his place.

Now and then either he or Logan would get free long enough to take a swing. But Logan delivered or received no more serious blows. There was considerable yelling and cursing. The Indians could not bother with their broken English, and their wild screams made the already desperate affair more chaotic. Two separate masses of men, colliding violently, moved clumsily about the drill floor as one, Strong at its angry core. Logan swung every chance he got.

They all fell down. The eyes of the Indians on the bottom bugged out from the weight of the Americans on top. Strong was swinging wildly at any and all. His blows lacked sufficient force to injure anyone though, and the Indians wiggled out from under him and jumped back on top.

Logan continued to struggle, but he could not break loose. He saw how Strong struggled also, all of them thrashing in the warm mud, fang and claw, like crocodiles in a shallow slough.

Mud? Logan thought. Where was the mud coming from? He looked at the rotary and stopped cold.

FORTY

They were drenched in mud. It ran six inches deep, in rippling waves. From the rotary it gushed three feet in the air.

"Strong?" Logan moaned. Strong was fighting for breath, his face bright red. He snatched at Abdullah Larry's arm still clasped tight around his neck like a sling.

"Strong!" Logan yelled. Rahiman saw the well and released his grip on Logan. Strong's assailants, still oblivious, pressed on. Logan pulled them off one by one, tossing them to the floor. Before they could scramble back to Strong, Logan grabbed their chins and yanked their heads to the rotary. That was all it took.

"Wake up, boys!" Logan yelled, more in awe than in fear. "She's comin' in!"

Strong, exhausted, lay flat on the floor until Logan's shouts reached his ears. "Strong!"

Strong gawked at the rising column of mud, now spewing ten feet into the derrick and washing out the V-door.

"Hey goddamy! What the fuck you doing!" Abdullah was perched over the monkey board, alarmed at the mud that threatened him. A damn good question, Logan thought.

Strong wiped the blood and mud from his eyes and looked again. "Uh oh," he said. He jumped to his feet like a cat. Logan stumbled unsteadily in his wake. By then the well was blowing hard enough for its mud to rain down on the floor. They both scrambled for the preventer controls. Neither one made it without falling twice on the slippery floor. For Logan, panic choked out all sense of pain.

"We gotta shut it in!" Strong yelled, dashing for his console.

"I'll close the hydril!" Logan yelled back, crawling on his hands and one good knee. He dragged his bad leg behind him.

"No! We'll never get a valve on that. I'll pull this collar out of the hole. When I do, close the blinds!" Logan saw the Indians, nervous, moving off toward the slide just as they'd been taught to do.

"Hey, where d'you think you're goin'!" Strong hollered. "I'll tell you when it's time to go! Get over here and handle this collar!" The crew took its uneasy position. Things did not look good to them.

The drill collar was rising out of the slips on its own, the mud bubbling around and through it. Mud shot halfway to the monkey board. Strong engaged the drawworks and began to pull the collar all the way out once the elevators actually caught it. Logan reached the preventer controls. His hand gripped the blind ram lever, mud dripping from his fingertips.

"Ripley!" Strong yelled. "Go for Barnes and Marshall! Make it quick!" Ripley, obviously relieved to learn that his duties took him away from all this, hurried down the slide, wringing the mud from his clothes as he went.

At last, the bit dangled above the well but was refused its center, the mud shoving it to one side or the other in an eerie, jerky arc. As soon as he saw the bit, Logan sealed the well. He heard the cadence of the accumulator, saw its lines jolt under the sudden pressure. Instantly the flow ceased. Everything grew quiet, save the wailing wind and the creaking of the elevator bales as the lone collar rocked back and forth across the rotary table. Mud covered everything. Together, Strong on his feet, Logan on his one good knee, they approached the well. They both leaned forward to peek in, each, Logan knew, afraid of what he might see.

"What d'ya think?" Logan gasped, his chest heaving.

"I don't know," Strong said, struggling for composure. "We lost a lot of mud. And this ain't no bubble."

Logan looked at the entire string of pipe standing on the rig floor. This time the well would be top killed—mud would be pumped against the sealed bore from the preventers down instead of pumped through the bit from the bottom up. It was the trickiest well-control procedure and the least successful, if Logan remembered his training correctly. He'd damn sure never seen it done in the field. It would all come down to how much pressure the walls of the bore could withstand and how hard Al Hisaab was pushing. There were at least a dozen different ways it could go wrong, all of which threatened the same disastrous result.

Strong's stare shifted to the pressure gauge on the choke manifold. Logan looked, too. The needle shot up to four thousand pounds and continued rising. "I just don't know if it can handle that," Strong said. If the brittle walls of the formation down hole fissured, Al Hisaab wouldn't need the well bore to vent to the surface. It would make its own way. "I just don't know."

It looked solid enough to Logan. He remembered that they'd pressure-tested the rams to fifteen thousand psi They had a ways to go, and there was still a lot of fluid standing in the bore—how much, he didn't know. But he was certain the pressure would soon stabilize. They'd caught it before, and they'd caught it this time.

Reassured now that the well was sealed, he studied Strong, whose anguished face suggested he had yet to find the same comfort. Logan drew back and smacked Strong's cheek with his fist to help him along. He was too tired to hit him very hard. Strong's head jerked a little from the blow.

"Not now, Doc," he said soberly, still focused on the gauge. "We're in enough trouble. Whatever the hell we were fightin' about can wait. It'd be best if you could help me figure out how we're gonna explain how we let it get this bad. Marshall's gonna kill us both."

"I'll come up with somethin'," Logan said. And then he thought about the ebb and flow of the night's events, from bad to worse and back again, and he had to laugh. Man, what a hitch this last one was turning out to be.

Strong watched him curiously for a moment. "I can't believe this is happenin'," he said, and then he too broke down laughing, white teeth flashing beneath a slick, dark coat of mud.

Soon the Indians joined in. They looked at one another, all at once slapping each other's backs. "Aie-whaa," Putti said. "We some crazy niggers."

"We'd have been some unemployed niggers if we'd lost this well," Strong said. "I'll tell ya that much." Strong returned to his console. He fidgeted with the knobs. "No wonder the goddamn flow alarm didn't sound," he said. "They'd shut it off."

Rahiman scooped up a handful of mud and flung it at Strong. Before long, they were all doing it until their faces were black. Logan wiped the mud away from his eyes to check the needle, now passing twelve thousand pounds. He stopped laughing. "It's gettin' worse," he said.

"It can't get any fuckin' worse." Strong smacked Rahiman in the back of the head with a big wad. When the mud began spraying out from the rotary in a nasty hiss, he froze. No more jokes.

"*Christ!*" Strong shouted. "It's them seals, man! Up the pressure, Doc!"

Logan crawled over to the controls and turned the valve. He kept twisting the handle, hoping to hear Strong tell him to stop. Finally, the threads came to an end. The blind rams were meeting at maximum pressure. And the mud kept coming.

Pieces of rubber shot out from the preventers. Logan, horrified, watched them teeter on the floor. Strong kicked one through the V-door. "We're in big trouble," he said. He turned to his crew, his sunken eyes dimming. They stood by, waiting for his orders, wanting to battle the well. Logan didn't see the first inkling of fear on those determined faces. Knowing things were about to get very rough on the floor, not one moved away.

"Go on!" Strong ordered, pointing to the slide in the shower of mud. "Into the wind." Abdullah Larry was the first to reach the chute. Putti followed. They did not hurry.

Rahiman stood fast. "I never go," he said.

"Get out of here, goddamn it!" Strong bellowed. "Don't you see?"

"I see!" Rahiman said. "I not afraid."

The mud was climbing back into the derrick now, its angry sibilance grating in Logan's ears. Small chunks of iron hailed down. High-pressured mud washed through the metal rams, cutting them like a blowtorch through butter. Soon the fluid would flow unimpeded from the well. When it was gone, the gas would come.

Strong dragged Rahiman by the collar and flung him down the slide. He marched back to the center of the floor and stood beneath the thickening column. He looked up into the derrick, its lower lamp lenses blinded by a film of smoking mud. Logan sensed that the *toz* was also strengthening. The wind cloaked the entire location in horizontal gusts. Everything looked grainy, like an old photograph or maybe a dream.

"Abdullah!" Strong cried. He signaled for Abdullah to exit on the Geronimo line anchored five hundred yards into the dark dunes. The Indian slipped out of his harness, freed the carriage from its sheath, and rode it to safety, his figure swallowed by the gathering storm. Logan thought he heard Abdullah make his Three Stooges noise, but he couldn't be sure against the combined clamor of the wind and Al Hisaab.

"Shit," Strong said to Logan. "I gotta do it." Strong slammed his fist against the rig alarm button. Logan could barely hear its throbbing rasp in all the commotion. Strong snatched the phone and ordered the location evacuated. When he hung it up Bull arrived on the elevator, terror frozen on his weathered face.

"You got the blinds closed?"

Strong nodded, wiping the mud from his face.

"Let's get the hell outta here then!" Bull shouted. "I didn't get this old by hangin' around somethin' like this!"

"You go on, Bull," Strong said. "I'm gonna play with it a little while!"

"You ain't got nothin' to play with, Strong. Let's go! You too, Doc! That's an order!"

Bull stood there waiting, begging him. Strong hesitated, then he went, disappearing in the dust and smoke. Logan's thoughts flashed to his dream. He was standing in the middle of it now, knee gone, well roaring, alone. Not alone—abandoned. Strong had walked right out, leaving him behind. A prickly rush, almost electric, gripped him. Unable to think clearly, he found himself gasping for breath. For the first time in his life, he felt he would die. And he didn't want to. Not snuffed out at twenty-seven years of age. Not here, in this awful place. "Strong!" he yelled, but there was no answer. He understood that if he was to survive, he had to get the hell off that floor. He started for the slide, determined to reach it. But he couldn't get his knees under him on the slick surface. He rolled over instead, wedging his fingertips between the joints of the rotted oak, and pulled himself along in a crawl.

The haze cleared as it had in the dream. Logan saw Strong waiting for the elevator. When it came he shoved Bull in, slammed the gate and pushed the button, sending the old man down to safety, Bull snapping at him every inch of the way. They argued back and forth until Strong walked away.

Strong fought his way back to the panel where Logan lay in the muck. Vaporized mud, steam, and smoke engulfed them both. The rig floor trembled.

"Go on, Doc," Strong said. "I'll load you on the elevator. I got this."

Logan shook his head furiously. "We're goin' together, Jamie!" he said. "I'm not leavin' you up here!"

"Suit yourself." Strong reached for the blind ram lever. "Let's open and close it back. Maybe it'll seal."

He tried several times. There was nothing left to close. The blind rams were gone. Pieces of them soon littered the floor. Strong closed both sets of pipe rams and the hydril after that, hoping to choke down the flow in stages and buy some time. The well blew each iron component in its turn out of the rotary, and they bounced on the floor with a dull thud. Even Strong had to know this was the end. The putrid gas, ripe with hydrogen sulfide, would reach the surface soon. Al Hisaab had made its intentions clear enough. Logan watched Strong's expression shift from determined grit to resignation. He saw it clearly in those gray eyes: Strong had made up his mind. He bowed his head in defeat.

"Let's go, man!" Logan screamed into his ear. "We ain't got much time. That gas'll lay us both out."

"All right," Strong said, his eyes closing for a second. "Stay with me."

Strong bent down, allowing Logan to drape his arm over his neck, and they walked together across the swamped floor toward the slide. He let Logan settle into the trough and nudged him gently with the sole of his boot. The next thing Logan knew, he was spitting sand out between his teeth. He looked back to make sure he was out of the way. But what he saw was Strong, still standing at the gate, yelling something Logan couldn't hear. Then he ripped out the wires that fed the elevator so no one else could use it, held up the palm of his hand to Logan, and slowly turned away under the black derrick. The haze absorbed him like the night does a shadow.

Logan started for the stairway. If he could reach the floor, he could bring Strong back down. All he had to do was talk to him. Strong appeared on the corner of the floor gripping a pry bar. He levered the stairwell loose from its mounts and kicked it aside to crash beside the Bombay Teahouse. Logan felt arms lifting him from the sand. Abdullah was on one side, Rahiman on the other.

"What the fuck you doing, Doc!" Abdullah said. "This well finish!"

And they carried him off toward the dunes where the other refugees were already waiting. Logan struggled to get free until Abdullah slung him across his shoulder. Logan turned his head to watch the last of the mud rip through the crown.

FORTY-ONE

⬦⬦⬦

Two pickups, their bright lights piercing the haze, came to a dusty stop in front of Logan and his bearers. Marshall was the first man out. He lost his hard hat in the wind as he rushed to Logan, his frantic glare fixed on the derrick above.

"What the hell happened up there, Doc?"

Logan caught his breath after Abdullah set him down. "The well came in on us when we were out of the hole. We closed the blind rams and that handled it for a while and we sent for you. But then the seals started leakin' and the rams washed out. That's what we got." He pointed to the well.

"Everybody off the floor?"

"No." Logan shook his head. "Strong's up there."

"Jackass!" Marshall looked to Barnes, who had just stepped out of the truck, but he didn't say anything. "Well, Strong'll have to look after himself. I can't send anybody up there after him." He turned to Barnes, who looked stunned. "Elvin, go back to camp and radio Dhahran. Tell 'em to alert the authorities to clear the area west of our position for at least a hundred clicks. Tell 'em to get in touch with well-control and send a crew out here. And tell 'em I said they might as well go ahead and contact Adair's boys. This is gonna be a bad one."

"All right," Barnes said, the towering gush of mud and steel mirrored in his eyes. But all he could do was stand with his hands on his hips and shake his head.

"Today, Barnes!" Marshall snapped, and Barnes jogged to his pickup and sped away. Marshall turned to Logan. "Can you walk?"

"Nope."

"All right. You stay put. You coolies stay with him. I'm gonna clear all the personnel out of here and group 'em to the east. Once I'm sure we've got everybody, we'll shuttle 'em back to camp."

Logan heard him, but his attention was drawn to the well. Mud caked the lights that lined the derrick. Metal fragments shooting from the hole had shattered some of the fluorescent bulbs. Logan could barely make out the tip of the crown. He knew Marshall longed for the breaking light of day. He would be able to see what he had then. No one liked wrestling with a well in the dark.

Soon enough the sky quit raining mud. The well sputtered for a moment, then came the sheets of white vapor. They formed a wavering cloud that draped over the rig floor, mixed with the dust of the storm, and converged into one seemingly endless, furious, boiling mass. The gushing roar never stopped.

"Take a head count, Doc," Marshall said, and Logan pulled his thoughts away from Strong to number dark and shaken heads. He was picking through Brother's roustabouts when the well exploded. The percussion landed them all on their asses.

Something on the floor, probably one of the busted lights, had ignited the gas. Logan felt the surge of blistering heat. Steam rose from the sweat and mud on his clothes. They had to move further east.

He managed as best he could, hopping with his arm wrapped around Abdullah's shoulder. He could feel blisters forming on his back, the pain dwarfing that in his knee. He felt the joints grinding, but little else. His hair broke off. He could smell it burning, the same stench he'd smelled in his dream. He covered his head and limped on, Abdullah begging him to hurry. Marshall, hand shielding his face, looked back briefly and waved him on.

There was plenty of light now. Abdullah, knowing they were both being burned, lifted Logan and carried him into the dunes. It was unusual for those sandy mounds to feel cool. Abdullah struggled, his boots bogging down in the sand, until Rahiman offered to help him. They went on. Once they were at a safe distance, Logan shook free and turned to look back.

The flames had melted the iron girders supporting the derrick.

The tower listed and then crashed across the mud tanks, destroying all in its thunder. The stands of drill pipe, once neatly stacked in the mast, scattered across the location, crushing the engine and electrical trailers, the pumps and crane. Everywhere shacks imploded from the heat. The tires on the pickup trucks melted and popped; the machines, paint bubbling, sank groaning to their axles in the sand.

Logan stared at the melting iron. A river of white-hot slag rolled across the sand. What was left of the stout substructure and blowout preventers collapsed piecemeal, their destruction as if by design, until every man-made thing cluttering the hole was burned away from it. Only the roar and brilliant blue of the earth-flame remained, its purifying pillar of fire entrancing those who had survived it. The ground trembled beneath Logan's boots, and a stench of rot hung in the churning wind. Al Hisaab spoke, and there was nothing to do but listen. The Rub al Khali had reclaimed its own.

"Would you look at that magnificent son of a bitch," Marshall said. He sank to the sand and wrapped his arms around his knees. "Let's just sit a spell." Logan crawled beside him, turning again to the well.

"You sure Strong was up there, son?" Marshall said.

"No doubt," Logan said.

"Hell, I'll believe he's dead when I kick his gangly body. You couldn't kill that son of a bitch with a stick. He's probably out there somewhere," he pointed at the desert that surrounded them, "wonderin' 'bout how much he can make sellin' ladies' shoes. Strong's destined to die with a beer can in his hand, unless of course I find him first."

"You won't find him, Marshall," Logan said. "Not one trace."

Silence followed. The fire loomed before them with greater menace, its flames continuing to build.

"I don't like the way it's lookin'," Marshall said. "I've seen a dozen blowouts, but nothin' like this. I wish y'all could've handled it. This ain't the one to lose."

Rocks and chunks of red-hot metal shot out like meteors from the well. Debris fell smoking to the dunes. The entire well bore was washing out from the pressure. In a few hours it would dig its own crater. "Best move back, boys," Marshall said. No sooner had he spoken than a stone the size of a basketball, smudged black and smoldering, landed with a thud in the sand. Logan, in awe, backed away.

"Let's get along to camp, men," Marshall said, rising.

They headed across the desert just as daylight peeked through fissures in the leaden sky. The gauzy dawn horizon could not match the brilliance of the great flame. Each figure in the desert cast two shadows, Al Hisaab's the darker and more defined of the two. Logan, carried by Abdullah and Rahiman, followed at the end of the long procession.

Marshall took slow, deliberate steps in the soft sand as if his legs were hobbled. The others trudged, heads down, behind him at his pace. The wind blew across their tracks, filling them with sand before Logan could reach them. Fatigued, he asked the Indians to stop to rest, and decided then to look back, like Lot's wife, at the evil thing they'd left behind. He cast his eyes to the dunes beyond. He saw something moving. A herd of camels milled along the flank of a shifting hill. Then he saw a Bedouin, the same Bedouin, he hoped, astride his lead camel, his robes flowing in the teeth of the storm. He was watching it all without any appearance of fascination or surprise.

Logan replayed those last moments with Strong. Knowing Strong as he did, living and working together for all those years, relishing the good times and enduring the bad, Logan could put the words into Strong's mouth. What he had said, and Logan was quite sure, was, "You were right, Doc. This is the last place. I've got nowhere to go."

Then he'd held up his hand to say good-bye and sunk back into the fog. He would have pulled up his driller's chair and taken his place before the rotary. He'd have lifted his hands high in the air, throwing his head back to gaze at the indignant black skies, waiting to greet Al Hisaab. "Let's see what this bitch's got" were probably the last words he had spoken.

Logan turned his face back to the flames when the notion struck him. Every image before him matched his nightmare identically. He was experiencing the same malevolent sounds and odors. The same terror. How was it then that he had escaped Al Hisaab's wrath? Why did his dream end as it had? He closed his eyes to recall it more clearly. He knew it well. He reviewed it step by awful step, up until the explosion, to the point where his body began to incinerate. Then he noticed the discrepancy. The boots being burned from his feet were lace-ups. Logan had never worn them. The screaming voice that echoed in his ears did not belong to him. The broken leg was thicker than Logan's, the clawed hands larger. He watched the flesh peel from the fingers. On the third digit was a ring that belonged to Jamie Strong. Then everything went blank.

Had Logan noted the dream's obvious inconsistencies; had he realized that, although he himself had begun the dream, it was Strong who had finished it; had he understood that he was being warned of Strong's imminent death rather than his own; had he confronted the dream rather than feared it, he never would have left Strong behind on the floor. Strong would have been the first man down that slide. It would all have happened differently if Logan had not been so afraid.

They wouldn't find Jamie Strong. Not one charred piece. That was how Strong would want it.

"Doc!" Marshall called. "C'mon."

"I can't!"

Marshall plodded through the deep sand back to him. "What's wrong?"

"I can't walk and they can't carry me all that way."

"All right." Marshall scratched his head. "You stay put. I'll send a truck back for you. One of you," he said to the Indians, "stay with him."

Logan expected Abdullah to volunteer, and he looked like he was about to. But Rahiman spoke first. "I stay with Doc."

"I don't know how long it'll take to make it back," Marshall told Logan.

"I don't care."

Marshall studied him. "Get yourself out of the wind. I'll come as quick as I can."

Marshall returned to the head of his column and on they went. Logan propped himself up and stared at the fire. He kept hoping to see the figure of a lone man walk out of the flames.

"He never come, Doc," Rahiman said. "He is gone."

Logan wanted to let his face drop into his hands, but one could not touch the other without agony. His whole body felt raw, and he knew the burns didn't stop at his blistered skin. He felt hollow, empty, seared right through to the bone.

"I'm sorry, Rahiman. It's all my fault."

"Not your fault, Doc. Strong was big asshole. Always problems with Strong. Now he pay."

"You don't understand."

"I understand plenty. Bad man gone. I never cry for him."

Logan turned to the Indian. "You can't judge him by how he acted out here. He was more than that. Strong grew up fighting. He had to fight for everything he ever had. And despite that, he still had the energy—the spirit—to fight for what he thought was right. He fought for me. And he fought for you."

"He never."

"He did." He heard his own voice cracking. "He wanted to see you get an AD's job. He knew you were smart enough, and good enough, and he tried to make it happen. I was with him when he went into Blount's office. He wanted to change the eighty-four-day work schedule, and he wanted you to be an AD. They laughed at him."

Rahiman's face went blank. He blinked his eyes while the information sank in. "I never know."

"Because he never talked about it. He didn't want you to know if it didn't happen. He didn't do it because he wanted you and the rest of the Indians to like him. He did it because he thought it was right. You don't understand. You didn't see the whole picture." Logan snatched a handful of sand and threw it to the wind. "You don't see the loss."

Logan thought about what his father had said to him all those years ago. "You got a cold heart, boy." It was intended as a superficial threat. But in truth, it was a warning. Who would ever be loyal to you, his father had asked him. And the answer to that question was Jamie Strong. Jamie Strong had been his friend.

It had been too easy for Strong's weaknesses to contaminate their relationship. Logan had condemned him for one indefensible act, committed in a state of emotional turmoil. Logan remembered better now, when it was too late, the things Strong had done for others. The many things he had done for him. Logan had come to manhood leaning on Strong's shoulders. Strong, in a desperate moment, had asked him for one favor in return.

So many times over the years, Strong had reached out to him, begged Logan to forgive him for his faults. Logan didn't have the capacity to reach back. Logan could chalk it up to his stormy relationship with his drunken father—his visceral contempt of flawed authority, his instinct to distance himself from relationships he could not repair. He could cite these reasons and make others understand why he had turned on Jamie Strong. But he couldn't convince himself that it had been anything but the will of his cold heart. He had obeyed it without question and looked on, detached, as Strong foundered. In the end, Logan had challenged Strong in the place he loved best, the one place in the world he called home. Why? Who better than Logan knew the mind of tormented men? What they could tolerate and what they couldn't? Who had provoked whom? Logan had cast aside twenty-seven years of experience and skill mediating the abusive bungling of troubled souls and decided, on a whim, to meet violence with violence. What kind of friend had Logan been? What kind of loyalty was that? Who had led Strong to the Empty Quarter and then pushed him over its edge to oblivion? Logan knew the answers to his questions. He knew who had committed the larger crime. And before him, in one heaping, billowing, screeching ruin, lay the cost of his error.

Logan felt the guilt burn within him, stripping insulation packed tightly a decade ago. A warming of some deep place that had known only the chill of so many wasted winter years.

"I never cry for him," Rahiman repeated with a haughty lift of his chin.

Logan put his head between his knees. He didn't care if it hurt. He started to tremble, and at last he convulsed. It had been years since he had cried, and once the drought was broken, the tears streamed down his cheeks. He watched them fall—cool and dirty—on the sand where they stood elliptical but intact. Even the Empty Quarter didn't want them.

FORTY-TWO

Logan lay in his boxers on his bunk, which he had shoved directly beneath the window unit. It hurt too much to sleep even if his mind would let him. He kept the room dark, allowing the cool air to bathe his blistered body, greasy from a thick coat of Pix's reeking salve. They would come for him soon.

His injuries weren't significant enough to save him from Momentum's fate. He knew he was in for his second grilling in twenty-four hours. In a way, Strong had stiffed him again.

He heard the knock at the door he'd long expected.

"Bring it on," he said.

It was Daniel, the houseboy. Logan hated to refer to a grown man as a houseboy, but Daniel always insisted. He was what he was, and he seemed proud of it. It was Logan who no longer had a title. Daniel stepped in quietly, hands locked behind his back, his gentle smile betraying the gravity of his mood.

"You awake?" he asked. It was too dark for him to see in.

"Yep."

"Feeling goot?"

"Not bad."

"Tool pusher say pack all your things, Doc. He say you take everything. Abraham waiting to take you to Dhahran. Leave in maybe one-half hour."

"Great. The inquisition. Okay."

"You need helping," he said, "you call Daniel, number one houseboy."

"Thank you," Logan said. "I'll be fine. Turn on the light, will ya?"

Daniel flipped the switch, shaking his head when he saw Logan's burned and battered body.

"Oh, very danger, no?"

"Very danger, yes. Now beat it, will ya? I've got a lot to do." And he did. He was leaving a day early and he was never coming back. Neither of which would be his choice. Momentum would do the choosing now.

"No problem," Daniel said. He paused. "Very sorry, Doc."

"It's all right. You're a good man, Daniel. You take care of yourself."

Daniel left the room, closing the door behind him. Logan roused himself from his bunk. His body ached, more from the fighting than from anything connected with his escape from the doomed rig. The blowout had done the rest. Every exposed inch of his body had been scorched. He slid his surplus duffel out from under his bed and began packing the items from his locker. He stacked clothes and other rig gear to the side. These he would give to the Indians. His Redwings, the only real prize, would go to Abdullah. He took his pictures down from the wall and placed them in the duffel. Momentum could deal with the rest as it saw fit. This phase of the operation didn't bother him in the least. He was ready to put all this behind him and move on.

There was another knock at the door. What now?

"Come in, goddamn it."

Marshall, the last man he wanted to see and the one he knew he must, stepped through the threshold. The brief hours of dark, cool, and quiet had come to an end. Grill time.

"It's good to see you, too," Marshall said, a nervous grin on his face. Logan was used to seeing Marshall on the rig, his home, where he commanded everything. Here at camp, he seemed out of place and ill at ease. He looked older out of the sun.

"Oh, I'm sorry, Marshall," Logan said. "I thought it was one of the Indians or maybe even that idiot Tate-Pixilate. He comes around and wipes another coat of grease on me about every twenty minutes. I think he's gay."

"I've always thought so," Marshall said, grinning.

Logan straightened his hair and slid his legs into his jeans. The denim stuck to his skin because of the salve. Oxley had safety-pinned one seam to accommodate Logan's splint. It was still too tight. Marshall studied his burns and bruises as he buttoned his fly. "You gonna make it, cousin?" he finally said.

"Yeah." Logan said. "For a guy who just blew up the southern half of the Arabian Peninsula, I guess I feel all right."

"Well," Marshall began, "that's why I wanted to talk to you before them other assholes in town get a hold of ya. You got a minute or two?"

"Actually, I've got about thirty," Logan said. Now he was glad Marshall had come. He was anxious to get it over with anyway. He knew Marshall was only the first in a long line of investigators. "You've always shot me straight. I'm gonna do you the same favor. It shouldn't have happened..."

Marshall cut him off with a wave of his hand. Logan was puzzled. This was the last reaction he had expected from the man whose exploration program he'd just ruined. Logan sat down on his bed, waiting. Marshall took a seat on the opposite bunk.

"I don't know what happened up there last night," Marshall said, "and I don't wanna know. I don't like it, I can tell ya that much. That hole meant more to me than anythin' I've ever done in my life. If you hadn't been hurt so bad already, I'd have wrung your neck."

"Lucky me," Logan said.

"You're that, all right, Doc. You'll never know how lucky you were. But when you get to Dhahran, your luck's gonna run out. Blount's gonna do everythin' he can to hang this on your ass."

"I know what's gonna happen," Logan said, and he damn sure did. He'd seen it happen to others plenty of times. He'd been through it himself in the North Sea.

He felt the impulse to defend not only himself but his crew, and he ran with it. "Once it kicked, we did everything we could to try and stop it. Our crew stayed with the well. Strong had to throw the Indians off the floor."

Marshall nodded. "I know y'all did your best, Strong especially." His tone shifted from friend to disappointed parent. Logan had expected this sooner or later. "But don't tell me y'all didn't fuck somethin' up. Old Marshall knows better than that. I don't know how we lost enough mud out of the well to allow the pressure to wash right through the goddamn rams. Somethin's wrong somewhere."

He shook his finger in Logan's face, not as a threat, just as a reminder. "But that ain't what I'm here to talk about. I just want you to know that I know, and that's all."

Logan nodded, breathing a sigh of relief. Marshall went on. "A drilling foreman ain't supposed to have a favorite. I never have before. But me and your daddy come from the same county. He went on to college. I carried my butt to the patch. We weren't friends or nothin'. But people talk. I'd hear a little somethin' every now and then. I know he's had his troubles. I know you've had yours." He crossed his knee. "Me and you's connected, Doc. We've got the same Arkansas roots. Same trade. I've tried to look out for ya, teach you a little of what I know. I wanted Barnes to let you drill in Strong's place, and I know now that I should've insisted. I guess that's neither here nor there after this mornin'. What I'm tryin' to say is that you're a good man. Your daddy'd be proud to see how you handle yourself."

Logan felt his throat tighten. "We're not close, Marshall. He went his way. I went mine."

"I know," Marshall said. "Like I said, people talk."

"And I can't think of anybody who'd be proud of me now."

"You'll get over it. That's why I'm here. I wanna help."

"Then shoot me."

Marshall chuckled. "There's a helluva mess out there in that desert, Doc, and them well-control boys cost a lot of money. The best thing about that is me and you don't have to pay for it. The Saudis get to pick up the tab on that, and they can afford it. They'll never flinch. We've shown 'em what they've got out there, and they'll settle for that, I guarantee. The situation'll sort itself out directly."

Marshall threw his head back and sighed. "Of course, we lost a man—a damn good man. I had my differences with Strong. You know that. But I respected him."

"He would've appreciated hearing that from you," Logan said.

"As for the rest of the crew, everybody's a little singed, but that ain't so bad. Nothin' else has happened that time and money can't fix. That oughta make things a little easier for you to bear."

"Frank Blount ain't gonna see it that way," Logan said.

Marshall nodded. "No, Doc, he ain't. Blount's been around a long time, same as me. We were never born, we just washed up over the shale shakers one day and went to work."

It was an old joke, not really funny the first time Logan had heard it, but under the circumstances he felt obliged to chuckle, seeing how Marshall paused to allow it. He did, and it hurt like hell.

"At any rate, he's like me. He's gonna smell a rat, right off, same as I do." Marshall paused, leveling his glance. "I guess you know Blount's gotta run you off. That's the way it works."

"I know how it works," Logan said.

"What we've got to consider now," Marshall said, "is damage control. You've got a future in this old oil field for as long as she goes. I'd like to see you land on your feet and keep with her."

"How?" Logan said. There was no way.

"You're gonna lie," Marshall said casually. He flicked a Camel out of his hard pack and slid it between his lips. He said he'd seen a movie once that had changed his outlook on things. He lit the cigarette and Logan shrank from the flame. He could swear he felt its heat.

"There was this fella," Marshall said, "a Frenchman, in bed with two women, and they were gettin' after it hot and heavy when his wife walked in. She screamed bloody murder, slammed the door, and was carryin' on in the den while she waited for the son of a bitch to come out and face her.

"This guy thought a minute and then helped them girls quietly out the back window. They didn't make a sound except for the rustle of fancy clothing like them French girls wear. Then he got dressed just as cool as a cucumber, fixed his hair, and walked out to see his wife. He kissed her on the cheek just like he was welcoming her home.

"At first, it knocked the wind out of her sails, but she came around soon enough. Naturally she was going on and on about his infidelity and the two naked women, and what wife wouldn't? Finally, he looked at her like she was crazy and said, 'What women?'

"It worked like a charm," Marshall said. "Pretty soon, she started to wonder if she'd really seen them or not. That Frenchman had the balls to turn things around in a hurry."

He slapped his knee and laughed. "Man, I learned somethin'

from that old boy. All ya gotta do is establish doubt. Human nature'll take care of the rest. Even Hitler said the bigger the lie, the easier they'll believe it." He cocked his head and winked. "Catch my drift, Doc?"

"I think so."

Marshall planted both feet on the floor. "Now when you wind up in front of Blount, you'll need to blame every non-Momentum personnel and every piece of equipment on that rig. Drag me into it all you want. But at no time should you indicate that you and poor Strong were in any way at fault, even though you and I both know damn well you were. I'll write up my own report, and I won't acknowledge any driller error. If we were back home, I'd have your balls on my wall. But here I can get over it. And if I can, Blount can."

He exhaled a plume of smoke. "I been wantin' to see Adair's men work anyway," he said. "It's gonna be quite a show around here. Sorry you won't be around to see it."

He daubed the ashes into the palm of his hand. "If you're careful—if you don't leave yourself out in the open—you can patch things up enough to go on with Momentum. Probably not here, of course, but with some other division." His eyes narrowed. "Understand me, cousin?"

"Yeah," Logan said, incredulous. "I believe I do."

"This might be a good time to leave contracting behind anyway. You oughta think about being a drilling foreman now, a company man. I could help you. I've got contacts worldwide. I'll give you my highest recommendation. I'd hate to see you leave the patch for good just because of one little mistake."

Logan couldn't believe it. Little mistake? "Thanks, Marshall," he finally said, and though it pained him, he cracked a smile. "That means a lot."

"There's one other thing for you to consider," Marshall said. It was the first time his tone was solemn. "If I was your age, I'm not sure I'd stay in the oil field. We're goin' the way of the buffalo and the blacksmith and ain't nobody gonna care. The future'll judge us harshly. I know that for a fact. They'll label us the dirtiest, most wasteful age in the history of mankind. I'm a part of it, but you don't have to be. If I were you, I'd think long and hard about gettin' out."

What a strange and wonderful man, Logan thought. Marshall

made him long to know more of his Arkansas people. See if they were cut more from Marshall's cloth than his father's rags. He'd never figured on that. Maybe he ought to drive back up there and knock on a few screen doors. Sit up under a sweet gum and dig his toes into that red clay. He'd once belonged to that place. Maybe he still did. At any rate, he knew he'd have a little extra time to kill once Blount got through with him. He just might go.

Marshall tossed his cigarette butt on the floor and ground it with his toe. Daniel wouldn't like it in the least. He stood up and smoothed the wrinkles out of his khakis. "Well, I gotta run."

"I don't know what to say."

"That's what I'm tryin' to tell ya. You don't say nothin'. The rest'll take care of itself."

Logan rested his forearms on his knees and looked down at the floor. "I'm real sorry, Marshall. This wasn't my first fuckup. It was just my biggest."

Marshall slapped his thigh. "And it's a doozie, too! Never seen one worse!" He leaned forward, as if to make sure Logan didn't stray. "But that ain't the issue here, is it, Doc?"

Logan shook his head.

"You'll be all right. Live and learn. This'll pass. And us Arkies got to stick together," he said with a grin. "Nobody else'll have much to do with us."

Logan reached out and shook Marshall's leathery hand. It felt warm.

"Thanks," he said. "I'll keep in mind what you said."

"You do that. You think about it hard. It's good advice from somebody that's been in your boots." He stopped. His expression turned grave. "Now I wanna know—just between you and me—what happened up there?"

Logan was about to tell him. He thought at least he owed him that. He caught himself when he understood that Marshall really didn't want him to. He shrugged his shoulders and said, "Mud gradient must've been too low. We didn't know what hit us."

"You got it," the old man said, and he stepped toward the door.

"Marshall?"

"Yeah."

"I was wondering about what you said. Why do you stay if you feel that way about the future and all?"

"Me? Ah, this train was already runnin' long before I got on it. It'll run on a while yet."

"Where's it runnin'?"

"Out." He winked his eye as he closed the door behind him.

Logan smiled and zipped up his duffel. The door flew open.

"What women?" Marshall said. He slapped his knee and pulled the door shut. Logan could hear his laughter fade as he walked away. How Strong would have enjoyed this briefing. But then, he probably never would have needed it.

Alone again, Logan slipped his darkest sunglasses over his eyes, grabbed his duffel, and stepped out into the heat.

FORTY-THREE

———◈◈◈———

Logan hobbled out to the crew truck, dragging his belongings behind him. The *toz* had blown itself out, leaving behind the bluest Arabian sky he had ever witnessed. He didn't see Barnes and was glad of it. Blount would be the final obstacle between Logan and home.

He passed by the ring of fire, its sand still smudged black from the diesel flames. He filled it in with the toe of his boot and went on toward the compound parking lot.

Ripley sat quietly on the heel of his trailer skid, smoking a cigarette. He'd showered, but he hadn't scrubbed behind his ears very well. "Dhahran?" the Englishman asked.

"Yep. You'll get your turn soon."

"There's fuck-all I can tell 'em, mate," Ripley said. "It was my week on the pits. First thing I heard was the alarm. Someday maybe you'll make it over to Yorkshire. I'll buy you a pint and you can tell me all about it." He grinned. "We'll sink one for Jamie Strong, eh?"

"Deal," Logan said. Logan offered his hand. "You're all right, Ripley."

"Steady on, Doc."

Logan left him and turned the corner. To his surprise, the entire Indian contingent, dressed in their finest loungees, shirtless, their bronze chests bare to the sun, had gathered to see him off. Abdullah stepped forward to take Logan's bags.

"What the fuck you doing, Doc?" he said. The very question he'd asked Logan the first time they'd met, and then hourly after that for almost two years.

Logan laughed. "I'm goin' home, Abdullah," he said.

"Goot," Abdullah said. "Soon Abdullah go his place also. Always he think of Doc, his big American friend. Doc teach Abdullah proper grammar English. Now he speaks too goot. Get goot fucking job my place."

"Please don't tell anybody you learned from me," Logan said. "I couldn't live with myself."

"No problem," Abdullah said, still grinning. Logan extended his hand, and the Indian nearly crushed it. Chavan, the welder, gripped it next.

"Okay, Doc?" he said.

"Okay."

"Plenty jig-jig now, eh?"

"I hope so, Chavan. Good luck with your marriage."

"Aie-whaa. No problem." He reached in his shirt pocket. "Want to see photo?"

"Sure." Chavan fished it out in no time. He'd just about worn the gloss off the print. "She's beautiful, Chavan. You're very lucky." Logan opened the truck door and Abdullah tossed in his duffel. Aboobaker waddled toward them, obviously having been designated the most creative and articulate, to present the official send-off speech. After several uneasy moments of preparation, he proudly delivered.

"Doc number one nigger," he said, his motion seconded by a contingent of bobbling heads. That was it. Logan would be remembered as the first among equals, niggers all. Short, sweet, apropos. The man was good.

"Ah, thanks, Aboobaker," Logan said. "I couldn't have said it better myself." He poked at Aboobaker's soft midsection. "Stay off the water, okay?"

"Not water," Aboobaker said. "Fat. I know long time." He grinned.

Chavan and Samuel helped Logan into the backseat of the truck. The vinyl was hot and stuck to his skin. He grimaced from the pain. He stretched his injured leg and sat up as best he could.

The Indians—roughnecks, roustabouts, welder, mechanic's helper, cooks and kitchen staff, and even Daniel—filed by the window to bid Logan farewell. He thanked them, held each of their hands for a moment, said something personal to each one. He winked at them all and smiled. Some had tears in their eyes. The only one to keep his distance was Rahiman. Always Rahiman.

"Maybe you come back?" Putti said.

Logan shook his head. "I don't think so."

"Is necessary?" he asked.

"Damn sure is. You take care. Watch after all Indian peoples."

Logan turned to Rahiman, who was leaning quietly against the TCN shack. "Rahiman, I left some clothes in front of my cabin. Give 'em to all the boys, will ya? I know you'll be fair. The boots go to Abdullah."

Rahiman nodded piously but held his ground. Logan tapped Abraham on the shoulder. "Let's go," he said. Abraham started the truck.

Logan looked at Rahiman, still standing there. Abraham engaged the truck. Putti began speaking to his younger crewman in Hindi. Rahiman waved him away, and then Abdullah tried. When that didn't work, the roughnecks shoved him up to Logan's window.

"Good-bye, Doc," Rahiman said quietly, his stare cast to the sand. Logan reached out and wrapped his arm around the back of Rahiman's head, drawing it to his shoulder. "Of all the Indian peoples," Logan whispered in his ear, "Strong loved you best."

Rahiman drew back, his warm brown eyes wild. "No," he gasped. "He never say."

"He say many times to me. He say Rahiman is the smartest, the bravest, the most like Jamie Strong." Rahiman shook his head, running his wrist across his tearing eyes. "I can say this because I know," Logan told him. "He loved you, Rahiman. Don't forget."

The Indians pressed forward, surrounding Rahiman, all touching Logan's outstretched hand one last time—the ultimate token of their affection. Logan let them go without another word.

"Let's go, Abraham," he said. "Time for music facing."

The Indians stood together as the truck backed away, waving those silly waves. Logan waved back in the same manner, and then he left them behind forever in a settling, powdery cloud of Rub al Khali dust.

In the distance, above the clatter of the rickety crew truck, Logan heard the angry rumble of Al Hisaab. He didn't think he'd ever forget it.

FORTY-FOUR

⬦⬥⬦

Logan, stiff as a statue, sat in front of the wooden desk, his arms locked across his chest. He peered helplessly at the floor. He didn't dare look up. He'd sooner walk into a mosque wearing an Elvis T-shirt, a six-pack of Budweiser in one hand, an inflatable love doll in the other, than be here in the Momentum division manager's office. His reception could not have been colder. All he wanted to do was get it over with. After that, he was a free man.

Blount read over his handwritten report, the labor of Logan's last lonely hour, drumming his hotdog fingers on the desk. The old man looked out of place in front of the computer and file cabinets, maps and charts. He was too grizzly to be at home in that corporate setting, too weathered to look comfortable in that button-down cotton shirt. Blount was patch first and last. Crude oil ran in those cholesterol-clogged veins. Logan thought he should be dressed in coveralls and a hard hat.

"This all you've got to say, Doc?" he said, his voice dull and gravelly. He let the paper slip from his grasp. From his expression, Logan could tell he thought it stank.

"That's it," Logan said. Blount leaned back in his leather armchair and massaged the folds of his face. It looked like Logan's old baseball glove, worn equally around the edges. The only difference Logan could see was that it had never been properly oiled and there was no place for the ball.

"I don't see an explanation here," Blount said. "A reason."

"That's because I don't know of one, Mr. Blount. It just hit us. And hit us hard."

"And there was nothing you could've done? Nothing, I should say, you should've done to prevent this?"

"We followed procedure to the letter. We couldn't hold that well."

"I sec," Blount said, his stern gaze unblinking. There had never been a blowout of such magnitude on this continent, he said. He told Logan he owed it to Momentum and its crews—crews Logan had worked with side by side—to provide him with enough information to prevent anything like it from happening again. He had hoped Logan's report at least might shed a little light that would be beneficial to everyone. It hadn't. Not at all. He was, he said, disappointed.

"Although I see shreds of truth in your statement," Blount said, "the whole picture remains curiously incomplete. For instance, I find quite a bit written about what happened after the kick, but next to nothing about what went on before. I find that troubling."

As well you should, you son of a bitch, Logan thought.

"It's my responsibility to report to Tulsa about this incident *in its entirety*." Logan got the message. "I can't do my job with what you've told me—and I intend to do my job."

Logan looked up. Bad idea. Once Blount's eyes met his, Logan's couldn't get loose. He stuck it out.

"Let's go over it again—just me and you—and see if we can understand what happened." I'm one of you, his expression said. You can be honest with me. Look me in the eye and tell me what went wrong.

"I've told you what I know." Logan pointed tentatively at his apocryphal report. "I wrote it down just like it happened."

"So you did," Blount said, running his fingers over his slick, wavy hair. "You contend that the preventers malfunctioned. Among other things. *Lots* of other things."

"That's right," Logan said. "They did."

"And how long had the well flowed before your crew shut it in?"

"Maybe thirty seconds or so," Logan said. "Somethin' like that."

The division manager's cold stare drove Logan's eyes back to the tile floor. He intended to look at one particular square for as long as he could. He reached for his report. He was pretty sure he'd written thirty seconds. He thought it wise to check.

"Thirty seconds," Blount repeated, snatching the report back. "Thirty goddamn seconds, you say. Uhmmm? A sixteen-thousand-foot well flowed for just thirty seconds, you shut it in, and it blew the goddamn rams out of the hole!" Even the veins on the manager's neck threatened to jump out and strangle him. "Is that what you're gonna sit there and tell me?"

"It's the truth, Mr. Blount," Logan said. This had to be the worst possible time to inquire about the fate of his contract bonus—five hundred a month, accruing for the last ten. Nevertheless, he had to remember to work it in somewhere.

Blount turned away, flipping through the ink-stained pages that Logan knew told him nothing. He spoke slowly, methodically, enunciating every syllable. "Let me get this straight. We had a dead well. We weighted up and circulated three different times, and the well was stable. We logged for three days. We did not drill any deeper into the reservoir, so there should not have been any pressure other than what we already had under control. Then it flows for thirty seconds—out of the blue, mind you. Maybe a hundred barrels of mud are lost at the most—that's what you're telling me—and the well blows out and burns down my entire goddamn location."

"That's about it," Logan said. He grimaced in pain, hoping Blount would notice and take pity on him. He damn sure hadn't so far.

Blount stared at him and said nothing. Logan nervously rubbed his aching knee. He wished his mother would call again. She had the number. She thought Mr. Blount was nice. She should talk to him now.

"Look, Mr. Blount," Logan said, rallying what was left of his nerve. "My record is clean and so was Jamie Strong's. In five years overseas we've never made a mistake. The last thing I ever wanted to do was blow out a well. But the reservoir kicked, we shut it in, and the preventer seals failed. We did what we could. I'm sorry it happened like it did."

"You're *sorry?*" Blount snapped, his face reddening. "Oh, well, as long as you're sorry, everything's okay, ain't it! Don't worry about the money. The insurance claims. The loss of life. The lawsuits. Everything's all right as long as you're sorry. The problem's solved. I'll telex Tulsa right away."

The heat from Blount's breath irritated Logan's burns. He wished he could bore a hole through the floor and crawl through the sewers to the airport.

"You know I can't prove it—that's the problem here—but I know a great deal of mud escaped from the well before you and Strong closed those rams. It flowed for a hell of a lot longer than thirty seconds before you acted. You better damn well know that I know! You must think I'm some kind of goddamn fool!"

"No, sir," Logan said. "I respect you."

"The hell you do," Blount said, waving Logan's report in his face, his proof of yet another, bigger lie. "You and your crew were up there with your heads up your asses while the hydrostatic head decreased to the point that my preventers couldn't handle the pressure. They never had the chance to just fail, and I know it."

He slammed his fist into the desk. Logan thought the top might cave. It looked like it'd cracked all right. Logan hadn't lied. Not about respecting Frank Blount, anyway. But in this instant, he decided he didn't like him. He never trusted corporate people who referred to company equipment as "mine." They were subjective beasts in an objective world. Marshall had already told Logan what would happen. Everything destroyed would be replaced. The real loss here was Jamie Strong, and it irked Logan that Blount constantly referred to "my rig" and "my preventers," but never "my dead driller." It made lying to this bastard so much easier.

"There was a failure, all right," Blount continued. "And I'm lookin' at it!"

"All I can tell you is the truth," Logan said. He was getting the hang of it.

"What do you know about the truth, Doc!" Blount's face flared brighter red, as if he'd dunked it in a barrel of caustic soda. Much to Logan's chagrin, it loomed closer, like the Hydra's head. He could feel its heat. In his hand, Blount held a file. Logan read his name on its label. "This ain't the first time you've had one of these little chats, is it?" He opened the file and picked through the documents. No doubt at the top of the stack was Logan's report of the North Sea incident. "You've covered Strong's ass before."

"No, sir," Logan said abruptly. "No, sir."

"No, sir, my ass!" Blount shouted. "I saw this coming. I wanted Strong out of my division. He was an accident waiting to happen.

Elvin Barnes always stuck up for him, just like you're doing now. We'll just see how Barnes feels about it once he's busted back to driller."

"Barnes had nothing to do with it," Logan snapped. Momentum loved scapegoats. "He wasn't even there."

"He's gonna be there from now on, I grant you that. He'll pull twelve hours on my brake until he learns to be a better judge of men."

Blount snatched Logan's report from the desk and wadded it up. "Do you realize it will take at least three months to bring that well under control and twice that long to replace the equipment you melted last night? Thirty million dollars gone, just like that."

Logan didn't look at him. He didn't see the point. "It took us by surprise."

"Well, I hate surprises, Doc, same as you. I'm sure it comes as no surprise that I'm reassigning you to domestic operations, effective today. Let Tulsa figure out what to do with you. I never want to see your face in my division again."

Logan knew this was a euphemism. There were no openings in Momentum's domestic operations. He'd never set foot on a Momentum rig again at home or anywhere else.

"My only regret," Blount said, "is that Strong ain't here to get the same."

"Strong's dead," Logan snapped. "He lost his *life* for your rig."

"And good riddance. He's an insurance claim now."

Logan shot up from the chair and reached for his crinkled report. He'd made his mistake, acknowledged, more or less, to Marshall. Now Blount had made his. It was one thing to blame Strong. Even Strong would have agreed that he deserved it. But it was quite another to trivialize his life. At first Logan had pitied Blount. He carried a heavy weight. But now he felt nothing but the deepest contempt, never far from the surface between management and field personnel. A general cloak of blame no longer would do. The time had come to get specific.

"You wanna know what happened, *asshole?*" Logan shouted, his gut wrenching in anger. "I'll tell you what happened. *You* decided to put a full crew of men on top of a preventer stack on an exploratory well that failed its test. Tulsa'll find that little detail in the drilling log. I wrote it myself. *You* decided to save a few hours of downtime instead of changin' them seals, and I damn sure heard Elvin Barnes suggest that you do it. I know Marshall Christianson heard it, too. Even the slickest Tulsa office worm would never have taken a chance like that on a wildcat well. A man's dead, Mr. Blount! And all because *you* were too chickenshit to lose three hours of rent money. I'll put that in my report, and then maybe it'll be your turn to sit in my place! That's what I'll tell Tulsa when Tulsa calls. You can count on it!"

"Hey, Ernesto!" Blount shouted. "Get somebody to take this man to the airport and out of my face. Give him his ticket, his passport—stamped Exit Only. And give him a kick in the ass. Momentum's done with him."

Blount marched around his desk and shoved Logan out of his office. He slammed the door. Logan took his papers from Ernesto, a Goan, the man with an Indian body and a Portuguese name, who said nothing as he pointed toward the door. On his way Logan noticed the well program—a blueprint—pinned to the wall. He'd never seen it before. They didn't bother showing it to the dumb bastards who actually drilled the thing. It diagrammed each depth to which they'd run the various strings of casing, all the way to the reservoir. What caught Logan's eye was the English translation of Al Hisaab. In parentheses, directly under the Arabic figures, was written: The Reckoning.

Logan's reverie was broken by Ernesto, who coughed into his fist. The Goan nodded toward the door.

Once inside the truck, driven by an Indian who wouldn't speak to him, Logan smiled to himself. Blount had cast Momentum's net a little too wide. He'd caught his own foot in the web. The fact was, regardless of how much mud they'd lost from the well, the preventers should have held. Something else, most likely the formation itself, should have given way long before the ram seals. Logan knew it and Blount did, too. Once Tulsa found out, Blount just might be standing behind him in the unemployment line.

A good place to leave things. Logan felt he'd performed as well as Strong could have done. Strong would've been pleased.

What women, indeed.

FORTY-FIVE

It had taken Logan twenty minutes to get an operator who accepted his credit card. He'd given her the numbers twice, once while dodging the Pakistani sweepers who perpetually roamed the airport floor. He washed down the last of his lamb gyro with some kind of weird-ass orange soda. The beverage did little to relieve the dryness in his throat. This was the phone call he dreaded making. It was the final phase of his salvage operation, and the one that mattered most. He broke out in a cold sweat when at last it began ringing. His head throbbed like it was in a vise. His heart nearly jumped in his throat. He leaned the top of his head against the wall, the receiver plastered to his ear, and waited for what could be the worst news yet. She answered.

"Caitlin?"

"Logan!" she gasped. In that one word, he thought he sensed her longing. Maybe he hadn't screwed this up. It was still possible everything would be all right. "I'm so glad you've called."

"I'm sorry, Caitlin. I know you've been worried. There's not really much else to say. I'm just so damn sorry. I've been an ass."

"I wish you would've let me explain everything to you. I couldn't believe Adam had the nerve to come back in uninvited, much less answer that phone. I knew you'd get the wrong idea. I couldn't have had worse luck. I threw his ass out of our house after you hung up." She paused. "I'm so sorry about all this, Logan. I know it upset you. Adam's not in my study group anymore."

"I don't care about any of that now. All I want to know is do you love me? That's the only thing that matters."

She did not answer immediately and it troubled him. "Yes, Logan. I do."

Logan closed his eyes, tossed his head back and sighed. He felt fresh, cool air fill his lungs, his blistered cheeks cracking as he smiled. "Will you still marry me?"

"Yes!" She laughed like a little girl, with genuine joy. It soothed him like no salve could. "But I've canceled the invitations. I didn't know what else to do after I got the telex."

"Let's do it in front of a judge, then. Let's go if we're goin'. I only want my mother to come. And my sisters. You invite who you like."

"You say when and where."

"As soon as I get the skin grafts and knee surgery. I want to look nice for the photos."

She listened. He could hear her breathing. He couldn't wait to lay his head in her lap and sleep. It would come so easy now that he knew there'd be no more nightmares. Once home with Caitlin, he could rest. "Are you all right, Logan? What's happened? You sound terrible."

"It's a long story. I'll tell you all about it when I get home. And I'm coming home to stay."

"I'm so glad to hear it, Logan. You don't know."

"I'd bought you a rug—a peace offering, I guess. When I was angry, I thought I bought it for me. But it was always for you, Cait. I wanted it for you."

"I can't wait to see it."

"Well, that's the thing. I don't have it anymore. I had to leave it behind. I left lots of things behind. I guess what I'm tryin' to say is that everything could've worked out a little better over here and we still could've gotten the same result. I'm sorry about that. The rug would have looked nice in the den."

"It doesn't matter. We can get another rug and whatever furniture we need. We'll just start over. I wouldn't care if we burned everything."

"I pretty much already have."

"What's goin' on with you, Logan?"

"It's gonna take a while to figure that out, Cait. I hope you'll be patient. I think I've learned to be."

"Just come home, Logan. We'll start from there."
"I'm on my way. I love you, Caitlin."
"I love you, too. We're going to be fine."

Logan ambled down the narrow aisle until at last he found his assigned place. It didn't feel right traveling alone. He'd get used to it. He stuffed his bag into the overhead bin and squeezed in. He wasn't about to remove the splint and attempt to bend his knee. He'd tried to explain his condition to the Saudi ticket clerk, one last attempt at an upgrade, but to no avail. He waved his American Express card next, explaining that at the very least he'd need a row of seats for the trip to Houston. Now he saw that even this had failed. They'd stuffed him in the rear of the plane, the section Strong always called "camel class." Logan had no choice but to carve out his own space. He'd learned the skill from Jamie Strong.

He went through the whole litany again to a Saudi traveler sitting in the seat ahead. At first the man was reluctant to listen, but he finally agreed to shift over to the next row, taking his things with him. Logan thanked him and pushed back the seat so he could rest his leg on its cushion. Arabs had a bad rap in America. Once they'd gotten past their suspicions—their assumption that a westerner had some sort of self-serving scheme in mind—Logan had found them to be a kind and gracious people. A flight attendant must have seen the commotion and arrived to see what the trouble was.

Logan recognized her immediately. She seemed to have a little more trouble with him, he thought, his features disguised beneath a thick layer of flaky cream. His whisk-broom hair certainly looked different. But she discerned him soon enough.

"You!" the purser gasped, her face as angry as when Logan had last seen it. She wagged her finger more rapidly than her acid tongue. "If you think for one minute that you're going to cause me the same amount of grief we had last time, you're sadly mistaken! I won't have it..."

Logan pressed his finger to his lips. "Ssshhh. It's all right, ma'am. I'm drugged." He took the pill container from his shirt pocket and rattled it.

"I'd better not have even a peep out of you," she said.

"Look, lady." Logan sighed, hoping to God he faced the last public relations problem Strong had bequeathed him. Just the same, he'd rather have another go at Blount than try and soothe this woman's justifiable rage. "Try, if you can, to understand me. I've had a hard day. I blew up half the Rub al Khali last night. It's still burnin'. I got my ass chewed down to the bone at my office. There ain't nothin' left of it for you. I'm tired. I'm hurt. I'm fried. I'm unemployed. And I'm very, very sorry I've caused you so much trouble. I hope you'll forgive me. I just want to quietly fly your friendly skies, like the brochure says."

"That's another airline, you jerk," she said. She scanned the aisle for his confederates, who she'd learned often scattered at the first sign of turbulence.

"You won't find him," Logan said. "He's not here."

"I'll believe it when we're airborne," she said. Out came the finger. She shook it at him. "Not a peep."

He wished he had the nerve to bite it. But he didn't possess Strong's passion for thwarting authority. Instead, Logan shook Pix's bottle again. "I'll be gone soon," Logan said. "I swear."

"And no drinks until we're out of Saudi airspace."

"I won't want them even then. A little water would be nice when you're not too busy."

"You don't even know what it tastes like," she scoffed.

"I'm willin' to learn," he said. "And you have no idea how thirsty I am."

Logan saw a curious glint in her eyes as she studied him. Mostly they were angry, but he thought he caught a spark of trust in there, too. It would be rewarded. She marched down the aisle, her heels listing with each step. Logan closed his eyes. All he wanted to do was sleep. His knee was swollen tight against its splint, throbbing unmercifully. It looked bad and felt worse. Job hunting would have to wait. He knew he wouldn't be doing much of anything for at least six weeks. With September the rains would return to Austin, providing the sun-scorched vegetation a second chance to thrive before the onset of winter. Rain promised renewal. And hope. And God's mercy. He thought he'd sit under the live oaks in Pease Park and let the cool raindrops drip from the leaves onto his face while he watched the land heal. And he knew it would. He longed to hear the torrents of Shoal Creek while he napped. Dry as a cow's bone all summer, it would run strong after a good September thunderstorm. How he'd missed the Texas rain.

He settled his head back against the rest. No spot felt exactly right. But sooner or later, he figured, he'd settle in. Time was the final variable in his particular equation. A solution was out there somewhere, waiting. Everything else was what it was. He felt the jet taxi in preparation for take-off. It accelerated down the runway and lifted into the ocher sky, the exhaust from the jet engines ripping that hole in the ozone layer just a little wider. To the south, past the white cities, the black highways, and the circular, irrigated farms of deep green, he thought he could make out the fringe of the Rub al Khali. The Empty Quarter. The last place. He'd never lay eyes on it again. He didn't have to. Logan knew its heart. And he knew also that he was free of it. Scarred. Wounded. Uncertain. Alone. But strong enough to keep striving and forever free. Sleep came easily when he thought of rain.

It has taken the earth eons to generate what we burn each day on our trips to the grocery store. Few hydrocarbons have been found older than sixty-five million years—the exact age when a meteor struck the Caribbean, shrouding the earth in a dust cloud for decades and dooming the great dinosaurs. And none have been found younger than one million years.

Ninety-five percent of the world's energy demands rely on these dwindling, nonrenewable hydrocarbon deposits. The United States is home to six percent of the world's population, but it consumes thirty percent of the world's energy and natural resources. Each American burns thirty times as much energy as any one person in the Third World. How we love our automobiles, central air, leaf blowers, and microwaves.

It is thought that all of the world's major oil and gas reserves have already been discovered and extensively explored. The most recent domestic American strike—Alaska's North Slope—contains reserves sufficient to fuel the United States' energy requirements for only two years. The Rub al Khali might buy us a brief reprieve, and one which we'll pay dearly for. But Logan Wilson left Arabco a little hickey to overcome before Saudi Arabia exports Al Hisaab's treasures. We'll see.

It is impossible with current technology to duplicate the earth's natural manufacture of fossil fuels. There is no real replacement on the horizon for oil and gas. Not yet. Experts predict, given our current rate of global consumption, that all fossil fuels will be exhausted by the year 2030. Marshall Christianson said it best. Where's this train running? It's running out. Soon.

David Marion Wilkinson
Austin, Texas

October, 1987 - September, 1988
December, 1995 - September, 1997

ACKNOWLEDGMENTS

I owe a great debt to the men of Atlantic Pacific Marine Corporation Drilling Barge #2. I first encountered the old beast in the fall of 1976. I still remember the names of my first crew: "Blackie" Alford and Frank "Catfish" Smith, toolpushers; Harry C. "Kinfolks" Dixon, driller; Jimmie Jessup, derrickman; E. C. Malone, motorman; Floyd Graves, welder; George Brouder and George "Skeeter" Davis, roughnecks; the Hillman clan (numbers 1 through 6) and "The Mule" and "Shorty" Soileau, drillers. I apologize to those whose names have slipped from memory. I remember the faces and personalities very well.

I also would like to thank the men of Atlantic Pacific #8 and the ill-fated Ranger #1, a jack-up that went over in rough seas off the Louisiana coast with great loss of life. I went overseas with the old Loffland Brothers outfit, working on Chevron's magnificent North Sea Ninian Central Platform and later for Loffland's Saudi Arabian affiliate, Nadrico Saudi Limited. These were all first-class operations, and I was proud to be a part of each. I can't list the names of the many lives that touched mine in these years, but I'd like to mention a few friends. Charles "Eddie" Fuller, Walter "Paul" Stahl, Walker G. Formby, Mike and Todd Gilliam, Bob Dees, Kenny Greene, and Jake Cross. Make 'em bite, boys. I've twisted off.

Living in a small, isolated compound in Saudi Arabia, I was exposed to very little of the country's culture. To enhance my experience, I consulted Robert Lacey's *The Kingdom* (Harcourt, Brace & Jovanovich, 1981) and Peter Theroux's delightful *Sandstorms: Days and Nights in Arabia* (Norton, 1991). I was even more ignorant of geology. Unlike Logan, I took virtually no science courses in college. To draft these sections, I had no choice but to plunder *Geology: An Introduction to Physical Geology* by Stanley Chernicoff and Ramesh Venkatakrishnan (Worth Publishers, 1995) and *A Short History of Planet Earth* by J. D. Macdougall (John Wiley & Sons, 1996). Please don't sue me. Special thanks to geologist Charles E. "Gene" Mear for reviewing and commenting on these sections. Thanks to Dr. Peter Abboud, Professor of Arabic,

University of Texas at Austin, for helping me name the fictional reservoir. And while there is some production in the Rub al Khali, to my knowledge it's nothing like what I've described in the novel.

Thanks to my friends William J. Scheick and Elizabeth C. Lyon for providing editorial direction and encouragement through the novel's early drafts. I couldn't have salvaged the manuscript without Elizabeth's help in particular. Thanks also to Robert Rorke. Special thanks to Sarah Nawrocki, who did a superb job editing; sharp-eyed and savvy Judy Bloch, and Elizabeth Vahlsing for her talent as a designer but mostly for her patience with her husband. I don't see how she does it.

I'm grateful to my readers: John Holmgreen, Barham Bratton, Aline Jordan, Donna Lee, Tommy King, Chandler Ford, Pat and Mack Barham, Barbara Minton, Lisa Minton, Mike Pugh, Mike Peebles, Louis Bratton, Lynn McFarland, and Bob Campbell.

I'm pleased to acknowledge the efforts of Anna Cottle and Mary Alice Kier. Like the best of agents, they were always at hand with wise words when I needed them most. I've waited so long to find you. Thank you both for your guidance and grace.

Thanks to G. Michael Pugh of Amarillo, Texas, for being the best friend I've ever had.

Thanks to my wife, Bonnie, who has always believed in me; and to our two sons, Dean and Tate, who make it all worthwhile.

And lastly, a word about Joseph Allen "Joe" McCue, to whom this novel is dedicated. A man with many of the strengths of the fictional Jamie Strong, McCue had none of his weaknesses. A novel requires tension, so I built some in between Logan and Jamie, when in fact there was none between McCue and me. I admired and respected him, trusted him with my life, and I hope he felt the same way about me.

After Saudi Arabia played out, we both drifted home. He got by all right, but eventually circumstances returned him to the patch. He continued to roam the world, and I envied him for it. The irony was that he likewise envied me for staying at home. We kept in touch over the years, although the phone calls became shorter and less frequent. Without new experiences to bind us, we didn't have much to talk about anymore. Then, in late summer of 1995, I received a phone call from a man I did not know, telling me he was, like me, a friend of Joe McCue's.

It seemed Joe had other plans in motion that last summer. He and another friend had launched a business. Joe had served his notice with the overseas drilling contractor that had last employed him, in Indonesia, I think. He agreed to pull one last hitch and then let go of the oil field forever.

At some point, there was trouble, the details of which I don't really understand. I know there was hydraulic pressure trapped in a line on the drill floor. From what I can gather, the problem should have been solved by the other crew. Joe inherited it, as was often the case. He was a rig superintendent by then, the top-ranking contractor on location. Just the same, he saw to the problem himself. Sensing danger, he cleared the floor of all hands. Shortly thereafter, there was an explosion. A piece of metal, a two-inch bull plug if my information is correct, shot into and possibly through Joe's body, which was knocked several feet back. He was taken by jet to Singapore, I'm told, where he lingered for several days. In the end, it wasn't the wound that killed him, but blood poisoning from the hydraulic fluid. I attended his closed-casket funeral in Denver. It was the saddest occasion of my life. Joe McCue was forty years old.

Of all the people I worked with in the oil fields, I never once thought Joe would be the one to lose his life. However fun loving and reckless he sometimes was in his personal life, he never took chances in the field. He was a stickler for decorum and procedure. He was competent, kind, fair minded, intelligent, generous, and, above all, a natural leader of men. The tragedy of his loss is far greater than any I could ever fictionalize.

This one was for you, old friend. I hope you like it. I can hear you saying: "You made yourself out to be quite the hero there, Doc." You were always my hero, big man. What a time we had. Know that you are missed.

David Marion Wilkinson, a fifth-generation Arkansan, has lived in Austin, Texas since 1975. He has worked as a carpenter, oil field worker, salesman, mortgage loan officer, legal investigator, and entrepreneur. His first novel, *Not Between Brothers*, was a 1996 Spur Award finalist in the "Best Novel of the West" category. It won the 1997 Violet Crown Award for fiction. David Marion Wilkinson is a member of Western Writers of America and the Austin Writers' League. He lives with his wife, Bonnie, and their two sons, Dean and Tate.